THE ARROGANCE
OF WOMEN

By the same author
A Rational Man

THE ARROGANCE OF WOMEN

TERESA BENISON

HUTCHINSON
LONDON

This edition first published in 1998 by Hutchinson

Random House (UK) Limited
20 Vauxhall Bridge Road, London SW1V 2SA

Random House Australia (Pty) Limited
20 Alfred Street, Milsons Point, Sydney,
New South Wales 2061, Australia

Random House New Zealand Limited
18 Poland Road, Glenfield, Auckland 10, New Zealand

Random House South Africa (Pty) Limited
PO Box 337, Bergviei, 2012 South Africa

A CIP record for this book is available from the British Library

Papers used by Random House UK Limited are natural,
recyclable products made from wood grown in sustainable forests.
The manufacturing processes conform to the environmental
regulations of the country of origin.

ISBN 0 09 179214 2

Typeset in Plantin by Deltatype Ltd, Birkenhead, Merseyside

Printed and bound in Great Britain
by Mackays of Chatham plc

First Blood

Quick as a fish in the shallows, the knife darts. The flesh parts and the blood wells and Adam looks down to see his disembodied hands, one grasping her wrist, the other twisting the tap.

The water gushes. It is streaked with blood – Tabasco, cochineal, Cabernet Sauvignon.

Images such as this proliferate like cancer. He might take a filleting knife to his memory, except he lacks the expertise to work on living flesh. He is a chef, not a surgeon.

There must be other cures. Fresh air and exercise.

Up on the headland, looking out to sea, he clenches his hands as the memories cascade: a caress, a threat, her nails scraping his scrotum.

Moonlight strikes the water like a blade, and the air is sharp with the cold. He turns up his collar and hunches his shoulders. Curiosity tugs at him, overriding caution. He steps closer to the edge. He has always been scared of heights. She also suffered an irrational fear – not of heights, but of the dark.

Face the fear.

Time and place, a Sunday morning in her abandoned church, a finger of sunlight struggling through a crack in the shuttered clerestory. The light from the stubby candles lined up along the broken altar rail, puddles the chancel steps. 'You're cheating.' His face is close to hers. Their breath mingles with the tang of hot wax. 'I don't call this dark.'

Face the fear.

He smells salt on the air and beneath his feet, the grass is stiff with frost. He takes another step forward. He has a dizzying sense of the landmass splitting away into the sea. Despite the cold, he has begun to perspire. His fear drags him forward. So easy to take just one more

3

step. A single stride, the body of a man shattered on the rocks, bones eroded by salt, bleached by the sun, winking like cockleshells against the black boulders. And hair – strands like weed clinging to the cracks and crevices, rising and sinking with the tide.

He rocks forward, but holds his ground. The landscape is secure. Behind him, the houses of Polruan scramble back along the hillside. The press of their presence is reassuring. He begins to relax.

Too soon. The pressure increases, but no longer reassures. Push me, pull me. He is compelled closer to the edge. He must concentrate. Polruan on this side of the river, Fowey on the other. The river widens and the estuary spreads its arms to embrace the sea.

The river spills into the sea.

When the tide turns, the sea will spill into the river. Nothing is forever. Nothing is what it seems.

Lifting his chin to the wind, he feels the slice of cold air on raw skin. This morning he shaved off his beard and he looks much younger. He's not yet forty, but the strain of the past year has put grey in his beard. The snip of the scissors and scratch of the razor and a new man emerges. If only it were that simple. He nicks himself along the jawline. First blood, a new beginning. He smiles, and takes it as a sign.

It had taken him nine hours to drive from Suffolk to Cornwall. He stopped once for coffee, again for a sandwich. He took a wrong turning at Liskeard and ended up on the road to Bodmin. It's late now and he's deadly tired. His eyes prickle from prolonged concentration, his shoulders ache and there is a persistent throb of cramp in his calf. For this reason, despite the hour, he walked to the headland before setting foot in the cottage.

'Pain defines.' Her voice rouses him. It is the distant knell of a church that has long since slithered into the sea. He struggles to focus and the words, though still remote, become clear. He hears the eagerness of her tone. She needs him to understand; it is important to her that he grasp her meaning. 'Pain sharpens the world, gives it back its edge. Listen Adam, please. It marks the line between here and now, you and me.' She moves closer and her breath stirs the hair on his nape. 'Like a paper shape,' her phantom fingers reach past him, snipping at the air. 'A paper dolly cut from a picture book.' Her fingers continue to scissor between him and the mercury sea.

He shakes his head; he must jiggle it loose, dislodge the memory.

He turns away from the sea and starts back to the village. The path is dark and he trips on hard tussocks of frosted grass. He turns his ankle on a rock. He is a city boy – Northampton, London, Bury St Edmunds. For a moment he cannot imagine what he's doing here, at the end of the world.

His decision to come to Cornwall had bewildered Babs. 'It's so far from everywhere. I'll never get to see you.'

'You can visit. We'll want you to visit; you could stay the whole summer . . .'

'We'll see,' she gave a watery smile and patted his arm. 'You haven't moved in yet. Besides, I'm not at all sure it's such a good idea. It isn't that I don't understand, don't think that. It's high time you made a fresh start – I would too, if I could – but why there, Adam? Of all places, how can you bear to live there?'

They have all lost so much, but though his own pain is a dead weight, a rock in the belly that shows no sign of passing, it is Babs who has lost the most.

The anguish remains, but the memories fade. Last November he'd woken suddenly from a bad dream. The details fled on waking, but the sense remained. He had dreamt of her. He recognized her voice, the shadow-puppet play of her body on the screen of his sleep. That much was vivid and intimate, but the puppet had no face. At first, panic paralysed him. It was as if he'd forgotten his own features. It wasn't possible. In a healthy individual the brain doesn't lose information, it's all in there somewhere – the line of her nose, the shade of her eyes, the jut of her chin. He has only to access that information. Lying in the dark he punches and pummels his memory. Recalling snippets of conversation, he tries to see her face as she speaks. He remembers their lovemaking – intense, terrifying, and faceless.

He has lost everything. He cannot even remember where it all began, let alone how it came to end the way it had.

The infection lingers. It bides its time, fermenting deep inside him. He must open the wound, let the salt air scour it clean. He needs to reconstruct the past, remember it all. Only then will he allow himself to forget.

To remember, and then forget. This is why he's come to Fowey and Polruan and the river and the sea.

His cottage waits. It looks like a shipwreck in the silvery gleam of

5

the moon, all broken spars and sagging timbers. His car is nudged against the front wall; there is hardly room to park in the narrow lane. As he approaches, he hears the whirr of the fan as it labours to cool the engine. He opens the boot and pulls out his sleeping bag, a box of supplies and a torch.

He came here last November. Because of the dream. She loved Fowey. 'It's like Venice,' she'd said. 'Too beautiful. Not part of our world. It shouldn't exist.' He'd taken a flat in a white stuccoed house high on the Esplanade. The long drive and the change of air gave him the best night's sleep in a long time. He woke late. Opening the curtains on the sun-winking sea, he was immediately enraptured. She had experienced this on her first morning, he was sure of it. He felt her beside him, laughing, stretching her arms and splaying her long fingers to the sun. Light, not darkness, is her element. Coming here had been the right move. To rediscover a person one should visit the places that matter to them. It is working already. He feels it now, as he sits in the bay of the window sipping coffee and watching the shifting light. How she must have loved it, the constantly changing colours and textures of the river as it moved from grey to blue, to silver and green in a dazzling catwalk array.

But if light is her element, it is also Simon's. As is colour.

A cloud shadows the estuary. He blinks and swallows the last of his coffee. How could it be otherwise? Find one and you find the other. That's the whole point of the exercise. Remember it all.

On the second day he'd taken the little orange ferry boat to Polruan. The village was more intimate than the town of Fowey. 'The best thing about Fowey,' the ferryman confided as he secreted the fare in a battered wooden box, 'is its view of Polruan.'

Leaving the ferry, he'd climbed a steep narrow street leading from the quay. He had no plan, he certainly wasn't house-hunting. He was drifting. Go with the flow. Lost in thought, he continued to climb. After a while, the city boy paused for breath and looked around. The day was overcast. Below, the river was silver grey, its texture stippled. He turned. Behind him a house crouched on a bank. It barely had a roof, the windows were boarded up and the garden was overgrown. The front gate had been broken off and tossed into the hedge. Adam pulled it into view. The gate had a nameplate. The name of the cottage was Eden.

Twice she'd fled to Fowey. Juggling the keys, he opens the door.

6

His torch casts a pale beam across the dusty flags. The stone walls radiate cold.

He should have followed her. Had that been his first mistake, or was there an earlier point at which he might have changed the course of things?

The second time, he did follow her.

He piles the vanguard of his belongings in the centre of the room. He hasn't thought ahead. He should have ordered fuel for the fire. At least he's brought some candles. He lines them up along the edge of the slate hearth. At the rasp and flare of the match memories start like pheasants rising from a thicket. He sets match to wick, moving from right to left. Bunching up his sleeping bag to make a cushion, he pulls a blanket round his shoulders and sits cross-legged to watch the candles burn.

His eyes blur with tiredness. His skin is stretched and tight. He blinks and sees her hand reaching towards the candles. Like a gaunt bird it hovers, then settles. The pads of her fingers almost touch the flame. Her flesh glows orange and rose, sunlight through blossom. He grabs her wrist, pulling her hand away – and she laughs like a child as the blister forms.

He rocks forward. His hands grip his shins and his fingers dig into muscle and bone. I can do it, I can bring it back, I know I can. I will heal myself.

He sleeps hunched in front of the candles and wakes stiff with the cold. He beats his arms and stamps his feet, and a shower of pinpricks tickles the backs of his knees. The cottage is damp and musty. If he carries on like this he'll die of exposure before winter is out.

He needs fresh air. He opens the door. The new morning is incandescent with sunlight. Standing at the top of his steps, he looks out across the river. It is a tall roost, but a safe one for a man who is scared of heights. He laughs out loud. The houses of Polruan tumble to the quay in a cascade of grey slate. The smart, white stuccoed houses of Fowey Esplanade march along the farther bank. He can see the house where he stayed last time and, a little below, the blockhouse from which a chain was once hung, spanning the estuary to keep the Spaniards at bay. Shading his eyes, he picks out the ruined castle on St Catherine's Point. Beyond, where the line of the sea meets the line of the sky, a tanker the size of a toy crosses his line of sight.

7

'Glutton for punishment, aren't you? That's a hell of a wreck you've got there. Are you doing it up?'

Adam starts and stares. The woman leaning on his wall is maybe fifty, fifty-five years old. She is dressed in jeans and a big green and black sweater, and wears her hair in an unflattering pudding-basin bob. Adam forces a smile. 'That's the general idea.'

'You'll have your work cut out.' She smiles. 'Still, never say die. I admire you. Welcome to Polruan. I'm Pam, by the way. Pam Fowler.'

'Adam Mason.'

'I run the art shop down by the quay. Art supplies, that is. Canvases, paint . . . You're not an artist, by any chance?'

'Not exactly.'

'Only we get a lot of those. And writers. Gets a bit much sometimes, always being on show, like living in a theme park.'

'I'm sure.'

'You get used to it. You know, I think I remember you when you looked round a while back. Have you come far?'

'East Anglia.'

She laughs. 'Flat, right?' Adam nods. 'Well, anything you need or want to know, pop over – only not this morning, I'm off to Lostwithiel.'

This is a small community. Pam may have seen her. She would have had to pass her door. She. No name, no face. It's a way of keeping the pain at bay. A woman's laughter and the knowing eyes of a child. Where does it come from, the myth of innocence?

He needs supplies. Milk, bread, meat. Last week he'd bought a stove from a camping shop in Bury St Edmunds. It has two rings and a grill. He may die of exposure, but he won't starve. He'll live by the seasons, anticipating each new crop and catch. As he strides down the hill, his palate fizzes at the thought of fresh mackerel grilled with lime, and scallops tossed in garlic butter.

He already loves this village. It is a good place to be, he can smell it and taste it. He will come through and build a future here. He'll put a roof on his house and replace the windows, make it warm in winter and cool in summer.

He will heal this house and heal himself and day by day, stone by stone, make a home here for his family.

1

Eleanor rarely visits Bury St Edmunds; it's too unsettling, like stepping through a television screen into a film of the past. Except it's more real. The sounds and smells and feelings crowd in on her, jostling for attention, obliterating the present.

When she became ill, Jess brought her back to stay with her mother. She'd panicked, but she trusted Jess. It had been the right thing to do and she's better now; it's time to go home.

On the way to the station they pass her old school and the memories scuttle and itch like spiders. The childish screams spin a web between past and present and she is able to distinguish the scrape of a shoe against asphalt, the rattle of chainlink as a knot of boys collides with the fence.

She recognizes the memory. It is her first day at school and there are two Eleanors in the playground: the quaking five-year-old and, just behind and to one side of her, the shadowy adult who sees as she sees, feels as she feels. Little Eleanor is unhappy. All summer this day has flickered like a storm on her horizon. The familiar world defined by her mother is about to change. Nothing will ever be the same again. Even Eleanor is different; the serious child staring out of the mirror isn't anyone she recognizes.

She's confused and miserable. Her shoes nip and she stands stiffly in her new dress and coat. It's as though she's wearing someone else's clothes. 'They feel all wrong,' she told her mother. 'They smell funny.'

In the playground, Eleanor and Babs stand apart from the other mothers. Eleanor doesn't mind. The crowd makes her uncomfortable; she's never seen so many children gathered together in a single place.

Eleanor and Babs live on the edge of town in a terraced cottage made of big blue stones, like bones. Dad is away a lot. Next door lives an old lady with a floury face like pastry that might crumble if she smiles; on the other side is Peter who's twelve and is learning to play the trumpet. His mother says he can't play in the house, so he leans out of his bedroom window to practise. When he's in the garden, Peter pulls faces at Eleanor and lobs stones at her mother's pet chickens if he thinks no one's looking. But Eleanor's looking. She glares at him and wills him to stop.

The playground is too big and too noisy. Eleanor clings to her mother's hand. Bab's coat smells of chicken food and plasticine. Eleanor clutches the soft folds. She doesn't want to let go.

A teacher herds them into a classroom. Eleanor sits at a table with five other children. Her new clothes prickle and chafe; it's like she's inside someone else's skin, or wearing a costume – like *Puss In Boots*, or *Cinderella*.

Who shall I be? She wants to laugh but the teacher is looking and she bites her lip to stay quiet. But the words are still singing inside her head: *You can be whoever you like*, they say.

She wriggles her shoulders and crosses her ankles and sits up straight. She looks around the classroom, at the bright painted alphabet boards and the trays of clay and paint, and this is when she sees the twins for the first time. They remind her of Rosalind and Gwynyth, her mother's chickens. Their fluffy ginger hair is the same colour and texture as the hens' soft under-feathers. Even their movements are alike. At playtime she follows and watches them. They stay close, warily observing, their nervous heads moving from side to side, here to there, peck peck peck. The other children stare and whisper, then an older boy starts to jeer and kick and herd them towards the fence. As they retreat they look even more like frightened chickens, and something happens to Eleanor. Her fear vanishes in a rush of anger. She runs to them and pulls at the boy. She is younger than him, but taller. She jabs her finger in his face, and says, 'It's rude to stare.'

These are her mother's words. Standing in the shadows, the ghost from the future hears the echo. But the boy doesn't hear, he remains defiant. He grabs Eleanor's finger. She twists away and kicks his shin. There is a movement behind her. Emboldened by her attack, the twins close ranks, and the boy backs away.

The twins became her friends. Every day Babs collected her from school and she'd chatter away about what they'd done and what they'd learnt and what games they'd played. Sometimes they came to tea, and now and again Eleanor went to their house.

'Their mummy can't tell them apart,' she told Babs. 'Isn't that funny? Their daddy can and I can, but she can't. Why doesn't she give them different dresses? Could you tell me apart, mummy, if I had a sister?'

Babs swept her on to her lap and pushed the wing of black hair off her face. 'That's a silly question. I'd know my Ellie anywhere.'

'But if I had a sister just like me . . .'

'Even then,' said Babs. She laughed and tickled Eleanor, and Eleanor chuckled and squirmed and tickled back. She didn't really want a sister; it was a lot nicer to have Babs to herself. She loved to play like this, to burrow her head deep in her mother's squashy chest and feel the slow bump of her heart, like a big secret animal kept hidden beneath her jumper.

2

Babs parks the car and follows Eleanor on to the station platform. It is a bitterly cold day and a creeping chill seeps through the soles of Eleanor's boots and makes her toes ache. She grinds her heel against the asphalt and, tugging her fake-fur hat down over her ears, adjusts her collar. The hat is black, as are her coat and boots.

'If only you'd wear something a little more colourful, dear,' says Babs with a sigh as she dusts Eleanor's sleeve. 'Black is so mournful, and it picks up every mark and speck. What's this?'

'Cat hair.'

'There you are, you see?'

'Don't fuss, Mum.' Eleanor wriggles her shoulders and her little flamenco-stamp echoes along the platform. Babs's face puckers. Immediately Eleanor regrets her show of petulance. A network of broken veins marks her mother's cheeks, and soft oyster patches have begun to swell beneath her eyes. Babs is getting old. Eleanor can't bear it, it makes her so sad. She really ought to stay with her. She is not a good daughter.

But some things never change. After all these years, she remains a misfit in this town – Babs Bycroft's changeling child, skinny and too tall for her age. In a photograph on her mother's sideboard her bright blue eyes stare freakishly from beneath her black fringe. If she closes her eyes she can hear the playground chants of Liquorice and Stick Insect, crowed from a distance because everyone knows Eleanor fights back.

You can be whoever you want to be.

She had hugged the knowledge to her. It was such a big secret, even Babs didn't know.

She craved variety and opportunity; she wanted to try on all the costumes, the flouncy dresses and the baggy check trews, until she found the outfit that was waiting, the one that would fit her like a skin.

She was eager to begin, frantic to leave Bury and go somewhere she wasn't known, start again.

Babs has never understood. She still thinks everything Eleanor has achieved could have been achieved just as well in her home town. Now Eleanor stands on the windy station and feels the distance gaping between them. She chews her lip, and her eyes prickle and ache. She is full to the brim with sadness and regret, but she's gone too far; what's done is done. She can't set time running backwards and she can't bridge the gap to her mother's side.

Babs touches her arm. In her mustard-coloured coat she looks like an overladen bumblebee and a rush of tenderness takes Eleanor's breath away. She cranes along the track.

'We're too early,' says Babs. 'Now isn't that you all over?' She's doing her best to sound jolly. Teasing is a sign of affection. 'Train fever.' She flicks yet another imaginary fleck from Eleanor's lapel. 'I've been thinking, would you like a coat for your birthday? I could come down to London, we'll go shopping, have lunch . . .' Her voice trails away. The distance widens. She's trying so hard but Eleanor doesn't know what to do. If she could be five again she'd climb on to her lap and burrow deep, and block out the years.

She blinks and focuses on her surroundings. The station is grey.

The yellow blob that is Babs leans closer and squeezes her arm. 'Ellie,' her voice is low and coaxing. 'I really don't think it's wise, you rushing off like this. Can't you stay a few more days at least . . .'

'I want to go home, Mum.'

'I know you do, dear, but who'll look after you?'

'I don't need looking after. Just look at me, fighting fit. And if I do need anything, Jess is there.'

'Be fair, dear, Jess has her own life. She's fond of you, but don't go taking advantage.'

'I'm not, but if things do get really bad, Jess is only five minutes away, or on the end of a phone.'

'Be a bit considerate, that's all I'm saying. Now you will be sure and give her my love, won't you? If you're determined to go, that is . . .'

'I have responsibilities. Oscar, for one thing.'

'Oscar's a cat, dear.'

'Yes, and he's been abandoned once already in this life.'

'Not by you . . .'

'That's not the point. Come on, have a heart, Mum.' She manages a smile but even as she speaks she grows cold inside. Babs is right. Nobody depends on her. Babs finds her eagerness to escape inexplicable and Eleanor wants to comfort her, put her arms around her, but she can't, she's frozen. Why? Why can't she show Babs how much she loves her? There must be something wrong, a loose connection, a missing component in her emotional make-up. 'I'm sorry,' she whispers.

'I know.' Babs's eyes glitter. A bell signals the approach of the train. Eleanor checks the ticket in her pocket. Babs stiffens her chins and forces a smile. 'Well, if your mind's made up . . . Are you ready? Have you got everything?' Eleanor nods. 'And you will ring, let me know how you are? And don't work too hard. You could come up again next weekend. Think about it . . .' She hesitates. The ice creaks beneath the weight of her suggestion. 'I do worry about you, Eleanor. Oh, I know you're grown up and all that, but I'll still be worrying when you're fifty. Promise me you'll take care, and don't push yourself. Be a bit sensible for a week or two, yes?'

It is a strange request. Apart from Chris, everything she has ever done in her life has been achingly conventional, sensible in the extreme. She works in a gallery, selling modern art. Brian Farraday thinks the world of her. Or he used to. What does he make of her now?

Where had it come from, that moment of wildness transforming her from crack shot to loose cannon?

The train arrives. The snaking carriages ease against the platform and a sprinkling of passengers stumble into the cold. Patting their collars and tugging on their gloves, they bow their heads against the wind and head for the exit.

Eleanor picks up her case. Babs says, 'Have you forgotten anything?'

'No. All present and correct. Don't fuss, Mum.'

'I'm not, I'm just checking.' She flutters her hands, dismissive, embarrassed. Eleanor gives her cheek a quick kiss and steps on to the train. 'Now, Jess is definitely meeting you at King's Cross?'

'Yes.'

'And you change at Cambridge.'

'Yes.'

Babs smiles and her chins quiver. A man in a quilted green body-warmer makes a dive for the next carriage. The doors give an urgent warning bleep and hiss shut. The train starts to move. Safe behind the mud-spattered window, Eleanor pulls off her hat and loosens her coat and watches her mother shrink to a tiny, wind-whipped jester waving vigorously and getting smaller and smaller until at last she's out of sight.

It would be much easier to confide in Babs if she didn't constantly blame Chris for all Eleanor's troubles. Poor Chris. Faced with a barrage of difficult choices, the silly man had spun like a weather vane.

She has yet to establish a full chronology. Her mind won't function; her thoughts sag like a badly knitted sweater.

What she knows for certain is that recent events were not triggered by a single drama, but had resulted from the relentless piling on of pressure until she woke one day to a world where the flicker of an eyelid sent walls and ceilings flying outwards and upwards, where objects dissolved at her touch and there was no colour anywhere, in anything.

She stirs in her seat. The train rattles and jolts through an expanse of bleak countryside. On both sides of the track fields stretch like raw

14

canvas smeared with early green. Seagulls skim the furrows, wheeling and diving. Someone once told her – a teacher, Dad, a friend – that gulls come inland when the weather on the coast gets too rough. She imagines the birds conferring, tapping their barometers and shaking their heads, debating their options as if capable of choosing one course of action over another.

Another memory – Babs in an orange dress, leaning over to straighten her collar. 'What's it to be, Ellie? Do you want a raspberry lolly or a cornet . . . the red dress or the yellow one? Come along dear, make up your mind.' Then Dad putting his arm around her shoulder as he offers a loaded choice. 'Now Eleanor, you can spend Christmas in Bury with Mummy, or you can spend it here with me and Laura and we'll go to the pantomime, or the ice show if you'd rather. It's up to you, pet, whichever you prefer.'

She feels it now, the sense of panic. Even as a child she understood that every decision was potentially the wrong decision – not just for her, but for others.

The responsibility is too great. It makes her shiver.

But seagulls don't have such worries and today they have chosen a Suffolk field in preference to the Norfolk coast. They have been joined by other birds, big and black with evil, wedge-shaped beaks. Crows maybe, or rooks or ravens.

Something startles the birds and they erupt in a jumble of grey, white and black, their wings like clipper sails. Eleanor turns away from the window. The man opposite is working on a laptop. His head is bent, the hair on his crown is thin. His stubby fingers bat at the keys. She crosses her legs. Her furry black hat, balanced on her knee, reminds her of Oscar. Oscar is a rescue cat and this past year she'd have gone crazy without him. Crazy sooner. He can judge her moods. When she's sad he reaches a soft paw to pat her cheek; at night he sleeps curled in the small of her back. When she's angry, he sits on the draining board and disapproves of her. So far as Oscar is concerned, anger is a criminal waste of energy. She's heard it said that the feline capacity for sleep has nothing to do with laziness and everything to do with conserving energy. For what? When's it to come, this burst of activity, this explosion of pent-up energy? On the Day of Judgement, perhaps?

She strokes the black hat and adjusts its position.

The man with the laptop is watching her. Glancing up, she catches him at it and smiles. He looks quickly out of the window and furrows his brow as if puzzling out a particularly difficult problem. Then, with an exaggerated grunt of understanding, he returns to his computer.

This is not unusual. People notice her. She wears her long black hair tugged back and fastened into a plait. Her face is distinctive, a triangle of jawline and cheekbones, a narrow chin and a wide mouth. People notice her, but she doubts they really see her. Not even Chris. He used to tell her she was beautiful and she would smile because although it was a lie, she does know a thing or two about illusion.

From a kiosk on Cambridge station she buys a cup of hot chocolate and a newspaper. Juggling these, she rummages for her phonecard and rings Jess to confirm the time of her train.

'Hey, Ellie.' She thrills to Jess's voice; it is the sound of homecoming. 'I'm glad you rang. I've just been talking to Babs.'

'Is she okay? Is she still upset?'

'Of course she is, she was hoping to pamper you a bit longer. She wants you to go back at the weekend.'

'I know.'

'I'll come too, if you like, if it'll help.'

When her train is announced Eleanor finds another window seat. She settles down and takes a sip of chocolate. It's too sweet and too hot and she burns her tongue. She snaps the plastic cap back on the cup. She opens the paper. None of the headlines grabs her and she's not in the mood to wrestle with the unwieldy pages.

Do mothers ever let go? Not when you're fifty, Babs said.

Jess understands. 'You're all she's got, Ellie. Be a bit gentle with her.' Eleanor remembers how, during her illness, she once woke to find Babs and Jess on either side of her bed – like a pair of vultures. That's what she thought at the time, but now her paranoia has ebbed and she remembers only their mirrored concern, Jess's smile and the frantic grasp of her mother's hand.

The train plunges into a tunnel. Eleanor's ears pop and the wavering image in the blackened window synchronizes uncannily with her thoughts. Yes, that's Jess, she smiles at the reflection, my mirror image – flaky on the outside, but strong underneath. She's such a sensible sort, is Jess.

There it is, that word again. Sensible. The train slows for the approach to King's Cross. The boy opposite scrabbles in the luggage rack and pulls down his jacket. Eleanor crams on her hat. She tugs at an earring and flicks back her plait.

Sensible. When did her life stop being sensible? She has to know. She must find the pattern, pinpoint the precise moment it started to go wrong.

Above all, she must make absolutely certain that it can never, ever happen again.

3

The train pulls into a satellite platform alongside the main station. Jess is waiting. She's wearing jeans and a sheepskin flying jacket and her hennaed hair is short and spiky. 'So you're back in the land of the living,' she laughs as they hug. 'Hey, Ellie,' she gives her shoulders a little shake. 'I've missed you.'

'Me too.'

'Well come on. Let's get going.' Jess grabs her case and frog-marches her out of the station. 'You'll never believe it, I've got so much to tell you.'

Jess's van is parked on a double yellow line and as she throws open the rear doors, a traffic warden approaches. Jess grins and shrugs apologetically. The traffic warden shakes his head and, giving a silent tut-tut, looks the other way.

Jess slides Eleanor's case alongside an old sofa stashed in the back of the van. As Eleanor buckles her seat belt, Jess pulls into the traffic. The dust embedded in the ancient stuffing shakes loose at every bump and makes Eleanor cough. Because Jess hasn't bothered to fasten it securely, the sofa slithers alarmingly at every corner.

'Is this legal?'

Jess laughs and shrugs. 'You're such a nervous passenger. Relax, Ellie, enjoy the ride.'

Jess plays cat and mouse with roaring lorries and aerodynamically unsound cabs. She knows London as well as any cabby and she ducks round corners and along silent backstreets and into another city. Her city. Ellie's, too.

Scary, Ellie getting ill like that. She remembers the phone call, the drive to the hospital, and Ellie sitting up in bed, white-faced and shivering.

No one had seen it coming. The process had been too gradual. Day by day Ellie had sunk deeper into the mire and the transition was so smooth that none of them had noticed until it was too late.

Jess blames herself. Losing Chris had left Ellie vulnerable, and Jess had run up the most enormous phone bill debating with Babs the best way to deal with this new, fragile Eleanor. When Ellie decided to move out of the flat, Babs was alarmed at the idea of her living alone. Although for Jess it was a personal disappointment, in principle she thought it a good idea. 'It'll give her a focus,' she reassured Babs. 'The new job, a new house, a whole new beginning – and it's not as if she's going far. I'll keep an eye on her, I promise.'

How could she have got it so wrong? She had misjudged the situation, and let them both down. Not that Babs blamed her. 'You did your best, dear, and to be fair, she did seem to be coping. She had us both fooled.'

A traffic light flicks to red and Jess stamps on the brake. Ellie says, 'Come on, Jess, what about it? I thought you had masses to tell me. Why so quiet?'

'I was concentrating on the traffic.'

'You never concentrate on traffic.' Jess shrugs. 'So? Come on, I've been away a month, don't tell me the whole of London has stood still . . .'

'Without you, everything screeches to a halt, you know that. Except me, of course. I've been busy as hell. I've just caned this bergère suite. You can tell, can't you?' She splays her hands on the wheel. They are the colour of raw meat and the nails are chipped and broken. She wiggles her fingers and laughs.

'You really should take more care, Jess.'

'Hark who's talking . . .'

Ellie smiles and displays her own hands. Jess envies her. Ellie has wonderful hands, lovely long fingers and perfectly honed and polished nails.

'Actually, I wasn't talking about your hands, Ellie.' Jess grins.

'Though anyone but you would have chewed them to the quick these last weeks. You make me sick sometimes, you know that? You're such a bloody perfectionist.'

'In my job . . .'

'You have to play the part, I know. You should try my job some time – give me a hand stripping this.' She gestures to the sofa. 'I need to get it done sharpish, I've a big commission coming through. Your Brian Farraday put me on to it. There's this guy he knows who owns a restaurant.' She pauses, considering. 'I think maybe my luck's on the turn. You should see him, Ellie.'

'Brian?'

'Don't mock. My pet restaurateur. He's gorgeous. Tall. And dark . . .' She gives an exaggerated shudder.

'Hey, this isn't like you.'

'I know. Amazing, isn't it? Anyway, like I was saying. Lovely, except he's got a beard, but there you go, nobody's perfect – and it's a very tasteful beard. Don't look at me like that.' She gives Eleanor's arm a little punch. 'I had to amuse myself somehow.'

'So this whole thing is up and running, is it?'

'Not exactly, but I'm working on it – and hell, where's the harm in a bit of fantasy? I know I can be a bit ratty about men, but Adam's a nice bloke. Adam – first man. If only, eh Ellie?'

'And you're working for him?'

'Sort of. He bought these chairs at auction. They're rough, need the full works – stripping, polishing, repair and recovering. It'll be time-consuming and they'll take up the whole workshop, so I need to clear the decks a bit. Hey, what is it, Ellie? You're not listening.'

She is listening. Threads are coming together, patterns forming. Her mind works like this. She's almost certain she's met this man. Brian Farraday. A restaurant. Yes. The day Brian offered her the job he took her to lunch. She remembers a tall man with curly, scalp-hugging hair and a tight beard and a shark's fin nose. He'd had to reach across the table to top up their coffee cups. 'He's got beautiful hands,' she says.

'What? Who has? What are you on about, Ellie?'

'Adam.' The pattern locks, the image sets in her mind. 'Adam Mason. I know him.'

19

4

Oscar is furious. The moment she opens the front door, Eleanor hears the bang of the cat-flap. She dumps her bag at the foot of the stairs and Oscar lumbers through from the kitchen and, seeing her, stops dead.

From the kitchen comes the gush of the tap accompanied by Jess's tuneless hum. Eleanor bobs down to Oscar's level. She really is unreasonably glad to see him. 'Hello there, puss,' she murmurs. 'How you doing?' Oscar blinks his big green eyes. She understands his dilemma. He is both pleased to see her, and piqued by her absence. Okay, so she's anthropomorphizing like mad – but who the hell cares? His confusion makes her laugh, but Oscar doesn't like being laughed at. He turns his back and sits down and starts to wash. She admires his dignity. He has a remarkably eloquent back. Disapproval and resentment chatter from every vertebra.

Jess leaves, banging the front gate behind her. Much as she loves Jess, Eleanor is glad to have her house to herself. She closes the door and draws the bolts top and bottom. She hears the rattle of Jess's starter motor. Leaning back, she spreads her palms against the wood and her fingers explore the fielded panels. The dimpled glass is cold against her shoulders. Such a relief that nothing has changed, the house is as she left it. The air she breathes she has breathed before. She starts to relax, muscles unclench, blood flows freely.

She tours the house, checking every corner and cranny. Trailing her hand along the dado, she relishes the slick surface of the paint and the opulent curves of the moulded wood.

At eighteen she had left Bury because she didn't want to go on being Babs's girl, and didn't want to be the bony, black-haired freak she encountered in her bedroom mirror day after day.

You can be whoever you want to be.

20

Easy to say, but to reinvent herself she needed a blank canvas, and it turned out that not even London, with all its scale and clamour, could provide the necessary degree of anonymity. Every area had a network of shops and services, and people soon noticed and acknowledged her. She moved from job to job, bedsit to flat, to no avail. She grew tired of the constant upheaval. That was when she answered an advert for a flatshare, and met Jess.

Not long after that she landed a public relations job with a hotel chain. She was good at her work and fond of Jess. She still got restless from time to time, but instead of moving house, she went walking.

The city excited and tantalized her with its noise and sudden silences. She was comforted by the way brick and stone, concrete and slate defined and fixed the environment. The sound of her footsteps ringing and bouncing off the walls drew her in, made her part of the changing fabric of the city.

People still notice her, but she no longer minds. She has reconstructed herself. Discovered herself, Jess would say. When people in the street turn and stare, they see a tall, stylish woman striding like an Amazon, but though they acknowledge her presence, she is still a stranger.

But these walks are not only about self-discovery. She is eager to learn the city and, like any explorer, she has her treasures, little corners of the capital she has made her own. There is St Mark's, for example, her abandoned church. She likes to sit in the boarded-up dusk, listening to the pigeons warbling in the roof space. She feels secure. The church is on a busy road and though its fabric trembles with the rumble of traffic, it has a stillness, an uncanny silence. The need to hide can be very strong. When she was little she built dens in all sorts of odd corners – under the table and sideboard, behind the sofa – and when Babs bought her a Wendy house, she hung a big crayoned sign over the door. 'Private', it said.

The church is in this tradition, somewhere to be alone, to recoup. She went there the day Chris died. Well, not the day itself, but the day she learnt what had happened. She climbed into the pulpit and it creaked and sagged but she didn't care. She tugged at the splintered wood. She made her fingers bleed and the pain was good; it placed her firmly in the here and now, stopped her sinking into the mire of the past.

Another treasure thrown up by her walks is a tiny park where no one goes in the daytime, perhaps because of the abandoned hypodermics, or maybe the feral cats. The cats look fierce and they smell but Eleanor aches at the sight of their jutting bones, at the way the skin hangs loose where the flesh has melted away. She takes them food. She would love to gather them up and take them away and look after them, but Oscar would never allow it.

It was on her way back from the park that she happened upon Farraday's gallery. She'd taken a series of wrong turnings. Suddenly she found herself outside a converted warehouse with a plate-glass window and a poster advertising an exhibition of sculpture by an artist called Andrea Harding.

Brian was a big man, tall and fleshy with a commanding voice. He took a liking to her and escorted her round the exhibition. He asked her what she thought and, without waiting for her reply, commented that surely only a female artist could come up with such wonderful foetal curves.

Eleanor frowned. 'Do you really think so? I'm not sure I agree. I don't think it's very helpful to categorize people according to your understanding of their sex.' Brian lifted an eyebrow. She stopped, her voice ringing in her ears. She was embarrassed. She knew nothing about art; any minute now he'd tell her she was speaking from the wrong orifice.

In fact he said, 'Is that so? Do go on.'

She had nothing to lose. She took a breath and continued. 'It's like you're falling for stereotypes. Women and curves go together, these sculptures have curves, therefore they must be by a woman.'

'A reasonable assumption, surely.'

'I don't think so. Although in my view she's as much at fault as you.'

'Andrea?' His right eyebrow, like a skittish black caterpillar, was on the move again. 'Tell me more.'

She bit her lip. She had a tight feeling in her chest, like a hand clutching her heart. The sculptures, the gallery, Farraday himself, moved her. She was not used to this. She said, 'She's catering to your prejudices. You, and people like you . . .'

'People like me?'

'Men.'

'A race apart, is that it?'

She shrugged. 'All I'm saying is, surely an artist should undermine expectations, not reinforce them.'

'It's a point of view, certainly.'

'You're laughing at me.'

'Not at all.' He rested a hand on her arm. 'But I do think you're over-simplifying.'

'Of course I am. This is a conversation, not a thesis.'

'Absolutely . . .'

Their argument collapsed in shared laughter, but she was still uneasy. A part of her wondered sneakingly whether he maybe had a point about Harding's work. The sculptures spoke to her in a very intimate way, evoking internal spaces and blood-lined caverns. And line. Outline. Definition. She wanted to run her hands all over them, feel her fingers slide against the stone, explore the contours and crevices.

She felt Farraday's bulk close behind her. 'Go on.' He conspired, and she could hear the smile in his voice. 'Touch.'

She touched. The stone was deliciously cool and smooth, its pale surface tinged a pinkish peach like the inside of a seashell. She placed her cheek against it.

He said, 'It's called *Redemption.*'

She discovered she had an eye for art, especially sculpture. Her responses were instinctive and Brian taught her to augment that appreciation with a more intellectual approach. 'But never lose the spontaneity of first reaction,' he cautioned. 'I cannot stress too much the value of instinct when running a commercial gallery.'

His analysis of the interaction between art and commerce intrigued her. 'Money enables,' he said. 'If an artist earns good money from his work, he's freed from the drudgery of day-to-day living. He can concentrate, move forward. My role is to help him in that.'

'For a percentage.'

'Of course. Taking a cut is nothing to be ashamed of.'

He took her to the Tate and to a variety of commercial galleries. He introduced her to the proprietors, and to some of the artists.

Jess thought the whole thing a hoot and laughed and shook her head when Eleanor tried to explain the irony of what was happening, how all her life she'd been searching for a self she could recognize – and now here it was, emerging naturally, almost of its own accord. She told her about the costumes, about *Cinderella* and *Puss In Boots*.

The outfit is slick against her skin, almost indistinguishable from it. 'This is who I am, Jess.'

And then Farraday took her to lunch at a restaurant called Jangles. It was tucked down a backstreet and the decor was plain, the atmosphere subdued. 'Not much to look at,' Brian murmured as he took her coat, 'but the food's good. The fellow that runs it only took over recently; the previous owner had a heart attack. Adam was his chef.'

They ate fresh salmon with a watercress sauce, accompanied by roasted peppers, mangetout and dauphinois potatoes. When Eleanor told Jess she was lunching with Brian, she'd laughed and said, 'So what's the score? He's rich but divorced, yes? Sounds to me like a nice, old-fashioned sugar daddy – but take care, Ellie. It doesn't do to take men too seriously, especially a man like that.'

Towards the end of the meal Eleanor's patience ran out. She'd heard all about how he'd financed the gallery, about his two marriages – one divorce and an estrangement – but so far not a word as to why they were here. 'You mentioned a proposition . . .' she said. 'Yesterday, when you asked me to lunch.'

'Ah, yes.' He smiled. 'Of course.' He mopped his lips and crumpled his napkin. 'Forgive me. The thing is, Eleanor, I've been wondering about this job of yours, at the hotel – do you enjoy it?'

'Yes, of course.'

'What in particular do you enjoy?'

'Well, for one thing, it forces me to broaden my way of thinking. If you just cut along the same old tracks, doing what everybody else is doing, where's the fun in that?'

He chuckled. 'Quite so.'

'Take your gallery, for example . . .' She hesitated, not wanting to seem pushy. 'Do you mind talking about the gallery?'

'Not in the least.'

'I've been thinking about ways you could extend your net, expand your audience, maybe enable a few more artists. It's nothing revolutionary, just a detail, but have you ever thought of distributing brochures to hotels? I've done some pricings and it wouldn't cost much to increase your print run.'

'Eleanor, this is exactly the sort of thing . . .'

'You'd have to give the hotel a cut, of course.'

'This is music to my ears. So now,' he replenished her wine and raised his own glass in a toast. 'I think we've reached the point where we should talk about us. We've got to know one another pretty well these past weeks, wouldn't you say? I'm impressed, Eleanor. You're a fast learner, you've a good eye and a quick mind.'

'I've enjoyed every moment.'

'Yes, I rather thought you had. So why not come and work for me? Don't look so shocked. Would you like to discuss the details now?' He pulled out his pocket book and scribbled some figures – a salary and a commission. He tore off the sheet and handed it to her, then waited. 'I don't expect an answer straight away.' His eyebrow twitched. 'But some indication would be nice. A smile, perhaps?' She laughed. 'We'd make quite a team, Eleanor.'

All the way home the adrenalin skittered through her veins. A role such as this would require a whole range of fresh costumes, not to mention an entirely new stage set.

Over supper she told Jess about Brian and the job – and her decision to buy her own house. Jess accused her of playing grown-ups.

'Maybe I am. So what? Who cares?'

'I care. I'll miss you, Ellie.'

'I'll miss you too.' She reached across to squeeze Jess's hand. 'But what we've got – you and me – that won't change, will it?'

'I don't know.'

'Jess . . .'

'No, okay.' Jess grinned. 'You're right, you need to do this – and of course it won't change anything between us.'

Eleanor adored the house the moment she saw it. The following day she dragged Jess along. Jess liked it too. She intended to involve Jess as much as possible at every stage.

The next weekend Babs came to stay and they both took her to see the house. She was less enthusiastic than Jess. 'What's wrong?' Eleanor demanded. 'What don't you like about it?'

'I don't understand why you're doing this, Ellie. You're barely over Chris, you've just taken on this new job,' she glanced at Jess, then back at Ellie. 'Is it really the time to be buying a house? And what about the area? Have you had a survey done? Look at this,' she flicked at the flaking paint on the windowsill. 'It's so run-down.'

'It'll be okay, I'll do it up. Jess is going to help me, aren't you, Jess? It's what I want, Mum. And yes, now is the time to be doing it.'

What happened next wasn't rational. It was strange, living alone, the house her sole responsibility. She went from room to room enjoying the solitude, but also fearing it. It crept up on her, oh so stealthily, the sense of having been abandoned. It was silly, because a great many people cared about her. They cared, but they didn't understand. Babs had never understood; Brian's main concern was the gallery; Jess had her own life. And then there was Chris.

No, it wasn't just Chris. It was the fear that she'd finally found her role – the outfit was snug, every dart and tuck nestled against her flesh – and she might never be able to change again. She was fixed now and for all time.

But it was Chris as well. What Babs and Jess and the rest couldn't see was how lonely she had become, how bleak life suddenly seemed as all her fears piled one on top of another.

The days shortened and darkened to night, and not even Babs remembered her terror of the dark.

Now, as then, the fear ripples inside her. It is a chill stream that makes her blood run slow and her quick mind sluggish. A stream. A river. Hungerford Bridge and the black Thames. The Festival Hall – a baroque palace with its bright lights and celebrating crowds, and Eleanor on the outside . . . and the music and the people, the stamp of her heels on the hard pavement and a blur of spinning faces, and the music in her head as her feet match her quickening heartbeat, and the stream heats, flowing faster and faster, and her hair flies out and the chill wind rising from the river whips her naked flesh.

5

All over now. She's better, strong and eager to be back at work. Today is Friday. Brian is expecting her on Monday. What will she wear for her first day back? She opens her wardrobe and strokes the sleeve of a jacket, pinches the seam of a skirt. She always buys the sharpest cut and the best fabric she can afford. She spends more of her income on clothes and make-up than anything else.

She decides on a dove-grey suit with a pencil skirt, a silk blouse a shade darker, and charcoal shoes.

The decision made, she goes downstairs. She's restless. She's been away too long. She belongs at the gallery; it is her true home and she can't wait to get back.

She makes coffee. She paces up and down. The mug scalds her palms. Oscar watches. Serene as a Buddha, he balances on the arm of the chair. He is absolutely still and seems to be meditating. She wants to laugh but instead tries to follow his example. It doesn't work. Her muscles twitch and her feet itch. She's a little unsteady – like that time before, with Hungerford Bridge shaking beneath her feet.

She hears herself laugh, a dry, breathy sound. Enough. She needs air; she'll go for a walk, maybe call on Jess and ask her to supper.

She has a long stride. The pavement resounds to the tap of her heels. The clamour and hardness of the city brings her back to herself and with every step the inner tremor subsides a little.

Jess's workshop is located down an alleyway, behind a dry-cleaner's. It has been raining and the cobbles smell sweet. In the winter dusk the fluorescent lights give off a sickly blue-white glow. Eleanor crosses the yard and pauses by the door. Jess always keeps the door open, because of the dust, she says.

She is stripping the sofa. With a series of deft movements she wedges the prong of her tack-ripper in place, gives it a thwack of the mallet then leans on the handle to prise out the tack. She works along the seat, wedge-thwack-prise, wedge-thwack-prise. Eleanor sways to the rhythm. Jess straightens and tosses the mallet and ripper aside. She pushes her fingers through her spiky hair. She's perspiring, her cheekbones glow. She bends back to her work, peeling away layers of velvet and calico, wadding, hessian and horsehair.

Eleanor steps across the threshold. She always feels awkward in here, teetering amongst the debris in her high heels and short skirts.

Jess looks up. 'You should wear jeans when you come here.'

'And wellies.'

'And a warm coat.'

'I don't have any jeans.'

'I know.'

'Are you busy? I was wondering about supper.'

27

'Busy as hell, but I've had enough for one day.' She flexes her stiffened fingers. 'Just give me five minutes to make a phone call.'

The telephone is in the back room. Eleanor half-listens. The call is to Jess's supplier. Hurry up, Jess, it's freezing in here. How can she bear to work in the cold like this? She slides her hands into the pockets of her jacket. Come to that, how can she bear to work in such a mess? Piled all around and pushed against the walls is a hopeless jumble of furniture, every piece at a different stage of dismantlement or reconstruction. Against the back wall is a bench. Eleanor's hand hovers above the array of tools. It is a seductive display. One by one, she fingers them. There is a small hammer with a magnetic head – she experiments on a cluster of tacks. Then there's the tack-ripper and a Stanley knife and next to this a selection of needles, all different shapes and sizes. One is like a sliver of new moon. Another is long and broad with a flat-tipped blade. She touches it tentatively with the tip of her finger. The metal is cold. She picks it up, and feels a deep, muffled response, a seismic rumble of fear.

I can control this.

She spans the needle across the pads of her fingers, testing its weight and balance. So sharp. She touches the point – the graze of a nettle, a split fraction of stillness. And silence. A whole new sensation. Can she make it come again? Try. She lays the tip of the blade against the ball of her thumb. She pauses. There is a murmur of excitement in her head, a fluttering in her veins. She presses down on the shaft of the needle. Yes, here it comes, a sting of pain and a deep, deep stillness.

In the ice-field silence the flesh whitens and the skin breaks. A bead of blood mists the steel.

'What on earth are you doing?' The ice cracks and the needle goes deeper. 'For God's sake . . .' A man's voice. Her head jerks up. He's staring at her hand. She looks back down. She's bleeding. She tosses the needle on to the bench and, pressing the ball of her thumb to her lips, sucks the wound clean. He is still watching her. Her skin feels rough and unfamiliar. Her blood tastes salty, and just a little sweet.

6

In times of crisis, Adam resorts to the kitchen. From the age of nine it has been his natural habitat. There's nothing so reassuring as the tick of knife against chopping board, the smell of bruised herbs, the weight of a sauce and its sheen as it coats the spoon.

He is delighted both by the action of cooking and the excitement of invention. He'll take a few basic ingredients – pasta perhaps, or some chicken – and off he'll go, chopping and peeling and pounding, his mind racing through his repertoire of spices and herbs. There's nothing like it, the thrill of it, the adrenalin rush. Cooking is an art form – complementary flavours, variety of colour and texture, presentation, display, showmanship . . .

The very things his restaurant lacks. There is no sense of theatre. In the food, yes, the food is dramatic enough, but the staging is bland. It's driving him crazy but his finances are stretched to the limit. Earlier this evening Kay had brought his books to the flat and taken him through them page by page, explaining his limitations. 'What am I supposed to do?' he demanded. 'We're barely ticking over. I've been talking to Brian Farraday. He hardly comes in these days – apparently his clients expect a little more pizazz.'

'You can't afford pizazz. Okay, things may not be as bad as I've made them sound, but after that business with the chairs I wanted to be sure you didn't go off and do something silly, like buy a new coffee machine or something.'

'I've got a new coffee machine. And what's wrong with the chairs? They're an investment.'

'They'll look ridiculous – all done up and tarty, and everything else gasping for a lick of paint. Just take it a step at a time, Adam. You're doing okay . . .'

'I'm sorry.' He poured another measure of brandy. 'But "doing okay" isn't good enough.'

'Then look at the figures.' She pushed a handwritten sheet across the table. Her projections for the next six months. 'Go on. Look at them. Unless you've got a rabbit tucked in your hat, it's got to be good enough for now.'

'You don't understand. I can't operate in a straitjacket. I'm not like you, I refuse to live my life in the third division.' He stopped. His words ricocheted round the kitchen. 'I'm sorry. That's dreadful. I didn't mean to say that – but look at me, Kay, I've got stuck in this bloody rut and I haven't a clue how to get out.'

Kay leant forward and touched her fingertips to his. Looking down, he saw a pair of disembodied hands that had nothing to do with him. Every day he drifted a little further from Kay.

'You'll get there,' she said gently. 'We both know that, but it won't happen overnight. Building a reputation takes time. Can't you try and be just a little patient?'

'No.' He sounds sulky, like a child. Kay's right, but he doesn't want her to be. Sensible Kay with her feet of clay. His dream is a gothic confection, a centrepiece of spun caramel and carved ice. Serve fudge ice-cream, says Kay, and be satisfied.

They go to bed unreconciled. He's ashamed of himself. She's beside him now, warm and loving. She moves. The bedcovers shift and there's a draught as she reaches for him. He feigns sleep and, rolling away, buries his face in the pillow.

When he was little, food was just fuel. Cornflakes and toast, sausages and beans. He was nine when his mother became pregnant and Gran started talking about the need to 'eat for two'. What else did his mother do for two? Did she piddle and crap twice as much? He watched her. He counted her visits to the toilet and timed her on the watch she'd given him for Christmas.

Then one day his mother had a pain. An ambulance rushed her to hospital, and Gran came to take care of Adam.

'Soup,' she announced that first afternoon as she puffed into the kitchen. She dumped her shopping bag on the table. Her glasses were all steamed up and her eyes blinked like ghosts behind the thick lenses. 'Always good to have a pot of soup on the go.' She ruffled his hair. 'Come along then, Adam lad, you going to give me a hand?'

His mother wouldn't let him near the kitchen knives. 'What

nonsense,' said Gran. 'Treating you like a two-year-old. You're a big boy, time you learnt. Come here.' She laid a cold hand over his. It looked like a map with its bulging blue veins and irregular liver-spots marking out towns and villages. But that was just on the surface. She showed him how to grasp the knife and press down on the blade. The tendons formed slender ridges under her thin skin. She was strong, was Gran. Deep down.

Gathering together a pile of carrots and leeks, turnips and onions, she set him to peel and chop. The kitchen was hot. Condensation streamed down the walls and made little puddles on the worktops. Gran hummed and tossed the roasted bones in the fat until they sizzled and spat. Tipping the bones into the pot, she added the vegetables and juniper berries and peppercorns, and Adam tied a bundle of bay, rosemary, thyme and parsley.

The pot bubbled and his mother's kitchen began to smell like Gran's house. His mouth watered. 'Is it ready yet? I'm starving. When can we have some, will it be soon?'

Gran laughed. 'No. We have to boil it up once a day to let all the flavours mix and mature. Like cheese. Or wine. Vintage soup, that's what we're making, Adam, what d'you say to that?'

Three days later Gran declared the soup ready. It was the day his mother came home. Alone. His baby brother was dead.

So Adam associates kitchens and cooking with crisis and comfort. He's not sure whether he's currently in a state of crisis, but he certainly needs comforting.

Kay has taken to leaving things in his flat. A magazine tossed in an armchair, her calculator and pens on the coffee table. Shampoo and a loofah in the bathroom. They've been seeing each other for six months and she's beginning to make assumptions. She has every right, but it makes him uneasy.

He can't sleep. He lies on his left side, but gets pins and needles in his arm. He rolls over, but that's still not right, so back he goes to start the whole process over again, all the while trying not to wake Kay, not to nudge her or make too much of a draught. She's breathing deeply. How does she do it, sleep like that, oblivious to him and the state he's in? Why doesn't she wake? No, he doesn't want her to wake. She'll insist on talking things through; she'll try to find out what's wrong, maybe go over the figures again.

31

He knows the restaurant isn't really doing so badly, but he lacks patience and gets frustrated by how far reality falls short of his ideal.

The idea of a piecemeal refurbishment had come, indirectly, from Rickie. When Rickie owned Jangles, Adam was his chef and, after his heart attack, he offered Adam a controlling share. He's a good partner; he likes to be kept informed, but never interferes with the day-to-day running.

'Trouble is,' Adam confided, 'serving good food's just not enough these days. We've got to be distinctive, we need a marketable identity. And that costs money.'

'It needn't, you know.' Rickie laughed. 'Don't look at me like that, Adam. I know in my day I was happy to let Jangles tick over, but that doesn't mean I never looked into the alternatives, wasn't tempted to make changes – and I'll tell you this, style doesn't have to be expensive. There are ways and ways of achieving an end.'

'Meaning?'

'Imagination. Innovation. I know you can do it,' he chuckled. 'I've tasted some of your concoctions.'

'It's hardly the same.'

'Sure it is. You just need to take a sideways look at things. No, no.' He shook his head as Adam drew breath to argue. 'That's all I have to say on the subject. It's down to you, now. The restaurant's your responsibility. Adopt and adapt, that's all I'm saying. Adopt and adapt.'

Adam was irritated. He thought Rickie was being sly and a touch cussed. He put the conversation out of his mind, but then a few weeks later he heard about an auction of bankrupt stock. He went to the sale. He saw the chairs. Adopt and adapt.

Kay was furious. It has nothing to do with her, but she keeps his books and grumbles if too much money leaks from the system. She doesn't understand. Okay, so the chairs are rough and they need a lot of work – but they're still a snip.

It was Brian Farraday who told him about Jessica Grant. 'She's a friend of a friend. Does up all sorts of odd stuff. Bit off the wall, but good, and she won't rook you. I'll give you her number.'

He met with Jessica. They discussed the timescale and cost of the project, and he took away some fabric swatches. It was these he was returning to the workshop this afternoon.

It had rained that morning. Dark puddles spanned the alleyway and he had to perform a strange, elasticated dance to dodge round them. Although her door was open, Jessica wasn't there. He stepped inside, and saw that she had another visitor.

He half recognized the woman. She was tall and slim. Her immaculate outfit included a ridiculous pair of high-heeled shoes, and she was as out of place here as a giraffe in a hen run.

The workshop looked as if the contents of a giant sack had been upended on the floor. Wadding and hessian and horsehair were strewn everywhere. Discarded tacks crunched beneath his shoes. The rough carcass of a sofa occupied the central space. The giraffe presided.

He sees her now. So severe. Her hair is tugged into a long plait that skids down her back. She's concentrating on something in her hand. He strains to see. He can hardly believe it. She is digging the point of a long needle into the ball of her thumb. He sees the bubble of blood, hears the sharp inrush of breath. His, or hers?

'What on earth are you doing?'

She starts. She stares at her thumb, as if only now realizing what she's done. She presses the wound to her lips, watching him as she does so.

She has the most remarkable cocktail-blue eyes. She sucks her thumb and smiles at him. And she, not the restaurant, is the reason he cannot sleep.

7

'Eleanor, dear, you're sounding much better – I'm so pleased to hear it.' Babs's voice flickers intimately along the telephone line. It feels as though she's right here in the room. 'How's work?'

'Work's fine.'

'That's good. I'm sure Mr Farraday's delighted to have you back. And Jess? Is Jess okay?'

'She's very busy at the moment, but yes, she's fine.'

'You must bring her with you, next time you come to Bury.' In the silence Eleanor worries at a loose wallpaper seam. 'You never did come back for that weekend.'

The first time she'd taken Jess to Bury had been for Babs's fiftieth birthday. She'd really wanted Chris to go, but he wouldn't take the risk.

Jess had loved Eleanor's home town. 'But it's great.' She laughed and gave a little pirouette. 'I don't know why you make such a fuss. I mean, just look at it, Ellie . . .' The flat-faced Georgian cottages flowed in a brick ribbon to the end of the street. Some of the doors were flanked by white pilasters and topped by graceful lunettes; others had boot-scrapers and dolphin door knockers and bright brass letter-flaps. 'It's like a BBC costume drama; Jane Austen meets George Eliot.'

Babs persists. 'Why not come next weekend? You and Jess.'

'I don't know. Jess has landed a big order.'

'In that case, come on your own. Or I could come down to London, how about that? I was going to buy you a coat, remember?'

'I don't need a coat.'

'Eleanor . . .'

'I'm sorry, I didn't mean to be sharp, but can't we just leave it for a bit?'

'If that's what you want, of course we can.'

'I need a bit more time, that's all. Things are starting to come together. There's nothing to worry about, Mum, honestly. Listen, why don't I ring you tomorrow and we can have a long talk, only I'm going out in a little while and I need to get ready . . .'

'Of course, dear. I mustn't keep you. Are you going somewhere nice? You and Jess, is it?'

'No. Not Jess.'

'Well, have a lovely time.' She hears a long intake of breath – Babs struggling not to swamp her with curiosity and concern. 'I'll talk to you tomorrow. You take care, Eleanor.'

'Of course I will. Bye, Mum.' She places the phone gently back on its cradle. If Babs knew where she was going and with whom, she'd be straight on the phone to Jess demanding to know who this Adam Mason was, where Eleanor had met him, and whether or not he constituted a threat.

Jess is annoyed about Adam. She makes light of it, but it goes surprisingly deep. A week ago she'd turned up on Eleanor's doorstep looking flushed and edgy. Instead of her usual greeting kiss, she shoved a bottle of wine into Eleanor's hand and pushed past her to the living room. Eleanor hovered in the doorway, nursing the bottle. Jess dumped herself on the sofa, kicked off her shoes and lodged her feet on the arm.

'Well, who bit you today?' Eleanor grinned.

'Nobody bit me. You going to open that, or not?'

Eleanor struggled with the wine. The cork was stubborn and the bottle fought back.

'What a wimp,' said Jess. 'Give it here.'

'No need.' Eleanor sprang the cork with a pop and filled Jess's glass. 'So,' she settled back on her heels. 'Let me guess. You've either pranged the van again, dropped a hammer on your foot – or Adam Mason's cancelled his order.' Jess grunted. 'That's it, isn't it?'

'No.'

'Well, it's something to do with him . . .'

'Screw Adam Mason.'

'Exactly.'

Jess glared at her. 'Listen, if you weren't my best mate, I'd be scratching your eyes out right now.'

'I knew it – definitely a bite, and the dog was rabid . . .'

'I saw him first, Ellie. Don't look at me like that, don't play the innocent. What did I say the day you got back from Bury? A gorgeous man, I said.'

'I remember.'

'Well then. Bags-I.'

'Fine.'

'Hands off.'

'Am I arguing? I must be missing something here. Do you remember what you told me, way back when we first met? "Men are like dogs," you said. "Sit, beg and roll over, that's all they're good for . . ."'

'And when you're done, pass them to a new owner. I know, Ellie, I remember. I've had one or two bad experiences – we both have – and I get a bit over-emphatic, but there's a difference between theory and practice, and Adam's different somehow, don't you think? You know, I really thought my luck had started to change.'

'Okay, so maybe it has.'

'No way. I saw how he looked at you. Cow-eyes or what?'

'I can't help the way he looked at me.'

'Sure you can, you're not trying. Dress in a sack, don't wash your hair . . .' Their eyes met. Jess swung her feet off the sofa and held out her glass for a refill.

'All right,' said Eleanor. 'Let's sort this once and for all. I go along with the dog theory, one hundred per cent, but if you think Adam's different, fine. Good luck to you. All I want is to be me, and in my experience, men always want me to be someone else. I promise you, I'm not interested in Adam Mason – not after last time. Think about it, Jess, you were there. Burnt fingers, burnt toes and nose. The field's clear, I swear.'

'It doesn't look it from here.'

'What you think you saw that day – he was just startled because he'd caught me playing the fool. He wasn't cow-eyed, Jess, he was pop-eyed with horror.'

'If you say so – but then why was he round at my place this afternoon fishing for your phone number?'

It took Adam Mason a week to telephone, which was long enough for Eleanor to make up her mind absolutely, definitely and for all time, that she was not in the market for another relationship.

When he finally rang it was after midnight. She was on her way to bed and he caught her off guard.

'Remember me?' His voice resonated. 'Adam Mason. We met at Jessica Grant's . . .'

'Yes.'

'It's very late, I know . . .'

'Yes.'

'It must seem odd, my ringing out of the blue like this.'

'Jess warned me, she said you'd asked for my number.'

'I hope you don't mind.'

'Yes. I mind.' He was silent. 'I'm sorry, I didn't mean to sound rude.'

'Of course not. It's my fault. I'm not very good at this.'

'No. Me neither.' Perhaps if he had been more polished in his approach, she'd have found it easier to turn him down. As it was, his awkwardness intrigued her. She said, 'I don't suppose you'll remember this, but we have met before.'

'You came to my restaurant with Brian Farraday.'

'I'm impressed.'

'I'd forgotten until I saw you at Jessica's.'

'You didn't catch me at my best. I was feeling a bit bloody.'

'Yes.' She could sense him smiling.

'So?'

'I was wondering if there was a chance we could meet?'

'I don't know.' Beg, sit, roll over – easy to say, but he's aroused her curiosity. What kind of man angles for a date with a woman who at their most memorable meeting had shown such a predilection for self-mutilation? 'All right, yes,' she says at last. 'I think I'd like that.'

But now, as she rests her head against the rim of the bath, she belatedly questions the wisdom of that decision.

'It doesn't have to be heavy,' said the now resigned Jess. 'Enjoy yourself. You deserve some fun.'

'We both do.'

She soaps the flannel and works it between her long toes. After Chris she'd sworn never to expose herself again.

Perhaps Jess is right, perhaps Adam is different. She remembers his alarm at the sight of her bloody thumb. She'd wanted to laugh. When Jess introduced them, his handshake was brisk and slightly embarrassed.

She stretches her arm and splays her fingers. Bath-water dribbles down her wrists. She can still feel the imprint of his grip. And then there's the way he'd looked at her – Jess has a point about that.

She sits up. The water has grown cold. She pulls the plug and steps out of the bath. Bubble-suds stream down her thighs and darken the toffee-coloured floorboards. She dabbles her toes in the puddle. Too much water. It will seep through the cracks and run down the joists and make a stain on her kitchen ceiling. This householder lark is a big responsibility.

The mirror above the sink is misted with condensation. She blinks, and the ghost in the mirror blinks back.

Babs had offered to give a hand decorating the house. Babs is into colour in a big way. She'd recently repainted her kitchen, and a flare of purple and orange dazzled Eleanor's inner eye. She said, 'It's okay, Mum, it's all in hand.' The next day she went shopping with

Jess. They bought two huge cans of magnolia emulsion, then visited a charity shop where they found a pair of curtains – mushroom-coloured with tiny green sprigs – and a wooden frame for the bathroom mirror which she painted blue and decorated with gold-coloured cockleshells. The shells remain a cause for concern. The gold is a bit Babs-ish. She must resign herself. No escape. A residue of bad taste lingers in her genes.

With a swipe of her hand she dashes the steam from the mirror. She shivers. Her wet hair clings like black seaweed; she feels its heavy drag across her shoulders. She extends her arms above her head and the air tightens her exposed skin. The sensation pleases her. She likes to be reminded of her body's boundaries.

It's late. She should get dressed. What to wear? Ridiculous to be so excited. She is about to have a quiet drink with the man her best friend fancies. And no wonder. Adam Mason has charm and a nice smile and the kind of voice that goes right through you.

When she agreed to the meeting he'd sounded excited as a boy. She'd found that rather touching, but when she asked where and when they should meet, he became confused. He hadn't thought it through, and that disturbs her.

She pulls her make-up basket towards her and peers into the mirror. It's an age since she last played this game. She remembers her first date with Chris. Three years ago.

She cannot excuse what happened. He'd never hidden the fact that he was married; she knew what she was doing. She saw the pitfalls, and marched straight into them.

Three years. She's a different person now, she cannot remember that other woman.

If she cannot remember, she'll have to invent. There are many sorts of costume; there are those that fit, and those that conceal.

She will paint a mask, and hide behind it. She traces the line of her cheek. Her skin is soft, and very pale. A naked face reveals more than a naked body and she sees the outline of angular adolescence skimming beneath the surface.

She begins to paint. She must make artifice look natural. He mustn't suspect. She tints her skin with a light cream, then adds a dusting of blusher and powder. Now the eyes. She colours her lids, patiently blending one tone into another. With the finest of brushes she outlines her lashes, then thickens and lengthens them. She stains her lips two shades darker than their natural colour. As she works, the ghost in the mirror vanishes and the new image acquires substance and form.

She rubs the last of the moisture from her hair and pulls it into a plait. She lingers for a moment, examining her reflection. The clothed face and naked body are a disturbing combination. Chris was sometimes scared of her, of what she represented. She had enjoyed his fear, it made her strong, but it had also meant that sooner rather than later, he was bound to return to his wife.

Eleanor has seen his wife. She is ordinary. She wears printed cottons and has a scrubbed, middle-class face. She is dull, which is why Chris came to her; she is also safe, which is why he wouldn't stay.

She closes her eyes. The images flicker like paper cutouts in a breeze. They are not real. She is not real; she cannot recognize this version of herself. Maybe it had all been a lie, maybe Chris had died for nothing.

She turns away from the mirror. The mirror lies. She must move on to the next stage. Padding through to the bedroom she scrambles across the bed that fills almost the entire space, and opens the creaking wardrobe door. The acrid honey smell coming from the muslin pot-pourri bags dangling round the necks of the hangers, makes her eyes sting. She bats away her tears with the flat of her palm, and pushes the hangers along their rail. Metal screeches against metal. Her fingers encounter silk and fine wool. She cannot choose. She allows her fingers to flutter and settle wherever they like. She pulls out a short, plum-coloured dress and holds it against her. She closes the wardrobe door and turns slowly in front of the mirror. Yes, this will do. She adds a silk scarf, shades of lilac bleeding to dark mauve. She swivels to catch herself at all angles. An all-round performance. The image fills the screen. She likes what she sees. The slim body and clean sharp lines that accentuate her height and colouring make her the perfect foil for Adam Mason, who is also dark and tall.

8

Adam is bewildered by the disjunction between how little he knows about Eleanor and the enormous amount of time he spends thinking about her. Two days after their encounter, he made a return visit to Jessica's workshop.

'I'm arranging transport for the chairs,' he said. 'When will you be ready for them?'

Jessica's narrow eyebrows shot up. 'You could have phoned to ask that.'

'Well, yes . . .'

'And don't tell me you were just passing.'

'Okay,' he smiled. 'Nothing gets past you, does it?' He waited, hoping she'd fill in the blanks, but no. How to go about this? He could dance round the houses, try to tease the information from her, or he could jump straight in. Yes, he is a practical man, there's something he needs to know, best ask outright, ridiculous to be so fey. He says, 'That friend of yours – you introduced us . . .'

'Lady Pincushion. What about her?'

'She's amazing.'

'I suppose she is, if you like that sort of thing. Do you, Adam?'

He felt foolish. 'To be honest, I'm not sure. Is she always so wacky?'

Jessica shrugged. 'She's had a hard time.'

'I see.' He paused, framing the question in his mind, trying to make it less like an interrogation. 'The two of you go back a long way, do you?' No response. 'Okay. I'll get to the point. Your friend made a hell of an impression on me the other day. I'd like to see her again. I thought we might have a drink, get to know one another . . .'

'That's between you and her. I don't see where I come in.'

'You can tell me where to find her, give me her phone number.'

40

'I barely know you.'

'I'm not a rapist, I swear . . .'

'I think I believe you.' Jessica smiled and relaxed a little. 'But Ellie's different. You said it yourself, she's a bit wacky. Hardly your average casual date.'

'I'll be gentle – kid gloves, I promise.'

She gives in, but he doesn't ring straight away. Again and again he replays the scene in the workshop – Eleanor and the blood and the needle. It makes no sense. She is too far removed from the normal run of his life and Jessica's right, he should leave her alone.

Yet where's the harm in a drink?

Her difference, her contradictions, excite him. She's like a waterfall flickering in sunlight and shadow, or a cocktail – all colour and light to the eye and deep layers of flavour to be explored by the palate.

This thought dances like fire on the rim of his mind as he rings her doorbell. She doesn't answer straight away.

He closes his eyes, and sees her eyes like blue Curacao, her hesitant smile and her blood-smeared thumb. A muscle pumps in his cheek. He hears her tread in the hall. The black cat watching him from the inner sill of the bay jumps down into the room.

There is a pub close by and they decide to walk. He is struck by how suited they are. She is tall and can match his stride. Kay has to trot to keep up. With Kay he checks his stride, a horse in harness. Now he steps free. Eleanor looks straight ahead. Her profile is stern and the straining hairline reveals her vulnerable ears, pinched white with the cold and pixie-pointed at their tips.

Why is Jessica so protective of her?

The barman forgets the lemon for the gin and tonic and is annoyed when Adam insists. The pub is crowded and noisy. She sips her drink. Leaning closer to make himself heard, he confides, 'I'm glad you agreed to come.'

'It was wrong of Jess to give you my number.'

'Well, she did treat it like it was classified, but I used all my powers of persuasion. I had to, I didn't know how else to contact you. I couldn't remember your surname, and I don't know where you work.'

'You work in a restaurant, don't you?'

The change of subject is abrupt and pointed. He tastes sharpness on his tongue, but swallows it. 'I own it,' he corrects her. 'It's called

Jangles, but you know that, you've been there.' Strangers jostle them, forcing them to stand closer.

'And you can just abandon it for the evening, can you?'

'I've an assistant, Tom. He's very good, and Mondays are generally quiet.'

'You should run a pub.' She bites her lip and glances round the bar. 'Scampi and lasagne . . .'

'Chips with everything.' He shudders.

'And peas. And dried-up cucumber garnish.'

He laughs and pulls out a packet of cigarettes. 'D'you mind?' As he strikes his lighter, a man bumps into Eleanor, slopping her drink over her hand. She recoils and shakes glistening drops of gin from her fingers.

'Eleanor, this place is dreadful.'

'I only suggested it because it was near.'

'Shall we go somewhere else?'

She hesitates. 'Where?'

He can't think of anywhere. He says, 'I don't know this area.'

'I suppose we could go back to my place. I'll open some wine. It won't be up to your standards, of course . . .'

'I'm not fussy.'

She laughs, but he can see she knows it's a lie.

When they reach her house she ushers him into the living room and goes round plumping up cushions and turning on table lamps. She says, 'I hope this is okay. I don't like overhead lighting, it's too harsh. Why don't you sit down? I'll fetch the corkscrew.'

Eleanor takes refuge in the kitchen. What devil had prompted her to invite him back when she could have brought the whole joke to a dignified close in the pub?

She had begun by being curious about Adam Mason. Her intention had been to satisfy that curiosity and then steer him in Jess's direction, but now she's not so sure.

She hunts for the corkscrew. She really rather likes the man. He makes her laugh, and his occasional awkwardness is touching.

It is also a source of concern. Something doesn't gel. Little tell-tale signs remind her of Chris.

Adam is also uncomfortable. He paces the room. Perhaps he should follow her to the kitchen. No. The state he's in he's liable to

42

go through her cupboards, assessing her spice range, checking nothing has overrun its sell-by date. A fine impression that'd make.

It isn't just Eleanor who's making him nervous, it's the house. She confounds every expectation. Nothing quite fits. He'd imagined her living somewhere more stylish – a modern flat with polished teak floors and calico rugs and furniture to be admired rather than used. He had not expected clutter. Eleanor's house lacks permanence; it feels like a stopover. And yet he suspects that this, like so much else, is contrived. The paper lampshades and threadbare carpet, the cardboard shoe box and the bookshelf in the hall with its ragged row of paperbacks, combine to make too articulate a statement. They suggest she might up and go at any moment, and he doesn't believe it. He'd lay money the house is owned, not rented. There are some signs of permanence, like the big black cat asleep in a tight ball in the seat of an armchair.

She returns and smiles and tells him to sit down. The sofa is squidgy and its springs ping. He laughs and edges along the seat. 'I thought your best friend was an upholsterer.'

'Cobblers' children. She's so busy, and now someone's lumbered her with a job lot of chairs . . .' She perches on the arm of the cat's chair and runs her thumb the length of a velvet ear. He asks the cat's name. 'Oscar.' She strokes the curved back, and Oscar uncoils and stretches to expose his tummy. 'He was a stray, scared of everything and everyone when I first got him. Now look at him, sleeping like a baby in the presence of a stranger.'

'The stranger being me?'

'Who else?'

'Then make an effort, Eleanor. Come and sit here.' He cannot believe he is being so crass. He adjusts a battered cushion, ostensibly to make room for her, in reality to cover his embarrassment.

She's looking at him and he forces himself to meet her gaze. Her eyes are blue and clear, but he's certain she's not seeing either the room or their situation quite as he sees it. He is like an actor who has wandered on to the wrong stage clutching the wrong script.

She says, 'I'm not sure about this. I almost didn't agree to tonight. Tell me what you're doing here, Adam.'

'I don't know.' Her eyes widen. 'It's the truth. What would you like me to say? What's the big mystery? If you don't want me here, just say and I'll leave.'

'It isn't that.'

'Then what?'

'I need to get some things straight, ask you some questions . . .'

'Go ahead, interrogate me.'

'When you rang to suggest we meet – well, there's something that's been bugging me ever since.'

'I was clumsy.'

'Yes, but more than that. I'm sorry, I have to ask you this, and I need you to be truthful.'

'I've nothing to hide, Eleanor.' She caresses Oscar's belly from chin to crotch and the cat emits a loud, deep-throated purr. 'I promise you,' he laughs to cover his awkwardness. 'I've led a pretty blameless life. In my line of work I'm too tired to debauch at the end of the day.'

She drains her wine and places her glass carefully on the mantelpiece. 'Not debauch, no . . .' she speaks almost musingly. 'But you are married, aren't you?'

'What? No!' His indignation is real, but a notch too high. He isn't married, but he's not exactly free. 'What on earth makes you say that?'

'Little things. You see, I can tell, I've been here before. Things you say, the way you behave . . .'

'Such as? What have I said, what have I done?'

He can hear himself, he sounds as guilty as hell. She turns to face him. Like the sun-winking sea, her eyes glitter on the surface, but are dark beneath. 'You're out of practice,' she says. 'You're at a loss when it comes to thinking up places to go. And you were too keen to meet here, at my home. You didn't want me stamping around on your territory.'

'That isn't so.'

'I know the signs, Adam. You're scared of being seen.' He stares at her. He can't respond; his mouth is dry and his throat aches. 'You see?' she says, and it's as if his silence is an admission of guilt. 'I knew.' She's standing now, towering over him. She's so tall, like a tree on a heath. 'I know how this goes, Adam, and it's dreadful. For everyone. I can't handle the subterfuge, living on the edge of someone's life, always last in their list of priorities. Some women can go with that, I can't. After Chris I said never again. If I'd realized sooner, I wouldn't have agreed to this evening.'

'I am not married.' He speaks slowly and clearly as he takes her by the shoulders. He is no longer thinking of himself and his own indignation, but of her. Her face is transformed by this something in her past; it has become gaunt, the structure of her bones achingly visible beneath the straining flesh. He lays his hand against her cheek. His framing fingers soften the stark outline. 'I am not married,' he repeats softly. 'I've never been. What's true of debauchery is true of marriage. It's hard, in my line of work. Long hours . . .'

'But there is someone.'

'Yes. But not how you think. It isn't serious. We don't live together. She moonlights for me, does my books.'

'Books?'

'Money. Talks to the bank. That sort of thing. I drifted into it, it's not right and it's over – it has been for a long time, but I'd got into the habit of being with her. Now you've shown me what a sham it is. That's why I'm here. I wouldn't hurt you, Eleanor. I wouldn't do that to you.'

He holds his breath, waiting for her to believe him. Her eyes are bright and close. A stab of mingled fear and desire is followed by a moment of surprising calm. She touches his hair, his temple; she drags a finger the length of his jaw and her nail snags in his beard. She leans closer. Her wine-flavoured breath brushes his lips. He inhales and his blood swells and his head swims. Although he can hardly see, he thinks she's smiling as she kisses him.

The connection is immediate – the spark or flare or whatever it is that tells him this is how it should be, is what he's been waiting for all his life. Her lips explore his, moist and hungry. Tasting her, he is eager for more but she still keeps him at a distance. Her hands push at his shoulders, their lips, tender and distended with desire, are the only points of intimate contact.

And then she releases him. Her hands fly from his shoulders and her lips close. She steps back. Her face is flushed, her eyelids lowered. He reaches out, then checks the impulse. She speaks softly, as if to herself. 'I can't do this.'

'Eleanor . . .'

'Is she waiting for you? Where does she think you are?'

'Who?' His mind flounders. Kay. She means Kay. He says, 'I told you. It's over.'

'Maybe for you, it is. But think about it, Adam, what about her?'

9

Adam lives on the top floor of a converted Victorian villa. He parks his car and, peering up, sees that the lights are on. It must be Kay. It had been a big mistake on his part, giving her a key.

'I called at the restaurant,' she accuses. She's sitting at the kitchen table with his cashbooks spread out in front of her. 'Tom said you'd taken the night off. You didn't tell me. Where have you been?'

'Out.' His face burns in the fluorescent glare. Eleanor's reproach is still ringing in his ears.

'Where?'

'Just out, Kay. You're not my keeper.' Again he sounds guilty, again he has no cause. A couple of drinks, a kiss and a misunder-standing – what does that amount to?

'I only asked.'

'Well, you've been answered.' He stops. 'I'm sorry, I didn't mean to snap.'

'It's okay.' She gives his fingers a reassuring squeeze. 'I know you're worried, but it's not so bad. The restaurant will be a success, truly it will, just give it time.' He tries to disengage his hand but she keeps hold of him. Kay's hand gripping his, Kay's caress and Kay's lips where just a short while ago it was Eleanor's touch and Eleanor's kiss. 'Adam?' She moves closer, and his body betrays him with Kay just as earlier it betrayed him with Eleanor.

And now, hours later, he lies awake tossing and turning in a fever of confusion.

He rolls away from Kay and clings to the edge of the mattress. Squeezing his eyes tight shut, he tries to concentrate on other things.

The restaurant. One of the things he regrets about running his own restaurant is that it leaves him little opportunity to do any cooking himself. He prices the dishes and keeps a general eye on the kitchen, but has to spend most of his time out front. That's where he first saw Eleanor. She came in with Brian Farraday. She'd made hardly any impression on that occasion, but in Jessica's workshop she'd near as dammit blown his head off.

He slides out of bed. Kay doesn't stir. His dressing gown is on the back of the door. The hanger rattles, but still Kay doesn't wake.

He collects his cigarettes from the living room and goes through to the kitchen. The room has two windows with views of the streets to the front and side.

He fumbles a cigarette from the packet and lights up. No self-respecting chef should smoke in the kitchen. No self-respecting chef should smoke at all. The sensitivity of his palate and his acute sense of smell are vital to his success. Yet sometimes he welcomes a deadening of these faculties, and tonight he feels a further need to break with established patterns. He takes a long, deep drag and the tip of the cigarette glows like a devil's eye in the dark. A light goes on in a house opposite. Someone else is unable to sleep and he finds that reassuring. He'll respond, signal to them that they're not alone. He visualises a network of insomniacs flickering their lights back and forth across the city.

Kay's papers are still scattered across the table. What's she been up to, beavering away over her figures while he was with Eleanor? He flicks through the sheets. She seems to have been working on another set of projections. She's good with figures. She works in a building society, but every so often he tries to persuade her to train properly. 'You could become an accountant,' he says. 'Get a real job.'

'I've got a real job. Leave me alone, Adam.'

That's Kay all over. No imagination. Not even enough to be an accountant.

How can he be so unkind? She's content with her lot – and good for her. Just so long as she doesn't thwart his ambitions.

But it was true, what he'd told Eleanor. He'd drifted into this relationship. When he met Kay he was uncommitted. His previous relationship had broken up months before.

He turns over another sheet of calculations. Kay's handwriting is plump and childlike. The figures remind him of soft toys. Eight is a fat-tummied teddy bear; two is a penguin; three . . . no, he's playing games. The figures are just figures, amounts of money spent and received, the stuff of which, according to Kay, his business is made. In his view it's made of something far more substantial, if less durable.

He tosses Kay's papers aside, opens the fridge and takes out a carton of milk and a block of butter. He fills a pan with water and heats it slowly to poach the eggs. He snips some chives from a terracotta pot on the windowsill, and starts to cook.

The process relaxes him a little. His thoughts become more evenly spaced. Something has gone awry in his life. There is a mismatch between how things ought to be and how they are. Nothing fits. It's like trying to align a painting to the landscape that inspired it. It can't be done. A transmutation has occurred which renders the one only faintly recognizable in the other. It's like that with the restaurant, and it's like that with Kay. She's not the woman he wants to spend his life with and, in fairness to them both, he's going to have to tell her. He may have already ruined his chances with Eleanor, but it's better to be alone than to be with the wrong person.

He rubs two slices of French bread with a clove of garlic, then browns them under the grill. The eggs are ready and, arranging them on the toast, he spoons over the sauce. As he sits down to eat, the door opens.

'What's going on?' Kay leans against the doorframe. Her hair is all spiky with sleep. She blinks in the light. 'What are you doing?'

'Eating.' He plunges his fork into the egg and the viscous, sunflower-yellow yolk spills over the bread and on to the plate.

'I can see that. It's four in the morning. You must be crazy.'

'Yes,' he whispers. An image of Eleanor stalks through his mind. He looks at Kay with a tug of regret. She's so sleepy and innocent. He knows what to do, but not how to do it. He forces a smile. 'How about some coffee?' he says. She nods. 'Come on, Kay, sit down. I think we need to talk.'

10

Jess isn't exactly surprised when Ellie turns up at her workshop. She makes tea but continues to work as Ellie goes over her evening with Adam. Somehow she just can't rustle up the required amount of sympathy. She examines her reaction. Is she jealous? No, she can honestly say that she's not. There's no point in grieving over what you can't have. Life goes on. If Ellie and Adam can get it together, then she's happy for them. Truly she is. Her real worry is that Ellie may screw up so thoroughly that in the end nobody gets anything out of it – and that certainly seems the way it's going at the moment. Just listen to her, trying to whip a minor glitch into a major disaster. It makes no sense.

'Food, drink and sex, Ellie – the bare necessities,' she allows her exasperation to show. 'Satisfy the appetites, then get on with the real stuff of life.'

'You know it's not that simple.'

'Okay, but I still think you're whipping this up out of all proportion. What did you expect? The man's entitled to a past, for God's sake – and we should have known, shouldn't we? What were the chances of his being unattached – slim or what?' She stretches a length of webbing across the seat of the sofa and bangs in three tacks. 'But credit where it's due, Ellie. The man was straight with you.'

'Only when challenged.'

'You see? You're doing it again: over-reacting.' She cuts the webbing, folds over the end and hammers in two more tacks. 'Adam Mason's not a chancer. Okay, so he's none too bright in a situation like this, but if he'd handled it more smoothly, wouldn't that have made you even more suspicious?'

'Possibly.'

'Definitely. If you want my opinion – and I assume you do,

otherwise why are you here – this has bugger all to do with Adam. It's Chris again.'

'No.'

'I know you, Ellie. Face it, Chris was out of his tree. What happened wasn't your fault. And whatever else, don't go offloading your guilt on Adam. It isn't fair. Give the poor sap a chance.'

'I would if I could – I want to, Jess – but I can't take the risk. You don't know what it was like. All I could think while I was with him was, what if it happens again? What if I screw up? You keep telling me what happened to Chris isn't down to me, but are you really saying that if we'd never met, he still would have died?'

'Probably. He was a loser, Ellie.'

'He wasn't, not really. It was me, I got it so wrong. It's true what his wife said, it was all my fault.'

It's almost a month since Adam broke with Kay, and he still feels dreadful about it. It was the right thing to do, but he hates being the cause of her pain. He'd felt so helpless. All he could do was stand and take it as she cried and shouted, calling him a liar and a hypocrite. He'd wanted to argue with that: it seemed too harsh when he was doing this precisely to avoid the lies and hypocrisy.

An unreasonable part of him blames Eleanor for Kay's misery. She'd forced him to confront the emptiness of the relationship. Without her, they'd have muddled on for years. They would probably have got married, had kids, generally played the game. But because a game is all it would ever be, he'd ended it, and now he's on his own again.

He's still in touch with Jessica. She's okay, is Jessica. She says he did the right thing with Kay, but she won't talk about Eleanor. 'Just give her time,' she says. 'You're not the only one with a past to put in order.'

Jessica rang this morning to invite him to a party. He is reluctant. 'I can't,' he says. 'I'm working.'

'Never mind. Call in when you're finished.'

'I'll see. I'll try.'

It is almost midnight when he closes the restaurant. Despite Jessica's assurances, it's never much fun being a latecomer at a party and he's tempted to go straight home.

No, he must face this. He has begun to demonize Eleanor, and it will not do.

If only he knew what he wanted from her. Does he want to be with her? To have a relationship with her? Perhaps. But she's such a far cry from anyone he's known. She's not straightforward like Kay. Her self-assurance is a coat she slips on and off at random. Jessica says she has a troubled past and is emotionally delicate.

'Then help me, Jessica, tell me about it.'

'I can't.'

'Who is Chris?'

'I can't tell you that. You must ask Ellie.'

Jessica lives in a pint-sized flat above a hairdressing salon. Adam identifies it easily from the pumping noise and the sickly blue glow that lights up the windows and makes shadowy silhouettes of the figures pressed against the shuddering panes. He pounds on the door, and the sound is absorbed by the pulsing, throbbing racket from above. This is definitely not his kind of party. He checks his watch. Twelve-thirty. He should go home.

He is about to turn away when the door is flung open by a man wearing a woman's clip-on earring and strips of photographic film pinned to his shirt. Grabbing Adam by his lapels, he pulls him inside. 'I'm a blue movie,' he announces, boastfully flicking his ribbons of film. 'Now,' he looks Adam up and down. 'Have you been invited, or are you a gatecrasher? No,' he gives a sad shake of his head. 'Invited, definitely.' He propels Adam ahead of him up the narrow stairs. 'You're far too unconvincing for a gatecrasher.'

Jessica is at the top of the stairs. She's drunk and she's wearing a long blue dress to which she's pinned paper fish shapes and trailing ribbons. She slides her hand down his shirt and tweaks his tie. 'I forgot to tell you,' she laughs. 'It's a themed party. The theme is blue. Even the food. We have Roquefort and Curacao and blueberry cheesecake. Are you hungry? And I'm the Blue Danube,' she tries to twirl but there are too many people and she blunders and trips and laughs. 'Come on, Adam Mason,' she shouts above the music. 'Let's have some fun.'

She slips her arm round his waist and drags him into the midst of the party. It takes a moment for his ears and eyes to adjust. The music is thunderous. Lampshades have been encased in cocoons of blue tissue paper, transforming the room into a night-darkened fish tank whose occupants nudge and blunder blindly – a heaving mass, like water approaching the boil.

He is glad to be tall. He cranes to see Eleanor, but cannot find her. Jessica still has hold of him and he dances with her, but he doesn't stop looking for Eleanor.

At last he sees her. She too is dancing. He bends downs, tries to speak to Jessica, but she can't hear him. He points to Eleanor and Jessica's face is indecipherable as she shoves him forward.

He forces himself through the crush. Hot bodies pump and bump against him. He smells drink and sweat and a chemical cocktail of cheap perfume.

He reaches Eleanor and touches her shoulder. She turns. Like everyone else she is wearing blue, but she has also painted her face – not just her eyes and lips, but her whole face is blue, cheeks, brow and neck. He stares. Eleanor laughs and disengages herself from her partner.

She is another person entirely tonight. She is close to him. He says nothing, there's no point. The music hammers in his blood. He has forgotten the meaning of silence. The thrusting dancers push them together. Her eyes are almost on a level with his. She smiles, and winds her arms around his neck.

Their bodies lock. They begin to sway and he goes with the flow of her body. They perform their own slow, undulating dance. Her breath is on his neck. The paint on her skin feels strange and chalky. He tightens his hold. Their bodies fit so closely he can scarcely breathe. His desire is like acid, corrosive and unstoppable.

11

The phone rings, an insistent trill that first merges with her dream, then breaks her sleep. It's Saturday, and it's late. Eleanor falls out of bed and stumbles downstairs. Her eyes ache and she's dizzy and she's thirsty, and the bloody telephone just won't stop ringing.

She grabs the receiver, drops it and retrieves it. 'Yes?' she barks.

'Eleanor?'

It's Adam. She slides her back down the wall and hunkers on the floor. She tries to recall Jess's party. Adam was there, she knows that much, but surely she dreamt the rest of it, the clinch, the scour of his beard – then what? Jess. That's it. Jess surfaced from the crowd and put her arms round both of them and the three of them danced together for a while, and then she'd slipped away, leaving Adam with Jess.

'Are you there, Eleanor?'

'Yes. I'm here. How are you, Adam? I didn't see you leave last night. I've the most dreadful hangover, have you?'

'No.'

'I hardly remember a thing . . .'

'Eleanor—'

'I'm sure it was a good party, they usually are.'

'I need to see you.'

'Why?'

'You know why. Come on, Eleanor, stop bluffing. I'm not fooled by all that hangover rubbish.'

'It's not rubbish and I can't see you and we've nothing to talk about . . .'

'Kay,' he blurts. 'I want to tell you about Kay.'

'You've left her. I know. Jess told me. Some other time, Adam, I have to go.' He is still speaking as she fumbles the phone back on to its cradle.

She crawls back to bed and sleeps till three. When she wakes, Oscar is propped on her pillow, snoring happily. She watches him, loving the meaningless feline smile and the dark line of his closed eyes, the indefinable quality of the fur on his muzzle, and the silly pinpricks from which his wiry white whiskers grow.

Jess should have warned her Adam would be at the party. It would have put her on her guard, then maybe she wouldn't have thrown herself at him like that. What on earth had possessed her? She was having fun, dancing with a total stranger, and then she turned and saw Adam, and he'd looked so out of place. A rush of feeling made her reach for him.

Jess says she needs to get a grip on life. She's been drifting too long and should get out there and take control.

Out there. Where?

Jangles.

She arrives at the restaurant at eight-fifteen. She dawdles outside, pretending to read the menu. It's Saturday night and the restaurant is busy, but not full. For some reason, she's reluctant to enter. *Take control.* Okay, Jess. I know.

And yet she feels like an imposter, as if the moment she opens the door a waiter will step up and take her by the elbow and steer her back into the street. He's terribly sorry, he'll say, but she really has no right to be here.

Nonsense. She has every right. Brian sometimes brings clients to Jangles. She straightens her back and summons the other Eleanor, the career woman who spends her days placating artists and closing sales with the sheer force of her personality. Her heels give a little tick against the pavement, and she pushes open the door.

Adam is startled, then he grins. A waiter approaches to take her coat, but he gestures him away, and takes it himself. She feels his hands on her shoulders. His touch is already familiar.

He seats her at a table. He will join her later. She orders spring chicken with braised leeks and a cream sauce and, as she eats, she watches him. It is her first opportunity for objective study. Their meetings so far have left her with a scrapbook jumble of impressions and a devastating sense of sexual rapport.

She tries to be objective. Gorgeous, Jess had called him, but that's going a bit far. She likes the way his black hair curls against his scalp, and his eyes are a particularly soft shade of grey, but his nose is a thin, hawkish beak, and he has a beard. She's not sure about the beard.

She compares his performance with her own at the gallery. Professionally, they have a lot in common. He proceeds from table to table, topping up glasses, chatting to his customers and producing dishes with a flourish. He moves well. He has a long stride and a tendency to swivel dramatically on his heel. Each time he passes, he meets her eye and smiles and runs a finger along the edge of her table. She laughs when he does this. It's a little too studied, a tad too contrived, but he's on show and he knows it and, like her, he plays to the gallery.

Suddenly she is confident. She can cope with this. The common ground is firm beneath her feet.

The restaurant begins to empty and Adam joins her for coffee and brandy. The coffee is espresso and comes served in tiny, chubby cups. He takes a sip and the coffee stains and moistens his lips. The desire to touch them, to wipe away the residue of froth, makes her smile. The tips of her fingers tingle with anticipation. She has not felt like this in a long time.

For a while they sit without speaking. Language has its limitations; some things are beyond words.

He signals for more brandy. The waiter is curious. At last Adam says, 'I meant what I said on the phone. I want to explain about Kay.'

'No.'

'But I need you to understand.' He swirls his brandy but doesn't drink. 'I blamed you at first, because it was you who set me thinking. I'd got into such a rut, and I'd let it run on because it was convenient, comfortable.'

'Safe?'

'That too. I'm not putting myself in a good light, but I am trying to be honest because I'd like us to try again. Is that possible? Only I've got hold of this ridiculous idea we could be special.' He raises his glass to suggest a toast. 'What d'you say, Eleanor?' She doesn't respond. 'Look,' he sets his glass back down on the table. 'You needn't be so suspicious. I'm not playing games. It hit me when I saw you at Jessica's – it was surreal, out of this world.' He laughs, embarrassed at his excess. 'A strike from the blue.'

'You shouldn't say that. It's over the top, it's scary.'

'Okay, so I'm going too fast, but I'd got in this rut and you lifted me out just like that.' He snaps his fingers and two waiters clearing a table glance up, realise it isn't a summons, and return to their task. 'Can't we try? What have we got to lose?'

She hesitates. She wants to say yes, but there's Chris to consider. Always Chris. 'I don't know, Adam.'

'Why not?'

'Well, for a start, I'm not very good at this sort of thing. Relationships. I tend to screw up.'

He leans forward, his elbows on the table. 'I know the feeling,' he says with a smile. 'Me too. You see? Didn't I tell you we were just made for one another?'

Once again Eleanor wakes disoriented, the victim of another memory lapse. Something happened last night. Chicken in cream sauce, apricot tart and fromage frais. And now she's in Adam's flat, in Adam's bed. She rolls her head on the pillow. His face is close to hers. He's sleeping deeply. It ought to feel strange, lying here with this man she hardly knows. She wants to wake him.

No, not yet.

Beyond his shoulder, the door to the living room is half open. Last night she'd waited till he was asleep before slipping out of bed and tiptoeing through to the living room. She flicked on the light. She'd not paid much attention to the decor when she arrived but now she sees that the walls are painted an unpleasant egg-yellow, and the furniture is second-hand and shabby. She knows almost nothing about him. Is this how he chooses to live, or was the flat this way when he moved in?

She fetches a glass of water and, before creeping back to bed, she angles the door so the light won't disturb him.

Because she doesn't want him to know – it sounds so silly at her age – being scared of the dark.

And now it's morning and the dawn mingles with the electrically generated glow to cast an unhealthy sheen across Adam's naked body. He's lying on his stomach with his arms splayed and his face pressed into the pillow. She props herself on one elbow and admires the shape of him, the angles and shadows of bone, the curves and planes. She thinks of Andrea Harding and her foetal stone. There is a particular place that catches her attention. It is at the back of his neck, just below the hairline. He's like a little boy – not anywhere else, only here in this one, pale, vulnerable spot. She extends a tentative finger. His skin quivers. It's like with Oscar when he's asleep and she brushes the fine hair at the tips of his ears until he flicks her away – though like Adam, he doesn't wake.

A frisson of fear, there and gone in a moment. Her blood thickens, ice-floe slow. His skin is smooth, the other was bloated – but like the other, like her, he is cold as a cadaver. Like, but unlike, because this life she can renew.

Very gently she strokes the dark hair, then moves lower to his tender nape, then lower still to the nudge of his shoulder blade. Her hair trails as her lips work along his body – surely this should waken him? She has never known anyone sleep so thoroughly, and with such abandon. She tastes his skin. It is cold and salty, he tastes of the sea and the sand – and yes, he's coming alive at her touch. His dark, dragon blood wells up, swelling artery and vein, flooding capillaries till they flush like coral. But still he doesn't wake, so she goes back again to kiss, to lick, to nip his nape between her sharp teeth. And he is resurrected at last as he moves beneath her, rolling over, and they are looking at one another – and looking and looking and looking, as if after today they will never see each other again.

'Eleanor.' He says her name like a spell. He laughs. 'This is wonderful. I knew it would be.' Her hair flows and ripples all round them, like liquid shadow, like dark water. 'Eleanor . . .' She sits up and her hair settles round her shoulders and over her breasts. He moves to kiss her, but she pulls back – a sudden fear that she is giving too much of herself too soon.

'What?' he whispers. 'What is it?'

'Nothing. The light . . .'

He frowns. 'We left the living room light on. Shall I see to it?'

'No.' She pulls him back. 'It's okay. It reminds me of something, that's all. Somewhere.'

'Where?'

'I'm not sure.'

Of course she's sure – it reminds her of her little church, all dusty and locked up and forgotten. Her great big, grown-up Wendy house. She smiles. She wants to tell him about it, but instinct insists it's too soon. 'A game . . .' she distracts him. Except it's not really a distraction.

'What sort of game?'

'I used to play it with Babs – my mother – when I was little.'

'What?' He laughs. 'Tag? Peep-behind-the-curtain?'

'No. It's to do with where you go and what you do when you want to get away.' He shakes his head; he doesn't understand. 'When things go wrong – like with you and Kay.'

'And you with Chris?'

'No.' What does he know about Chris? What has Jess told him? 'Not like that.'

'But it's not really a children's game?'

'No, it's anybody's game. So, let's play.' She leans over him and laughs and shakes her hair in his face. 'Tell me, Adam, where do you go?'

'To the kitchen, usually.'

'And that's your favourite place of all?' He shrugs. 'Where else?' The need to know isn't rational, but it's urgent. She must have this insight as a token of his goodwill. She kneels above him and he lies very still, looking up at her. Last night had been shockingly intimate. For a while she'd lost sight of herself and afterwards she'd needed the light to see the shapes around her, to claw back some sense of herself and her place in the world.

He touches her. His hand is large, but rather beautiful. Shapely fingers, well-proportioned knuckles and neat, well-scrubbed nails. He strokes the pale skin of her inner thigh. This time, it is her flesh that quivers. She observes the reaction as if it's happening to someone else. But it isn't. The yawning, flickering desire is hers alone. He is still watching her. People do that; they notice her, watch her. Adam does more. He reads her. The masks don't fool him. His hand becomes still. He says, 'I'll take you, if you like.'

'Take me where?' She has forgotten their conversation. His words and hers have long since dissolved into the air to be supplanted by sensation.

'To all my other favourite places.'

She shakes her head and laughs. 'Not now,' she reaches for his hand, and presses it against her thigh. She strokes him from wrist to fingertip and the movement, at first gentle, becomes faster and harder as she coaxes him to action, so that this time it is her he touches, inside and out. She leans over him, her lips against his ear, her tongue exploring cartilage and crevice. She speaks on a breath. 'My turn first. I'm going to show you.' Her bucking body moves of its own accord, her voice is jagged with laughter and desire. 'Come on, Adam, hurry – this is my favourite place of all.'

The Runaway Likeness

The storm hits at two in the morning. Adam wakes to an explosion, a cannon charge hitting the seaward wall of the cottage. For a moment he doesn't know where he is or what is happening. The noise is horrendous. There is a scream like the screech of a demented tea-kettle. It is the wind in the scaffolding. The whole house shakes. He struggles to free himself from the sleeping bag, but is trapped in his cocoon. The opening cannon shot multiplies to a barrage. The windows rattle. A scaffolding pole breaks loose and swings and clangs like the clashing swords of boarding pirates.

Get a grip.

He locates the zip of the sleeping bag and tugs. A cotton thread catches in the teeth. He wrenches it free and scrambles out into the cold.

Batten down the hatches – there are no bloody hatches.

He stumbles to the window. The tarpaulin whips and cracks like a loose sail. Trees and shrubs whip and thrash, now exposing, now concealing the lights of Fowey. He clings to the window-frame. Every stone and timber strains and creaks. Any minute the house will be ripped from its moorings.

He should never have come here. He recoils from the window and stumbles back to his makeshift bed and the half-dead fire and the burnt-out candles.

He'd had fair warning of the storm. Pam had told him it was coming, and the builders had packed up early. They had been working since daybreak and he was edgy with their clamour, with the constant smash of their hammers and the clump of their feet against the fragile slate. All day the house has groaned like an old man in the dentist's chair, but now they adjust the ropes on the tarpaulin stretched across the roof, and lash their ladders to the scaffolding.

From the landing window Adam watches the dark clouds come rumbling over the hills. He is alarmed at how readily the grey of the river melts into the gun-metal sea. There is no horizon. The sea vaporizes; it loses its identity and becomes indistinguishable from the sky.

Batten down the hatches. He locks the doors and lights three candles, one for each of them. He prepares his supper – fish in a bechamel sauce, basmati rice with crushed cardamon pods. The meal is bland. It lacks variety. His standards are slipping. He drains the last of the wine and stokes the fire and shuts down the vent before crawling into his sleeping bag.

He lies back, contemplating the shadows cast by the guttering candle flames. Strange shapes flicker and jump across the cracked, bumpy surface of the ceiling. It is almost midnight, but still the storm does not come. The wind is relentless, but as yet there is no rain. He is secure. His house is a ship, perched high on the crest of a wave with the sea and the sky spread out before it – and he holds the helm, and sometimes it seems both he and the house rock and keel to the swell.

But he is a dream-time sailor. Here and now in the middle of a real storm, he crouches on the floor with his hands clamped over his ears, rocking back and forth to still the terror and block out the frenzied elements.

Jesus Christ, what a fool. Where do they come from, these crazy, romantic notions – the laughable idea that the house is a ship with its broken spars and torn sails? If it is a ship, then it's the *Ship of Fools*, tugboat to the *Titanic*, the *Marie Celeste*.

Take heart. Eden has stood rooted to this spot for two centuries or more. It is hardly likely to fall tonight.

He unclenches his hands from his ears. The storm continues to rage, but the house is still. It does not rock or crack. It creaks a little, but all houses creak. The battle is outside. In here, he is secure.

Tea. That's what Gran would do, she'd make some tea. He fills the kettle from the standpipe in the kitchen. The hiss of the gas is lost in the racket of the storm – but he is no longer afraid. He brews his tea. Lapsang Souchong. He returns to what's left of the fire. The tea is hot and tarry and he clasps the mug in both hands.

Why is he doing this? He's never seen the point in roughing it, has never felt the urge to hike or camp or go white-water rafting. It is certainly not for the thrill of it, the adrenalin rush. He is doing it to purge himself.

Closing his eyes, he tries to imagine Eden healed and whole. He sees it in summer with the golden gorse blazing and the newly painted stucco glittering like sea-foam in the sunlight. He hears laughter. There are curtains at the windows and a terracotta pot by the door spilling a cascade of pink petals on to the grass.

He will make it a reality.

Tomorrow he will start work on the kitchen. He will demolish the internal wall between the kitchen and wash-house, strip the walls to bare stone, and re-lay the flags. It's the first time he's fitted a kitchen to his own requirements. In Jangles he'd kept Rickie's layout. Jangles-Two and Jangles-Three had also been bought as going concerns. Adapt and adopt.

The morning after the storm he gets up early. Taking a pickaxe to the wall may not be the most professional approach, but it's quick and effective. The muscles across his shoulders and along his arms strain and ache as he raises the axe; the muscles in his back lock to control the downward lunge. His whole body shudders with the impact. He is conscious as never before of the power of his body, its mechanism and structure.

By midday he's exhausted. Muscle and blood throb and protest. He strip-washes at the kitchen standpipe. As he lathers the soap along his arms and across his chest, he notes the changes in his body. There is a hardness to it, as if a ratchet has been tightened and secured. Adjusting the small, cracked mirror lodged on the window-sill, he makes a half-hearted effort to shave. Despite the difficulties of living rough, he is reluctant to grow back his beard. The mirror returns a distorted image. Or has he really changed so much since coming here? The face in the mirror is gaunt. His collar bones jut.

Refreshed, he crosses the river to Fowey. He does this often; it gives him a different perspective on Polruan.

A jazz band is playing in the pub by the quay. He goes in. The bar is long and narrow. It looks newly renovated with its stone-clad walls and light, wood-panelled ceiling. The music booms. He sips his whisky. The spirit roars through his blood and the ache ebbs from his bones. He orders another. Propping himself against the bar, he turns his attention to the music. A line of boards define the performance area. They are painted a dirty cream, with the words

Hot Jazz scrawled in the kind of scarlet lettering more usually used to advertise hot dogs.

Although he is virtually tone-deaf, there is something visceral about this music; it runs in his blood. His body thrums to the pump of the horns and his fingers fidget to the rhythm. He surrenders to the music. Go with the flow. His mind wanders. His gaze drifts and is arrested by a face he recognizes. It's his neighbour, Pam Fowler. The bar is crowded and she hasn't noticed him. She sits alone at a corner table with a sketch-pad wedged on her knee, and is totally absorbed in her work. Her hand moves swiftly across the page, darting a line, fixing a detail.

The band whips itself to a frenzy. For no reason Adam can discern, three horn players rise to their feet, continue to play as before, then sit down. Apart from the drummer, they are all grey-haired and middle-aged. He wonders what they do for a living. What kind of occupation doubles with playing in a jazz band? They probably work in St Austell or Truro. He allocates professions – one is a building society clerk, another a dentist; the guitarist might work in the open air – a farmer perhaps, or a shipbuilder.

The music hits a crescendo. The horns rise again, the drums roll – and the band takes its break. As he drains his glass and turns to leave, Pam catches his eye. She smiles and beckons him over.

'What's all this, then?' He gestures to her pad.

She laughs. 'I told you. You live in a theme park now. Sit down and I'll show you. Can I get you a drink?'

'I was about to leave.'

'Okay, you needn't have a drink, but stay for a minute. I was trying to draw you. Every so often a face jumps out of the crowd. Look.'

He takes the pad. The page is filled with studies of the band, but in the top left corner he finds himself. She has sketched a beakish profile, a faraway expression and a shaggy mane of dark, curly hair. Others have tried to draw him. He remembers a child's stick figure with a big nose and great splayed hands; and a more professional attempt – Lucifer tossing an omelette.

'You've an interesting face. All bone and angles. Like a weathered figurehead.' She laughs. 'That sounds a bit personal, I hope you don't mind. Are you sure you wouldn't like a drink – by way of recompense?'

'I'm sure.' He returns her sketch-pad. 'Do you do a lot of this?'

'It's a compulsion – catching people off guard. It's totally anti-social, but exciting. Sometimes I can fix people – like this. I really feel I've caught you. But sometimes I see a face, I sketch the individual parts, but I can't bring it together – I call it a runaway image, like a beetle scuttling into the undergrowth.'

The next time he sees Pam she's on the quay sketching passers-by. Despite the blustering wind, a hint of spring has brought out the day-trippers. She waves and he goes over to her. 'I thought you'd be in the shop.'

'The season hasn't started yet. I'm making the most of it. Which reminds me, I've worked up that sketch I did in the pub. Pop over some time and I'll give it to you.'

'I will.'

'Good.' She squints up at him. 'Now what is it? You look different today. Ah yes.' She admonishes him with her pencil. 'You've cut your lovely hair.'

'You piqued my pride. I looked like a tramp in your drawing.' He joins her on the bench. 'You must feel exposed, working out here with people constantly peering over your shoulder and asking stupid questions.'

'It doesn't worry me.'

'It worries some people. I knew an artist . . .' He stops.

'And she tried to paint you, did she, this artist?' She taps his arm. 'And threw a wobbly when you tried to look?'

'No, it wasn't like that.' Further along the quay, a fair-haired child squabbling with his brother recalls Simon's pinched and angry face. He cannot think what prompted him to make such direct reference to his past, and to a complete stranger.

But that's the point. Pam knows nothing of Adam or Simon or Eleanor. He can confide with impunity. He takes a breath. 'He would get hysterical if anyone saw his work before it was finished.' As he speaks, he remembers that Simon had come here, and it's possible Pam has met him. He says, 'He visited Fowey a while back.'

'When?'

'Five or six years . . .'

'Before my time. Was he professional, should I have heard of him?' The memories gather, nudging at the edges of his mind. A parade of colour, the pageantry of the murals, the aggressive portraits. And a haunting seascape, the view from the headland. Pam is waiting. She says, 'We get a lot of amateurs, weekend-painters . . .'

'No. No, Simon was for real. Simon Whitburn.'

She frowns. She closes her pad and leans her elbows on her knees. 'You know, I think I may have heard of him. Yes. I read an article. He does murals – is that right, is that your man?' He nods. 'In the States,' she becomes enthusiastic. 'And a couple in this country. Restaurants, yes?'

'My restaurants. The London ones, that is.'

'How about that.'

'Well, not quite.' He corrects himself. 'I sold the restaurants, but they were mine when he did the murals. That's what I meant about getting hysterical. My livelihood was at stake, but I wasn't allowed to see until he'd finished. I had to take it all on trust.'

'But there must have been preliminary sketches.'

'Barest outlines.'

'According to that article, he's got a hell of a reputation . . .'

'He has now, he didn't then. That was the beginning; it was how he got started.'

She is watching him again. Like Simon, observation is her trade. Can she tell from the lines of his face that his connection with Simon is more than that of artist and patron?

'I've had enough for now.' She tucks her pad, along with the pencils and pastels, into her shoulder-bag. 'I feel like a walk to the headland. Why don't you join me?'

The fighting boys have transferred their attention to a bedraggled black and tan mongrel. They imitate its walk as it shambles across the quay, and when it cocks its leg against the railings they giggle and pretend to do the same. A gull watches from its perch.

'We could get some wine,' says Pam, 'and a couple of pasties, have a picnic.'

There is no view of the sea from the lower end of Fowey Esplanade. It is a long, narrow road. Along the seaward side a row of flat-faced terraced houses crowd the pavement. The view belongs to the houses opposite. Perched on their craggy bank, they crane to glimpse the river and the sea beyond.

Pam tells him she moved to Fowey when her marriage broke up. 'We split the proceeds of the London house and I bought my cottage. The shop's rented. It's touch and go sometimes, but worth it. I love it here.'

The view opens out. He has walked part of this route before. From Readymoney Cove he climbed through Covington Woods and then, instead of going to the castle, he took the higher path to Allday's Fields and Coombe Farm.

They reach the headland. Pam has no fear. She clambers over the rocks to the ruined castle. He hangs back. He calls after her, 'Simon painted this . . .' but the wind tosses his words aside. Pam beckons. He takes a step, then shakes his head and retreats.

Simon's seascape. She used to call it her portrait. He hadn't understood at the time, but he understands now. Nothing is what it seems. Sometimes she seemed like the cliffs, upright and strong. But he'd known from the start that her strength was an illusion. The constant wash undermines the headland; sooner or later the land-mass is bound to crumble into the sea.

Clutching the corner of the castle tower, Pam leans over the edge. Just watching her makes him feel sick. The headland reverberates to the crash of the sea and the roar of the wind. He turns away, looking for somewhere sheltered for their picnic. He finds a concave area of stone and stubby grass. It is shielded from the sea and the view is of Fowey and the river twisting inland.

Lerryn, Golant, Lostwithiel.

Pam sits by him. They drink red wine from plastic beakers. The pasties are cold, the meat tough. 'D'you know about the pilgrims?' she says. 'They came through here en route from Ireland to Compostella in Spain.'

It occurs to him that he too is on a pilgrimage and has come here looking for enlightenment and absolution.

Pam takes out her sketch-pad. She outlines the castle ruin and the line of Polruan beyond. At first she works in silence, but after a while she says, 'I have to say, Adam, for all the company you've been I might as well have come here on my own.'

'I'm sorry.'

She glances at him. 'Are you going to tell me what's wrong? Or do I guess? Could we be in failed romance territory . . .?'

'No.' He crumbles a fragment of pastry into the grass. 'Nothing like that. It's just this place. We were talking about Simon Whitburn earlier and I've seen a painting he did here. I'm trying to line it up with what I'm seeing.' He shrugs. It's an inadequate explanation for his preoccupation. He pulls out a crumpled packet of cigarettes and offers them to her. They spend a few intimate seconds huddled round the wavering lighter flame.

Pam leans against the rock and inhales. The smell of tobacco taints the keen sea air. She says, 'It happens sometimes. It's like I was saying about getting a likeness on paper. Landscapes can be the same. Plus of course you always bring something of yourself to any painting and that's bound to change it, give it a different slant or perspective. Often as not you don't know you're doing it. Is this making sense?'

'There's a transmutation?'

'Something like that. And not just painters. You too, Adam.' She waits, but he doesn't respond. 'You're so serious. You don't give much away. Here's me prattling on, you've virtually had my entire life story, but what do I know about you?'

'That I ran a restaurant.' He laughs. 'Three restaurants . . .'

'And you know Simon Whitburn. It's not much. I want to know what you're doing here. Why Polruan? It's a culture shock after London, I should know. And what about family? Do you have any family?'

He stares at her. The nicotine stings his tongue. 'When the house is ready . . .' he begins. He remembers. That's what he said to her: when the house is done, we'll think again. We'll talk then. To Pam he says, 'I hope my family will join me, in time.'

She's triumphant. 'So you are married, then.'

He stares at the river. Polruan flickers at the corner of his eye. He knows without seeing that beyond Polruan, St Saviour's Point is a dizzying cliff and a jumble of black rocks – and that the sea is calm, lilac and turquoise and silver-grey. And he knows that the shimmering surface is just a façade, a glittering carapace masking dark, psychotic currents.

Pam's hand rests on his arm. She leans towards him. Her ridiculous pudding-bowl haircut has been smashed by the wind. Her eyes are grey. Her lashes have no colour. She waits for his answer.

'Yes.' The breeze lulls to accommodate his words. 'Yes,' he says, and it's as if the whole world is listening. 'I am. I'm married.'

1

White. Like being in a lunatic asylum. White walls and white lights angled to pick out the lurid splashes of colour punctuating the walls. His paintings, his first ever private view – and he's hating it.

Acid-bright, the lights bite the corners of his eyes and make them water. Irene says stay away, but Farraday insists. 'Got to get used to the public eye, Simon. Come and glower, it's expected.'

'Why?'

Farraday laughs. 'Just one of those things. Performance art, perhaps? I try not to analyse too much. Trust me.'

Irene had had an affair with Brian Farraday. Before Simon, before her marriage. He imagines his mother's tiny, paint-splattered form engulfed by the portly art dealer. Or atop him like Jonah riding the whale. It would take a brave whale to swallow Irene.

It was Irene who'd shown Farraday his work. 'He wants to see more, Si, how about that? He's keen. Who knows, you might get an exhibition . . .'

Simon sat hunched on the tube, his portfolio propped against his knees. He mentally catalogued the contents, and the list assumed the rhythm of the train. Maybe when Farraday saw what was on offer he'd lose interest. When the tentative suggestion of an exhibition was withdrawn, Simon would go back to Irene and tell her what a bastard her ex-lover really was.

It's almost as if he doesn't want to succeed. The train slows to a halt, then accelerates again. It's not success he fears, but failure.

The gallery turns out to be less formidable than he'd expected. Farraday takes him by the arm and draws him in. 'You're surprised,' he chuckles. 'Didn't Irene warn you?'

'Not about the gallery.' Her only warning had concerned Farraday himself. 'He looks a brute, Si, but don't be fooled. He's a pussycat really, and he's got a first-rate eye.'

'Who needs the West End, tell me that, Simon. Cramped, expensive – whereas here . . .' Farraday gestures and pirouettes like an elephantine ballerina.

Swivelling on his heel, Simon takes in the broad space, the sweep of the walls and the browsing punters – a surprising number, given the location and time of day.

Farraday strews the contents of Simon's portfolio across his desk. 'These are very good.' He flicks rapidly through the sheets. His fingers are delicate and agile – another surprise. 'I like your style.'

'My mother said you would.'

'Ah yes.' Farraday looks up. His face, like his body in general, is heavy but animated. His expression moves swiftly from pleasure to disapproval. 'This is perhaps something we should get straight from the start.' He jabs at the desk. The chunky gold ring on his little finger glints in the sharp light. 'This has nothing to do with your mother.'

'So if I'd wandered in off the street you'd still be giving me your time and attention?'

'I confess I might have put you through the filter system. Then again, timing is important. Now, for example, is a lucky time for chance callers. Eleanor, my ferocious assistant, is off sick.'

Farraday is laughing at him, and he doesn't like it. He doesn't know the rules of this game. He needs to be reassured, to have a complete stranger, an independent witness, tell him how good he is.

To hide his confusion, he strides to the far end of the gallery and turns to look along its length. He digs his hands in the pockets of his cracked leather jacket and wonders, are his paintings strong enough to survive in this barn of a place? He imagines them melting into the walls, being absorbed into the fabric of the building. It's a little Dali-esque, but it's a powerful image and he files it away for future reference.

Farraday says, 'You do see what I mean about space? I find it distressing when a painting has to shout to be heard above its neighbours.'

'I think there's almost too much space.'

Farraday grins, 'I confess I had a wobbly moment as I was hanging my first exhibition. Contracts signed, conversion work completed and the invoices flooding on to my desk. Not a good moment to start questioning the wisdom of the whole enterprise. But my nerve held, as you see, and all's well. If the exhibits are small we erect partitions. Not that we'll be doing that for you. Your colours and forms are very strong. They will benefit from the space.'

'They won't get lost?'

'Absolutely not, trust me. They will leap off the walls, both visually and commercially.'

'But who comes here?'

'Ah, I see. You think people only visit the East End to buy cheap clothes and potatoes, and art has no place in the scheme of things? Well, it's all a question of marketing, Simon. I offer what the majority of central galleries can't. Space, and the chance for a display of social one-upmanship. We all like to discover the gem that has eluded the rabble – an improbably sited restaurant serving the best fish with the rarest sauce; a shop tucked down a back street with goodies flown in direct from Scotland – saddled venison, partridges with the heather still clinging to their little toes . . .' His fingers flutter expressively. He's laughing again. Life and art and business, they're one big joke to Brian Farraday. 'And then, there's us. Me. Farraday's Gallery.'

'And it works, all this marketing and psychology?'

'Certainly it does. The real beauty is that we're never stale. The gallery is constant, as am I – but the displays change all the time. I'm engaged on a ceaseless quest for new artists, unknowns, names of the future . . .'

'But you can't guarantee any of this.'

'Unfortunately not, but with luck it becomes self-fulfilling. And not luck alone. My eye for talent, the hype, the location – a combination that puts the odds on your side. Trust me,' he says again. 'I know what I'm about.'

Simon is riveted by Farraday, by his heavy jowls and mobile features, by the restlessness of his movements. His fingers itch for paintbrush or charcoal. He wants to draw him, to capture his uncontainable energy. He is utterly three-dimensional. He will need to both flatten him out and mould him into the two-dimensional canvas. He will show it all, the staccato gestures, the gaze that flickers back and forth, here and there, hardly resting for a moment. How on earth can he judge the merit of a painting when his eyes never linger on any one canvas for more than a few seconds?

Somehow he does. His livelihood depends on it. With a sweeping glance he takes in every detail. His mind is a catalogue of subject and colour and form, fixed, indexed and cross-referenced to the market.

Concentrating on the strewn collage he has made of Simon's work, Farraday says, 'You're offended, Simon. You prefer to think art is about beauty and expression.'

'Isn't it?'

'Up to a point, but it is also about communication, and communication is unavoidably two-way. You need an audience, Simon. You neglect that at your peril.'

'That's where you come in. Me, I just paint.'

'I hope to convince you otherwise. You're good, I'll give you that much. Not Turner prize material – not visceral enough – but if you were crap I'd tell you. Even if Irene is your mother.'

'You mean that? Only it's something I do need to know . . .'

'I promise you.' Brian pats his shoulder. 'I have a foolproof shit detector and when the alarm goes, I'm ruthless.' Simon laughs, but is still only half convinced. 'So, it comes down to this.' Farraday closes the portfolio and leans on it with the flat of his palms. 'I'm going to show your work, but on the condition that we do it my way, or not at all. Agreed?'

At the other end of the gallery, two potential customers shuffle and murmur. Brian Farraday is waiting. Simon takes a deep breath. 'Okay,' he says. 'Agreed.'

They have met several times since then to discuss the exhibition – which paintings are to be shown and how they should be hung. Posters and leaflets have been designed, printed and distributed, press releases and invitations sent out. Now, at last, it is happening.

The gallery has become a backdrop to a startling parade of colour – crimson and aubergine, indigo and buttercup – the dresses of the women and the patchwork array of the paintings.

'We'll pull in a good crowd,' Brian reassured him. 'Now Eleanor's back we're guaranteed a party atmosphere. Isn't that right, Eleanor?'

Eleanor Bycroft glances up from her desk and smiles. 'It's looking that way, yes. We're getting some good responses.'

'There you are.' Brian is triumphant. 'If Eleanor says so, it must be true. It's how it works, Simon. If we can get a good buzz going we should be able to lighten enough wallets to make it worth our while.'

Simon tries to look grateful, but the whole enterprise has started to sound unbearably commercial. The circus gathers momentum, but he cannot see where it connects with his reasons for painting. The sales matter – he's not a fool, he knows that and he hates having to scrape around for money – but it's the process of painting, the act of creation as a form of meditation that he loves. In the close silence of his studio, observed only by the fat pigeons stalking the roofs opposite, his mind soars, sending images and colours reeling across the canvas. Everything else – the gallery, the crowds, Brian Farraday and Eleanor Bycroft – is just play-acting.

Irene had said it would be like this. 'Don't get me wrong, I want you to succeed, Si, but so far as the rest is concerned, count me out.'

Dad said, 'Give the boy a break, love. It's his big day.'

'Big day or not, he ought to be warned.'

'Well, I'm pleased for the lad. Come on, Simon, put your coat on, I'll buy you a pint.'

As he crossed from the bar, a swilling glass in either hand, George Whitburn was accosted twice. 'Customers,' he explained with a shake of his head as he handed Simon his drink. Dad was a butcher. Simon had always thought it odd that though his father invariably knew his customers' favourite cuts and the depth of their purses, he could rarely conjure a name. He took a sip of beer and wondered what kink in his genetic tail had made him a painter rather than a butcher.

As Dad's small white hands gripped the straight sides of his glass, Simon had a mental flash, a bloody snapshot of his father's fingers rootling around in a fleshy socket of meat, a faint sucking, squelching sound as he eased out the glistening knob of blue-white bone.

Simon rotated his glass on the stained beer mat. He and Dad were very different, and yet they knew each other well. Dad was the one person who might understand what he was going through right now, but Dad had something else on his mind. The levels in their glasses sank slowly but at a more or less even rate; the volume of noise rose and fell as people arrived and departed. Simon fetched the next round.

'Thought it best to get out of the house for a bit,' said George at last. 'Only your mother, you know . . .' He dug in his pocket for a packet of cigarettes, tucked one between his lips, then repeated the process in search of matches. Simon waited. George shook out the match, then puffed and puffed again before continuing. 'Try and go a bit easy on her over this, Simon.' Simon requisitioned an ashtray from the next table. 'The exhibition, and all that. She's a bit . . . well, it's not that she's not pleased for you, don't get me wrong, but it's hard. She never quite made it herself.'

'She didn't do so bad.'

'But for her it's never been enough. She reckons she never really got out of the third division.'

'And she thinks I'll succeed where she failed? I'm not that good, Dad, that's what scares me about all this.'

George moved the charcoal tip of the burnt-out match to and fro among the debris in the ashtray. 'Oh, you're good, Si, and it's not just your mother that says so. You've got talent and people are prepared to back you. It's what she wants for you, but she's a mite jealous, that's all. Try and be a bit gentle with her, eh? That's all I'm asking.'

This whole business is tying him in knots. He should be ecstatic. Recognition and status, they're what he's always hankered after – ever since his first mural. The memory makes him smile. He's in his mother's kitchen and Irene is working on a papier-mâché model – not for him, but for an exhibition. He becomes bored with splashing his paintbox colours on to the paper she has provided. He wants new paper, clean and crisp, not these recycled sheets with his mother's sketches on the back. He turns to the patch of wall next to the back door. The door is open and in the yard Pablo the cat is playing with a torn paper bag. Pablo is ginger. Dipping his brush in the jar of water, Simon works up the rusty tablet of colour and tries to paint Pablo's outline, but the surface of the wall is shiny and the paint gathers in globules and won't form a line. He fetches crayons. Mum is too absorbed in her papier-mâché rhino to notice. Crayon is better. Pablo takes shape. Instead of a paper bag, he draws a mouse. A disembowelled blue mouse with scribbled red entrails. He is five years old.

Acorns to oaks, from that to this, a sticky summer evening at Farraday's gallery. No Irene and no George, just Simon and his paintings, exposed and vulnerable. He digs his fingers into his coarse blond hair. His nape is damp. He pours another glass of warm wine. Maybe it's the heat, or perhaps he's coming down with a bug; either way, none of this feels real.

Voices shimmer all round him, individual words dissolving in a hum of contempt. And then a sudden clarity, a voice like glass. 'He has a bold hand with colour. Vicious, almost.'

Irene had said, 'I think you're a fool, but if you can't stay away, watch what you say. Give them half a chance and they'll twist every word, make you sound pretentious or sulky, make you fit their idea of what being an artist is about. Treat it as a life class, keep your eyes open and don't get side-tracked.'

He takes her advice. He studies them, the tailors' dummies and shop-window mannequins downing Farraday's wine and readjusting their poses between each pronouncement on his style, ability and vision.

'Mingle, Simon,' Brian had said. 'Flatter the punters, make them feel they're in the presence of a great talent . . .'

He can't do it because he doesn't believe it. He cannot connect with these people. They crowd the gallery, chattering and gesticulating, and though he moves amongst them, they do not notice him; they brush him away as they would a scrap of lint on their oh-so-expensive clothing.

He is suddenly deeply conscious of his cheap shoes scuffing Farraday's polished floor. He hears and feels the crackle of synthetic fibre against his skin, and knows that if he dares to open his mouth, his accent will crack their cultured prattling like a peacock's scream.

Turning away, he notices a grey-haired man in an open-necked shirt leaning towards a painting, placing his nose an inch from the canvas. He appears suspicious, as if about to catch it out in a lie. Simon edges closer until he is standing alongside. He glances at the man. He has an irresponsible urge to speak to him – not as the painter, but as a critic. The painting isn't a favourite and Brian's approval had surprised him. Two teenage girls are engaged in a cat-fight against a backdrop of mock-Tudor suburbia. The black tights of one are gashed and tattered, her short skirt has wrinkled up to show a babyish glimpse of pale blue knickers. An advance review dubbed it a profound social comment. Bullshit. He'd witnessed the fight outside a pub in Hackney. The background is a memory collage of places he's seen from the top decks of buses and images culled from magazines and television. The subject had interested him for as long as it took to paint, no more. He had given it nothing like the level of thought the reviewer suggested.

'Not conscious thought, perhaps,' Brian said. 'But you're a

product of your world. You communicate by expressing your experiences as honestly as you can. Do that, and you inevitably say more than you know. That's art. When it becomes a deliberate effort to blazon a message, that's politics.'

Simon takes another surreptitious glance at the man who seems so riveted by this particular piece of unconscious polemic. He consults his catalogue. Simon leans towards him and whispers, 'It's a fake, you know.'

The man straightens and turns to see who has spoken. He is not impressed. He scowls. 'Indeed,' he says, and closes his catalogue and moves away.

So much for mingling. Simon takes another gulp of wine. On the far side of the gallery a woman in a crimson dress turns towards a painting and raises a languid arm to indicate a detail. Beneath the shadowed hollow of her armpit, the bodice is cut away to expose the grapefruit swell of her breast.

And Simon sees it as a real grapefruit, its skin pitted, a segment peeled away to reveal pale pink flesh, glistening juice and a seeping stain creeping down her immaculate dress.

'Glad to see you looking more cheerful, Simon.' Brian materializes at his side. 'We can congratulate ourselves. The punters are impressed, and we know the critics like you.'

'For the wrong reasons.'

'Let's not go into that again. You know what I think.'

'That anything goes so long as it turns a profit.'

'That's a little harsh. Don't be so touchy, Simon, this is your big night. Let me top up your drink.'

But Simon's blood is up. The accumulated uncertainties and insecurities of the past weeks wheel like screeching bats. He feels neglected and undervalued and exposed. 'This is fucking rape,' he mutters.

'I beg your pardon?' Farraday is unsure whether to be angry or amused.

'Rape,' Simon says again, more loudly. One or two heads turn. Good, now they see him. 'Public violation . . .'

'Not a lot of public here.' Brian's hand is on his shoulder, steering him away from the crowd. 'Dealers and critics mostly.'

'Something should be done about it.' He digs in his heels; he's hysterical but he's gone too far and he can't stop. 'Castration's too good . . .'

Brian gives a bark of embarrassed laughter. 'Cut off their pretensions? Don't think I haven't been tempted.' He glances round, then puts his face close to Simon's. His breath is a mixture of wine and peppermint. 'Actually,' he confides, 'that's not strictly true. We do have a reasonable sprinkling of buyers.'

'But have you sold anything? You see, if this fails, you won't touch me again, will you? Not you, not any dealer . . .'

'It's not going to happen like that. Maybe we haven't sold any as yet, but Eleanor's working on it. Look at her.' Simon glances behind him to where Eleanor Bycroft is engrossed in an earnest conversation with a man in a red shirt. 'She's good, Simon,' Brian reassures him. 'Take it from me, she's bloody good.'

'Sorry, but I can't see her doing much good.' He turns back to Brian. 'She's a chilly sort, if you ask me.'

'I'm not asking you. Funnily enough, I don't put a lot of store by your insight when it comes to women. And as for Eleanor, ice to Eskimos, Simon; ice to Eskimos.'

'If you say so.'

'I certainly do. You should cultivate her. She could do you a lot of good, push your work . . .'

'Isn't it her job to do that whether I cultivate her or not?'

'It's a question of degree. Now do please try and lighten up, Simon. It's going pretty well, they like you.'

'D'you see him over there, the fashion victim in mustard and green? D'you know what he said?' Pursing his lips, he imitates the disdainful tone. '"All very fine and good, but a blind man can see he's a decorator at heart." That's liking me, is it?'

'It's what you are, Simon. How often have you lectured me about the need to generate an income? I warned you there'd be flack about those murals, but it'll die down. Give it time. Trust me.'

'Trust him,' said a voice behind him. A woman's voice. 'I really would if I were you.'

'Eleanor,' Brian welcomes her. 'How's it going? Simon's feeling a trifle insecure and I'm trying to convince him he really is on the way up.'

'I'm sure you're right. The first rungs are always the hardest.' Her tone is sympathetic, but her attention is not focused. Her eyes flicker about the room and Simon is irritated until he realizes she's poised to pounce at the merest hint of a sale.

A life class, Irene had said. He studies the woman called Eleanor. She really is rather striking, tall and dressed all in white, her black hair tugged into a thick plait.

Brian says, 'I've been telling Simon the two of you should get together, have lunch one day soon, or dinner.'

'Yes,' she says. She does not smile. Her face is unreal, severe as a Byzantine Virgin. 'Yes,' she says again. 'I'd like that very much.'

2

It's very late and Simon can't sleep. Brian's cheap wine fizzes in his veins. The evening has been a disorienting mix of scorn and approval, excitement and unease. His mind reels from a jumble of impressions, comments half heard and less than half understood. To have wanted something for so long, and to have achieved the dream, how many people manage as much? He should be grateful, and he is, but it's not enough.

Maybe he should find a less stressful way of making a living. Like going into business with Dad, or setting himself up as a painter and decorator. He's got a head start, there.

If only he had a choice, but he hasn't, it's a compulsion. Even now, when he's dead tired, the images shimmer and dance as his restless brain endlessly rearranges their random jumping until composition, narrative and form materialize and crystallize and he is ready to begin.

Night.

The night is white, a shrieking canvas he is frantic to fill. He pulls up a stool and leans forward, his charcoal poised above the blank sheet pinned to the easel. Eleanor Bycroft's striking image hovers between his hand and the paper. He starts to work, long strokes, an outline, a dashed detail. But too soon the adrenalin skitter of anticipation gives way to the dragging undertow of disappointment. A growing pile of torn and crumpled paper marks the passing hours.

He's puzzled. Something's wrong. He shouldn't be struggling like this. He'd left the gallery thinking he had everything he needed to draw her. The tilt of her head, the line of her neck, the butterfly veins at her temples and the deep, lilac shadows in the hollow of her neck. Her beauty teeters on the brink of ugliness. He's giddy, he can see her, but can't draw her. He manages an outline, can reproduce the shapes and angles, but something vital is missing. The essence of her escapes him.

He hesitates to try again. He should give up, move on to the next project, the next fee.

He hears her voice. His nerve-ends ignite. By the end of the evening she had sold several paintings, including that of the fighting girls to the man in the open-necked shirt. 'You see, Simon?' Brian was triumphant. 'Didn't I tell you?'

Simon shrugged. Eleanor said, 'It must be strange, being on display, having your work discussed like this.'

He glanced at Brian. He was tempted to repeat the rape argument, but refrained.

'Perhaps you could try to detach yourself a little. You know, like the real Simon Whitburn's not here at the moment, you're just occupying his body for a while.' He stared at her, not understanding. 'All I'm saying,' she explained, 'is that none of this is real. It's just a means to an end, Simon.'

It was the business about the two Simons that caught his attention. It occurs to him now that she may also have been talking about herself.

Yes, he could be on to something there.

Hard and soft, deep and superficial. He has to understand and understanding, for him, means visual exploration. She refuses to come into focus; there is an amorphous quality to her that's driving him crazy, but he won't give in. He will conquer her, fix her to the paper like a butterfly with a pin.

He closes his eyes and counts to ten. Then fifteen, then twenty. One step at a time. Start with the details. Her hair is sleek, her eyelids smudged a delicate grey, her lashes heavy. Her eyes are terrifying, dark pupils ringed by irises the colour of a summer sky.

A childhood picnic. His mother and father, cheese sandwiches and lemon barley water, a shiny red inflatable ball. And the merciless sky. So much of it. The heath drops away, exaggerating the curvature of the earth, exposing him to the hard sky, bright and indifferent as enamel.

The flick of Eleanor's hand obliterates the picture. Her hands. He can see them. Thin, bony. The little finger is unnaturally long, the nails cared for, honed. Instruments of disembowelment. Hold on to that. Imagine their touch. A lingering caress, a pressure that threatens. The hair on his nape prickles.

He sketches quickly. The hands take up almost the entire sheet. They are unmistakable. Anyone who knew her would recognize them.

The sense of achievement is intoxicating. He remembers nothing of the exhibition or those attending, only empty space and white light and Eleanor Bycroft. He pins up a fresh sheet. Keeping half an eye on the successful sketch, he tries again for the whole woman.

And fails. His charcoal falters. Falling, it traces a dark arc across the paper. Eleanor has gone. He cannot see her any more. He repeats the litany: a tall woman with dark hair and blue eyes and sharp nails. But they are only words; they are without substance.

3

Jess is in a bad mood. Adam Mason's chairs are in a worse state than she'd realized – every stretcher-joint needs to be cleaned, glued and cramped back into position. The work is tedious. She's sick to death of the chairs, and she's sick of Adam Mason.

No, not fair. It's not Adam, it's Ellie. It's ages since she's seen her.

She cleans the last of the glue from her hands. It's nearly lunchtime. No point hanging around waiting for something to happen. If Ellie won't come to her, she'll go to Ellie.

She drives to Whitechapel. It's the first time she's been to the gallery. Ellie occupies two distinct worlds and her instinct has always been to steer clear of the professional daytime one. Until now.

She's tried ringing her at home, of course, but Ellie's never there and Jess has too much pride to go quizzing Adam.

Who'd have thought she'd miss her so much? They'd met when Ellie answered the ad for the flat-share. Jess had taken one look at her and thought, no way. She only let her in because when she turned her down, she wanted it to seem a considered decision.

As Ellie wandered from room to room, Jess scuttled ahead to clear a path through the debris of clothes and newspapers strewn across the floor.

'You don't need to do that,' said Ellie with a smile. 'If you're not tidy, then you're not tidy – you won't change if I move in, will you?'

'I'd probably drive you crazy.' Jess shrugged. 'You look an orderly, well-balanced sort of person. I tend to be a bit haphazard.'

'I have my haphazard moments. I eat chocolate in the bath and collect second-hand books . . .'

'Books?'

'I choose them for the comments scribbled in the margins. It's not a very tidy hobby.'

Jess was puzzled. The mannequin standing by her window ought to be a devotee of *Cosmopolitan* and airport paperbacks. Jess tried to imagine her browsing in a cramped second-hand bookshop, reaching a volume from an upper shelf and getting dust on her jacket, then walking to the till and catching her heel in the wormy floorboards.

Appearances deceive. She began to suspect a whole other woman lurking beneath the layers of fine jersey and silk.

'Can you cook?' She decided to stall.

'I can microwave.'

Jess grinned. 'Are you in a rush, or have you time for a cup of tea?'

Boiling the kettle and dunking the fennel tea bags allowed her to gather her thoughts. Her biggest nightmare in the flat-sharing game was the fear of getting stuck with someone dull. She handed Ellie a mug of tea, and leant back against the sink. 'Biscuit?' Ellie shook her head. 'I've been thinking.' Jess sipped her tea and pushed her fingers through her spiky hair. 'I could maybe squeeze in one more bookcase, perhaps a shelf or two . . .'

'A trial period?' Ellie suggested. Jess nodded. 'No commitment, and no offence when you tell me to get lost. I really think we could make it work.'

Jess thought so too, but to begin with they were careful with one another. She struggled to keep her newspapers in a neat pile, and Ellie tried not to get chocolate flakes on the bath towel. They said please and thank you, and took it in turns to cook adequate but uninspired meals.

Then one evening Ellie came home from work flushed and exhausted, and said, 'Look, we've eaten in every night since I came here. I think it's time we loosened up a bit.'

'Fine by me.'

'I've heard about a restaurant not far from here. Turkish. Do you know it?' Jess shook her head. 'Apparently it hasn't been open long. What d'you say, shall we give it a try?'

The restaurant was tiny with a low ceiling and walls draped with rust-coloured hangings. Crowded benches flanked refectory-style tables and the pungent atmosphere was hot and noisy and welcoming. Jess threw Ellie an approving look as the waiter shooed the existing diners along the bench to make room for the newcomers. When they were settled he brought a menu and Ellie ordered two glasses of raki. 'No water,' she called as he turned away. 'And no ice – just as it comes.'

The waiter grinned. 'What the hell have you ordered?' Jess had to shout above the clamour.

'Wait and see. You'll like it.'

'Promise?'

'I promise. Listen, Jess, have you noticed how many bland people there are in the world? Skimmed milk and mild Cheddar, alcohol-free beer . . .'

'What?'

'Well, you're not like that. I could easily be, but I'm fighting it.' The waiter brought their drinks and a dish of pickled chillies. Jess rotated her glass, examining the clear, viscous liquid. Ellie laughed. 'Don't be so suspicious. Have you ever had ouzo?' Jess nodded. 'Well, raki is to ouzo what Ricard is to Pernod.'

To go with their main course of spiced lamb and rice, they ordered a jug of red wine. 'Gutsy,' said Eleanor, appraising her glass.

'Robust,' suggested Jess.

'Yes, that's a good word. Robust – full of strength and sex and purpose.'

It was late when they staggered back to the flat. They opened another bottle and, curling up on the sofa, flicked through the TV channels until they found a film, *The Wicker Man* – Edward Woodward, and an assortment of ducks and goats being burnt alive by the pagan fringe.

Ellie lived with Jess for two years, Chris came and went, then Ellie got the job with Brian Farraday and moved out of the flat. The move had not spoilt their friendship. It had taken Adam Mason to do that.

Jess parks her van two streets from the gallery. She misses Ellie like hell, but she's also angry. Friendships matter, they shouldn't collapse in the wake of a man. She wants to take Ellie by the shoulders and shake her and remind her of Chris, and what a risk she's taking.

The gallery's plate-glass window looks on to the street. Ellie is talking to a man, presumably Brian Farraday. She's laughing and gesticulating. Her long nails flash.

The figure in the window both is, and is not familiar. Jess realizes, with a clutch of alarm, that this isn't really Ellie. This is Eleanor – bright as jet and hard as diamond – and Jess is a little scared of her.

Eleanor looks up and sees her. She is startled, then pleased. She beckons Jess in.

Jess is always teasing Ellie about being out of place at the workshop, but here it's she who feels gauche and rather silly. On every side of her, garish canvases stud the walls; at the far end of the gallery, two women in suits examine a glossy brochure.

Jess sniffs. A faint whiff of glue emanates from her sweater, like steam rising from a dung heap.

Eleanor shows no sign of having noticed. She kisses Jess's cheek. 'What a surprise,' she says. Even her voice sounds different, somehow both breathy and clipped. 'Brian, let me introduce you. This is my friend, Jess Grant.'

'Hello there.' He pumps her hand and welcomes her. He seems a nice man. 'I've heard so much about you,' he says. 'In fact, I put some business your way a while back.'

'Adam Mason. Yes. I'm sort of skiving off that job at this very moment. Tell me, Mr Farraday, do you allow Ellie out for lunch?'

83

'As a reward for good behaviour,' he chuckles. 'Yes, certainly. And please, call me Brian.'

There is a café not far from the gallery. It has polished steel tables and French pretensions. Ellie has coffee and a *pain au chocolat* and Jess, who is suddenly starving, opts for a *croque monsieur* and a bowl of French fries. Ellie laughs, 'I can't order a thing these days without trying to guess what Adam would say.' Jess stares out of the window. Adam. Why must she talk about Adam? 'I bet he could tell the variety of potato they've used for your chips – probably the soil and the county they were grown in as well.'

'Mild Cheddar,' murmurs Jess.

'Hey, that isn't fair.'

'Maybe not, but what's the big deal? He's just a cook, Ellie.'

'Gorgeous, you said.'

'Don't remind me.' She feels a smile coming on. It's tough, staying angry with Ellie. 'Okay,' she concedes. 'So he's a flash cook. So what?' She nibbles a chip. 'Want one?' she proffers the bowl.

Ellie shakes her head. 'This isn't like you. You never come to the gallery.'

'Do you mind?' The chips are hot, she's burnt her tongue.

'Of course not.'

'Only it must be weeks since I last saw you.'

'I sent you an invitation to Simon Whitburn's view.'

'It's not my sort of thing, you know that. I've called at the house and rung several times.'

'I was probably with Adam.'

'And that's going well, is it?'

'Look Jess, if this is about Adam . . .'

'No, it's not. It's about us. It's like you've abandoned me, Ellie. We used to be friends, remember? We did things, went places together.'

'Life moves on, things change.'

Jess chomps on a piece of cucumber garnish. Change. Change always hurts. She cannot think of a thing to say that doesn't make her sound like a spurned lover. 'Anyway,' gesturing with the remains of her cucumber, she makes an effort to distance herself from her anger. 'Never mind all that. You're looking great. Farraday obviously adores you. I take it this Simon person's view was a success?'

'Pretty much, though Brian could have promoted it better.'

'Have you told him that?'

'Certainly I have. He doesn't pay me to pull my punches.' She leans forward, elbows on table. 'What is it, Jess? Why are you laughing?'

'Because I can't imagine anyone persuading you to do that.'

'Okay, so I speak as I find . . .'

'As Babs would say.'

'Yes, she would – and all I'm saying is, it's a shame I was away when Brian was putting the show together. He hasn't maximized Whitburn's talents. He does murals as well, you see. He's a bit touchy about it, but I think we could have persuaded him to let us use them for publicity.' Jess's continued laughter brings Eleanor to a halt. This is Ellie at her best; her eyes glittering with excitement and her face buzzing through a series of reactions like a film on fast forward. It is what she loves about Eleanor, her bright, hard-edged energy, and her fragility.

'What's so funny?' Eleanor demands.

'Nothing. You're just back in the flow, that's all. It's great to hear you enthusing about your work again. I've missed that. I was afraid you'd lost it. You were getting too dependent on Adam, and that's dangerous, Ellie. Don't ever forget what happened last time.'

'It isn't the same.'

'I know that, and I know Adam – he's not like Chris, he's a good bloke – but there's more to our lives than the sum of our men. Take what's on offer, Ellie, but try to keep a little distance between you.'

'Distance?'

'I know it isn't easy. Something in us needs their attention. Weird, right? I feel it too, don't think I'm immune. Just try to keep a hold of who you are. Do you understand, Ellie?'

'Oh yes, I understand.' Ellie's voice is suddenly toneless and Jess feels the gulf reopening between them. 'You're afraid we'll close ranks against you – me and Adam.' Eleanor shakes her head slowly, as if amazed at the revelation. 'And you'd prefer to see some daylight between us, that's it, isn't it? You're looking for a chink in the armour – a pinhole, a crack, some weak spot where you can slip in . . .'

'No! How can you say such a thing? Don't do this, Ellie. I'm your friend, remember? I care what happens to you. Don't twist my words.'

4

Most mornings Adam is first up. He makes coffee and brings it into the bedroom on a tray, and wakes her with a touch. She has grown used to this intimacy. Dependency, Jess would call it. 'I worry about you, Ellie. You've a knack for getting hurt. I wish you could learn to be happy in your own right.'

If only it were just a question of learning, if her body would do as her head dictated, then she wouldn't go chasing after love like this. If she could be totally self-sufficient, that'd be great, but life's not like that. Jess may kick against it, but dependency is the natural state and the only thing to do is make the best of a bad job.

So, if we are biologically determined to lean on another person, we'd better make sure we choose someone safe.

These days she has her own key to Adam's flat, plus a sponge bag in his bathroom, and a change of clothes dangling in his wardrobe. On Sunday mornings Adam likes to go to Holland Park. He prefers to get out early, before there are too many people about. Eleanor resists. She crawls back under the duvet and tugs the pillow round her ears. She explains for the umpteenth time that she's not at her best first thing in the morning, and Adam insists her debility arises from habit – and that habits can be changed.

'Come on, sleepyhead.' He laughs and, locking his arm round her waist, compels her to walk in step. His step is light this morning, and there is laughter in his voice, but Eleanor is unable to respond. Her encounter with Jess has disturbed her; she has a hollow sensation in the pit of her stomach.

'Isn't this great?' Adam tightens his grip and gestures to the surrounding park. 'You'd hardly think you were in the middle of the city.' She doesn't respond. 'Of course,' he says, 'I keep forgetting, you're a country girl, aren't you?'

'Absolutely. Bury is so rural.' The words skitter across the surface of her mind. 'Cows in the high street, pigs in the kitchen. We sleep three to a bed, on mattresses stuffed with straw . . .'

'Okay, I get the point.'

'I simply don't know how I've coped so long, all alone in the big city.'

He laughs. 'I'm sorry. Pax?'

She shrugs. Adam has never been to Bury, he knows nothing of her childhood and has not met Babs – and yet even in his eyes she is defined by her past.

As they round a corner, a squirrel stages an ambush. It leaps from a fence post to the middle of the path and splays its feet and waits. Adam always brings some nuts and, bobbing down, he presents a selection on his outstretched palm. The squirrel considers the offer. Its grey tail switches back and forth. It makes a decision, and edges close enough to snatch a nut.

'Shall I tell you a secret?' says Adam. 'When I was a kid I couldn't say squirrel. I called them squiggles.'

'Am I supposed to find that endearing?' He glances up. She forces a smile to take the sting from her words. The fact is, she does find the story endearing. The little boy in him enchants her, but since Chris she has been wary of enchantment.

Adam straightens. The indignant squirrel scuttles up the tree and spread-eagles itself against the bark to watch them.

They stand face to face. Almost in a whisper he says, 'I don't understand. What is it? What did I say?'

'Nothing . . .'

'You're so sharp this morning. You're a strange one, Eleanor Bycroft.'

'I've never pretended otherwise – you were given due notice.'

'A Government Health Warning . . .'

'I'll get it printed on my thigh. Next to the bar code.'

She had left Bury to start afresh. She'd wanted to shake off the preconceptions and intentions of others, and in all her relationships she has tried to maintain exactly the kind of distance Jess recommends. That had been Chris's appeal. He was once a week, every week, and would never be anything more. Above all, he would never want her to be other than she was.

But what was she? What is she?

The worm inside had corrupted her resolve. She began to want more from Chris.

And now Adam. The distance narrows, boundaries are weakening. AdamandEleanor. A single word, a single being. She sees and despises her weakness.

She stiffens her shoulders. She must try to be logical, look the facts in the face. She knows next to nothing about Adam Mason. It isn't possible to utterly know another person, she must rely on trust, and trust needs a solid base. Stick to the facts. Adam had ditched Kay to be with her; it is therefore likely that one day he will ditch her for someone else. She cannot know his thoughts. She has been deluded before.

The evidence is conclusive. She would be a fool to continue. So why will it not go away, this debilitating tenderness, the persistent desire to touch and embrace?

Jess is right. Men come and go, but friendships are forever.

Anger spears enchantment. She will shake herself free. These past weeks every thought and action has revolved around him. Even her work has been affected. Her professional neglect of Whitburn's show deserves Brian's rebuke.

Adam Mason has infiltrated her life – mind, body, and heart. She wants to shout at him, hit out, frighten the squirrels, send them tearing into the branches, screeching like monkeys. And Adam after them, a long-limbed, furry ape.

But it isn't really his fault. He only wants what most people want, and what she is determined to resist. They are vulnerable to one another. How can he understand her reasons for reacting as she does?

'Eleanor?' His voice ruptures her thoughts and brings her back to the real world, to the park and squirrel. He catches her by the hand and draws her close – but the gulf between them is enormous. 'It's so hard.' He brushes her fragile temple and the straining line of her hair. 'I don't know what you're thinking.' There is an ache in his voice; he wants to absorb her thoughts through his fingertips. 'Eleanor . . .'

'I want to go home,' she blurts.

'Soon.' His fingers trail her cheek and come to rest in the hollow of her neck. Her pulse taps against his fingerpads. No, not hers but somebody else's pulse, someone else's fingers. 'I've been thinking,' he says. She tries to turn away, but he holds on to her. 'We're together so much these days, aren't we?'

'Too much, perhaps.' She refuses to look at him.

'No.' He laughs. 'That's not what I'm saying at all. I love being with you, and you seem to quite like it.' He grins, then becomes serious. 'Okay, you're a bit off key this morning, but as a rule . . .' She stares at him. He's nervous. Why? 'So I've been thinking,' he continues.

'That's what Brian said,' she interrupts. She wants him to stop. This is getting too personal. 'When he offered me a job.'

'Is that so? Well this suggestion is just as significant. I want us to be together even more. I want you to move in with me.'

'Move in?'

'Why not? You and Oscar.'

'No.' She pulls away.

'It makes sense, Eleanor.'

'It makes no sense. We barely know one another . . .'

'That isn't true – and anyway, I know I want this.'

'Well I don't.'

'I don't believe you.'

'And you think you know what I want, what I feel, better than I do?'

'No, but we are good together, you can't deny that. Okay, maybe it's too soon, I've jumped the gun – I've been thinking it over and over. For a long time I didn't know what I wanted, but now I do. At least say you'll think about it.' She shakes her head. 'I care about you, Eleanor. I don't understand, you don't seem to value that.'

'I do.'

'Then think about it.'

'I don't need to. Kay was on the brink of moving in with you, wasn't she?'

'What the hell has that to do with anything?'

'Don't play the innocent. You dumped Kay, and now you're on your own and so you're scouting round for a substitute.'

'No.'

'Tell me what you want, Adam. What you really want.'

'Okay. I want you to step outside yourself and take a long, hard look . . .'

'And see what?'

89

'How little of yourself you give.'

'Adam, no – you couldn't be more wrong.' How can he think such a thing? 'That's the point, don't you see? That's the trouble – I'm giving you so much, I'm losing sight of who I am.'

'You know exactly who you are, and you choose not to share your life.'

'It's not a choice. I want to share with you. I do try, Adam.'

'Then try harder.'

'All right, if that's what you want.' She chews her lips. It's true what he says, but it's not that she hasn't tried. *Step outside yourself.* She has done her best. She has shared her time with him, and her body, but she has not shared her thoughts or her shaky view of the world and her place within it. These things are too personal.

She gives a little stamp of her feet. The gritty hardness of the path reassures her.

'All right,' she says again. 'I'll share something with you. Come on.' She starts to walk away, then turns. 'What are you waiting for?'

'Where are we going? Eleanor?'

She speaks slowly, as if explaining to a child, 'You say I don't share my life. You tell me I don't allow you any insight into the things that matter to me. Well maybe you're right, so I'm going to show you something. Whether you understand or not is up to you.'

The Victorian church is no longer in use; it is many years since it rang to hymn and sermon. The building is flanked by a parade of shops selling newspapers and ice-cream and second-hand electrical goods. Immediately next door is a launderette. Hunched against the window, an old lady in a dirty yellow headscarf smokes a tired cigarette. None of the washers or dryers is in operation.

On the padlocked door of the church the message *Lucifer Lives!* has been spray-painted in red. Eleanor gazes up at the façade. Her hand seeks his. 'Come on,' she says. 'I know a way in.'

She pulls him after her along the side of the building. They step over takeaway cartons and discarded cans. The side door is boarded up, but the shuttering is loose and the wood is springy. If pulled in just the right way, it makes a gap wide enough to duck inside.

This is the best, her favourite place of all. The windows are mostly covered, but from a single crack high in the clerestory, a spiral of daylight twists across the aisle and pews, and the dust drifts and swirls in the greenish, watery light. There is a faint smell of salt and incense, and a coral flush from a fragment of stained glass high above the altar.

She has been harsh with him, and she's sorry. She slips her arm around his waist. 'Your eyes get used to it after a bit. Are you okay?' He nods. 'So, what do you think?'

'I think it's sad. This space could be used, made into a hostel for the homeless or something.'

'I didn't realize you had a social conscience.'

'What's going on, Eleanor?' He frames her face in his hands. 'You don't seem to like me very much today.'

'It's not you, it's me. Or rather, it's what you say about me. Too close to home, perhaps. It's true, I don't share easily and I realize that makes it hard for you. You see,' she manages a smile, 'I admit it.'

'That's great, but what are we doing here?'

'I think that in order to know a person you need to visit the places that matter to them – and this place matters to me, Adam. It matters very much.'

'Okay,' he says. 'I'll go along with that.' He turns slowly, taking in the space, the high vault and the fragile arches flanking the nave. 'But is it safe? We shouldn't really be here, should we? I mean, this is breaking and entering.'

'It's entering. It was already broken.' She gives his arm a little pinch. 'We're not doing any harm, not getting in anyone's way. Nobody comes here.'

'You can't know that.'

'Look,' she points to the dust lying thick on the floor. Footprints lead to the altar step. 'Those are mine. I was here last week. No one's been here since. People are superstitious, I suppose, or they haven't found the way in. I don't know. It doesn't matter. I've been coming here for months and never seen sight nor sound of anyone.'

'Why? Why come here? It's cold and dirty, and it isn't just that it's structurally unsafe – you could be raped and murdered in here and no one would know.'

'Look, Adam, if you want to know about me, know what I am, I'll show you – but I can't guarantee you'll like what you see. If that's a problem, then let's leave now.'

'No.'

'Good. So now I'll tell you why we're here. Have you noticed how people connect with places and buildings? Why is that?' She doesn't wait for his reply. 'I think buildings and landscapes are metaphors for what we are or what we'd like to be – and that's what's so exciting, because if we can change the landscape, then maybe we can change ourselves.'

'And this place?'

'Is what I am.' She approaches the chancel steps. A row of stubby candles is ranged along the altar rail. Over time, the wax has run, dribbling down and draping the wood with an uneven fringe. She breaks the tip of a stalactite and rolls the nub of wax against her palm. Adam stands close behind her. She hears the grind of his shoes against the stone-flagged floor. His breathing is erratic. He is afraid. Good. Two can play at enchantment.

She digs some matches from her bag. The match rasps along the roughened side of the box and flares with a hiss. She moves along the candles, going from right to left. The smells of the church are supplemented by spent matches and hot wax.

Adam says, 'I think we should go.'

'Why? Not scared of spooks, are you, Adam? It's okay, I'll look after you . . .' As she speaks there is a great flapping and blundering up in the roof space. Dust and feathers shower down. Adam steps back, stumbling on the shallow steps. 'Holy Ghost,' she explains with a laugh.

'What?'

'Pigeons. Look.' She kneels and retrieves a fallen feather. Still kneeling, she holds it out to him.

Strange that, although afraid of the dark, she is not afraid here. Perhaps because the church is not really dark, but subject to a perpetual dusk. It is full to saturation with echoes and shapes. The air resonates, it has substance, she pushes against it. Like fighting a tide.

She stands. Adam is still close. She was right to bring him here. In this place she is her own self again, distinct from him. She touches his face. His beard is rough against her palms. Her fingers search out the substructure of bone. She's unsure whether his unsteady breathing arises from fear or desire. He closes his eyes and his lips and allows her fingers to explore the moist inner surfaces. Then he closes on her, trapping her, exploring in his turn. She feels the slither of his tongue, the press of his teeth – and knows he feels both desire and fear, and that it is a powerful combination.

Power. She feels so strong. All hesitation is gone. She leans against him and his body clenches her, gripping with arms and thighs, his frantic mouth on hers. She runs her hands down his body and it thrums with life. Easing herself back, she looks into his face. The candlelight distorts, but she sees how closed and concentrated he is. His curiosity dissipated, he is almost unaware of her, conscious only of the functions and demands of his body.

She fumbles with his zip and he throws back his head and moans. The tight coils of his beard dissolve into the bristle of his neck. He tries to swallow and his throat works and his Adam's apple bobs.

Trick or treat.

She has him in her hand. She is in control now and she is stronger than ever. What can he do? Nothing. Jess is right. Friendship is all. Men are such fools. She holds him and he is helpless. All his strength is concentrated here, in her palm. Many eggs, one basket. She stifles her laughter and her hands flex involuntarily, one gripping his buttocks, the other his engorged penis. His fingers dig into her shoulders. There is a frozen moment, and then he comes with a spurt and a yell and she has to bite her lip and hold her breath to choke it back, the gagging laughter that threatens to bellow and echo and bring the stones of the church tumbling around them.

5

It's Thursday evening. Eleanor tidies her desk and prepares to go home. Maybe tonight Adam will take her call. Maybe not. The message is clear, she has gone too far.

Brian emerges from his office brandishing a large manilla envelope. 'Eleanor, my sweet, could you drop these off at Simon's on your way home? I've photocopied some reviews, only the good ones, of course.'

'What's wrong with the post?'

'Nothing, but your bus virtually goes past his place. Come on, Eleanor, don't make the poor boy wait till morning – and don't look at me like that. You've been neglecting him, and that isn't like you. He needs to be reassured. It's time you made an effort.' The reproach is deserved. She takes the envelope. 'Now remember, he's very insecure is our Simon, he needs careful handling.'

'And you honestly think I'm the one to do it?'

'You have the necessary subtlety.'

'I have the subtlety of a bulldozer these days. I know you're right, Brian, I haven't given him anything like enough attention, but just at the moment, I'm afraid I might blow it.'

'I have every confidence . . .'

'I know, but my judgement is shot and if I'm honest, Simon Whitburn irritates me.'

'Simon irritates everyone, but he's not so bad. You've got to crack this, Eleanor. We'll be doing a fair bit of business with him in future – I've agreed to act as his agent.'

'Why? He's okay, but he's not that good.'

'He shows every sign of being a commercial success.'

'Even so . . .'

'And I promised his mother.'

'His mother?'

'Irene. Now we have a problem, there. Irene doesn't have much time for the razzmatazz and she's passed her prejudices on to Simon. I really do need your help, Eleanor – we must counter the Irene effect.'

'I see.'

'So you'll run my errand, yes? Court our Simon with wine and reviews. Make an evening of it, take time off in lieu, come in late tomorrow.' He squeezes her arm. 'That should please Adam.'

She agrees because she owes Simon Whitburn, and because she has nothing better to do. It's more than a week since she last saw Adam. Taking him to the church had been a bad idea.

Struggling for breath, his voice tight with panic, he'd said, 'Jesus, Eleanor, what the hell was that about?'

He'd looked ridiculous with his shirt flapping and his trousers gaping. 'Was it good?' she demanded. 'It was, I can tell.' Where did those words come from? She wanted to be tender with him, but she couldn't, she was frozen. Never mind scaring Adam, she scares herself sometimes. She watched as he cleaned up, then folded himself gently away with his large, elegant hands. She wanted to say she was sorry, to hold him and duck her head and kiss the hurt away. Instead she laughed at him and said, 'This is me, Adam. You wanted me to share, isn't that what you wanted . . .?'

She rang him twice the following day and again on Tuesday, but he didn't return her calls. She thought about talking to Jess, but that would only complicate matters.

She will talk to no one, she will concentrate on her work. The gallery is an excellent source of distraction. Despite her irritation with Simon at a personal level, she sympathizes with his frustration over the reactions to his view. Like him, she hates the posturing, the need to compete with the paintings in the things that are said and done. The people that attend such functions are too sure of themselves, too indifferent to the work on show. Why do they need to pontificate, why can't they just stand in front of the work and silently drink it in? It's what she does. Then again, maybe they're the wise ones. It may be delicious, but it is also unnerving how easily colours and shapes and ideas absorb themselves into the body's fabric, stamping their mark indelibly on every cell.

Simon's work demands attention. His paintings are disturbing and vibrant – garish, Jess had called them. He uses primary colours and bold outlines, and plays with perspective. Sudden tunnels of illusory space rip open the otherwise defiantly two-dimensional canvases. He mixes abstract and figurative with startling effect. A city nightscape made up of rectangular blocks of grey, highlighted with orange and yellow, thrusts itself to the front of the picture-plane. A dark alleyway dives into the canvas. At the far end, silhouetted figures suggest a violent exchange.

She is seduced by his work. He depicts the darkness, then illuminates it. He gives form to shapeless fears, reveals the horror and then contains it.

Teach me, Simon.

She senses a gap between what he paints and what she sees. She must know his intention, find what lies behind his haunting colours and strange perspectives. She is determined to see his murals.

Teach me. He paints an exit from danger. In defining the world he has discovered the means to abscond without losing himself.

She is hungry for his secret.

Simon spends the afternoon with Irene. On the way home he stops off for a Chinese takeaway. King prawn curry, fried rice and noodles – Irene would have a fit. The extra noodles are a particular defiance. He decides to eat straight from the foil containers and is in the process of prising off the lids as the doorbell rings.

It's Eleanor, looking as though she's come straight from work with her teetering heels and her grey suit and ivory silk shirt. His tee-shirt is less than fresh, but she doesn't notice, she's too busy taking in the array of cartons on the low table behind him. The smell of oil and spices hangs heavily on the air. Why does he feel caught out like this? As if he gives a shit whether she approves his eating habits.

'Brian asked me to call and give you these.' She proffers an envelope and a bottle of wine. He takes the envelope. 'Reviews,' she explains. 'He thought you'd want to see them as soon as possible.'

'Good reviews?'

'I haven't read them, but I imagine so. He wouldn't want to depress you.'

'Thanks.' He waits for her to leave, but she stays put. He remembers the wine. He gestures to the bottle, 'Should I open that?'

He closes the door. To his surprise she ignores his only armchair and settles herself on the floor. She draws up her long legs and her sculpted knees look distressingly vulnerable. He wants to tug her skirt to cover them. Instead he hands her a glass and she sips her wine and examines the takeaway cartons. He sits facing her. 'Are you hungry?'

'Peckish,' she smiles and, without waiting for a more direct invitation, leans forward to pluck a fat pink slug of a prawn from the runny curry sauce.

Those hands. He can't help staring. Birdlike. He laughs. Most people would think 'birdlike' meant fine-boned and delicate. He has talons in mind, birds of prey. A kestrel plunging to the kill.

'What's so funny?' she demands.

'I was thinking of Farraday. Why did he send you here? I could have waited for the post.'

'He wants us to get to know one another.'

'Really?'

'I was away when he took you on, so I didn't have a lot to do with the publicity for the exhibition. He expects me to be more involved. Do you mind?'

'No.' He sounds grudging. He wants her to leave. He wants her to stay. What he really wants is to explain his need to paint her, but he suspects that at best it would sound ridiculous, at worst pretentious.

'I very much like your paintings.'

'You don't have to say that.'

'I know, but it's true, so I thought I'd share it with you.'

'Thanks.'

She laughs. 'I know,' she says. 'It's hard to take a compliment. I have the same problem. But they are special, Simon. And then of course there are your murals . . .'

'Fucking wall-paintings.' She's startled. 'Sorry,' he mutters.

'You don't need to apologise, though I'm surprised. It seems an extreme reaction.'

'You heard what they said at the view.'

'You must grow a thicker skin. It's like that sometimes. There's a particular type of person who doesn't think they've had a good evening if they haven't found an opportunity to snipe at the artist. You were unlucky, they were out in strength that night, and to be honest, the murals are a bit of an Achilles heel.'

'You said it.'

'But I've an idea how we might change that.'

'Really?'

She hesitates, 'I need to work out the details.' She shakes her head and laughs. 'Don't look so worried, I'm always scheming. It'll probably turn out to be unworkable, so best forget I said anything. For the time being, just hold on to the fact that it isn't real. It's all just a game.'

'I don't like games.'

'I do. The wonderful thing about games is that they have rules. Rules set boundaries. I like boundaries.' She stops, takes a breath before continuing. 'Look, Simon, don't think I'm unsympathetic. All this must seem a million miles from what's in your mind when you're painting.'

'That's right – but you're not exactly toeing the official Farraday line there, are you?'

'Aren't I?'

'Farraday's always telling me not to forget the audience.'

'Well, you can't survive without an audience and you need to bear their prejudices in mind in order to overcome them. Be reassured, Simon – there are ways of turning perceptions around.'

'How?'

'Well, to begin with I think it would be helpful to revise the way you view the murals. You're too defensive. They're part of your repertoire so there's bound to be some cross-fertilization between the murals and the canvases.'

'I suppose.'

'I would love to see them.'

'You can't. They're all in private houses.'

'I'm sure they're very good.'

'They pay the rent.'

'Okay, so maybe they don't represent the pinnacle of your artistic achievement – but I still say they're relevant and you shouldn't be ashamed.'

Her eyes are bright as she leans towards him, her face is animated and her hands chop the air to underscore her argument. He is more intrigued than ever. He wants to take her and transform her, flatten her on to canvas, define her. Confine her. He must find a way to see her clearly.

His mother is always saying, 'Don't go at life full pelt. Ease up, Si. Take a breath now and then.'

He takes a breath, and says, 'I know what you're saying, but it's hard to take them seriously when everyone else is so scathing. I do them because I need to eat and pay the rent – and they're too lucrative to give up.'

'I don't think you should. Think about it. Are you really saying they stand alone, that nothing useful ever comes out of them?'

He shrugs. 'Maybe sometimes.' He thinks for a moment. 'I did a bathroom a few months back – a big house off the A1. It was an underwater scene; the guy wanted a shark coming out of the wall at the foot of the bath. Open mouth, teeth, the lot.'

'Amazing.'

'Not really, but the colours were good, and the line. Sinuous. It might work as an abstraction.' He shrugs. 'Okay, I see what you're getting at, I may well work it into a painting one day.'

'You see?' She is triumphant. 'Cross-fertilization.' Simon tops up her wine. 'Now I think we should change the subject before I come up with some crack-brained scheme or opinion and we fall out.'

'Would Brian fire you?'

'I doubt it. He'd blame you – artists are notoriously difficult.' She pulls a foil container towards her and examines the contents. 'Simon, this really is a terribly unhealthy diet.'

'That's because I have a crack-brained scheme of my own. I'm going to die young and make a fortune.'

'Now that,' she gestures with a dripping prawn, 'is a hell of a career move.' She pops the prawn into her mouth then sucks her fingers. 'I must remember to mention it to Brian.'

'Irene would go spare, of course.'

'Naturally. I'm sure she's a very loving mother and your death would distress her a great deal . . .'

'No, she'd take that in her stride. It's the means to the end she'd object to. Irene is into healthy eating. Natural yoghurt and fennel tea.'

Eleanor shudders. 'My friend Jess drinks fennel tea. What about pinto beans, and wholewheat pastry? Don't tell me your mother makes wholewheat pastry . . .'

They finish the curry fingerful by fingerful. Simon opens another bottle. He's enjoying himself and so, it would appear, is Eleanor. There is a disjunction, a mismatch, between Farraday's Eleanor and the woman sitting on his floor, sharing his supper. It's as if she's allowed him to glimpse behind the mask. Because that, he realizes, is what she presents to the world with her hair pulled back and her eyes carefully coloured and defined. Then, having created the image, she needs to mould a personality to fit, and it doesn't always work. That's why she's so difficult to draw. The mask is on askew, the eyeholes aren't aligned. He should see a flicker of blue behind, but there is only darkness.

It makes him reel, the knowledge that to draw her, to define her, is to control her.

He says, 'I want to show you something.'

He fetches a folder from a stack against the wall. Sweeping the debris of their meal to one side, he pulls out a series of sketches worked up from memory: Eleanor at the gallery, sitting at her desk with her glossy head bent; Eleanor at his view, straight and tall with

99

her head thrown back. In the third sketch she has half turned to gaze at the viewer. Eleanor the Amazon, Boadicea with her knives.

He waits for a reaction. It is a long time coming. The silence deepens. The spark of understanding is extinguished. Surely he imagines the gradual stiffening of her shoulders, the slow uncoiling of her spine and the almost imperceptible sway of her neck as, like a cobra rising from its basket, she forces him to meet her eye. The questions gather in his throat. What do you think? Is it good? Shall I paint you? I do so want to paint you.

The questions refuse to come, but she hears them anyway. She taps her nails against the paper. Her hands are shaking. 'This isn't me, Simon. Whatever made you think it was me?'

He should have known. It's just another caricature, a cartoon figure, a tiny marionette with Eleanor's outsize hands. Does she recognize them? Probably not. 'I'm sorry.'

She shakes her head and the action frees her. 'It's not your fault. People don't really see me. You're a painter, you must know that some people never come into focus, no matter what you do. Well, that's me. I'm dreadful in photos, too. It drives my mother crazy.'

'Let me try again.'

'No.'

'If I get it right, we can give it to your mother.'

'I said no. I'd really rather you didn't.' She's gentle now. He wants to touch her. Where has it come from, this sudden, smoky sadness? It feels so intimate to be sharing it with her.

And then he understands. Even now he isn't really seeing her. The sadness is no more real than the rest. Eleanor Bycroft knows exactly what he's seeing, because she knows what she's showing him. She has colonized his thoughts, and she dares him to see through her.

6

The restaurant is closed. Adam is in his office, checking the takings. They are slightly above average. Kay would say this proves her point and that, given time, business will improve. There is a part of him that misses Kay. She is an orderly, uncomplicated person. What you see is what you get. Whereas Eleanor . . .

Eleanor. He has thought of little else these past few days. It's more than a week since she last telephoned. What does he expect? When she rang he refused either to talk to her or to return her calls.

With Eleanor what you see bears no resemblance to what you get. Sometimes she is so precise: everything about her, her manner, her mode of dress, every gesture, is fine-tuned. But like the turtle in its shell, her armour disguises a baffling softness. No, that's not quite it. Soft implies gentle. Fragile is closer to the mark, but it is a dangerous, brittle fragility.

He remembers the church, the glitter of her eyes, her nails scraping his scrotum, and a desire so intense that his blood runs like acid in his veins, and his brain is permanently seared with her image.

He leaves the restaurant intending to drive straight home, but at the end of the street he turns right instead of left.

Eleanor's house is in darkness. He knocks anyway. Silence. He knocks again. The hall light comes on. Through the dimpled glass he sees her approach. She leans against the door, pressing her cheek against the pane. He glimpses the distorted glitter of her eyes and the dark smear of her hair. 'Who is it?'

'Me. Adam.' She steps back. Slowly she draws the bolts and opens the door a crack. 'I know it's late,' he says. She frowns. 'Perhaps I should go. I'm sorry. I'll ring you.'

'No.' She opens the door wider. He has woken her. She wears nothing but a crumpled, wine-red tee-shirt and her bare feet wriggle against the floorboards. Her loose hair, muzzed by sleep, straggles her shoulders. She says, 'You say you'll ring, but you don't. I left so many messages with Tom it became embarrassing.'

'I've been busy.'

'Well, you're here now. You'd better come in.'

He steps inside and she locks the door. He says, 'I couldn't ring, I didn't know what to say. I'm so bloody confused, Eleanor.'

'Me too.' Although her tone is sharp, everything else is blurred and indistinct. This is what he fears the most, and what he loves the most. Her bewildering contradictions reflect his own emotional immaturity. He has no experience of anyone like her.

He says, 'I keep thinking we should talk, but we misunderstand one another all the time. That's why the phone's no good. Then I thought, maybe if we're face to face . . .' He stops. Her head is cocked on one side, and her hair drifts in a tide across her shoulders. Her expression is vaguely sceptical, and he realizes he's got it wrong again, that this is not the moment for talking. She is standing very close to him and she smells of oranges and sleep. She slides her arms round his waist. This time she is so gentle, and when he kisses her she opens to him so that only now does he fully grasp how guarded she has always been – and how well she has disguised the fact.

They go upstairs. Her manner is so changed that even her weird and slightly gothic bedroom doesn't alarm him. The tiny room is filled almost to capacity by a big bed with a caramel-coloured bergère frame and a feather mattress. There is a satinwood wardrobe in the alcove formed by the chimney breast. In front of this a wrought-iron pricket spikes a fat candle the colour and texture of unsalted butter. Scrambling across the bed, she retrieves a box of matches from the windowsill. She sets match to wick. The speckled mirror on the wardrobe door doubles the flame. Next to the bed is another sconce with a stub of candle. She lights this also.

She kneels on the bed. He starts to undress and she strokes the backs of his hands and this tenderness is so sweet that his breath catches in his throat and he closes his eyes and gives himself over to the sensation, to the feel of her skin beneath his sliding hand, to the coral-flush of her blood and her subtle movements of tentative invitation.

And all around him the smell of her and the taste of her, the tang of the sea, of citron and salt on her cheeks.

He wakes and rolls over and the bed beside him is empty. He lies still, listening for the rush and gurgle of the shower. Nothing. In that case, she'll be downstairs. He strains to detect the aroma of brewing coffee or the chatter of a radio. Still nothing. Tea then, and the morning paper. He assembles a scene lifted straight from a TV ad, all golden light and clean lines and muesli. He laughs. That's more Kay than Eleanor. Rewrite the scene with Eleanor as the star and it will be stewed tea and burnt toast. Last time she'd stayed at the flat he'd cooked a breakfast of scrambled eggs with chives and cream and strips of smoked salmon. He'd presented it on a frosted glass plate, dusted with chopped parsley and accompanied by freshly squeezed orange juice and real coffee, Tanzanian Chagga. He could do with a cup now. The desire is so strong he can taste it.

He goes downstairs. In the kitchen Oscar sits in front of his empty food bowl, fastidiously washing his face. He pauses for a moment, paw frozen in mid-air. He's weighing up the chances of extra rations. 'Sorry, Oscar. You'll have to wait till the boss gets home.' Oscar resumes his washing and Adam fills the kettle and goes in search of coffee. There are mugs and a cafetiere, but only a jar of supermarket own-brand instant.

He extends the hunt. Tucked behind the bread bin is a canister of English Breakfast Tea.

What on earth had prompted him to suggest they move in together? The question had sprung from nowhere. Thank God she'd had the sense to turn him down. Okay, so he's missed her this past week and he's glad they're together again, but anything further would be disastrously premature. She is still too distant. Sometimes he can be with her, and yet not with her, as though a glass shutter has dropped between them.

He knows so little about her. He remembers what she said about a place being a metaphor for a person. In the light of this, he considers her kitchen. It seems it was last fitted out during the nineteen-seventies. The decor is all dark pine and mustard and brown tiles, and the sink is fire-engine red. There is a radio and a notice board with no notices. The bread bin contains half a sliced loaf. Something and nothing. At one level the room has little to say about Eleanor, except that she doesn't subscribe to middle-class obsessions with real coffee and fresh bread, and she probably wears sunglasses to wash up.

Then again, the room has everything to say about Eleanor. A lack of evidence can be as telling as an abundance.

Oscar finishes cleaning his face and peers up at Adam with unblinking amber eyes. 'So,' he hunkers down to the cat's level. 'Tell me about her. You know her better than anyone. Does she make a habit of disappearing first thing in the morning, not a word, not so much as a note?'

'Yes, she does.' She laughs; she's standing behind him. She's dressed for work in a beige suit and a burgundy shirt. She tosses a newspaper on to the table and sits down and crosses her long legs. The point of her wine-coloured shoe taps his knee. He encircles her ankle. She says, 'And do you make a habit of talking to strange cats?'

'No, it's a first.' He releases her and stands up. 'Would you like some tea?' She nods and he fetches the pot and another mug.

'You seem to have made yourself at home.'

'Just the kitchen.' He pours the tea. 'I've a thing about kitchens. Do you mind?'

'Each to his own.'

'That's very generous. Would you like breakfast? I'll cook something, if you like.'

She shakes her head. 'The cupboard's bare. Anyway, I have to go to work soon.'

'Why not ring in sick?'

'That's a rather irresponsible suggestion for an employer to be making. What would you say if Tom did that?'

'If he only did it the once, I'd never know.'

She studies her tea. 'All the same, it's a dangerous precedent.' She smiles, 'Then again, I'm usually very responsible, and just once wouldn't hurt . . .'

'Of course not. So, it's settled?'

She laughs. 'Yes, but only because I was on duty yesterday evening and I'm due some time in lieu.'

'It's all a big cheat, then?'

'I'm afraid so. But listen, Adam, don't go cooking anything, I'm really not hungry.'

'At least have some toast to go with your tea.'

'You're a persistent man, Adam Mason. Okay, toast – if it'll make you happy.'

He hunts the marmalade and Eleanor flicks through the paper. It's

104

a very cosy scene. He tops up the teapot and sits down. 'Goodness,' says Eleanor, folding the newspaper and laying it aside. 'You really are terribly domesticated, aren't you?' The false note surprises him. At some point between pouring the tea and buttering the toast, while his attention was engaged elsewhere, her mood has changed. She is tense. Her face is rigid, her hands clenched. He reaches out, half expecting her to pull away. Her skin is cold. Her knuckles gleam like tallow. To distract him, she says, 'You've got lovely hands, did you know? Has anyone ever told you?'

He looks down. His hands are large, but she's right, they are quite shapely. He compares them with hers. 'Yours are beautiful.'

'No.' She unlocks her fingers and spreads them on the table. 'Claws.' Her voice is clipped. His abdomen tightens and his skin prickles at the memory. She says, 'You looked so at home, pottering around in my kitchen. I'm so sorry about the other day, the church and everything.'

'It's okay.'

'No, it isn't. You've been avoiding me. You think I'm crazy. You're probably right.' She scrapes at the table top with a long, polished nail. 'You say I'm secretive, that I don't tell you things about myself – but is it any wonder? If I look too deep, who knows what I'll find swimming around in the dark. Did I hurt you?'

'What?' The sudden switch wrong-foots him.

'In the church.'

'I see. No, but I thought you might.'

'That's the point. I can't reassure you, can't say I never meant to hurt you. Maybe I did. I wasn't thinking, I just reacted. But it's good that it happened. If you decide to continue with this, you need to know what you're getting into.'

'Do you want to continue?'

'I don't know.' Her fingers lace the mug and he imagines it scalding her palms. 'I think so, but I need to explain things to you – things that don't even make sense to me.'

'Try.'

'It's hard,' her voice is barely above a whisper. 'If I put it into words, it sounds silly, but it's real, Adam. It's real to me.' He holds himself very still. He wants to hear this. Nothing must distract her. 'Sometimes the world isn't as solid as I'd like it to be, as it seems to be for people like you and Jess and Brian. The ground shakes. Like a train crossing a bridge. Different things bring it on. There's this exhibition at the gallery at the moment. Simon Whitburn's paintings blur the boundary between the real and imaginary worlds. For me. The critics don't agree.' She shakes her head in frustration. 'I said this would sound ridiculous.'

'It doesn't. Go on.'

She bites her lip and continues in a rush. 'It's almost as if I'm seeing the world refracted through moving water; straight edges waver and colours blend and shimmer. What I am, what I was and what I seem to be – it all mixes together, I can't separate out the elements. It's so scary, Adam, and I have to do something sharp, something decisive to bring myself back. I focus on sensation. Remember Jess's workshop and the needle? Pain, Adam. It sharpens the world wonderfully, gives it back its edge.'

'I see. I think.' He manages a smile. 'So now tell me how the church fits into this.'

'I can control it there. I go in and everything comes together. The church is a metaphor. It looks solid outside, but inside it's crumbling away. That's me, Adam. The world is disintegrating round me and I grab at anything and anyone that'll bring me back.' She lifts her head. 'So there you are, now you know I'm weird.'

'No. You're not.' He casts around, desperate to help her. 'I know the feeling.'

'How do you know?'

'It's like being scared of heights. What you call disintegration, the feeling that the world is dissolving round you, I've had that, it's vertigo.'

'It's not the same.'

'It is. Everything you describe. I've been scared of heights all my life. Listen to me. You have to convince yourself it's only in your mind that this is happening. I'll tell you a story. I went to the top of St Paul's once. It was perfectly safe but I was so scared I thought jumping off was the only way to end the panic. Imagine that. I grabbed at the balustrade and clung to it until my fingers bled. Pain brought me back, just like you. And I'm not talking about when I was a kid, either. This was five years ago. I know what you're feeling, Eleanor, I do understand. I can help you.'

7

The phone rings and Simon curses. He's working on a tiny oil, maybe eight inches square. Eleanor's hands, inspired by Dürer. He wedges the handset against his shoulder and scrubs at his fingers with a scrap of rag.

'Simon.' Brian's voice booms down the phone line. 'How goes it? Working good and hard, I trust.'

'Remind me to invest in an answering machine.'

'I'll take that as a yes, shall I?'

'As you like.'

Brian laughs, 'Well I've obviously caught you at a less than amenable moment, so I'd better get straight to the point. There's been a development. I need to talk to you.'

'What sort of development?'

'Don't sound so worried. It's good news, but I'd rather not discuss it over the phone.'

'I'll call round some time.'

'No, Simon.' From the other end of the line comes the admonishing crack of a pen against the plastic handset. 'I need to talk to you now, this afternoon. It's important.'

On the way to Whitechapel Simon runs through the possibilities. Perhaps another gallery has expressed an interest, or maybe Brian has landed a commission, or a minor newspaper wants to do an article.

Eleanor greets him with a sharp nod and ushers him into Brian's office. 'Well,' says Brian with a grin. 'Glad you could make it. Sit down, Simon, sit down.'

'So what's the hurry?' Simon pulls up a chair. Eleanor perches herself on the edge of the desk and Brian settles back in his chair and steeples his fingers against his chin.

'Hurry?' Brian smiles. 'No hurry, as such, but we've had an idea and we're eager to put it to you.' He glances at Eleanor. 'I hear the two of you had a very productive dinner the other night.'

Every time Simon looks at Eleanor he sees that other woman, the one who'd sat on his floor sucking curry sauce from her fingers and dabbing at spilt grains of rice.

'Of course, I knew it would pay dividends,' Brian continues. 'Getting you together.'

'It wasn't really dinner.' Simon drags his attention away from Eleanor. 'We shared a Chinese takeaway, that's all. I can't see we achieved so very much.'

'Maybe not,' says Eleanor. 'But it set me thinking.' She grips the edge of the desk and tucks one narrow ankle behind the other. 'I warned you, didn't I, about my tendency for crack-brained schemes?' He nods and shrugs. 'We were talking about your murals, at the time.'

'And I told you I do them for the money, because I can't live on what you get for the canvases.'

'The dilemma being that the murals buy time for what you consider to be your real work, but they also undermine the status of that work.'

'So what? None of this is news.'

'No, but Brian and I have talked it over, and we've come up with a cunning plan.'

Simon waits. He thinks of the painting drying back at the studio, and considers the model here before him, her beautiful crone-like hands clasping her stockinged knee.

'I said you should revise the way you think of the murals.'

'How? Rent money, that's how I think of them . . .'

'No, you must stand up for them. They must have taken considerable time and trouble to complete – we should capitalize on that.'

'The thing is this,' says Brian, 'we need to devise a way for the murals to work for the paintings, rather than against them.'

'I'm going to prove the critics wrong, Simon.' Eleanor's eyes glitter. 'A mural can be a significant work of art. Think of Paula Rego – and there's a college in Cambridge . . .'

'I'm not Paula Rego.' Panic catches in his throat. What are they hatching? 'And I don't paint fucking colleges. Bathrooms, Nell. I told you. I paint bathrooms.'

She leans forward and places a calming hand on his arm. Brian says, 'Simon, that is your biggest problem and it's one we have to address. Everything you've done to date is in private hands and isn't generally accessible.'

'So what is this grand plan? You're going to turn me into a graffiti artist, is that it? Okay, fine. Point me to a bridge, a warehouse wall. Why not? Shit, Brian, I never thought you'd go so far.'

Brian bangs the desk with the flat of his palm. 'You can't have it both ways, Simon. You prattle on about the need to make a living, so now we've found a way, don't go all fancy and artistic on me because it's as phoney as the crowd at your view and I won't have it. Play it that way and we'll call the whole thing off. Empty walls don't scare me. There's an army of people out there panting for the chances you're being given.'

'Great. If that's how you feel . . .' He stands up, ready to storm out. Brian seems set to let him, but not Eleanor.

'There's no need for this,' she says softly. 'Brian, this isn't like you.' For a moment Simon thinks they may have scripted this. Eleanor says, 'We're on your side, Simon, you must believe that. This is in your interest as well as the gallery's.'

Brian leans back in his chair and smooths his grey hair with a plump hand. 'What we'll do is get you a public commission. A mural in a bathroom is little more than customized wallpaper, but the same mural in a public space could well be art.'

'And it's that easy, is it? We just wander out and nab a commission? It's not how it works, Brian.'

'I know the system and we'll work within it, but we'll speed things up, give the process a tweak.' He glances at Eleanor, and gives a half wink.

Simon hates this conspiracy, the way they seem to be manipulating him. He should have followed his instinct, stood up and stormed out. Sooner or later they'd have begged him to come back. But the moment had passed. He looks from one to the other. Eleanor is in control here. What is she up to? His skin is dry and taut. He's light-headed. He senses his future careering out of control. Out of his control. Too many people want a stake in his life – his mother, Farraday, now Eleanor – they bully and coax and generally coerce him into their vision of his future. And they're succeeding. He knows his weaknesses, he cannot fight them.

'What do you mean, "tweak"?' He sounds sullen, but he can't help it. 'What are you proposing to do?'

Eleanor and Brian swap another glance. He wants to bang their heads together. He'll paint it one day – sly collusion and a pair of cracked skulls. Brian rotates the ring on his little finger. 'Restaurants.' He offers the word as a throw-away. He gives a half dismissive shrug, 'I don't know why we didn't think of it before.'

'Because it's naff? Teashop watercolours, hollyhocks and picket fences . . .'

'Pussycats and steeples.' Brian laughs. 'No, Simon, we've something better lined up. Tell him, Eleanor.'

'We persuade a restaurant to let you do a mural, we don't charge a fee because it's free advertising, and we unveil with a flourish, lots of publicity, maybe a simultaneous exhibition.'

Brian leans across the desk. His eyes are more bloodshot than usual. 'We'll work out the details later,' he says. 'But the idea is sound. What do you think?'

'I think it's crap.'

'Thanks a bunch, Simon.'

'I'm sorry, but you did ask.'

Eleanor says, 'It could be big.'

'Really? And what the hell would you know?' Her eyes widen. He shifts uncomfortably in his chair, and relents a little. 'All right then, tell me about this grand plan. You bushwhack some poor sap, sell him the scheme – how do you propose to convince him? You haven't seen the murals. They could be rubbish . . .'

Eleanor shakes her head. 'They're not. I have seen them. It wasn't difficult, just a dab of rudimentary detective work. And they are good. It'll work, Simon.' She smiles. 'And as for the poor sap, I've already got someone in mind.'

'I think it's a brilliant idea,' says Irene. Her approval astonishes him.

'Do you? Well I think Brian Farraday has flipped, gone ga-ga. The man is totally out of his skull. That woman and her barmy ideas will ruin him.'

Irene is working on a series of illustrations for a children's book. She adjusts the sheet pinned to her board. 'Don't you believe it.

Brian's no fool.' She considers her illustration. A streetwise teenager loiters outside a launderette. There is something familiar about her. Irene turns and smiles. 'Don't scowl, Si. It's an interesting approach, that's all I'm saying. Don't dismiss it out of hand, it could work.'

'It's too commercial.'

'So is this.' She gestures to her board. 'What's wrong with that?'

'I didn't realize you'd changed so much. These days you measure success according to volume of sales rather than quality, do you? You used to have standards.'

Irene shrugs. 'I'm simply saying she could have a point. There's nothing wrong with a mural if it's handled properly. You see things small-time, Si. Expand.' She spreads her arms. 'Think of Giotto, think of Paula Rego.'

'Fuck Paula Rego.'

Beyond her shoulder, the illustration springs into focus. She has stolen the girl from his suburban cat-fight. She's toned her down a bit for the teenage market, but it's definitely the same girl. Irene shifts her position to block his view. 'Now, then,' she changes the subject. 'Why don't you tell me about this Eleanor woman. She seems to have sprung out of nowhere . . .'

He should say something. Not about Eleanor, but about Irene's plagiarism. There have been other occasions, though less blatant. He should say something, but he knows how she'll respond. She'll deny it. Even presented with the incontrovertible proof of his painting, she'll outface him. 'Tell me, Simon, who's to say who influenced who? Genes, Si, and upbringing. I could claim everything you've ever done derives from me. You know as well as I do, there's no such thing as an original idea.'

8

Adam knows nothing about art. Although he has never in his life been inside a gallery, a few days ago he took a stroll past Farraday's in the hope of glimpsing Eleanor. He was in luck. The plate-glass frontage made a stage set of the show space. Eleanor was deep in discussion with a prosperous-looking man in a voluminous overcoat. Adam could tell from the efficient slope of her shoulders and the tight, hacking gestures of her hands that she was working up a sale. He could also tell from the way the man watched her that he'd made up his mind, but was reluctant to close the deal and bring down the curtain on Eleanor's performance.

Loitering at an angle that excluded him from her range of vision, Adam continued to observe. When they shook hands he saw the flicker of her nails, and remembered their caress.

This evening, sitting across the supper table from her, the memory remains acute. It is the first time he's been to her house for a meal. She is not a good cook. He'd suspected as much from his survey of her kitchen and he relishes her inadequacy. His ascendency in this one field gives him a buzz. She uses cheap olive oil and puts too much poor quality vinegar in her salad dressing. 'I like it with a bit of bite,' she explains. She also overcooks the pasta. It doesn't matter. Given the circumstances, good food would be a waste. He cannot concentrate, not with Eleanor facing him across the table, dressed all in black and mopping pale oil from her plate with craggy scraps of bread.

'The thing is this,' she says, her lips glistening, 'Simon Whitburn has talent. Okay, he's not brilliant, no Michelangelo, but he's good, and he's commercial – though don't tell him I said so.'

Adam shifts his pasta to and fro. This isn't making much sense. He says, 'I'm a bit adrift. I seem to have missed the start of this conversation.'

'I want you to come to the gallery and take a look at his work.'

'Why? I know nothing about art.'

'You don't have to. You remember the other day you were telling me how the restaurant is only just ticking over, that you need a new identity, a new image?'

'So?'

'Murals. Simon paints murals.'

'You must be kidding. I've only just paid Jessica for the chairs, the purse is threadbare and the bank manager's getting restive. I can't go getting involved in some half-baked project . . .'

'It's not half-baked.'

'Even so —'

'Don't you trust me? This is my job, Adam, it's what I'm paid for, and it could work for you and for Simon. Think about it. It'll be great publicity and it won't cost you a penny.'

'I don't know. It sounds dodgy.'

'Don't be so timid.'

It wasn't very fair of her to call him timid. Kay had always been the timid one. He said he'd think about it, and he did. Two days later he rang to make an appointment at the gallery.

'Good to see you, Adam.' Brian greets him, pumping his hand. 'I thought we'd begin by letting Eleanor give you the grand tour, then we'll talk business.'

Eleanor links her arm in his. Simon Whitburn's vivid canvases festoon the walls and as they promenade, she draws his attention to her favourite works and offers suggestions as to how they might be adapted for his restaurant. Brian follows at a distance. He seems highly amused by it all. 'We could arrange access to one of the murals,' he says. 'If that would help.'

'I can't imagine it would mean any more to me than what I'm seeing here.' Adam likes Brian, but he's wary of him. He straddles the line between art and commerce and it must be pretty uncomfortable at times. Today he's having trouble assessing exactly what's going on behind those moist, pouchy eyes. It has never struck him before how closely Brian resembles an overweight beagle.

Beware of the dog.

If he goes ahead with this, he'll be relying heavily on Eleanor.

He has to admit, the idea of the mural is very seductive. He's even had one or two thoughts about the effect he'd like. Jessica is covering his chairs in a heavy-duty fabric the colour of oxblood. In his mind's eye he extends this to the whole restaurant. He sees warm colours, deep reds, tapestries, mahogany panelling – a medieval banqueting hall. Of course, all these things are beyond his means. Or they were until Whitburn came on the scene. He has no qualms when it comes to authenticity and historical accuracy. If Whitburn can conjure a semblance of mahogany and tapestry – at no cost to himself – he would be a fool to say no.

9

Eleanor can't see anything or hear anything or feel anything. She opens her mouth to scream, but no sound comes. Her silence joins the bigger silence and she has no sense of who she is or where she is, if anywhere.

But she has been here before. She knows this non-place of dense matter. No memory, no sensation. A black hole.

Adam is afraid of heights and she is scared of the dark. When she was little Babs tried to combat her fear by calling a halt to bedtime stories of witches and goblins who perform their wickedness under cover of the night. She replaced them with innocuous tales of children embarking on unlikely adventures, stories that made no impact whatever on Eleanor. When Babs considered her old enough to dispense with the nightlight, she'd lie rigid as a stick with her eyes tight shut and her fists clenched at her side, waiting for the house to grow quiet. Then, when all was still, she'd creep on to the landing and switch on the light. Snuggling back under the covers, she'd will herself to sleep by staring at the yellow strip seeping under the door.

As for the stories, Babs had got it wrong. Eleanor loved the goblins and spooks, they were her friends, they occupied the night and gave it shape and purpose. What the darkness concealed wasn't the problem. She knew perfectly well that the big lump in the corner was her chest of drawers, that the silvery sheen hovering by the window wasn't a ghoul, but the glimmering reflection of moonlight in the mirror. None of these troubled her. It was the nature of night that made her quake. As an adult she has learnt to articulate her fear, but she has never conquered it. Darkness isn't a supernatural, malevolent entity. It is absence. Absence of light. As a child she was told that because colour derives from reflected light, at night all objects are colourless. 'But how would you know?' ten-year-old Eleanor protested as she chewed the corner of her pillow. 'How can you tell, when it's too dark to see?'

And where does this leave Simon? The visual world belongs to him. If he lost it, he would be devastated. He must fear blindness above all things. Light and colour are crucial to him. Sometimes she cannot understand how the whole world doesn't freak out the moment the sun sets.

There is another dream, equally persistent. She is a bird condemned endlessly to circle the earth, frantically passing through time zone after time zone, and night is behind her – its gaping jaws and stinking breath stir the feathers of her tail – and if the night catches her, it will swallow her, and she will become part of the darkness forever.

When Simon showed her the sketches he'd done of her, he'd tried to distract her from the lack of resemblance by talking in more general terms about his work. He follows his body-clock, he'd explained. If unable to sleep, he doesn't fight it, he works. 'But I thought artists needed light.'

'Not always. Degas veiled his windows. Not that I compare myself to Degas.' He described his night-time sessions. 'It's like the night turns white,' he said. 'It becomes a sort of canvas.'

If only. I want that. I want the night to be a screen stretched taut to receive my dreams. I want. I can't have. It would take an act of faith, and darkness isn't a matter for belief. It is a scientific fact that if there is no light, then there is no colour.

So what happens to Simon's paintings – anyone's paintings – come nightfall? How permanent are they? What happens when the gallery lights go out? If only she could believe the colour stayed – that this was Simon's particular magic.

In the absence of faith, she makes other provision. Next to her bed is a candle sconce. From a hook below hangs a drawstring bag containing sections of candle. Every night she puts a piece of candle into the sconce and goes to sleep by its flickering light. Babs, if she knew, would worry about the fire hazard.

The thought excites her, a flood of crimson, brazen flames filling the darkness, pushing back the fear, blinding her with colour.

And then sometimes, like tonight, a dream wakes her after the candle has guttered out. She is twenty-eight years old, but the fear still halts her blood and stills her heart. She once had a friend whose dog, a briard the size of a bear, was also scared of the dark. Take him for a walk and as soon as the streetlights were behind him, poor Benji would start to whimper and shake. Lucy said he was scared because, being so black and hairy, he couldn't tell where he ended and the night began. Eleanor didn't laugh. She knows how terrifying it is to lie in the dark with no sense of shape or form, either of the objects around her or of her own body. It is as though she's leaking into the darkness, dissolving into the night, and come morning, there will be nothing left but the stalactites of dead wax hanging from the candle sconce, a tousled mound of sheets, and the cold imprint of her head on the pillow.

10

'Medieval pastiche. Thanks, but no thanks.' Simon has been asked to join Brian and Eleanor for dinner at Mason's restaurant, and they are treating him like a painter and decorator. He knew it would be like this, he should never have listened to her.

According to his mother and Farraday the whole point of his exhibition had been to persuade the critics to take him seriously. Simon Whitburn, a name to conjure with. Buy now, before prices go ballistic. Then along comes Eleanor all sparkly-eyed and enthusiastic, and the next thing he knows he's back on the decorating circuit, expected to transform Mason's third-rate backstreet caff into a medieval banqueting hall.

'Don't sulk, Simon.'

'I'm not sulking.' He pushes his plate away.

Adam signals Tom who removes the plates and crumpled napkins. 'I owe you an apology, Simon,' he says. 'Like you, I was persuaded to this and it clearly isn't a good idea. I think it would be in everyone's interests if we forgot the whole thing.'

'Adam, no.' Eleanor is surprised and annoyed.

'He's not interested, Eleanor. He's uncomfortable with the whole idea, and I can't say I blame him. Leave the poor man alone.'

Eleanor leans towards Simon. He is acutely conscious of the Byzantine arch of her brows, the scar-like parting in her hair. 'What exactly is the problem, Simon? I thought you'd agreed to this.'

'I didn't know we'd be getting into the theme-park business.'

'That's an exaggeration.'

'Perhaps I got a little carried away' Adam smiles and tops up Simon's wine.

'I don't see what I stand to gain. What about my paintings?'

Adam ventures a glance at Eleanor, 'We thought perhaps a catalogue . . .'

'And an acknowledgement on the menu,' she adds. Simon stares. 'You can design that as well. What d'you say, Adam?'

'That's not what I call art,' Simon snarls. 'That's design. Graphics. It's not the same.'

'You're riddled with prejudice.' Eleanor laughs. 'It's a brilliant idea. Total integration. Menus, stationery, the whole bit. A complete look.'

'And costumes for the serving wenches – who'll design those? Don't do this to me, Eleanor.'

Their escalating voices draw attention from the other customers. Adam intervenes. 'We needn't go so far,' he says. 'I think even my taste balks at serving wenches.'

'Oh, I don't know.' Eleanor smiles. At Adam, not at Simon. It is a slow smile, beginning with a flicker, then broadening and deepening until Simon's fingers twitch with the desire for charcoal or brush. Then Eleanor reaches across to score the back of Mason's hand with her nail. The charcoal snaps. Mason withdraws his hand and Eleanor turns to Simon. 'I promise you,' she says softly. 'This will work. It's a one-off. Think of the publicity. One more mural, Simon, that's all it'll take. Get it right this time, and you need never do another.'

11

In the end he agrees, but he's not fooled. She's lying. If he gets it right – and he will, because this is how he pays his bills, and he's good at it – word will get around, but the wrong word. It will be a case of 'just one more', and 'just another one, Simon,' and another and another until he's so busy trying to keep up with demand he won't have time to do any real work, and he'll live his life and die and no one will ever have taken him seriously.

But he needs the money, and perhaps Eleanor has a point – where is it written that commercial success and artistic status can't ride in tandem? 'Build for the future.' That's what Dad says. 'Keep a little butcher's shop, and a little butcher's shop will keep you.' It is the culture he was raised in, the culture that corrupted Irene. Now it makes its mark on him. He has been offered the freehold on his flat. Security. Permanence. If Eleanor can pull off this party trick of hers, he'll be able to afford it.

He will do the mural. He will show Nell Bycroft his worth, make something of his life, get the recognition he craves and nothing, not even Adam Mason's chivalric fantasies, will get in his way.

The kick of determination, like a rush of desire, knocks the breath right out of him. Reaching for the corkscrew, he opens a bottle of Merlot, tosses the cork aside and slops the wine into a glass.

Earlier today he visited the library, coming away with an arm-breaking stack of books. They're piled in front of him now: a Victorian reproduction of illuminated medieval manuscripts, a magnificent bestiary and two hefty volumes on gothic architecture. He sits hunched over his wine, alternating between turning the pages slowly and flicking rapidly, allowing the glimpsed images to super-impose themselves on his retina. Minutes pass. Wine floods his veins and flushes his skin. Piece by piece he assembles a repertoire of shapes, of flaming crockets and arabesques of stone, of fantastic beasts, gargoyles and grotesques. He reaches for his pad and smooths the page. His fingers perform a skittering dance as, fizzing like sherbet, his mind skips from image to image. Patterns form, then scatter and reform like filings chasing a restless magnet. And then the pattern fixes. He has it.

It is a dizzy moment that has nothing to do with the wine. He knows this feeling, has had it before, exhilaration matched to a fear that melts his guts. What if he can't do it? What if he lacks the skill to translate the three-dimensional images in his mind on to a two-dimensional canvas? It happens every time, the giddiness and self-doubt as he perches atop the big-dipper ride, a moment of suspense before the irretrievable, stomach-lurching plunge.

He always feels this way, and he always pulls it off. Painting is his life. No false modesty. He's got what it takes. There is only one subject he cannot master, and he'll conquer her one day.

Eleanor is curious about his murals. Several previous clients have phoned to report a visit from Eleanor Bycroft. She has examined their murals, taken photographs and asked all sorts of questions about his working relationships and methods. More than this, she has quizzed Simon directly. He stonewalls and baits her by playing the temperamental artist. He's faking, of course. Self-annihilation has never enticed him. No drink, drugs or wild parties for Simon, only long hours and aching muscles and eyes that sting from lack of sleep.

Again and again he refuses her access to the Jangles mural. Mason is also banned from his restaurant. Simon gets a kick out of that. That's real power.

No, it isn't. It's another illusion.

Mason is up in arms. He complains to Eleanor and threatens white emulsion.

'Speak to him, Simon,' Eleanor urges. 'Reassure him. He's out on a limb, out of his depth. Be a bit diplomatic. This is a friendly arrangement, there's no contract . . .'

'Slipped up there, didn't you?'

'Maybe, but I thought we were civilized, mutual friends working for our mutual advantage. Make an effort, Simon. Please?'

She invites him to supper. 'An informal chat,' she says. 'No Brian, just the three of us. Let's see if we can't resolve this.'

Simon takes particular care scrubbing the paint from his fingers. He pulls on a clean shirt and a stain-free sweater. Stopping off on the way he buys a bottle of wine. He knows nothing about wine but it cost enough, so it must be good.

Eleanor takes the bottle, kisses his cheek and ushers him into the living room. Mason is already there, ensconced on her sofa with his long legs stretched out and his ankles crossed. He looks like he owns the place.

It makes Eleanor smile to see them together. They have little in common apart from her – and she is a different person with each of them.

She's nervous about the evening, but also excited. Adam and Simon, home and career – does she really have the skill to bring together these diverse aspects of herself?

Simon is also uncomfortable. He spends so much time peering over his shoulder to see who's gunning for him, it's a wonder he ever gets any work done. He is particularly sensitive to any hint of conspiracy.

When she suggested the evening, Adam offered to cook dinner. 'I don't think so,' she said. 'For two reasons. Firstly, if you cook, it's bound to turn out too formal. That's not a criticism, it's just that I know you like to do things properly, and it might make Simon feel awkward.'

'And secondly?'

'I don't think we should broadcast our relationship. Simon is already fantasising that Brian and I are ganging up against him – God knows what he'll do if he thinks you're in on the act.'

'Well, if that's the way you want to play it, I'll be discreet. But he's not a fool, Eleanor, he's bound to pick up on it.'

Adam does his best, he is not openly affectionate, but he can't help playing host. He opens the wine and points Simon to his seat. Eleanor makes a weak joke about how he's never off duty, but it doesn't matter; Simon is far too on edge to be bothered about Adam. He fidgets with his glass and jabs at his chicken. 'Don't you like it?' she asks.

'It's all right.' He takes a bite. 'It's great. I didn't know you could cook as well, Nell.'

'Hidden depths.' She glances at Adam, who is trying not to smile.

'I'm surprised you didn't invite Brian.'

'This has nothing to do with Brian. It's down to the three of us.' She's trying to give Simon a conspiracy of his own but he's too paranoid to notice. 'Would you like some more chicken?' He nods and she ladles another portion of casserole on to his plate. Adam declines. 'Forget Brian,' she urges. 'I see the Jangles mural as an amalgam of my acumen, your skill and Adam's vision.'

'His vision? What about mine?'

'Yours too, but it's different. Adam's taking a commercial risk. That's why we need a progress report.'

'I'm progressing,' he says grudgingly.

'Could you be more specific?' Adam is curt. 'What stage have you reached?'

'The scaffolding's up.'

'And have you started painting?' Eleanor tops up his wine. 'Or are you still priming?'

'I've started.'

'Well, that's great, isn't it, Adam? It's good to know everything's on schedule and underway . . .'

'There is no schedule. I'm not building a garden shed or putting in a new toilet . . .'

'You know that isn't what I meant.' Mostly she can tell when he's playing games, but tonight she's not sure.

'So when do we get a look?' Adam interrupts. He's been fretting about this for days; he hates not being in control.

'When I'm finished.'

'Now hang on, this is my restaurant, let's not forget that detail.'

'He knows that,' Eleanor lays a hand on his arm. 'We won't get in the way, Simon, I promise – but you must give us something to be going on with. All this secrecy's great fun, but Adam needs to be reassured. Imagine how you'd feel if someone barred you from your studio. Well, it's the same for Adam – he can't bear being locked out of his kitchen. Look at him,' she laughs. 'He's in a terrible state.'

'Is it any wonder?' Adam protests. 'All I've seen are a few vague sketches and some colour samples. I need more than that.'

'You don't trust me . . .?'

'Of course he trusts you.'

'On what grounds?' Adam doesn't much like Simon and he can barely contain his irritation. 'I know nothing about him, Eleanor.

You produce him from nowhere and I'm expected to give him carte blanche – this is my livelihood the pair of you are playing with.'

'We're not playing, Adam. Simon, can't you make a little concession?'

'No.'

'For heaven's sake.' Adam looks from one to the other. 'Let's call a halt to the whole business right here. I don't have to put up with this . . .'

'Neither do I.' Simon pushes his plate away. 'This is how I work, take it or leave it.'

'Simon, hold on —'

'Those sketches,' – he jabs his finger at the table – 'they're ideas based on what you asked for, but they're not fixed, they could change. It happens sometimes. I paint something, it makes me think of something else, I paint that. Organic.'

Eleanor looks at Adam. 'That does sound reasonable, doesn't it? I think we can trust him. I mean, look at it this way, I don't suppose you relish an audience when making an omelette.'

'It's hardly the same,' Simon spits.

'But for Adam it is, that's the point – don't you see?'

He doesn't see. Won't, can't. He goes home in a rage and for a whole week Eleanor leaves him alone. Then she issues another dinner invitation. He says he's busy. It's a lie, of course, but he's scared of another spat, afraid to look a fool in front of Mason.

The trouble is, having turned her down he spends the entire evening wondering whether Mason had also been invited. If so, he'll be there now. They'll have reached the brandy. What are they talking about? Him? Yes, he's the one thing they have in common. They are grumbling about his rudeness, his intransigence. Unless they haven't given him a thought – that would be much worse.

What if he went round to the house? He could sneak up the path and peer through a chink in the curtain – and see what?

The screen is blank. He cannot imagine the scene.

He pours another glass of wine and consoles himself with a sketch of Adam Mason who, with his curly dark hair and his beard and hawkish nose, is the very spit of the devil.

12

The mural is finished. Fire and snow. The tables with their blue-ice napery and sparkling glass cut a swathe through Simon's fantastic landscape. Where wall and ceiling meet, a trompe l'œil pole with mock ormolu brackets supports a magnificent, Venetian red tapestry overlaid by an ivory trellis entwined with foliage. This in turn is home to a splendid variety of birds and butterflies and insects. So convincing are these, so vivid, that even Simon is startled by their rustling and chirruping – in reality the chatter and chink of the diners. At regular intervals along the wall, monkeys and gryphons and cloven-hoofed cherubs peel back broad tapestry folds. The erratic shadows thrown by the candles adorning each table create an illusion of movement, as if the fabric stirs to a breeze from another world.

And it is in this other world of revealed secondary space, that he has placed his own work. Each parting in the tapestry exposes a diamond-shaped painting distinctively and irrefutably the work of Simon Whitburn. In the panel facing the entrance, a satanic- looking chef with a remarkable resemblance to Adam, slides an omelette from pan to plate in such a way that it seems about to fly out of the wall. In another, a market stall presents a vegetable battlefield. Tomatoes, carrots, pumpkin and swede are strewn, piled, split open – a gutted marrow suspended from the crossbar parodies Van Cleve's butchered ox. Simon's favourites are the fish, iridescent monsters weaving through opalescent water. Below, a crab attempts to haul itself out of the frame. One surreal claw extends into real space.

'Amazing, Simon.' Eleanor comes up behind him. 'You've done it, it works wonderfully – and you've found a way to include your own work. I knew you could do it.'

123

'Thanks.' He sounds grudging. 'But I did it for the money, so you'd better sell some paintings.'

She laughs. 'We'll do our best.'

He believes her. Like him, she's good at what she does and tonight she's whipped up a tornado of interest. According to Mason the restaurant is fully booked until the end of the week after next, but he can't help wondering whether the well-dressed diners know what the evening is really about. She's done everything she said she would. As well as the general publicity, the invitations had been explicit, stressing Simon's name alongside that of the restaurant and Farraday's gallery. But will all this palaver sell any paintings? He squints at the pile of catalogues on the table by the door, trying to gauge whether it has diminished during the course of the evening. It's hard to tell; perhaps Mason has replenished it. He turns to Brian. He's absorbed in his meal. Now and again he exchanges a word with Nell's friend Jess, who'd apparently had something to do with furnishing the restaurant.

Brian is eating wing of skate with black butter and pimentos and it looks good enough to paint. Simon watches as he eases the moist flesh away from the translucent bones. He says, 'You can eat those.' Brian looks up and frowns. 'The bones. Skate bones.'

The atmosphere tonight is very different from his private view. That had been a surgical occasion, involving a clinical dissection of his work. This is more like a medieval fair.

He drains his wine and settles back to enjoy the effect of his handiwork. It's true, a mural is redefined by location. This is a lot more than customized wallpaper. This is art. Or near as dammit. Interactive art. Again and again a detail catches the eye of a diner who, with a toss of the head or a flick of a fork, draws it to the attention of their companion.

It is the ultimate ego trip. He's proud of what he's done. He's taken Mason's crude ideas and mixed tradition with innovation to transform them into something utterly new.

Brian finishes his fish and tops up Jess and Simon's wine. 'This is great,' Jess leans across the table and gestures to the crowd. 'Just look at them all.'

'You must come to the gallery,' says Brian. 'Get Eleanor to bring you to our next view.'

'Will it be as good as this? I'm having a whale of a time. This is better than a night at the theatre.'

'Exactly. Eleanor knows how to put on a show. Isn't that right, Simon?'

'I suppose.'

'Tut-tut. Did you ever meet anyone so grudging, eh Jess?' Brian mops his lips and gestures with his crumpled napkin, 'Look at that, Simon, they've been topping up the catalogues all evening. We'll be getting sales from this, you mark my words.'

'We'd better. I'm broke.'

'Simon,' says Brian with a wink at Jess, 'is always broke.'

Simon shrugs and smiles. He doesn't want to quarrel any more. He's eaten well and drunk a lot and he's feeling rather sleepy. He slouches in his chair. His eyes grow heavy. The customers, so strident at the outset, have also mellowed. The shrill scrape of conversation has softened to a mild buzz. All around him the candle flames strike tawny echoes in the curves of the brandy glasses.

What about Eleanor? Where is she? He swivels in his seat. There, over by the bar. At some point, it seems hours ago, Mason had beckoned her to introduce her to someone. She is still with him. She strode across to Mason's side, unashamedly startling with her distinctive colouring and her splendid hair piled on her head, the fine strands straining at her nape. Her dress is stunning, electric blue and tight-fitting. A lightning bolt. The back plunges almost to her waist. She moves, and the knuckles of her spine ripple, supple and deadly as a conger-eel. He laughs. Are conger-eels deadly? He starts to turn, to ask Brian, then thinks better of it. It doesn't matter. Scientific accuracy is less important than the metaphor. He stores it away with all the other hints and shadows and allusions that will one day empower him to paint her.

And then he notices Mason's hand. It is large, and surprisingly elegant. It grips Eleanor's arm just above the elbow. The fingers tighten and release. Eleanor responds, turning to look at him. She smiles. Just centimetres separate them, an intimate space, a shared breath. Mason's hand slips to her waist and his thumb nuzzles the inverted apex of her dress. She responds with a subtle flexing of her spine, from the small of her back to her fragile nape.

'Quite a couple, eh?' Simon is startled. 'Those two.' Brian nods in their direction. 'That's right, isn't it Jess? Eleanor and Adam. You must have realized, Simon.'

'No. I had no idea.'

'Adam's a good bloke. They seem right together, don't you think?' Simon shrugs. He has nothing to say. 'You know, Simon,' Brian shakes his head reprovingly, 'I worry about you sometimes. You're an artist, you're supposed to notice things.'

'I do, but not this.'

'Too close to home, perhaps?' Brian glances at Jess.

Simon grunts and drains his brandy. Brian's right, he should have realized. That dreadful supper, and the time before, at the restaurant – Nell's long nail scoring the back of Mason's hand.

He should have seen, but he hadn't. He didn't want to see. Eleanor belongs to his world. How can it be otherwise with her colouring and that amazing face, hard and delicate all at once, and those hands, gesturing, expounding, explaining his work? Okay, he knows there's a cross-over point, a bridge into Brian's world. It drives him crazy, but he loves that too – Eleanor the entrepreneur. He cannot see a single thing she has in common with a man like Adam Mason. Brian has made a mistake.

It is after midnight and they are preparing to leave. Adam helps Eleanor into her coat. His hand rests on her shoulder. It is an intimate, proprietorial gesture. Earlier, as the customers departed, they stood side by side, saying their farewells like a married couple seeing off their dinner guests. He is prepared to admit that physically they are well-matched. Both tall, with dark hair. Eleanor's eyes are blue, Mason's a muddy grey. Brother and sister. A pair of bookends. But not lovers. Please, don't let them be lovers.

13

Eleanor tugs the duvet under her chin. Adam laughs and pulls her towards him; their long legs tangle, their fingers lock. They kiss, and continue their analysis of the evening. 'I think it was a roaring success,' says Eleanor.'

'You would,' he laughs. 'It was your baby.'

'You don't think I'm being objective?'

'Did I say that? Anyway, you're right. So far as Jangles is concerned it was a triumph, but what about Simon? I thought the idea was to promote his paintings.'

'And we did. The invitations had his name plastered all over them, there was a whole stack of catalogues right by the door, and as for the murals – I don't see how anyone could have failed to notice those.'

'I know, but I was watching them. They picked up the catalogues the way people take handouts in the street. They didn't look at them.'

'Don't worry, they'll take them home and they're big and glossy and they'll go through them later. I don't see why you're so concerned. Simon's my responsibility.'

'I feel sorry for him. He's out of his depth and he doesn't make an impact on people. He should have been the star tonight.'

'He doesn't really like being on show. Look, if we sell a couple of paintings and maybe pick up a commission or two, he'll be more than happy. Now please, can we stop talking about Simon.' She pinches his arm and ducks her head under the duvet. She hears his sharp intake of breath. Fear and desire.

She wakes the next morning muddle-headed and mildly hung over. She glances at the clock and moans and digs her head under the pillow. Her eyes feel gritty, her mouth dry. Adam laughs and runs his hand the length of her sinewy back. She wriggles away, squirming down under the feathery mound.

'It'll take your mind off your hangover . . .' he suggests. She doesn't respond. 'It'll take my mind off my hangover.' Still nothing. He whips away the duvet. 'How about a walk? Let's go to the park. Fresh air. Blow away the cobwebs.'

The morning is damp and drizzly. The mounds of copper and bronze leaves have degenerated into a squidgy mass lining the edges of the paths. Eleanor is not happy and he's not sure whether it's the park, the hangover or something else. He tightens his grip on her waist. Joined-at-the-hip, they trip over one another's feet and laugh and hold on ever more tightly.

Two boys on rollerblades glide past, deftly avoiding all obstructions, the sodden leaves, the stones. Their movements are fluid, swimmers of the air. Eleanor envies them. Her mind flies after them, clinging to their sleeves – go with the flow. The tail of the mirage flicks its defiance.

Adam pulls her back. 'Feels strange this morning, doesn't it? Bit of an anticlimax, I suppose.'

Yes, that's exactly how she feels. Last night she'd been in her element. Everything fitted. She looked right, she felt right, she knew all her lines and the stage set was perfect. All her efforts of the past years, the striving to recreate herself, had culminated there. Not because of Adam, but because of what she has achieved on Simon's behalf.

This is who I want to be.

'It happens sometimes,' she says. Her mind races as she analyses her feelings. Life is about progress, about the movement from here to there, to elsewhere. Last night had been an arrival, a grand coming home, but now she must turn her mind to the next stage, the next departure. She cannot stand still because if she does, life might leave her behind.

'You see,' Adam continues, 'I'm not used to this. The peaks and troughs tend to be closer together in my trade.'

'Really.'

'Does this happen after every opening?'

'More or less. Can we go home, Adam?'

He turns to peer at her. 'Aren't you well?'

'I'm fine.'

'Well then, let's stay a bit longer.'

'I don't want to.'

'Why ever not?'

'For God's sake, Adam, what's with the interrogation? I'm cold and I'm tired. Isn't that enough? Why d'you have to make such an issue of it?'

She sounds hysterical. Where has the panic come from? How can she explain?

She feels exposed. Every sound, smell and sensation is heightened. It's as if her skin has been ripped away, and now there are no barriers between her and the cold, rasping air and the insistent clatter of the park, the scrape of shoes on asphalt, the tear of claws on bark, the grating sound of clouds scouring the treetops.

'Eleanor?'

'I want a cup of coffee.' She clings to what is ordinary, to their rituals, the games they play. 'Tanzanian Chagga.' She nuzzles his cheek and nips the lobe of his ear. She can smell him. Last night the air had been thick with the tang of paint, and now it clings to his hair, mingling with the brandy fumes and cigarette smoke and her perfume.

'And croissants,' Adam joins the game. He too is relieved to return to normality.

'Hot croissants and chilled quince jelly.'

'Contrasting flavours.'

'And textures.'

'And temperature,' he says. 'You're learning. I'll make a connoisseur of you yet. Eleanor . . .' He catches her arm and pulls her close. Her hearing is normal now, but her field of vision has narrowed. She cannot see the russet trees or the cobwebs spanning the twigs, only Adam. He says, 'You worry me when you withdraw like this, for no reason.'

'There's a reason.' She tries to lighten her tone. 'I'm never at my best in the morning, you know that.'

'Do you remember the day we went to the church?'

'Of course I do.'

'It began here. Right here, by this tree.'

She glances up. 'Did it really? I'd forgotten. It looks different, and the squirrel's gone.'

'But nothing else has changed, has it? You still don't trust me; you're fending me off all the time. This business with the restaurant and Simon, it was just an interlude. You and me, we're not going anywhere, Eleanor, we're frozen.'

Does he realize how closely he echoes her own thoughts? Are they so much attuned that they realize at exactly the same moment how out of sync they are?

'Where do you want to go?' she asks. 'Because if this is about me moving in with you . . .'

'No, it isn't. Not directly. I don't think that would work, do you? Not until I understand you better. All that stuff about hiding our relationship from Simon – it set me thinking. It's almost like you're ashamed of me, because I'm not an arty type like him and Brian. All I am is a common or garden businessman . . .'

'That's ridiculous. You're always talking about the art of cooking . . .'

'Then what is it? What's wrong with us?'

'I don't know. The thing about not telling Simon was just a question of expediency, and I'm sure he knows now, after last night.'

'Okay, but what about us? We're in a rut, Eleanor.'

'You said that about Kay. Is that what you're doing? Are you dumping me?'

'No. I'm asking you to help me to understand.'

'How?'

'Chris. Tell me about Chris.'

Sharp as a gunshot. Her body recoils. Her head swims and she gapes as if drowning. The pinch of his fingers brings her back. 'Who told you about Chris? Jess, you've been talking to Jess, haven't you?'

'No. Or rather, I tried, but she won't tell me anything. But you, you mention him now and again, and it's as if I'm supposed to know . . . There's something about him and it's getting in the way, keeping us apart. I need to know, Eleanor.'

'It's over. It was done and done with long before you came along.'

'But the hurt's still there, I can tell, and if you still love him, where does that leave me?'

'What I feel for him, what he did to me – it has nothing to do with us.'

'But it does. Sometimes you're so strange, so distant, and I'm certain he's behind it. I'm scared whatever happened between you is poisoning us. He's the reason you're how you are. Isn't he? I'm right, aren't I?' She cannot answer. She doesn't want to look at him, but can't help herself. She is paralysed; she cannot turn her back or move her head. 'Talk to me, Eleanor.'

If it didn't hurt so much, she'd be angry. Long ago she'd locked Chris up, put him away – what right has Adam to go bringing him back?

And Chris. After all this time, nothing has changed. He's still a part of her, occupying a space that should have been hers. The scream twists inside her, spiralling up through her gut, and her body convulses, suppressing it, transforming it to a croak. 'He was married.'

'That much I guessed.' His face is close to hers and she can see the tight texture of his beard, the faint creases, the latticework of pores, all exaggerated as if viewed through a microscope.

'I made a mistake.' The words loosen the blockage, the dam breaks and back it floods, a great black torrent of misery. The bitterness at having been taken in by Chris. It makes her dizzy – still, after all this time – the dark abyss between the man she thought he was and the man he turned out to be. 'I'm such a fool, Adam. You wouldn't believe it. Or perhaps you would. You want it all, don't you?' She hears the harsh crack of her laughter. It belongs to someone else. It comes from somewhere else. 'Chapter and verse, is that it? Okay. I'll tell you.

'I truly believed,' she takes a deep, shuddering breath. 'I truly believed that what we had meant as much to Chris as it did to me. I loved him. I thought he loved me. I was wrong.' She looks into Adam's eyes and sees Chris's narrow, peevish face reflected in his dilated pupils. It is the face of a drowned child rising to the surface of a pond.

'Eleanor . . .'

I will conquer this. I will not let it start again. If I tell Adam, make it into a story, maybe that will help. 'I would have taken risks, I would have made tremendous compromises for Chris. But he didn't want me to take risks, and the compromises he was looking for weren't the ones I was prepared to make.'

'He went back to his wife?'

'He went back to his wife.' There is comfort in repetition. She sees her standing on her doorstep, blank faced, dumb but accusing. Her lips are numb. She chews them, seeking sensation. 'I met her, his dull little wife, overweight, with a scrubbed middle-class face and suburban values. You think I'm bound to say that – but I won't lie, it's true. She was a total nonentity, the sort of person you talk to only to forget what they look like and the sound of their voice and everything they say, the moment they're out of sight.'

'Isn't that a little harsh? I mean, next to you, almost everyone is a nonentity.'

She laughs. The tension eases. Her own lie dissolves into his. If he can believe that, that's wonderful. She won't be the one to enlighten him. She must not lose this. She loves to be with him. Maybe they can move forward together. He is solid and he gives her something to push against.

And he is right to ask about Chris. She has said it herself, that he should know what he's getting into. 'The thing about Chris,' she speaks slowly, very carefully, 'is that so far as he was concerned, every decision, every choice I made was the wrong one. And it's crippled me. I'm scared, Adam. That's why I'm so cautious with you. What if I go on and on for the rest of my life making all the wrong choices and hurting people, hurting everyone I care about? I don't mean you to feel left out, or to think I don't care or am ashamed of you in some way. Nothing could be further from the truth. But sometimes it all seems too much and I don't want to be here, I want a dark hole to crawl into, somewhere where I can't see anyone or hurt anyone ever again, somewhere no one can see me . . .' He is holding her by the shoulders. She can feel the dig of his fingers, the brush of his body. She needs his help. 'Look at me, searching for a gap in the stars.' Her laugh is like breaking stone. 'But even that won't work. The light's too bright, it hurts my eyes – you know me, Adam, surely you've realized by now how scared I am of the dark.'

14

Simon hasn't seen Eleanor in over two months. Hasn't seen her, doesn't want to see her. He's trying to forget. He can block out their meetings and verbal wrangles, but there's more to Eleanor than that. She's got inside his head somehow, tramped across his imagination leaving a forensic trail that strikes up echoes in everything he sees and does. He tries to ignore it, but in his line of work he can't afford to turn a blind eye to anything. But if he can keep it at that, insist her hold over him is purely professional, he'll be okay.

It doesn't help that Irene is taking an interest. 'I'm curious, Si. She sounds interesting, your Eleanor. I thought I might invite her for supper.'

'Not my Eleanor. If you're so keen, you should get Brian to introduce you. He's proud as a bantam cock.'

'Don't be so tetchy, Si, it doesn't suit you.'

'I'm sorry, I've just had enough. I'm sick of Nell Bycroft and all that shit about the restaurant. She was playing games. She was bored, so she interfered and got her boyfriend's restaurant tarted up gratis. I'm last week's plaything, yesterday's news.'

'You're taking this a little personally, aren't you, Si? Okay, she's got a boyfriend – so what? The way I see it, she's succeeded in what she set out to do – you've sold some paintings, got your name put about. That's why you went along with it. Yes?' He shrugs. 'Well then, what's it to you if she's moved on?'

'Nothing,' he mutters. 'Nothing at all.' This is ridiculous. He ought to be able to confide in Irene. She's a painter, after all – it must have happened to her. Isn't that how she met Dad, saw him in a pub and wanted to paint him? Maybe it's Dad he should talk to. 'Okay, so I'm getting it out of proportion.' Irene's eyes narrow. 'Now what?'

'Give her a ring, go and see her. Nothing ventured, Si . . .'

So Irene thinks he fancies Nell but doesn't have the balls to do anything about it. Well it's not like that, or if it is, he can't get his head round it. Too late now. The speed of change has utterly wrong-footed him. He'd thought he and Eleanor and Farraday were the team, with Adam Mason just a temporary player. He couldn't have got it more wrong.

After the opening, when the guests had gone, Brian phoned for a taxi and offered Simon and Jess a lift. Mason said he was going in the other direction and would take Eleanor. Brian gave Simon a knowing look. Simon felt sick. He said, 'You two take the taxi. I'll walk.'

It was a misty night. Moisture speckled the pockets of air round the streetlamps. It was a shock exchanging the warmth and security of his medieval fantasy for the bleak London street. It would have made sense to go in the taxi, but he couldn't face Brian's heartiness, or the endless speculation about Adam and Eleanor. He kicked a discarded can into the gutter. The clatter and chang of aluminium on stone reverberated through his skull long after the can had come to rest. Suddenly the world felt less than substantial. Brittle as eggshell. A stray blow, a light tap, would crack it open.

No, it's not the planet that's fragile; he's the one in danger. He must go home. Home is safe.

He starts to walk. Slowly, with exaggerated care, he places first one foot, then the other down on the pavement. Most likely he looks drunk, but he isn't. He knows only that it is important not to jar his fragile bones.

Why did Nell go off with Mason? Brian can't possibly have got it right. The fool misread the signals.

But if it's such a big mistake, why didn't Jess say something, and why do his bones ache like this? What's this crashing in his head?

Anticlimax. Nothing more sinister than that. For weeks he's lived and breathed Mason's bloody mural – day and night, eating and sleeping, shitting and piddling. No escape. And always there, hovering in the background, Eleanor. What will she think? Will she like it, or will she shake her head and sigh, and tell him it's not appropriate?

Eleanor sitting cross-legged on his floor, her long nails tapping against his drawing. 'This isn't me, Simon. What made you think this was me?'

At one point while painting the mural he thought he might slip in a portrait. She was unlikely to recognize herself. Then again, maybe he'd come close enough that anyone who knew her would see he'd tried. And failed. Mason's portrait was obvious and excusable. 'Don't you think it rather endearing,' one punter commented as he admired the satanic chef, 'this Whitburn fellow taking a gentle pop at his patron? I must say, I like that. The man has a sense of humour.' Simon considered owning up to his authorship, but in the end he didn't because any discussion might expose the portrait as an expression of malice rather than humour. Doubtless Adam recognized himself, but what about Brian? He was too vain to identify his own features in the lugubrious face of the catfish. As for Nell, the whole point would be to capture her likeness and as it's never a good idea to be seen to fail, Eleanor is absent. Unless, of course, you count the crab.

He can sort of understand Brian's mistake about her relationship with Mason. During the course of the evening she'd spent a fair amount of time at his side, but then that was all part of the show. The scheme had been her idea, naturally she'd want to oversee its success. And fair's fair, she had tried to include him. Several times she had drawn him into the circle and introduced him to Mason's customers. 'This is our artist,' she said. 'Simon Whitburn.'

'Our' artist. Adam and Eleanor's pet with his hog's bristle tail and painted clown's face, cavorting at her command, turning tricks for the trade.

Since then he's kept away from the gallery and done his best to blank her out. She's not a person or in any sense an individual, just an accumulation of data stashed in his image bank.

These days his dealings with Brian are mostly by phone. He rings to report any sales and, at the end of the month, Simon receives an account. However, a week or so ago, Brian phoned in a state of excitement. 'It's working, word's getting round, Simon. I've just had a call from the director of a small computer company. The man had lunch at Jangles last week and was impressed with what he saw. He took a brochure, consulted his board and they want to commission a painting for their conference room.'

'Sounds like wallpaper to me.'

'Now, now. Isn't this precisely what Eleanor predicted? Corporate art. The birth of a reputation. Rejoice, Simon.'

'What do they want?'

Brian rustled some papers on his desk. 'Ah yes, here we are.' He read out a list of dimensions and a sum of money.

'I told you,' said Simon. 'Books by the yard.'

'Maybe, but they don't have to be bad books, now do they Simon? Work within the system, build a profile and the future will take care of itself.'

'If you say so. And Nell . . .'

'Eleanor and I have invested a lot of thought and effort in your future; we can't have you going all arty on us now.'

He can't afford to say no, and Brian knows it. He has committed himself on the purchase of his freehold. He agrees to a meeting. He says, 'Will Eleanor be there?'

'No, just you and the clients. See what you think and if you agree, I'll go to see them and talk terms.'

'Right.' End of conversation. No further excuse to talk about

Eleanor. After weeks of silence, he is desperate to know what she's doing. Is she still with Mason? Is she settled in her job, or liable to move on? Above all, is the thing with Mason likely to last? Always assuming it exists in the first place.

Brian is his only source of information, but his lips are dry and sealed. The words will not come. Not that it matters. Brian would certainly resist. Good-natured gossip is one thing, hard information another. He'll probably tell Simon what he already knows – that so far as Eleanor Bycroft is concerned, he has no right to information.

It is mid-morning. Simon perches on his stool before a persistently blank canvas. The grey-white light washes over him. Bulging, warbling pigeons clutter and strut the rooftops.

He's had an idea for this commission. He will explore the relationship between old and new, human versus machine. He sees a cubist collage of keyboards and VDUs superimposed over a spectral figure, flowing line and drifting hair indistinctly emerging from the back of the canvas to fuse with the grid of computer hardware, creating a new synthesis, a different reality.

Eleanor. Who else could it be, but Eleanor? Or a version of her, the best he can manage at the moment. He recalls his sketches of her hands. Yes, this is the way to tackle her. He will paint her bit by bit in ever updated versions until one day he catches himself unawares and finds he has succeeded in fixing her to the canvas.

As for this new painting, he can see it clearly but can't get started. He takes a walk round the studio. He cleans tubes of paint and lays them in neat rows. He shakes out and refolds his paint rags, arranging them within easy reach. He fiddles with the easel, adjusting it to just the right angle. Then he adjusts it again. The pigeons grumble their derision.

He cannot put this off any longer, he must get started. Where, how? He needs a springboard. He shuffles through a folder of unfinished sketches looking for something to get him going. Bullshit. Knowing what he wants, he lacks the confidence for the first stroke. His new brushes wait. They bristle and mock. The blank canvas glares.

I will conquer this. What is she anyway? Nothing, just sinew and bone, artery and vein, a lattice of azurite and coral and blue-grey, blood-thrumming muscle. His mind teeters on the brink. He starts to work. His hand dashes across the canvas, broad strokes outlining, shaping, chasing his inner vision. And what about her mind, frantically working behind those cruel blue eyes? No mystery there. Just matter infinitely folded and refolded; ganglia and synapses and electrical pyrotechnics, charged impulses flashing and jumping from point to point like contacts in a computer.

15

Eleanor stands full-square in front of the canvas. Her back is rigid. Even her plait is stiff with resentment. There is a tickle of hysteria in the back of his throat. He always knew she'd hate the painting, but didn't think she'd ever see it. It is destined for the conference room of a private company. She is unlikely to wheedle her way in there.

Yet she had managed to see his murals. He mustn't underestimate her.

He works every day from dawn till dusk. He is totally absorbed, exhilarated by the organic processes of composition and form. He builds the painting up, layer by layer, oil followed by acrylic, concentrating on texture, line and mass. He limits his palette to beige shading to brown, chromium oxide to Prussian blue. For weeks he's lived with this version of Eleanor materializing out of the network of computer hardware like a mould growing through the canvas.

And now she is here in person.

Because the conference room is large, the painting is massive. If he had any sense he'd have covered it. He has a sheet as big as a ship's sail piled in the corner, it almost needs a rigging to get it in place. But he doesn't cover the canvas. What brings him crashing to his knees is vanity.

Hearing the doorbell, he half hopes it's Brian.

He angles the canvas so the painted surface isn't visible from the door. He's pleased with his achievement. It's a triumph. But despite this uncharacteristic bullishness, he has allowed no one to see the painting. He wants to whet Brian's appetite, force him to ask permission to view.

Crossing to the door, he anticipates his reaction. The sharp intake of breath, the dart of his gaze as he absorbs the layers of nuance, the oblique – and to those in the know, not so oblique – references. He is eager for reassurance.

Except it isn't Brian who's come to call. It's Eleanor.

She smiles. 'Hello, Simon.' She sounds almost shy. Her eyes flicker past him and he glances over his shoulder to reassure himself that though she can see the canvas, the painting itself is not visible. 'So how are you?' she continues. 'I haven't seen you in ages. I'm often tempted to pop in, but I know you don't like an audience while you're working . . .'

He stands with his back pressed against the closed door. Just like last time, he wants her to go, and he wants her to stay. He says, 'I hate it, and to be honest, it isn't too convenient just now. I'd prefer you to telephone . . .'

She laughs and shakes her head. 'Listen to you, one commission and you think you're David Hockney.'

'You know about the commission, then?'

'Yes, of course I do. It's why I'm here. The clients are pestering Brian for a progress report.'

'I told you, it's not convenient.'

'Simon, you can trust me, you know that. I just need a quick glimpse and then I can make up a story to keep them quiet . . .' She gives his arm a squeeze and stalks to the middle of the studio. She's wearing a lilac suit with a short skirt and grey stockings. She swivels slowly on her heel, taking in the discarded sketches, the bundles of brushes and the table covered in paints. His reaction is too slow to prevent her confronting the canvas.

There is a long silence. Even the pigeons hold their breath. At last she says, 'So this is it, then?'

'It's not finished . . .'

She has the most expressive back. He remembers an expanse of glowing flesh, the caress of Mason's thumb, and here it comes again, the contorted conger-eel twist as she straightens her shoulders and flicks her plait and says, 'It is, Simon. It is finished.'

'You don't understand.' His voice has no volume; it emerges as a glove-puppet wheeze. He feels the grief flowing from her, like an incoming tide. No. There is no way she can recognize herself in the anatomical spectre looming through the collage of technology. It is a figure reduced to its component parts, separated from and integrated into the computer hardware. But with Eleanor's hands, and a cloud of dark hair like mountains seen from a distance, and flashing, electric blue eyes.

'How could you?' she whispers.

'How could I what?' He is defensive. Angry and guilty.

'Do that.' She gestures to the painting.

'I've done nothing . . .'

'You have, you know what you've done.' She swings to face him. 'You've no right.'

'It's my painting, Nell. It's nothing to do with you.'

'The fuck it isn't.' His language in her mouth. Her mask skids sideways. He always knew she wasn't real. She is a composite person, a reflection.

She touches the painting. He hears the scrape of her nail against the canvas. 'Don't do that. It's not dry.'

She examines her nail. Then the painting. Then him. 'You haven't signed it.'

'I'll sign it when it's done.'

'It is done.'

'No.' They square up to one another, a pair of squabbling infants – 'tis-'tisn't . . . 'tis-'tisn't.

'Sign it.'

He doesn't move. She approaches the paint table and idly pushes and delves amongst the jars and tubes. 'What are you doing? Leave those.'

She makes her selection. She glances at him, brandishing a crimson acrylic left over from a previous painting. 'Won't you sign it?' Her reasonable tone is shot through with something else. What? Irony? No, there's a threat lurking in there somewhere. 'Last chance, Simon.' She waits. 'No? All right. Fine. I'll do it.'

'No.' He makes a grab for her hand, but too late. She clenches her fist and the tube buckles and spouts its contents and with the flat of her palm she smears a bloody gash from bottom left to top right. She turns slowly, examining her hand, as if unable to believe what she has done. There is a moment of stillness and silence.

It is too much for him, the savaging of his painting. He grabs at her. His nails bite into her wrist. She is strong, much stronger than he'd imagined – and determined. They are locked together, frozen in this moment.

'Fucking bitch.' His grip burns. Eye to eye, muscles straining, lips parted. And pain – sudden and sharp as her shoe impacts his shin. He twists her arm and her face convulses and she shouts and the veins pulse in her neck and her eyes sparkle, and she is laughing as she lunges at him, as she sinks her sharp teeth into the tender lobe of his ear.

16

'My God, Ellie, I thought you'd killed someone.' Jess ushers her through to the back room of the workshop.

'I think I nearly did.'

A few moments ago Ellie had stumbled across the yard looking first like an accident victim, then a murderer. Now she perches on a stool, proffering her hand like a little girl who's fallen off her bike. 'Don't play the innocent with me,' says Jess. 'You look like fallout from a horror movie.' She takes Ellie's hand and turns it over. 'Paint?' she says with a sniff and a frown as the sickly fumes fill the tiny room. 'What the hell's going on, here?'

'Nothing. I had a disagreement with Simon, that's all.'

'A disagreement? You know, Ellie, there are times when I wonder what planet you're on.' Soaking a rag in white spirit, she cleans her fingers with rough thoroughness. 'There. That better?'

'You've got a real maternal streak, d'you know that?'

'Maybe, but I keep it pretty much under wraps, so don't you go telling anyone.'

'I promise.'

'Good. Now, about this disagreement, are you going to tell me what it was all about?'

'Paint,' says Ellie with a shrug. 'It's only paint.' She laughs and pulls her hand away. 'We argued about paint . . .'

'Okay, be cryptic if you want, but you've ruined that suit, so I hope it was worth it.' Eleanor looks away. Jess is uneasy. This isn't like Ellie – at least, not Ellie when she's well and in control, the way she'd been at Adam's opening. She takes a breath. 'Tell you what,' she tosses the rag aside and stands up. 'How about I make us some tea?'

She fills the kettle. Ellie sits hunched on the stool. She has retrieved the rag and is dabbing ineffectually at the crimson paint staining her skirt. Jess touches her shoulder as she pulls up another stool. She half expects Ellie to recoil but she doesn't; she looks up and smiles and says softly, 'I scared you, didn't I?' Jess nods and Eleanor reaches a hesitant finger to stroke her cold cheek. 'I'm sorry. You mustn't worry about me, Jess. This was just a glitch, he hit a nerve. I'm okay, really I am. And despite appearances,' she grins, 'I didn't kill anyone.'

'So we shan't be interrupted by screaming sirens and flashing blue lights?'

'Sorry to disappoint. But you know, it may only be red paint, but there was a moment, a point when I nearly did, or could have . . . I was so angry. No, it was more than anger. There was this rage. Like something inside me trying to get out. Something physical. I was scared, Jess. He's done this painting . . . you should have seen it. It was like he'd got inside me. Like he'd found me out. Could it happen, do you think? Painting me like this, could he come to know me better than I know myself?'

'I suppose it depends how well you know yourself.'

'Don't be flippant, Jess.'

'I'm sorry.'

'Shall I tell you what he's found? He has discovered that I don't exist. That I'm nothing, no one. Only what people make me. Bone and blood.'

'Ellie . . .'

'His father is a butcher, did you know that?'

'Are you sure you're not hurt? Maybe you should see a doctor.'

'I don't need a doctor.'

The kettle comes to the boil and Jess makes the tea. Fennel tea. They sit in silence. Eleanor doesn't know what to say; she can't explain. She cradles her mug. She's sore all over. Her muscles ache and she is conscious as never before of her body, its mechanism and design. She feels inside her the very structure Simon has painted.

But Simon has painted more than that. He has seen the child she'd been, gawky and flailing and freakish. He has seen the adult Eleanor, busily constructing an intricate web to obscure the past and support the future. And he has revealed that past, shown the child fighting through to the foreground, to the daylight. She is about to be unmasked.

Jess is speaking. Eleanor surfaces slowly. 'Ellie? Ellie, why did you come here?'

She is startled. 'What do you mean? Where else would I go?'

'Adam?'

'Adam would never understand.' She closes her eyes. The fennel-scented steam rises up to calm her and she breathes it in. It condenses on her cheeks, penetrates her pores – but it cannot reach the part of her that had thrilled to the fight, to the flush of blood, the clench of muscle. Energy. Definition. Line.

Today's events have set her apart from Adam and from Jess. She cannot expect anyone else to understand.

Only Simon.

And yet it's true what Jess says: she could have – should have – gone to Adam. Adam is gentle, he would have soothed her with a touch, no need for fennel tea, though he would probably have wanted to cook for her. She has never met a man like him. She loves his kindness and innocence; his unlikely strength gives her something solid to push against.

So what perverse instinct had stopped her going to Adam?

She sips her tea, and thinks of Simon. Suddenly she glimpses the root of her fascination. Adam may give her something to push against, but Simon Whitburn goes one better. Simon pushes back.

A Different Kind of Loving

The coast is on fire. The canary-yellow gorse blazes along the edge of the cliff. The high clouds roll, tumbling sunlight across water. The sea is azurite streaked with turquoise. The clouds gather and it becomes dark, then just as suddenly the labrador sun shakes itself free and the water glitters bright and fast with a million silver sequins.

Adam holds his breath. The rapid changes in light and colour – and texture too as the breeze stipples the water and scatters the sequins – fill him with wonder.

These months of self-imposed isolation have been hard. He receives fat letters from home and responds with a scribbled note on the back of a postcard. 'The answer is there, in Polruan,' he'd told his wife. 'I have to go. I need to know why she did what she did.'

The answer lies in the landscape; it is lodged in the rocks, dispersed throughout the sea and sky, in the blazoning light and the air like sherbet.

They say what she did was an act of will, that she'd moved from point to point along a fixed route, her destination always in view. He alone cannot believe it. Like Canute he struggles to hold back the tide that condemns her.

Pam is curious. He has described a marriage on the edge and the desire for a new beginning. 'Polruan and Eden are a part of that.' His explanation comes close to the truth, and misses it by a mile.

'You're being deliberately obscure,' says Pam. 'Like a brooding lead in a romantic novel.'

She's right. It's amazing the way the human mind builds walls round unthinkable subjects. Amazing, but dangerous. Such walls solve nothing, they merely obscure. It is not an original discovery, but more valid having arisen from personal experience. Behind his barrier of brick and stone, the wounds continue to fester.

But his mind shies away from the pain. It says, 'Look at the sea, isn't it beautiful? Your new home is taking shape, isn't that exciting? Don't think about those other things, forget.'

Such forgetfulness almost destroyed him. He feels it now, the panic of those last months spent in Bury St Edmunds, the sense of dislocation, the way the world he knew – his whole identity – began to unravel.

He has come to Polruan for a reason, and Pam's questions remind him of that.

Which isn't to say it isn't true – all that about the beauty of the landscape and the sea, and the mounting excitement as, day by day, he imposes his personality on Eden.

He was right to come here. This was her favourite place of all. He will never leave. He lifts his head to the screech of a gull. He will never tire of the sea. It is like Eleanor. Beautiful. Deceptive. Compelling.

Despite distractions of mind and climate, he is succeeding in his task. His Eden, his broken shipwreck of a house, is beginning to heal. The roof is sound and the repointed chimneys salute the sky. The scaffolding is down, the flaking stucco cleaned and patched, the windows replaced and the kitchen fitted. Two nights ago he invited Pam for a celebration supper. 'I thought we'd christen my new stove.'

He has prepared a dish of monkfish served with mangetout, new potatoes and salad. He replenishes her glass. Pam eats slowly. He watches, eager for a reaction. She teases him with her silence. Eventually she grins and says, 'Top marks to the French stove. This is close to being the best meal I've had in a long time.'

'Close?' He is piqued and amused. 'And as for the stove, I did have a little input myself . . .'

They finish with cheese and fruit and coffee. Pam lights a cigarette and offers one to Adam. 'Now then,' she flicks her lighter. 'What's next on your list of home improvements?'

He pulls a face. 'Weatherproofing the outside. I've bought some paint, the stuff they use for lighthouses —'

'I thought you were scared of heights.'

He takes a long drag on his cigarette. Face the fear, isn't that what they say? It's what she would have said. He can hear her. The phrase encapsulates her paradox, the clash of strength and fragility.

Fear was the one thing they'd had in common. Hers of the dark, his of heights. In the end she had faced her fear alone.

No. Not quite alone.

He wedges the ladder against the front of the house and lodges stones round the base. One step at a time. Slowly he climbs. Don't look down. Or up. Or sideways. He hangs the paint can from an upper rung and, staring straight ahead, starts to work.

It's hard to ignore the view. The changing sky and the sea taunt him. The body of a man shattered on the rocks. Bones like cockleshells and hair like weed, rising and sinking with the tide.

Fear starves his brain of oxygen. Bye-bye reality.

Get a grip.

He dunks his brush in the paint pot and transforms another dull patch of stucco to brilliant white. He works methodically. He needs a rhythm to counter his dizziness, to silence the roaring in his head. But now the roaring is outside. A steady thrum. The air vibrates. Stiff-necked, he glances sideways. A tanker edges along the river to the sea. The throb of its engines suffuses the landscape. His left hand grips the ladder. His fingers ache, the bones in his wrist jut. His flesh is white. The blood no longer flows. His other hand works frenetically, scraping the paintbrush back and forth. He mustn't be distracted. The faster he goes, the sooner he'll finish and be back on firm ground.

For all this speed he makes little progress. He could bring in a professional, but he hates to be beaten. Anyway, this is why he's here. To scour the pain with fear.

To remember in order to forget.

'Don't look round,' Pam calls with a laugh. 'I don't want you falling, but I saw you up there and I just have to draw you.'

'Again?'

'You're an interesting subject, all bones and angles . . .'

The afternoon slides into evening. He is unspeakably tired. His arms ache and the effort of bracing himself against the treacherous ladder hour after hour has bruised his shins and given him cramp. He joins Pam, perching on his wall. She offers a cigarette and shows him her sketch.

She has depicted his fear. The ladder keels at a crazy angle. He clings to its rungs, a jumble of gangling limbs and flailing paint-brushes. He laughs out loud. Pam says, 'You see? Nothing in the world is fixed. Everything's a matter of perspective.'

Perspective. Another reason why he's here, to get a new slant on the past, to see the players differently – himself and Eleanor, Simon and Jessica and Georgie.

Pam tears off the sheet and hands it to him. 'A present,' she says. 'Send it to your wife. Will she understand, d'you think?'

'Yes.'

'And your daughter?'

He stares at the gawky figure in Pam's drawing, and remembers. He sees a blue-eyed, dark-haired child – and another, fairer. The faces are indistinct, the features of the one blurring into the other. He has no photographs, no drawings, only disintegrating memories.

Lerryn, Golant, Lostwithiel. The river twists inland. The sun sets in a crimson blaze. It's as if the whole world is on fire.

Past and present should come together here, merging one with the other as the river blends with the sea, as day dissolves into night.

But his past refuses to join with the present. It is being consumed. The children are wraiths. His other life is hardly real.

He stares towards the setting sun. 'What am I doing here?' His beloved landscape offers no answer. 'Am I really healing myself, or am I running away?'

He knows the answer. Living in the past is painful, but the past is known, a river contained by its banks. Here in Polruan the river opens its arms to the sea and the present spills into the broad, undefined future.

He closes his eyes. The falling sun scorches his lids. He puts his cigarette to his lips and inhales deeply.

A breath of cool air touches his cheek, and in the long silence of the dying day, he hears her say his name.

1

Simon's encounter with Eleanor has left his ego battered and his shin bruised. The lobe of his ear continues to bleed. He dabs it with a paint rag. A chemical on the rag makes it sting even more.

He tries to work but she gets in the way. He sees her face swollen with rage, her bloody hand raised – it is a stunning image. He wants to paint it. He wants to forget.

He can still feel her, the furious crush of her body, her long limbs locked with his, the clench of their muscles, the roar of blood. Face to face. Eye to eye. She will not let him go.

He pours a drink. Vodka. Another. The day passes. He sleeps without dreaming and wakes to find nothing has changed. His anger is raw, like scalded flesh. He goes to the gallery. Eleanor is not there. Farraday is in his office, an end-of-the-pier exhibit behind the wall of plate glass. He glances up. Simon storms through the door. 'She's a bloody liability, that woman.' Farraday replaces the cap on his fountain pen and leans back in his chair. 'D'you know what she's done, has she told you?'

'This would be Eleanor, would it?'

Brian's trying to stall, but there is a momentum to Simon's anger. 'She cons her way into my studio, all sweetness and light, then fucks up three weeks' work in as many seconds.'

'Now Simon—'

'You've got to do something. Come on, Brian. What's up? Nothing to say about your precious protégée? Eleanor this, Eleanor that,' he mimics. 'The sun shines out of Eleanor's arsehole.'

Brian suppresses a smile. 'I merely asked her to find out how the commission was coming along.'

'She's a vandal, a graffiti artist. A lunatic.' The words gag in his throat. He'd always known the painting would make her uncomfortable, but it had gone further than that. It had frightened her. 'You've no right,' she'd said.

It's true, of course, he has no rights where she's concerned. He's a parasite. The strength and anger drain out of him and he slumps in a chair.

'What exactly did she do?'

'She hasn't told you?'

'Not in detail.'

'She wrecked it.' He rubs his hands over his face, as if to scrub out the memory. 'It was her,' he admits.

'A portrait?'

'Not exactly. I was just having another go at getting her on canvas. I suppose it's possible she saw something I didn't realize was there . . . Where is she, Brian?' He sits up straight. 'Call her, get her in here, I need to talk to her.'

'Not possible, I'm afraid. She rang in sick; she's taking some time off.'

'Is she at home?' Brian shrugs. 'Shit, Brian, don't pretend you don't know.'

'She's gone away for a few days. She needs to recoup. Eleanor can be a little fragile, Simon, she needs careful handling. As do you. I had hoped you could be friends. You really do have more in common than you realize.'

2

Eleanor was seven when her father left home. Their last holiday as a family was spent in Cornwall, in a cottage on the north coast, near St Agnes.

Babs was happy and full of plans. If she'd had any premonition, she didn't let it show. All her energies were focused on Eleanor. She wanted Dad to teach her to swim, but Eleanor didn't want to and Dad didn't insist. He didn't care what they did.

Halfway through their stay Babs suggested a trip to Fowey. They parked on the outskirts of the town and Eleanor skipped to the entrance of the car park and clambered on to a low wall to get a better view. The grey houses tumbled down the steep hill. The water glittered like sun on broken glass. There were boats on the river, little yachts with spiky masts. 'Hurry up,' she shouted. 'I want to go down, I want to go down.'

She ran on ahead, swinging dangerously on the railing that flanked the path. She passed a big Victorian school with gables and tall windows. The angle of the path allowed her to see over the wall and into the playground. It would be lovely to go to school within sight of the sea.

They reached the quay and found a kiosk selling Cornish pasties. 'I'm hungry,' she said, tugging on Babs's hand.

'Let's have a picnic, shall we?' Babs laughed. Dad grumbled. Babs said, 'Oh, don't be so childish.'

They bought cherryade which they drank straight from the bottle. The pasties were lukewarm. Eleanor nibbled the meat and potato and onion, and fed the pastry to the gulls. The swooping, bullet-headed birds scared her as they struggled against the wind, checking their flight to anticipate and catch the scraps of pastry. Babs sat on the wall with her knees drawn up and her eyes scrunched against the dazzling water. She wriggled her toes on the hot stone and shouted encouragement. 'Look, Eleanor, that one there – he keeps missing. Try again. Don't leave him out. He's coming round again. Oh, well done.'

When the food was gone, Babs pulled out the guidebook. 'Listen to this.' She had to shout above the squalling of the indignant birds and adjust her hold on the book as it flapped in the wind. 'Back in the olden days they used to put a chain across the river to stop enemy boats coming in. How about that . . .'

Eleanor imagined the black water and the floundering ships, their masts snapped like twigs and, borne on the wind, the shouts of the sailors, the screams of drowning men.

'It'd take more than a chain to stop a U-boat,' said Dad.

Even after all these years, Eleanor delights to think the little town's security was assured by such simple means.

And now she's back, and she is the one seeking security.

She rents a three-storey cottage halfway up the hill. The living room has a bay window with a view of the town and the river and the tumbling village of Polruan on the farther bank. From the dormer window she can see where the river widens to embrace the sea. A strong breeze snags the water, teasing white tufts from the waves. An indifferent tanker crosses her line of sight.

She leans on the windowsill and breathes in the cold, tangy air. The instinct for flight is powerful. So much has happened, too much has changed in too short a time. Her work at the gallery reached a climax with the Jangles mural. Not only was the publicity good for Brian and Simon, but last week a West End gallery had made a convincing attempt to poach her.

The project has knitted together two disparate parts of herself. The private woman who bewilders Adam, the Eleanor who can never quite shake off the failures and misjudgements of her past; and Brian's assistant, self-assured and self-aware, an art form herself as she struts his gallery selling paintings and devising schemes for marketing and publicity.

She was born for this. The Jangles mural is a triumph for her as well as for Simon. She is whole again.

Or so she'd thought, until Simon shot it all to hell. His new painting is a graphic reminder of where she comes from, and how far she still has to travel.

Adam. He deserves an explanation. She rang him at the restaurant. 'I'm going away,' she said. 'I need some time to think.'

'About what? About us?'

'Partly. You accuse me of hiding – well, I hide from myself as well. It's time I conquered that, so I'm going somewhere peaceful to try and get a new perspective on it all. Maybe then we can move forward. You want that, don't you? It's what you said . . . You do understand, don't you, Adam?'

No, he doesn't understand, she can tell. It hurts him that she should want to do this alone. 'I could come with you,' he said. 'Can't we work this out together?'

She is bad for Adam. Life is simple for him; he moves in straight lines, from here to there, and cannot understand her inability to function this way. There are no straight lines for her, only big dipper loops and spaghetti junction tangles. She can't see where she's going, she can barely follow the thread. It makes her unpredictable, and Adam can't handle that.

It would be a kindness to break with him, to withdraw, leave him to Jess. It would be a sensible and selfless thing to do. Adam needs someone without secrets, someone straightforward, but not dull. That's where Kay had got it wrong, but Jess is just the ticket. She is secure in herself, she has no need to hide.

And anyway, fair's fair, Jess had seen him first.

Eleanor pulls back from the sill and closes the window. She likes this house. It stands like a tower on the hillside. A fortress. She goes downstairs and bolts the doors front and back, then wanders from room to room, marking the bounds of her new territory. The living room runs the depth of the house; the kitchen is a tacked on lean-to affair. The bathroom is on the first floor. The stairs to the second floor are perilously steep.

There is a wood-burning stove and a pile of logs. A primal instinct prompts her to light a fire. A forest glade. Light dispels dark and the flame strikes fear to the heart of the wolf.

The flames flicker. The house is silent. The heat intensifies and she begins to relax. Rocking slowly back and forth, she abandons herself to the rhythms of her body. Possibly hours pass, possibly not. She loses all sense of place and time and self.

She needs this distance to see the pattern. The flickering light and the insistent, cradling motion induce a trance-like state, and she manages to do what Adam once asked of her: she steps outside herself, and sees herself as others see her.

Since Chris she has been too concerned with her own needs and reactions. Her friends have been kind, but sooner or later they are bound to kick back. She snatched Adam from under Jess's nose, and Jess let him go because Eleanor's need was the greater, and because she genuinely believes friends should take priority over lovers. Whichever way you look at it, she has abused Jess's beliefs, has used them to justify her actions.

Then there's her mother. She has neglected Babs but Babs doesn't complain because, like Jess, she knows what a tough time Ellie has had and is prepared to make allowances.

This cannot continue. She must make an effort, to the benefit of others as well as herself. If she'd been less self-absorbed, Simon's painting would not have posed a threat. She thinks too much and she feels too much. She must direct her energies outwards.

Perhaps Simon's paintings could help her in this. It's an exciting thought – if she could transform him from a threat into an advantage, then maybe, just maybe . . .

The adrenalin dances in her veins, but the sense of purpose is tentative. The ground still shakes beneath her feet.

She wakes with a jolt to find the fire has burnt low. She gingers the ash with fresh logs. It is almost midnight and she's hungry; she hasn't eaten since lunch – a dry scone in a motorway service station. She prepares a bowl of porridge and carries it back to the living room and the fire.

Sometimes she sees her life as a board game. No sooner does she get all the pieces in place for a victory, than someone kicks the board and everything is scattered and she has to start again.

And again, and again, and again . . .

Everything she'd thought known and fixed about herself has been turned upside down and inside out. She'd loved Chris. Losing him, she'd thought she'd never feel that way again. Then she met Adam. Adam was different. What they had was both like and unlike what she'd had with Chris, and she counted herself lucky to be given a second chance.

Simon. Simon pings into her mind like Zebedee. If things were on their head before, they are well and truly scrambled now.

It had taken her unawares, the violence of their exchange, and her delight in that violence. They had wrestled for a moment, like children squabbling in the playground. She'd wanted to laugh. She had laughed. She tasted his blood.

What sort of a person am I? I didn't know I could be like this.

But Adam knew. He'd been at Jess's workshop, had seen the needle and her blood, and then there was the church . . .

'It all fits,' he would say. She can hear him so clearly. 'This is what you are.'

And she would have to agree. 'Yes, this is what I am, it's what I've always been. But until now, I never realized.'

3

Every day she goes for a walk. Sometimes she goes into the town, sometimes to the headland, or across the river to Polruan. On her first morning she went out for supplies and, catching her reflection in a shop window, saw at once how out of place she was in her city coat and city shoes. That afternoon she drove to St Austell and bought some boots and a pair of jeans and a big puffy coat.

This is much better, much warmer. She's struggling along Fore Street with her head bent against the wind. Her hair is loose and the wind whips the long strands across her face. She laughs out loud. Her hair is the wing of a great black bird, a devil-albatross. Reaching the quay, she leans over the wall and allows the gale to buffet her. What if I were to let go? she thinks. If I were to spread my wings . . .

I would fly. I would, I know it. Into the wind and away.

She finds a café, warm and friendly with net curtains and crocheted white place mats, and orders tea and scrambled egg. When Adam cooks scrambled egg he adds all sorts of exotic and inappropriate ingredients – smoked salmon and chives, prawns flamed in brandy and moistened with cream. He once asked her what she thought. 'It's okay,' she said. 'But it's not scrambled egg.'

Here the dish is served plain – not even a sprig of parsley.

The following day she goes to Readymoney Cove. Dad called it Moneypenny Cove, and Catchpenny Cove – she never could remember its real name. Dad was like that, plenty of puns and silly, nervous jokes. As an adult she sees it as a reaction to Babs. Babs was too much for him, she'd swamped him. She experiences a stab of sympathy for her mother. Dad hadn't understood, had never tried. 'For God's sake, Barbara,' he'd say. 'You're always chasing skitter-bugs.'

Dad wasn't comfortable with Babs, and he wasn't comfortable with

Eleanor. She was constrained with her father, but another child entirely with Babs. It's like that now, with Adam and Simon.

Adam and Simon perceive her in such different ways and, like a mirror, she casts their images back at them. She is the moon to their sun; she has no light of her own.

So, if the moon takes its light from the sun, would the moon's colour alter if the sun changed? And would that diminish its importance?

Ridiculous. She does too much of this, spinning in circles, then rocketing off at a tangent. The moon can't change and neither can she. Her head aches. This has been going on for days.

She tries so hard, but she can't stop the tide of self-questioning. Every answer spawns another question, every question fragments into a dozen more.

It begins to rain. She hurries along the Esplanade. The tarmac glistens; the sky is smudged and grubby like a discarded palette. Today the town is both dingy and dramatic. She identifies with this wild schizophrenia. Maybe she'll stay a while longer. Maybe forever. At least then she won't be hurting anyone but herself.

No, she won't stay, she can't. The city will pull her back. She can already feel its hooks tugging at her flesh.

But if Simon were here, he could conjure a memento. He would transform the day. Taking the clouds, he would endow them with energy and life. He would make the gloomy river welcoming. Cracking a whiplash of errant sunlight through the cloud, he would light up a silver-gold pathway and send it snaking and cracking, hypnotically dancing across the waves. He would capture it all, and he would give it to her.

She only has to ask.

She turns off the Esplanade and stops at the bakery for a Danish pastry. The rain eases as she starts up the hill but the wind continues to lash and billow her hair. She digs her hands in her pockets and hunches her shoulders against the cold. At last she scrambles up the steps to her cottage. It's good to be home and in the warm.

Waiting for the kettle to boil, she brushes the stubborn tangles from her damp hair. She feels at home. At home and very safe. She pauses to listen to the battling wind as it rattles the windows in their frames.

She takes her coffee and bun through to the living room. She doesn't bother with a plate but tears open the bag and uses it to catch the crumbs. Leaning her elbows on the table, she idly pulls at the pastry, then shakes her head in irritation as tendrils of hair trail in the sticky glaze. As she removes the last traces of sugar, there is a knock at the door.

Agnes at the bakery and Jan from the newsagent's are the only people she knows in Fowey. Neither are likely to call, so it must be a hawker or a Jehovah's Witness. She continues to rub at the sugar in her hair. It's a dull day but she hasn't switched on the lights. If she doesn't answer, it'll look as though she's out.

She remains perfectly still and holds her breath. Not a sound. The caller knocks again, this time an impatient staccato rap. 'Damn.' She drains her coffee and sucks the last of the sugar from her fingertips, then opens the door.

A chill rush of air greets her. A powder of rain makes her blink. It takes a moment to register what she sees. The dishevelled figure on her doorstep scowls and pushes his fingers through his wet hair. 'Hello.' His grin is too bright, too focused. 'I thought I'd never find you – talk about the back of beyond.' She continues to stare. 'Come on, Nell, look lively – you going to let me in, or what?'

4

She doesn't move. The sugary tip of her middle finger lingers at her lips. Her mouth is dry. The pastry has left a chemical residue on her tongue.

Poor Simon, he looks so cold and fed up. His leather jacket is new and stylish, but city-thin and streaked with rain. She thinks of her new boots, her jeans and sweater and her lovely warm coat.

What is he doing here? Revenge, an eye for an eye? She has ruined his painting, so she owes him the cost of a canvas at the very least.

He is watching her. Observation is his trade and suddenly she is painfully conscious of her loose hair and lack of make-up. She is a bare canvas, he the artist. He will paint her. Last time he tried, she had recognized herself – what if next time she doesn't? Or worse, what if he fixes a fictional Eleanor to the canvas so firmly that she has no choice but to conform? His canvas is her prison. She struggles to force a way to the front of the picture plane . . .

The man must be clairvoyant on top of everything else – she has just described the very painting she destroyed.

He has already seen too much.

Yet there is a chance she could turn this to her advantage. If she offered him a constant and coherent image, and if he painted that image – then her own vision of herself would be fixed for all time.

And if she wanted to change, he could paint the change she devised. A new costume, another role. *I can be whoever I want to be.*

It's risky. She would have to exercise great vigilance.

No. This is witchcraft. She clenches her fists. Nails bite, knuckles strain. Pain defines. I am here, this is me – this vacillating, unfocused mess – and Simon Whitburn, for all his magic, cannot change that.

It seems minutes have passed. She hasn't moved, neither has he. Time has frozen.

No. Time endures, it is they who have stopped. Down the hill, Agnes continues to sell her sugary buns, and the wind still blows and the little boats in the harbour rock and racket against their moorings. She hears the distant, metallic ting of rigging on mast. Only she and Simon have ceased.

Ludicrous. And another ridiculous thought, rising like cream – with her hair this way and her face unpainted, he might not recognize her. Any minute now he'll find his voice and ask if she knows an Eleanor Bycroft, and she'll say no, no one of that name lives here.

'Look lively . . .' He has already recognized her.

He says, 'What's up, Nell? Cat got your tongue? It's freezing out here.'

'I know.'

'So come on then, let me in.'

She steps back. He enters with much exaggerated shivering and beating of his arms. 'Don't overdo it, Simon.' He hangs his jacket on the back of the door. She says, 'I suppose you'd like some coffee, or tea or something . . .'

'You don't sound very pleased to see me.'

She stares at him. Why has he come, what does he want? After their

158

last encounter, why on earth would he think she'd be pleased to see him?

'I'll put the kettle on.'

He follows her to the kitchen. The room is small and he stands close behind her. The wind knocks the fat pods of the unpruned roses against the windows. The lead to the kettle is faulty. She hears the crackle of escaping electricity. There is a pile of cutlery on the draining board. Her fingers brush the handle of a broad-bladed knife.

Simon says, 'You look different.'

'No,' she lies. 'Just the same. What do you want, Simon?'

'Hey, Nell, steady. Take it easy.' He touches her shoulder. The adrenalin rush is like the sting of neat alcohol. She rummages a teaspoon from the cutlery on the draining board and reaches a mug from the cupboard. The kettle sighs. 'I know it must seem strange, me coming here like this. I don't know why I've come – or what I want, come to that – but I do know I upset you and I didn't like it, you running off like that. At first I thought, shit, the bloody woman'll pay for this. But now I don't know . . .' She spoons instant coffee into a mug and pours on boiling water. A beige scum, flecked with brown, rises to the surface. 'I just don't know, Nell.'

'How did you find me?' She adds milk to the coffee.

'I asked around. Brian was cagey, so was Jess. So I went to see Mason. A right state he was in, poor bastard. Says he hasn't heard a word, not so much as a postcard. Still, if he'd wanted he could have found you. I did.'

'How?'

'Brian's got a temp in,' he shrugs. 'He forgot to warn her it was a secret. I just told her you handle my stuff personally and I needed to talk to you pronto.'

'As easy as that? Brian'll probably sack her, you do realize?'

'Only if you tell him.'

'About Adam . . .'

'Fuck Adam. Adam's not here, Nell.'

'I need to know . . . Don't look like that. I don't want to pick a fight.'

'No?' He's laughing now, and he's very close. His eyes sparkle and his body exudes the smell of the studio. He has worked with paint all his life. The chemicals are a part of him; she imagines the molecules twisting and tangling with his DNA. He says, 'Sure about that, are you, Nell?'

Simon thrusts his face close to her. He must be crazy, coming here. Half a dozen times during the course of the drive he'd thought of turning back. His feelings alternated between rage and remorse. Try as he might, he can't get a handle on this.

The woman's a headcase, that's not in doubt. She's like those tribesmen you read about, the ones that think you steal their soul if you take a photo.

He should have turned back, but he didn't and now he's here and he's found her and he doesn't know what to do or say. The bloody woman has immobilized him. He wants to tell her what a liability she is, that Brian must be out of his skull to let her anywhere near his artists. And he wants to tell her how sorry he is, to stroke her cheek and twine his fingers in her hair and say, 'I know I went too far, I overstepped the mark, I'm sorry . . .'

He'd lost control. He'd responded to her attack by attacking back, and Eleanor had returned his fire with fire. The bruise to his shin has not yet faded, his earlobe remains tender.

So which of them is owed an apology?

She is sitting in an armchair by the window with her knees drawn up under her chin. She looks different, disconcertingly vulnerable with her hair all loose like that. But her hands are the same, and the gut-lacerating nails. His spine tingles, his skin prickles and the hair on his arms lifts.

It's touch and go whether or not she'll let him stay. He can almost taste her fear and mistrust. He must tread carefully, consider each word and gesture. He suggests dinner, sensing she'd feel safer in a more formal environment, and just for once he seems to have got it right. Relief softens the hard contours of her face and the room's atmosphere becomes lighter, more breathable.

Most of Fowey's restaurants turn out to be closed for the winter. When eventually they find one, they are the only customers. They order fish. With the skill of a surgeon she lifts the flesh from the bone. He remembers the mural and the catfish, and Brian Farraday flaking a portion of skate from a handspan of translucent bones.

He watches her. The absence of make-up blurs her outline, makes her seem less in control. With every movement her hair shimmers and snakes. He has a sudden flash, a snapshot of Eleanor on a cliff-top, sculpted by the wind, engulfed and supported by a voluminous red velvet gown with ermine sleeves. Her ballooning hair is crowned by a golden filet and her ugly, beautiful fingers clutch a lily to her breast.

Shit, what a cliché. Time and again she slips through his fingers, leaving nothing but echoes, the imaginings of others.

The weather deteriorates. The windows are streaked with condensation inside and rain outside. They finish their coffee. He helps her into her coat and rests his hand on her shoulder. It is a proprietorial gesture.

Stepping out of the door, they are assaulted by vicious rods of rain. Arm in arm they bow their heads and struggle along Fore Street. He hears a breathy, gasping sound. He glances sideways. 'Don't you just love the wind?' she says with a laugh as it lifts her hair, hurling it against his cheek like a sea-soaked hawser. 'Isn't this wonderful?'

The steps to her cottage are steep and lit by a single lamp. The treads are wet and they slither and slip and clutch at one another. Gripping the icy railing, they haul themselves up.

They are both drenched. They stand in the living room and laugh as puddles form round their feet. Eleanor bobs down and riddles the stove and adds another log. Simon crouches behind her. She can hear him breathing. What if he touches her? He doesn't touch her. He moves away.

'Try and get warm,' she says. 'And take off those wet clothes. I'll fetch a towel.'

She scampers up the stairs. Her feet clatter and reverberate off the narrow walls. She's too keen to escape. Does it show?

She strips with a twist and a rush. Her skin is damp and clammy. She curls her toes against the boards. It was mistake, letting him come here. What's he doing down there? And what is she playing at, hiding up here? If she dawdles too long he'll come looking for her. Her bathrobe hangs from a metal hook on the door. She pulls it on and knots the belt, then fetches the towels from the bathroom cupboard.

Simon has stripped to his underpants. He sits hunched on the floor in front of the fire with his hands splayed to the heat. The flames make his skin glow; they sketch his fingers in scarlet.

'Here.' She tosses him a towel. Perching on the edge of the sofa, she begins drying her hair. The towel is warm. She thinks of Babs lifting her from the bath and wrapping her in a big scratchy towel and rubbing her until her skin became a stinging, crimson shell.

She shakes her head. Her hair is still wet; it clings to her cheeks and neck. She continues to rub, all the while watching Simon. He looks innocent sitting there on the hookey mat with his blond hair all spiky, and his body curled round and focused on the fire. When she was a little girl she went into the woods and found a baby bird. She picked it up. The nest was too high to reach. She cupped the tiny body in her palm and it trembled so, the poor little thing, all pink and raw and covered in pimples.

Brian likes to tell her that she and Simon have a lot in common. Until tonight she hasn't been able to see it. But tonight he is not as substantial as usual. The lamplight gives his flesh the radiance of a candle shining through honey. When he moves, the shifting shadows alter his outline. As one part of him blends with the darkness, another emerges. There is something soft, almost unformed about him as if, even at this late stage, a change of heart on his maker's part might transform him utterly.

He tosses the towel aside and half turning, grins at her. Her own eyes are a tawdry blue, the colour of cheap paint. Simon's eyes have the strength and iridescence of antique enamel. On her sixteenth birthday Babs had given her a dragonfly brooch the body of which was just such a lustrous blue.

He shifts his position. He is very close. The atmosphere is charged. A storm is brewing. What does it mean, this spark, this flare . . . of what? Antipathy or affinity. Does it matter which? Her feelings for Adam are easily identified, but this defies reason; it is a different kind of loving.

She should get away, go upstairs – plait her hair and paint her face, resurrect the other Eleanor, the one who's so damn good at seeming in control, who coerced the reluctant Simon into painting Adam's mural, who destroyed the painting that came too close to truth. She quakes inside, but outside she is strong.

Simon stands up and reaches for his shirt. It is still damp and it clings to his skin. 'Where are you going?'

'I've booked a room at the Ship.' He fumbles with his buttons. 'I told you.' It seems so long ago. Her hands continue to tug at the tangles in her hair. He makes a gesture towards her, then checks it. He says, 'I'll see you tomorrow.' She nods. 'Okay. Sleep well, Nell.'

5

The baby bird died. Eleanor made it a bed of cotton wool and dropped milk-soaked bread into its gaping, yellow-rimmed mouth. But still it died.

She took it to the Abbey Gardens in Bury and launched it on the river in a pink plastic soapdish laden with daisies.

The river flows. The debris gathered from the bank sinks and floats and tangles with the rubbish on the mud-silted floor – the bicycle frames and trolleys, the bodies of cats and the bones of dead men.

Chris. He bobs up from nowhere. It needn't have ended like that. Chris was a coward, but it was her fear that destroyed him. If only she'd opened the door that night. He'd pounded and pounded and all in vain – and the water swept over the bank again.

The baby bird died. She wakes to brilliant sunshine. Fists pound on her front door. A hoarse voice shouts her name.

Quick, oh do be quick – don't let it happen again. She stumbles across the room and trips over her shoes. They are still wet from last night. She throws open the window to a translucent, rain-washed morning. The last wisps of cloud drag their feet across the hills. At the sound of the sash, Simon steps back. 'You okay? I couldn't make you hear. I nearly broke the door down. Hurry up, Nell, let me in.'

She ducks inside to look for her keys. It would be wiser to pack him off back to London.

The keys are like silver fishes on the flat of her palm. Her fingers curl round them. Simon waits. 'Put the kettle on,' she says as she tosses them down. 'I'll be with you in a minute.'

She dresses slowly, pulling on her new jeans and a thick burgundy sweater. There is a cracked mirror screwed to the wall next to the door. Her hair swings loose. She gathers it in her hand and pulls it back from her face. It doesn't work, that other Eleanor doesn't belong here. She shakes her hair free, and goes downstairs.

Simon is slumped on the sofa with his legs outstretched and his ankles crossed. It's how Adam had sat in her London living room, looking like he owned it all, the sofa, the house, and her.

Simon's mug is balanced on the arm of the sofa. He flicks through the paperback she'd bought in St Austell. She'd started reading it yesterday at breakfast – before her walk, before her visit to the baker's shop.

Simon looks up. He points to her coffee on the corner of the mantelpiece.

That time in his studio, in the midst of their tussle, she had seen in his face that the thrill of it, the pain and desire, were shared. Veins stood proud in his brow and neck. His twisting grip burnt her arm. There was dread in his eyes, and longing, and an uncertain flickering round his lips as he hardened.

Everything she felt, he felt also. He feels it now.

She takes a gulp of scalding coffee. It makes her wince. She goes into the kitchen. She doesn't know why. She comes out again. She opens the front door and breasts the cold sunshine and inhales the tart sea air. The rooftops tumble down to the river. A rusty tanker noses its way upstream.

She goes back inside. Simon is reading. She says, 'I still don't know why you're here.'

He closes the book and lays it aside. 'Not sure I know myself.'

'It's a long way to come on a whim.'

'It was more than a whim. Jesus, Nell, I don't know which of us is more to blame.'

'The painting . . .'

'I should have consulted you?'

'Yes.'

'But it's not a portrait or anything. It just sort of happened.'

'You let it happen.'

'What the hell was I supposed to do? I told you, it's an organic process, things grow of their own accord – for Christ's sake, you weren't supposed to see the bloody thing.'

'Which makes it okay? It's fine for others to gawp so long as I don't know about it?'

'No.'

'Then what?'

'I don't know what you saw, Nell, but whatever it was I didn't put it there, and no one can see it but you.'

'I don't believe you – and even if I did, it doesn't matter. You took a risk on my behalf without my consent. You're arrogant, Simon. Who the hell do you think you are? You're not so great, you know? Not yet.'

'Without you, I suppose you mean?'

'And Brian. Let's not forget Brian.' She's angry and hurting and she wants to make him suffer too. Her voice is both a part of her, and not a part. 'Why did he show your work, can you tell me that? Because of its merits, its commercial potential – or because way back in the stone age he screwed your mother?'

'Shit, Nell —'

'Perhaps he's still at it – who knows? What d'you think?' He hits her. He grabs and strikes and she yields to the blow, then resists. It is just like before. Pain and desire. 'How does it feel?' she hisses. 'How does it feel to have the things that matter to you gutted this way? Rape, Simon. Remember?' Her voice is close to his ear. 'Violation.'

He sees again the woman with the grapefruit breast, and the man insisting he's a decorator at heart. He releases her. He slumps on to the sofa.

She stands over him. 'I'm sorry,' she says, 'I shouldn't have said that about your mother.' After a moment, she sits beside him and rests a tentative hand on his arm. 'I was just trying to make a point . . .'

'And I over-reacted . . .' The mark of his hand has reddened her cheek. 'Jesus, Nell, I'm sorry too – about the painting. And this.' He touches her jaw, her chin, her lips. 'But you don't know what you do to me.'

'What we do to each other. The things I said . . .'

'You didn't mean it, you were goading me and I deserved it, but through it all, and despite everything – you're bloody amazing, Eleanor.'

'That's a bit back-handed,' she smiles.

'You are, though, and I want to paint you and it's driving me wild. If you were ordinary I'd have got you first time. Some people are like that – I capture them in a couple of strokes, an outline, a gesture or expression, because there's nothing to them, only what's on the outside. But you're more than that. I try and try and I can't get it right. I manage bits, like your little finger and those pointy tips to your ears; I

165

catch a mood, just enough to keep me going, but never the whole picture. It's driving me crazy, Nell.'

'No . . .'

'It's true. You think I'm exaggerating, but I'm not.'

'You must stop this.'

'You wanted to know what I was doing, what that painting was about, well I'm telling you. I'd got hold of a little bit of you. Start from the inside, then clothe the body – sinew and bone, then flesh and skin, and one day the whole you. It's all I want. If I can get it right, if I can paint you, then there's nothing in this world I can't do. Do you see? For fuck's sake, Nell, tell me you understand.'

6

'You drive me crazy, Nell . . .' Chris used to say things like that, and then he'd tell her that he loved her, and she believed him, but she should have known it wasn't true because he also said she was beautiful, and that she knows for a fact to be a lie.

Once a week Chris came to London to stay at the hotel where she worked. They had dinner and went to see a play or a film, and then they spent the night together.

'It suits us,' she told Jess. 'Nothing heavy. No commitment.'

'Just the way you want it?'

'Yes.'

'And when you want more? Don't fool yourself, Ellie, it'll happen, it's bound to – but you'll never get anything but leftovers from him. He won't leave his wife. Men are such gutless bastards.'

'No.'

'You think your Chris is different? Okay, ask him. Tell him you've had enough, you'll leave him if he doesn't leave his wife. I'm telling you, it's just a game to him. An ego trip. He's a philandering hypocrite, just one more married man screwing around.'

But she hadn't listened to Jess. Months passed. Increasingly their few hours together were over too quickly. There was no contact during the rest of the week. They tried writing, but it didn't work. She would come down in the morning to find an envelope addressed in Chris's spider-spoor scrawl. A manilla envelope. It could be worse, it could have been typed. What distresses her now is her naivety. The anticipation, the way she'd ritualized the event. She would place the envelope prominently on the kitchen table, then feed Oscar and make coffee. Only when these things had been done would she return to the letter, scanning the pages for a personal word, some indication of real feeling. The disappointment was always acute. He wrote in a clipped, officious tone, careful to say nothing intimate. He was too self-aware; he had the mind of a lawyer. Perhaps he was afraid she might sue, or show his letters to his wife.

This had been the sum total of their affair. Weekly visits and a handful of sad, inadequate letters. She wanted more – and that brought terrors of its own. Commitment. The responsibility made her dizzy, but if the only way to be with him was for his marriage to end, so be it. She would not shirk the consequences of her actions. She would have taken it on, all of it: the hostility of his children, his trauma, his guilt – they could have worked it through. He had only to trust her.

But he didn't trust her, and he didn't love her. So much emotional energy, so much pain. In the end, it was all for nothing.

In the end. After the flood. Fists pounding on a locked door. 'You can't come in, go away. Go back to your wife. Leave me alone.'

Another scary thing – how easily we heal. A bloody gash, flesh ripped to the bone, and the injury is closed and bound, becomes a red weal, a white scar. A buried memory.

But buried memories, like buried feelings, are most dangerous of all.

She needs to see, a clearer vision.

What do people see when they look at her? Do they see her at all? Perhaps not. They have troubles of their own. But she looks, she looks and sees and is fascinated by the shadow-play surrounding her, by the way everybody she meets, strangers, family and friends, struggle to project an image greater than their physical selves.

Simon's painting had reminded her of this, and of its futility. We are a collection of body parts, nothing more.

Except for Babs, of course. She smiles at the thought of her mother.

In Babs, image and reality match; she is so full of life, constantly chasing new ideas and different enthusiasms. Dad had hated it. 'So what's this month's daft scheme?' he'd say. The word 'daft' had confused Eleanor. She'd taken it at face value, thought it another of his sharp-edged jokes, but a month after the holiday in Fowey, Dad had walked out. He didn't leave to be with someone else – that might have been more bearable – he left because he couldn't endure to be with them.

Now he lives in Surrey, a carport-and-microwave life with a Persian cat and a new wife.

The idea of such a life turns her blood to water. Might she and Adam end up like that?

Now Babs would never settle for anything as bland or constructed as a pedigree cat. Eleanor remembers coming home from school to find half a dozen orange-footed ducklings skidding across the kitchen lino.

She laughs out loud as the memories eddy and swirl. She sees the long, narrow garden and the hens, Rosalind and Gwyneth, ruffling their tan feathers in the dust. Espalier cherries dig their twiggy fingers into the crumbling brickwork. They strain and lust for the sun. All in vain. The fruit remains green, and the size of marrowfat peas. She remembers Babs's pokerwork sign. She hasn't thought of that in years: the smell of singed hair as her mother leans over the kitchen table, the tip of her tongue protruding in concentration. And later, Eleanor fidgeting from foot to foot, the nails cupped in her hands as Babs fixes the sign to the back gate. 'All done,' she steps back. Together they admire her handiwork. *Beware of the Tortoise*. They do not have a tortoise.

It hadn't been easy, sharing space with such an energetic, such a bloody interesting mother.

To see herself as others see her. Brian and Simon and Adam all have her firmly in their sights, but what do they see?

Brian doubtless sees a reflection of himself. Like him, she loves both art and the commerce of art. 'Money is freedom. My money and enterprise give artists like Simon the opportunity to develop their talent.' As for Simon, he sees her because she provokes him. She prods and probes like a hyperactive child and it's hard to ignore.

Which leaves Adam. Goodness only knows what Adam sees.

7

Simon is keen to make the most of his stay in Cornwall. He wants to go
to the Tate at St Ives, and Eleanor agrees. It is on her list too.

The journey takes over an hour. As they accelerate past a minibus
full of schoolchildren, Simon says, 'Irene's been going on about the
new gallery ever since it opened. She'll be jealous as hell when I tell her
we've been. Apparently it's not just the stuff inside that's so great, it's
the building as well. I'll send her a postcard.' He glances at her. 'From
both of us, yes?'

'I don't know her.'

'But she knows about you. I'll take you to see her when we get back.'

It's specking with rain when they arrive in St Ives. They park in the
town and walk to the gallery. The building is either stunning or
quaint, Eleanor can't decide which. It perches above the beach like a
sugar-mouse banjo. She detects a hint of seaside-architecture, shades
of Art Deco.

She says, 'I thought it would be bigger.'

They enter via a flight of shallow steps located at the drum end of
the banjo and pass through a brick and glass amphitheatre. The main
exhibition space is situated in the arm of the instrument. The image of
the banjo pleases her. She can almost hear the sea air twanging in its
strings.

Simon's got hot feet, he can't keep still. 'What about this, then.
What do you think?' He pulls her towards the Patrick Heron window.
The stained glass glows. A magenta pyramid pierces a cobalt plane,
jostling a constellation of asymmetrical forms. Yellow and red and
orange – the colours invigorate, the shapes excite. The composition is
unstable, forms teeter. Although by nature and structure the window
is fixed, its heart is in flux, its spirit changing constantly according to
light and viewpoint.

But Simon isn't looking at the window, he's looking at her. 'Great, isn't it? Photos don't do it justice.' Her hand finds his. 'Hey, Nell,' his voice is low and eager, 'if you like this, just wait till you see his paintings.'

She is reluctant to leave. She thinks of her church, abandoned and desecrated – and the fragment of window that remains unshuttered and which, when the sun is right, casts a coral flush across the altar.

'Nell . . .' He's as impatient as a child. 'Come on.' He tightens his grip. Her fingers curl.

She finds Heron's painting a disappointment. It is a still life, a table with crudely painted jugs and bowls placed at jaunty angles. 'Look at the line,' Simon urges. 'Look at the colour . . .'

'But it's so superficial.' She remembers Brian's dictum: instinct first, rational analysis later. 'An unsuccessful Cézanne, a failed Matisse.'

'Judge it on its own merit, Nell.'

'I can't. How can you look at it out of context?' Simon doesn't answer. An artist is being criticized and his fellow-feeling is aroused. 'Come on, don't be like this, don't take it so personally.' She hooks her arm in his. 'It's only an opinion, not worth falling out over.' She leans against him. 'Where to next?'

Although the gallery is smaller than expected, there's a lot to see and Simon wants to discuss the exhibits in detail. They agree and disagree in almost equal proportion.

When they are thoroughly exhausted they walk into town and find a café with a view of the bay, and eat a late lunch of salmon and pasta in a claggy lemon sauce. Simon eats carelessly; he is very different from Adam. Eleanor pushes her plate away. She's tired, but also happy. Their verbal sparring, their aesthetic differences, are every bit as exhilarating as their physical skirmishing. Her skin glows and her fingertips tingle. She splays her hands on her lap. They are translucent, insubstantial, but as she watches, something strange begins to happen. An inner energy summons a chaotic haze of microscopic particles; fragments whirl and bind to create a stronger form. The outline strengthens, her flesh gathers substance, roundness, shape. Life flares through her, tearing along her veins – a galvanizing force flooding her with energy. She reaches out. She flexes her fingers and, touching Simon's cheek, makes a tentative grab for the future.

8

That evening they have a picnic supper at home – a bottle of wine, bread and cheese and fruit. Simon is content just to be with her and to watch her. Okay, so they snipe at one another, say and do hurtful things, but there's no malice there, certainly not on his part, and he thinks not on hers either. It is a reflex, for both of them. In her own way, she's as uncertain about life as he is. They are two of a kind.

She sits by the fire with her back propped against the sofa. She pares a sliver of Cheddar and eats it from the knife, and Simon sees a Dutch interior, a Cézanne still life.

He says, 'Today was great, wasn't it?' She nods and nibbles a dried apricot. 'We make a good team.'

She looks at him, eyes narrowed and divided by a deepening frown. 'How can you think that, after what I said about your mother?'

'I don't suppose Irene would mind, so why should I? Besides, when I think of what you've done for me . . . I know I kick and spit, but you were right about the mural, and now this commission – where to next, hey Nell?'

She stares into the fire, but doesn't answer.

'Okay,' his laughter is edgy, nervous. 'Short term, no rush. How about tomorrow or the day after, we go back to St Ives, take a look at the Barbara Hepworth museum. You'll like it. Brian says you're mad about sculpture—'

'Not tomorrow.'

'Any time – hey, we've got the whole week.'

'No.'

'Don't you want me to stay?'

'I think you should. It's a good place to work. You can have the cottage for the rest of the let, but I'm going back to London.'

'What? No, please, don't do this, Nell. We're just getting to know one another. Brian's always saying we've a lot in common . . .'

'Brian gets carried away.' Her voice is suddenly cold. 'And besides, he has only a very limited influence on my life.'

'Right.' His chest feels tight, and his hands are cold. 'I get the picture. This isn't about Brian, is it? It's about someone else with influence – like Adam Mason.' She looks away. 'Brian says you're an item. You know the crazy thing? I tried to deny it, I didn't want to believe it. But before coming here I went to see him, and he was really cut up at not knowing where you were, and so now I'm thinking, maybe it's true. Tell me, Nell.'

'It's none of your business.'

'Sure it is – and you know why? Because Brian's right. We are alike. The same things excite us. You know it's true.' She refuses to look at him. Her three-quarter profile is etched against the light spilling from the table lamp. Her hair is all mussed. He wants to brush it, feel it stretch beneath the stroke, lift to the static. He wants to see the long black threads tangling amongst the bristles. 'You and Mason.' His voice is harsh. 'I told myself it was a business thing. Jesus, what a fool. You're fucking him, aren't you?'

Now she turns. Her eyes are bright and her face stark white. 'Yes, I certainly am. Is there anything else you'd like to know?' Her voice is sickly sweet with sarcasm. 'Times? Dates? Number and Richter scale of orgasm – mine, his . . . off the dial, Simon. You cannot begin to compete.'

There is a roar in his throat, it comes from her – a whiplash cracking and binding him to her. No thought, no decision to act, just impulse and rage. It isn't even him who's pinning her to the floor. The floor is hard. He is hard. The man who isn't him is erect and thrusting. Do something, Nell, say something. Stop this. I don't want to be doing this.

Yes, I do. Deep down, I do.

But her face is all closed up. No expression. No rage or scorn or desire. It had been there before, last time, he couldn't be wrong about that. He is frantic to see it again, that inward-looking, blood-suffused yearning, the rasp of her breath and her hands on his body, her long fingers exploring the landscape of muscle and flesh, learning the substructure of bone.

He sees none of these things. Only indifference, and distance. He releases her. His two selves converge. He pulls back. He says, 'If that's the way you want it, go on, go back to London. If that's what you want – you and Mason. Just remember it was me who found you, it's me that's here, not him. Don't fool yourself, Nell. He could have found you if he'd wanted to.'

9

She's been driving for hours and she's exhausted. She stops at a motorway service station. Its pick-a-stick construction is all hard lines and primary colours, and it smells of cement and new paint. Lowry figures throng the foyer and clot the area by the toilets. The shops sell food, magazines, toys and tapes.

She needs caffeine. The coffee shops are distinguished only by slight styling differences. The plastic seats in one are a watery blue, in another tomato-red. They have different logos and different shaped menus, but they smell the same and their prices are almost identical. She orders coffee and a toasted teacake. The coffee arrives in a plastic cafetiere. It is not Tanzanian Chagga. Adam. She has a sudden sense of him, a deep longing. What they have together is good, a rapport that goes beyond language.

Could she and Simon ever have that? Could Adam have it with Jess?

Within the first couple of days in Fowey she had half decided to pull out of their relationship, to make a clean break and start again. But now she's not so sure. It would make a lot of sense to stick with Adam. Maybe even marry him. Man and wife, like Babs and Dad. Well, not much like. That hadn't been for all time, but then marriages aren't, despite what people say. Look at Chris.

All at once, she remembers Chris's wife. She cannot recall her name, but can see quite clearly her round face and her lank hair crimped by an unsuccessful perm.

Adam – their future stretches before her, a hazy landscape where one feature blends with another, melting towards the horizon. Simon offers a rougher terrain. Jagged mountains and precipitous paths and unmarked swamps. To negotiate these will require constant vigilance. She will stumble, and sometimes she will fall, but she will know with every step, every jolt and bruise and broken bone, that she is alive.

10

Eleanor leaves for London. Simon waves her off and goes back inside. The silence of the cottage is tangible, it takes form from the air. He is trapped between fear and understanding, he's angry and he is also jealous. A tiny fist yanks at his gut. The gaps in his thoughts are full to bursting with Mason's name and Mason's face.

Pull yourself together.

He wanders into the kitchen. He's hungry. He'd been in such a hurry to catch her before her early departure that he'd skipped breakfast. Next to the kettle is an open packet of biscuits. He nibbles at one as he climbs the stairs. It's stale and powdery and it sticks in his throat. He balances it on the banister post and dusts off his hands.

He opens the bedroom door. A shaft of light, a spotlit stage: the night of the opening, Mason's hand clasping Eleanor's arm. He zooms in on the elegant, bruising fingers as they flex and slide lower, as Adam Mason's thumb explores the small of Eleanor's back.

The man is all show. He can pose as much as he likes, but he's no match for her. Whatever they'd had, Nell and the chef from hell, it's over. He's sure of it, he knows it to his bones.

The bedroom has a bay window with a view of the town and the river. The bedcovers are folded back. A single hair, like a strand of black weed, is caught in the pillow lace. He buries his face in the linen. It smells of her. Tugging off his sweater and jeans, he slides naked between sheets still fragrant from her touch.

He sleeps in her bed, but cannot capture her dreams. He wakes.

The wind tumbles the clouds across the sun. Patterns dance and skitter across his ceiling. The golden darts and toffee-coloured shadows recall a painting at the Tate upon which they had managed to agree.

'Look,' she called, pulling him by the hand, swivelling on her heel. 'Simon, look at this. Isn't it fantastic?'

They are in a crescent-shaped gallery overlooking the amphitheatre. The broad curve of the window gives a panoramic view of the beach. The painting hangs at the far end. The scale is modest, but the effect dramatic. The artist's palette echoes the gold of the sand and the changing greys of sky and sea. The artist is John Wells and the painting is *Sea Bird Forms*. Using the sunlight and shadows flitting across his ceiling, Simon reconstructs the painting. Shades of pewter: scimitar-wings slicing the air, a whiplash of polished bronze shearing through the crap and flim-flam to reveal the heart of the matter, the very point of connection.

Okay, so they fight like cats, but at a visceral level they do connect. He thinks in pictures – sees himself as a ginger tom and Nell as a sleek black queen – but he needs words as well, and language is inadequate. He has no choice but to fall back on cliché. The biggest cliché of all – he loves the bloody woman.

This morning she'd climbed the low wall in front of the cottage and, shading her eyes, gazed out across the glittering water. Calling to him and resting a hand on his shoulder, she said, 'Will you paint it for me? I want you to paint it all, the hills, the estuary, the sea – and the sun, I want you to bottle the sun for me.'

He'd shrugged and said, 'I don't know. Maybe.' But now he thinks, yes, I will paint it for you.

He climbs to the headland. It is the perfect day for such a project. Images swarm like gnats, jostling for attention, each one clear cut and assertive – but most vivid of all on this bright morning, the memory casting the darkest shadow, is Eleanor with her rain-soaked hair and the glow of the fire and the rattling tattoo of the rain on the windows.

The air is razor clear and cold as death. He goes to the edge of the cliff and belly-flops on to the grass. His fingers dig into earth and stone. The sea pounds at the rocks, grinding them one against another. The whole landscape vibrates. His body tingles from chin to groin.

Then all at once the scene fixes. He sits up and scrambles back from the edge. He begins to sketch. He rearranges and enhances what he sees, discovering a form of composition in this chaos. His hand sweeps across the page as he strives to create something not exactly figurative, not entirely representational – not abstract, either, but something new and explosive.

Although the wind buffets his hair and his body shrivels with the cold, he can't stop. The excitement escalates – right off the Richter scale.

Hey now, two can play at that, Nell Bycroft.

11

Eleanor arrives home. The house closes round her. She is secure. Oscar follows her into the kitchen where she feeds him and opens her post. She considers ringing Brian to say she'll be back at work early, then remembers he's taken on a temp and it's probably best not to upset his arrangements. She needs to think. The whole point of Fowey had been to get her thoughts in order, but the scheme had backfired big time. So now what?

She decides to go for a walk. It is a cold day. Not the healthy wet and windy cold of the Cornish coast, but a bone-aching city cold. The light is different, too. There is a deadness to it. Everything is grey.

She goes to St Mark's. It's always a relief to find the church unchanged. She has a nightmare that one day she'll turn into the street to find it has been demolished, and a supermarket erected on the site.

She pulls at the board blocking the side entrance. It is spongy and slimy and it slips beneath her fingertips.

Inside, the atmosphere is musty and the church reeks of disuse. Kneeling at the altar rail, she sets a match to the candle stubs. The flames flicker and the honeyed light spills over to puddle the chancel steps. Holy Ghost and his friends warble in the rafters.

What would Simon make of this? Turner painted churches, all

pointed arches and glancing sunlight and piles of picturesque rubble. Turner painted the real thing, but this Victorian heap is more in line with Simon's status.

Why does she snipe at him so? It's a reflex, says Jess. Self-defence. 'He could do a person harm, could Simon.'

She's right. Simon is dangerous. He niggles and excavates her psyche, and reproduces his finds on canvas – he is a pirate, a bounty hunter. She remembers the painting, and her thunderous fury. She's never felt anything like it, a deep, blood-rolling geyser of rage. At first she thought she'd contained it – the illusion of control – but then she saw her bloodied hand and, looking up, a crimson slash rending the canvas.

And yet, for all his painterly pyrotechnics, Simon is a copyist. A good one, granted, but a copyist all the same. He describes only what he sees. There is no deep understanding, nothing but dressed canvas smeared with paint, the smell of oil and turpentine, and the unwilling scrape of a brush.

One of the candles gutters out. She strikes another match and watches as the blackened wick blossoms into flame and the wax melts to form a clear pool in the shallow dip around the wick. The pool swells, pressing against the rim. There is a pause before the rim breaks and the wax dribbles, then tumbles, then cools against the side of the candle in a frozen cascade that is both fragile and strong.

The wax jacket supports and contains the wick, and the wick burns on and on and on . . .

I am like that. I melt and reform, I change shape, reinventing myself so often, sometimes even I don't know who I am. But I know now. I know that the real me is strong and eternal like the wick – and yet that part of me can exist only with the support of my other, more fragile, containing, self.

The clarity of the vision makes her head spin.

And yet it is no more than a reaffirmation of the truth she discovered as a child, the realization that she could be anything or anyone she wanted to be – and that, whoever she decides to be, whichever costume she chooses to wear, it is the choice of her true self.

She struggles to her feet. She has to tell Adam. He must understand that although a part of her – an important part – does need Simon, it is him she loves.

There is a phone box next to the launderette and she rings the restaurant. Tom answers. There is a long silence while he fetches Adam.

'Eleanor.' His voice cracks down the line. 'Where have you been? Where are you ringing from?' She tells him. 'I see.' His tone is harsh; he is still hurting.

'Adam . . .'

'Your artist friend came to see me.'

'I know.' She clenches the greasy handset. 'Adam, I've got to talk to you.'

'Really.' His voice is distant. She imagines him holding the phone away from his face.

'It's important, I need to talk to you now. Will you come to the church?'

'I'm working.'

'Let Tom take over for an hour or two. Please, Adam. I have to see you.'

Maybe after last time it's not such a wise move, bringing him here. But then if Adam can't accept her for what she is, surely it's best to find out sooner rather than later?

She checks the candles, then retreats along the nave. She crosses the west end and is halfway up the north aisle when she hears a scrabbling at the side door. There is the crack of strained wood, a fleeting change in the movement and constitution of the air, then silence.

She waits. There's no hurry. She must choose her words carefully. If she starts prattling on about candles and wicks, he'll think her off her head.

She ducks behind a pier. The shadowy movement becomes more distinct as he reaches the rail and the row of candles. Even from here she can see how the cooled wax hangs like melted flesh.

Adam is very dark and very devilish as he stands silhouetted against the candlelight with his black hair and beard and his dark overcoat. She presses her cheek to the pillar. She embraces cold stone. An effigy. A dead lover. She trails the stone with her fingers. She is like this, cold as Carrara marble, strong as a monument. But brittle, also.

Samson in the house of the Philistines, cracked pillars, a broken roof and tumbling walls – triumph in death.

She laughs aloud. Adam hears, and lifts his head and turns. She follows his progress down the nave and across the west end. She listens to the soft scuffle of his tread as he approaches.

His face glimmers in the almost-dark. He has seen her. His voice is hushed, a whisper of dust as he says, 'Eleanor? Is that you?'

Who else would it be? They face one another. They do not move, they do not speak. Every word they have ever uttered, every taunt and caress, shivers in the air between them.

His face is pinched. He huddles into his upturned collar and she experiences a rush of tenderness. She has behaved so badly, dashing off, not telling him where she was going or when she'd be back, then summoning him here, to this cold, creepy, unenchanted place.

Not so. It is the most enchanted place she knows.

'Adam.' There is a moment, the merest flicker of hesitation before he comes to her.

This is good. She loves the feel of his head beneath her hands, the tight, crisp curls, the shape of his skull and the tips of his ears, white and chill as a dead man's flesh. She wraps herself round him. His body is hard and warm, cocooned by his coat. Her long hand spreads across his back and down to stroke and clench.

He starts and recoils and tries to disengage. 'Not again,' he whispers. 'Not here.'

'It's okay.' There's a fluttering in the roof. 'Holy Ghost is watching.' She laughs softly. 'Adam . . .' she draws him to her, and he no longer resists. He delves inside her coat. His hands explore her waist. They are large and strong and they move upwards. His thumb seeks out the place between her breasts. His clothing skids over his body as her fingers probe – concavity and crease, convexity and contour. She slides her thigh under his coat and he thrusts at her, crushing her against the pillar.

This is wonderful – I know what I am. Adam and Simon, candle and wick. But more than that, this space between hard body and harder stone. He cannot force his way through to reach the stone. He thrusts again. They are fully clothed, yet never has she known such intense, such pure desire. It begins with a faint tremor deep inside, then escalates through her body, growing in intensity and pitch as her breathing racks in time with his. She hears herself shout, feels the whiplash crack of her body against stone: once, and again, then one last time. Then stillness. He pins her to the pillar. Without him she would fall. She has no strength, and cannot catch her breath. His face is pressed to her neck. His breath is hot. He says something. She cannot hear him. Maybe he says her name. He strokes her cheek. His fingers catch in her hair and loosen it, and he buries his face in the tangled strands.

But then comes a sharp intake of breath, and a jerk of alarm. He recoils. 'Simon.' There is a space between them, a rush of air chills her overheated body. 'I can smell him. In your hair, on your skin . . . on me. I can smell him on me.' She's going to fall. She presses back against the pillar. Like a climber on the rock-face, her fingertips seek the cracks in the stone – and Adam's mouth is like that, a faint crack in the scrub of his beard, and his face is grey, like rock glittering with mica. 'You've been with him,' he whispers. 'And now you're with me. I don't understand. Why?'

The ground drops beneath her feet. The darkness closes in. She pushes herself away from the stone and stands upright.

Adam backs away. 'Is that what it was all about, going off with no explanation?'

'I did explain.'

'And then Whitburn coming to see me, playing the innocent. Jesus, Eleanor, you've made a fool of me.'

'No.'

He does not trust her. He's wrong, but she hasn't the breath to argue. Even if she wanted to. She has lost the will to fight. The day has been too long; too many revelations in too short a time have left her dizzy and confused.

She edges round the pillar and takes two unsteady steps along the aisle. Adam remains in the shadows. She takes two steps more – firmer, this time – then another three. And now she's walking faster, much faster, and she's out of the church in the grey London light and striding past the launderette and the phone box, running for the bus and scrambling up the twisted stairway to sit on the top deck with her hot cheek pressed against the cold glass, and her long fingers gripping the chromium rail of the seat in front.

12

Simon returns from Fowey with a whole stack of drawings, aspects of the town and the river and the sea, together with quick studies of people, of faces spotted on the quay or in the pub. And memories. Eleanor on the chocolate-coloured sofa with her knees drawn up, and the fine blue veins in her ankle like the mesh of a butterfly's wing.

Now that he's home he'll work the sketches up into paintings, starting with the seascape. When it's done, he will give it to Eleanor.

The painting she'd destroyed – it seems so long ago – is turned to the wall. He sets up a new canvas. He knows what he wants, he can see it, feel it. He begins. He thrills to the scrape of bristle against canvas. He forgets everything and everyone. He is full to overflowing with memories and images and ideas. His hand darts back and forth, testing a line, adjusting a colour – again and again and again, until it all comes right.

A casual observer might easily miss the point. They would see a conventional estuary and seascape. But it is not at all conventional. The rocks are alive, they teeter. The composition is unstable. The entire landscape is poised to leap into action. He has shown the power of the cliffs, and their fragility. Erosion. Century follows century and every day the shoreline disintegrates a little more, then reinvents itself.

Exactly so. He is painting Eleanor.

He works frenetically, building colour, deepening the field, intensifying the sense of mass. He speaks to no one, ignores the phone, hardly eats.

His anger is gone, as is his jealousy. He has forgotten Adam as he has forgotten himself. There is only Eleanor. Eleanor and Nell. First and last.

13

Adam is also ignoring the phone. Eleanor has left three messages at the restaurant. He has told Tom he is permanently out to Eleanor Bycroft. At home his calls are screened through the answering machine.

To begin with her messages are brief. Would he ring her? Would he ring her soon? Please would he ring her soon . . .

After a few days they become more complicated. She needs to talk, to explain, she hates there to be such bad feeling between them. Her voice is painfully familiar. It speaks to a deep, dark part of him, a place he cannot locate. If he could, he would cut it out. He stands by the telephone with the tips of his fingers pressed against the black recording box. The vibrations fracture his nerves.

Years ago he had a girlfriend who worked in a restaurant. It was a standing joke that no matter how vigorously they bathed, the smells of the kitchen clung to their hair and skin. In bed they played like truffle pigs, each snuffling out what the other had cooked that night. And so it had been with Eleanor in the church. He had buried his face in her hair and taken a deep breath, and inhaled a chemical cocktail of turpentine and oil and God knows what else. Simon.

Yet even now, despite his conviction, he is eager to hear that it isn't true. He imagines her charging into the restaurant with her black plait flying. She would make a scene. He'd hustle her into his office and close the door, and she'd turn and face him with her hands on her hips and her face full of scorn, and tell him how wrong he was. That he hadn't smelt Simon. It was perfume. Cheap soap. Anything. Anything at all but the truth.

It doesn't happen. Days pass. A week. Then more days. She no longer phones. He could ring her. Or go to the gallery. He doesn't. His pride is hurt. And anyway, he can tell from her messages it's not reconciliation she's after. She wants to be understood. Forgiven. Well, I don't forgive you, Eleanor. I never will.

He wakes early on Sunday. He can't get back to sleep so he goes to the park. A cruel frost has lined each twig with spikes. A Christmas Crown of Thorns.

'*Be careful what you wish for.*' Gran's voice shivers out of the mist. 'You can't predict the future, Adam, so take care. You might make a wish without thinking it through, and then it won't turn out the way you want. It might turn out meaningless, or even dangerous.'

A giraffe in a hen-run. Finding Eleanor in Jessica's workshop, he'd thought, this is what I wish for, to be consumed by love, to know its sting, to feel it coursing like a virus in my bloodstream – and now here it is, a bolt from the blue, straight between the eyes. *Be careful what you wish for.* He had not completed his wish. The bolt must go both ways. One way only, and you have nothing to show but a hole in the head and a burnt-out brain.

He's had enough of Holland Park. There are too many imps perched in the trees; too many memories crack with the ice.

Tucking his scarf more tightly under his chin, he quickens his step. He turns a corner. He stops. He almost doesn't recognize her. She's wearing jeans and a puffy, wine-coloured coat. Her hair is loose. He stares. She looks up and her eyes are smudged and poorly defined. She says, 'I called at the flat.'

He stays rooted to the middle of the path. A jogger skirts him with a disapproving puff. 'You look frozen.'

She rubs at her cheek. She's wearing navy mittens. 'Just a bit.' She smiles. 'I thought I'd find you here. It's Sunday morning. Early walks, blow away the cobwebs . . .'

'I've nothing to say to you, Eleanor.' His voice is as cold as the morning. He can't afford to show any warmth. She is not to be trusted.

'What you said,' her voice is barely above a whisper. 'What you think – it isn't true.'

'Then why take so long to deny it?'

'I was confused.'

'You didn't look confused. You didn't sound it, either, when you rang me and summoned me there. There's no point to any of this, Eleanor. I could smell him . . .'

'He followed me. That's all. I went to Cornwall and Simon followed me. You didn't.'

'I left you alone because that was what you wanted. Time to yourself – that's what you said – and I respected that.'

'I know.'

'And even if I'd wanted to follow, I'd no idea where you'd gone.'

'Neither did Simon.'

'And if I had come after you?'

She stares past him at the frost-encrusted trees, at the mist that hangs like Miss Haversham's veil. 'I don't know. It may have changed things. How can I tell?'

'It's not a lot to go on, is it? I'm sorry, Eleanor, but this isn't my style. It all hangs on too slender a thread. You don't know, you can't tell, things might have been different . . .'

'Nothing in life is totally predictable.'

'That's a cop-out and you know it. Let's call it a day, shall we? Jesus, I don't know why we're even having this conversation. We're too far apart – and it's not really to do with Simon and what did or didn't happen in Cornwall. Simon's just a symptom of what's wrong, another example of how you keep changing course without telling me. I can't play that game, Eleanor. I'm no good at second-guessing. I care about you, but I can't be with you, not any more.'

She doesn't speak, she doesn't move. She watches him with her hands clenched tight in her ridiculous mittens. The blue of her eyes holds him a moment longer. A bird flutters in the tree above. A powder of dislodged frost dusts her hair. He takes a step backwards, then another. He twists his ankle on a stone, swears on a breath and turns and walks away.

14

Simon arrives at Eleanor's house with the bubble-wrapped parcel clutched awkwardly under his arm. Wedging it between his raised knee and his chin, he rings the doorbell.

Yesterday he'd visited the antiques market in Camden Passage in search of a frame. In an upper room of an arcade he found a stack of prints hidden behind an ugly sideboard. One print had an elaborate gilded plaster frame. He brushed away the dust and examined it front and back. There was no price tag. A woman sat in the corner reading a newspaper. He called to her and, glancing over her half-moon glasses, she quoted a price. He shook his head and returned the frame to its stack.

The woman smiled knowingly, and put aside her paper. 'Well then, let me just look. There may be some leeway.' She reached a stock book from a shelf and flicked through it. She closed the book and, looking from Simon to the frame and back again, suggested a figure. It was still a lot – but hell, he's doing this for Nell and he's got to get it right.

He took it home and, placing it alongside the painting, saw at once that it was a good choice and worth every penny.

Even so, he's a little nervous. What if Eleanor doesn't like it? Adjusting his hold on the parcel, he gives her doorbell another punch, then bangs on the glass for good measure.

The door opens. 'Simon.'

'Special delivery, ma'am.' He wields the parcel like a trophy.

She laughs and tugs at his arm, pulling him inside. 'It's nice to see you,' she says. 'What have you got there?' She plucks at his parcel. 'Come on Simon, tell . . .'

'Wait, hold on. Let me put it down.'

'In here.' She ushers him into the living room. On the sofa is a plastic basket piled with clothes. An ironing board is angled across the room. Eleanor edges past him and bends to switch off the iron at the socket. Simon shoves the linen basket to one side and wedges his parcel against the back of the sofa. He takes a penknife to the string.

He hesitates and glances at her. 'Listen, Nell, why don't you go and put the kettle on or feed the cat or something?'

'Why should I want to do that?'

'Because I want this to be a surprise.'

'But it isn't. It's another painting – and I bet I even know the subject.'

'Okay, but I want you to see it all together, not a bit at a time as I unwrap it. Come on, Nell,' he pleads. 'Play the game.'

She shrugs. 'Okay.' She gathers up a pile of precision-ironed pillowcases and blouses. 'I'll take these up to the airing cupboard, but it won't take long, so you'd better be quick.'

As he peels back the last of the bubble-wrap, he hears her tread on the stairs. 'Hold on a minute,' he shouts. 'I'm not quite ready.' He adjusts the angle of the painting, stands back to check its impact, then goes out to her.

'You know,' she says. 'I don't much like being ordered about in my own house.'

'I'm sorry.' He senses an imminent change of mood. She makes him dizzy with these turn-abouts; it's no wonder he sometimes goes too far. He takes a breath and makes an effort to be patient. 'It wasn't meant to be an order, it was a suggestion.' The alarming scowl continues to furrow the Byzantine scoop between her eyes. He catches her by the wrist and, with the ball of his thumb, smooths away the crease. 'There,' he says as she pulls back. 'That's better. It's okay, Nell, I won't hurt you. Come on, come and see your painting.' He hesitates. 'Just one thing – another suggestion – will you close your eyes? Please?'

'I'd rather not.'

'Hey, Nell,' his hold becomes a caress as he strokes the tender skin on the inside of her wrist. The veins swell. Blue. Vulnerable. 'Don't be stubborn, this is for you.' She smiles and closes her eyes. He leads her forward and places her in front of the painting. 'Okay, are you ready?'

'Yes.'

'Go on, then, you can look.'

They stand side by side, hand in hand like children. He waits. He wants to know what she thinks, but is afraid to ask.

Does she see what he has done? Can she tell that he has painted her again? Although at one level it is a seascape, at a deeper level it is Eleanor who suffuses the canvas. The seaweed strands whipped by the tide are the snake-locks of her hair. The line of her nose and the planes of her cheeks are the slabs of rock tumbling recklessly to the sea. The steely light reflecting off the waves is the façade she presents to the world. The currents beneath are the real woman, the visceral Nell.

She fidgets. Her fingers clench his. She understands. 'Well?' he whispers. 'What d'you think?'

She says, 'I like the frame.'

'Shit, Nell!'

'God, I'm sorry. I don't know why I do that.' She bites her lip and leans against his arm. 'Yes,' she says. 'It's very good, you know it is. It's the best likeness yet.'

15

It's late on Christmas afternoon and Jess stands naked in front of her dressing table mirror. Behind her, sprawled on the bed like an abandoned ghost, is Adam's present to her – an ivory silk kimono.

Sitting down, she pulls the robe across her lap and fingers the nubbed fabric. She is almost certain it wasn't originally intended for her. It is altogether too serious a garment for her wardrobe. She laughs at the verbal conceit. She doesn't have a wardrobe, not a real one, just a rail in an alcove, the overflow strung out along the picture rail.

Adam will insist that he and Ellie are a thing of the past, but Jess knows otherwise. She can tell from the frequency with which he asks after her and from the way he says her name, that a part of him still yearns to be with her.

'Well hell, that's just the way it is,' she speaks out loud, addressing first a handful of bunched silk, then her speckled reflection in the dressing table mirror. 'So don't go fooling yourself.' Standing up, she gives the kimono a shake prior to putting it on. 'The fact is, this little darling is yours only because Ellie buggered off to Venice with Simon. Your precious Adam has no other reason, no ulterior motives for showering you with gifts.' She leans forward and pulls a face at the image in the mirror. 'Hey, are you listening, kid?'

Last Christmas she'd gone to the Norfolk coast with Ellie and Babs and, because it was mild, they'd picnicked on the dunes in the lee of the pines. But this year Ellie is with Simon, and Babs is visiting a friend in Ireland.

Remembering previous Christmases had made Jess feel abandoned and, as she suspected Adam was in much the same state, she rang him. From his studied vagueness she was reassured that, like her, he had no plans for the holiday. She told him about last year. 'It seems to me,' she said, 'we should say to hell with them all and have a picnic of our own. It doesn't have to be Wells-next-the-sea, in fact I'd strongly advise against Norfolk. How do you feel about Brighton, or the South Downs?'

They decided on Brighton, but Christmas morning dawned dank and uninviting and when Adam arrived with his hamper they examined the sky and consulted Ceefax, and decided to stay at home.

Adam's idea of a picnic does not involve fishpaste sandwiches and orange squash. He tends more towards the game pie and quail's eggs and salmon in aspic school of thought. As a consequence they eat too much and drink too much. Afterwards they flop on the sofa, laughing at their excess, and exchange presents.

The kimono tumbles from its wrapping like thick buttermilk. She allows it to flow through her fingers. 'Try it on,' he suggests, and she flees to her bedroom, glad for the chance to hide her embarrassment.

She mustn't let him see that she knows the kimono was really for Ellie.

Or so she'd thought, but now, as she holds the robe against her and turns first this way then that in front of the mirror, she realizes her mistake. The colour and texture of the creamy silk perfectly complement her warm skin and glowing hair. It looks absolutely right on her – and would look very wrong indeed juxtaposed to Ellie's stark colouring.

Goosebumps form along her arms. She feels a little lift of excitement. She is ready now, eager to feel the fabric slide against her skin. As she draws the raw silk over her shoulders, she pictures Adam in the next room, sampling the raki that Ellie had bought her. She'd had a glass herself after lunch; its warmth still swirls in her belly.

The robe is surprisingly heavy. When she swings her hips, it flies open. She laughs, and fastens the sash and returns to the living room.

'Wake up, Mr Mason.' He is sprawled on the sofa and she stands before him, hands on hips. 'Tell me what you think. Is it me?' She parades back and forth, opening her arms to display sleeves like butter-coloured flags. 'Semaphore,' she says, gesturing. She catches his hands and pulls him to his feet. 'Not that I ever learnt semaphore. They kicked me out of the Brownies. They told my mother I was subversive.' She tugs him closer. 'Hey now, Adam Mason, about this robe . . .'

'D'you like it?'

'It's lovely. Thank you.' She brushes his lips and, when she hears his sharp intake of breath, she kisses him again. He responds tentatively at first, but then more positively. She has to stand on tiptoe to reach him. This is so good. She always knew he would feel like this, taste like this – delicious. The man is a chef, after all.

But then he pulls back. She drops down on to her heels. 'It's okay, Adam. Don't look so worried, relax.' She touches his cheek. He's frowning. She runs her finger from the bridge of his nose to its tip. 'What is it? Is it Ellie?' He shrugs. 'That's silly, don't let her ruin your life. This is so right – can't you feel it? I've always liked you, right from the start – before you'd ever heard of Ellie Bycroft.'

'But you're her friend, Jessica.'

'You're saying it would be okay if we were strangers?'

'Yes, I suppose so . . . No, maybe not. I don't know.'

'Shall I tell you about friendship? When Ellie snatched you from under my nose, I let her. Okay, maybe I didn't have much choice, you were far more interested in her, but the point is, I didn't try to compete, and I certainly didn't resent what she had with you.'

'I had no idea.'

'Didn't you?' She considers him for a moment. He does not rise to her bait. 'Well, maybe not. In any case it wouldn't have made any difference. I'm fond of you, but I'm not a fool. Look, all I'm trying to say is, what's past is past. Just for once I'm thinking of myself – and let's be honest, what happens now is no skin off Ellie's nose.'

'But I let her down . . .'

'And she picked herself right up and went to Venice with Simon. I bet they're having a whale of a time. I can just see it, can't you?'

'No.'

'Come on, you're not trying, Adam. They're two of a kind. Ellie and Simon in some grand palazzo, cracking the marble . . .' She senses his pain, but she can't stop. He has to see what he's up against; he must understand once and for all that he has lost this battle. 'I'll bet they're fucking the daylights out of one another even as we speak.'

16

It is raining in Venice. It rained the day they arrived, but they didn't mind. As the water taxi sped away from the airport, Eleanor pressed her face against the rain-streaked windows, eager for her first glimpse of the city.

On the flight over she'd told Simon she expected to be disappointed. 'Why? You'll love it. It's so romantic, Nell, all those canals and churches and masks . . .'

'What about the murders and the red dwarf?' She added some more gin to her tonic and nibbled an airline-standard peanut.

'That was just a film, Nell.'

'Don't you see? That's my point. Venice doesn't belong to the Venetians, any more than the Parthenon belongs to the Greeks or the Colosseum to the Italians. It's a common image. We all know what Venice looks like – or what it's supposed to look like. The original is bound to fall short of our imaginings.'

'Don't be such a pessimist.'

'I'm a realist. Preparing myself for disappointment is a safeguard against disappointment.'

But in the end she is not disappointed. The water taxi leaves the airport far behind and the low skyline of the city, the terracotta roofs, the domes and campaniles, swell towards her through the rain and the mist.

The myth has substance after all. She has passed through a cold, dark forest and come upon a sunlit glade to discover a unicorn grazing.

She turns to Simon. She's smiling, but there are tears on her cheeks, though she doesn't realize until he brushes them away. She blinks, and sees that his eyes are also bright.

They disembark at San Marco. The hotel is close by and, though tired from travelling, neither of them wants to rest. Dumping their bags, they collect a map from reception and go exploring.

The first thing that strikes her about this city of contradictions is its uncanny silence – the kind of silence that for her is more often the aftermath of pain.

They walk the streets, muffled against the rain, losing themselves in a maze of alleys and campi and narrow canals. The buildings rise straight and sheer from the water. Huge patches of stucco have fallen away to reveal crumbling brickwork and gaps in the mortar. It is a city of boundaries, yet formless when seen from within. The alien echo of their footfalls resounding off walls and water has a quality all its own.

They stand on a bridge. Silence and stillness surround them. Their breath plumes and joins with the mist. Then, out of nowhere, a sound. The faint throb of an engine. The water laps almost soundlessly against the sides of the canal. A barge rounds the corner. Its load is shrouded in a tarpaulin and its distinctly industrial air adds another dimension to the city.

The barge approaches the bridge and passes under them. Silence returns.

Eleanor grips the iron balustrade. She is moved beyond words by this fragile city that has lasted a thousand years. She tries to imagine the very first settlers. Whatever possessed them to build their future upon such shifting sands?

It just goes to show how a risk can pay dividends.

Sometimes the quiet unnerves them. They walk close together, they link hands. They are lost now, but it doesn't matter. They come upon a campanile that leans so recklessly, it seems the pressure of a single finger would be enough to send it toppling. In one broad campo is a palazzo so twisted on its foundations that it appears as if viewed in a fairground mirror.

Day after day they walk the city. Now and again, when the rain becomes too heavy, they duck into a church. They even spend a morning in the Accademia, but they always return to the streets.

Of all the sites and monuments they visit, the tetrarchs of San Marco delight her the most. Two men in armour, locked in an embrace, are carved from purple porphyry. Simon checks the guidebook and discovers that, like the quadriga above, they were plundered from Constantinople. She is fascinated by the way they have been incorporated into the building's fabric. She leans close, touching the cold, damp stone, allowing her fingers to explore the grooves in the armour, the hawkshead pommel of a sword. Simon is beside her, one hand gripping her waist, the other extended to explore the smooth line of a brow, the rim of an eye, the roughened wound where a nose has been lost.

And all the while, the rain trickles and floods, duckboards span the square, a woman in high heels staggers and trips.

The downpour increases and they shelter beneath the loggia of the Doge's Palace. The sky is the colour of dirty wadding. A squall sends a chainmail curtain of rain swinging across the lagoon. Eleanor leans against Simon. He laughs. 'Look at that sky,' he says. 'And the rain on the water – does it remind you of anywhere?'

'Yes,' she says. 'It does. It reminds me of Fowey.'

17

It's six-thirty on a Wednesday morning and Adam is making scrambled eggs. Eleanor always said he was incapable of cooking the eggs plain and it's true, he cannot resist adding just a little something extra.

But this morning he will keep it simple. He melts the butter in a pan and, cracking the eggs on the side of the bowl, whips them with a dash of cream. Next comes a hint of tabasco and a generous shower of coarsely ground black pepper.

Eleanor is very much on his mind and so when he hears a knock at his door his first thought is that it must be her.

His second thought is that he's a twenty-four carat fool. He hasn't seen her in months. Not since before Christmas. It is now April. He hasn't seen her, has not sought news of her. When Brian brings clients to the restaurant it is an unspoken rule that Eleanor is not mentioned.

There are times when he despises himself for the way he's erased her from his life. She'd tried to explain, but he wasn't interested in her lame justifications. It was almost as if he'd been looking for an excuse to break free.

From this distance he cannot see how they could ever have had a future. They are too different. She had been a distraction, an exciting episode in his life, and now it's over.

The knock on his door is repeated; his visitor rattles the letter-flap and calls his name. It is not Eleanor.

'Were you hiding?' Jessica grins. 'I knew you were in there. You've a reputation as an early riser. I thought, I'll winkle him out somehow, if I have to shin up the drainpipe to do it. Is it okay if I come in?'

'I'm not dressed.'

'Don't be coy. I promise I'm not here to seduce you. Do I smell coffee? Tanzanian Chagga, right?'

'Right.'

'Ellie was always going on about you and coffee, she says it's a hoot.' She sniffs Bisto-Kid fashion and pushes past him.

'What is this, Jessica?'

'I haven't seen you in a week or two, that's all – so I thought, why don't I pop round, make sure you're still in the land of the living.'

'At six in the morning?'

'Six-thirty.'

'Has Eleanor sent you?'

She pulls a face. 'Somehow it always comes back to Ellie, doesn't it? Try not to look quite so disappointed, Adam.'

'I'm sorry.'

'It's okay. Let's change the subject, shall we? You know, I really love this room.' She swivels to admire his kitchen. 'All these windows, a view down both streets. It's like a tower, a castle turret. You're safe here. You can spot the enemy a mile off – plenty of time to stoke the boiling oil. Double virgin olive, of course.'

'Jessica —'

'What?' She hikes her bottom on to the work surface, kicks off her shoes and pulls up her knees to sit cross-legged. 'You're looking good, Adam. A bit tired, but good.'

He shakes his head and smiles. She looks like a leprechaun. She's let her hair grow. It has lost its aggressive spikes and clings to her scalp like a hennaed bathing cap.

'Okay,' she says, relenting. 'I suppose there's no escaping it. You want to ask about Ellie, don't you? Well, she's fine.' She runs her

fingers along the edge of the working surface. 'More than fine.' Her
nails are broken, her skin is raw and chafed. He finds her total
unselfconsciousness rather touching. She says, 'Adam, the smell of
that coffee is driving me wild. I know how choosy you are about your
breakfast companions, but if we skip the foreplay, couldn't you make
an exception?' He stares blankly. 'Is there any chance of a cup?' He
hands her a mug and she eyes the bowl of uncooked eggs and the
abandoned balloon whisk. 'So what's all this, then?'

'Breakfast. Scrambled eggs.'

'Right, yes. Ellie's told me about your scrambled eggs. Smoked
salmon and prawns.'

'Something else she thinks is a hoot.'

'Now let's see if I can remember.' She marks off her list on her
fingers. 'As well as coffee and scrambled eggs, we have croissants with
chilled quince jelly, brioche and apricot jam spiked with Armagnac . . .'

'Is that what you talk about when you get together, my eating
habits?'

'Your culinary skills and your dick.'

'Jessica, please . . .'

'Sorry. Bad taste, right? Just a joke, Adam, you're making me
nervous. Don't look so worried, it's just that Ellie thinks your cooking
is sexy.'

'Really.'

'And while we're on the subject, that's a great dressing gown. Invite
her here, let her watch you cook dressed like that, and she's all yours. I
think she's crazy to let you go.'

'Like you said, I was the one who ended it.'

'Technically, yes. But listen, are you really saying you don't want
her back?'

'Words of one syllable – no I don't. Now can we please drop the
subject?'

'Yes, in a minute, but I've something to say, and it isn't easy for me,
Adam. Ellie and I are close, and I've left you in no doubt about my
feelings for you.' She pauses, but he can think of nothing to say. He
turns on the stove to reheat the butter. 'Okay,' Jessica shrugs. 'Let's get
back to Ellie. She's had a tough time these past few years, what with
Chris and everything – but you know that. Then you come on the
scene and the two of you hit it off, and I thought, hey now, don't be

selfish Jess, isn't this just what the doctor ordered?' He gives the eggs an extra whisk and tips them into the pan. 'And I wasn't wrong, except I didn't allow for Simon. Simon . . .' she muses. 'Now there's a spanner in the works if ever there was one.'

'I'd rather not talk about Simon.'

'Okay, but tell me this, can you honestly say you've let her go?'

'Yes.' He continues to stir the eggs. They scramble, bind, become solid. He pushes the pan away and turns off the heat.

'Only I keep remembering that time in my workshop, the way you looked at her; and you haven't taken up with anyone since – despite some pretty tempting offers.' She pulls a rueful pout. 'You must understand, I'm just trying to get at what you really feel.'

'I feel nothing.' He tips the ruined egg into the bin, scrapes out the pan and fills it with water. 'You know what happened. What was I supposed to think? She went with him. Call me old-fashioned, but we were a couple, and she went with him.'

'She didn't.'

'I'm not stupid, Jessica. It's like food, like cooking – I could smell him on her.'

'Haven't you ever been in a room with a smoker and come out reeking? It doesn't mean you screwed the person, does it? You just shared their space for a while.'

'If that's how it was, why didn't she explain?'

'Because you didn't give her a chance.'

'You're saying she didn't sleep with him?'

'Not in Cornwall, no. I assume they got it together in Venice but I don't know for sure. I don't get chapter and verse any more. Look, I wish you wouldn't fight me, Adam. I'm on your side. We could change this. It's not too late.'

'It is. She's made her choice.'

'No, what she's done is allow Simon to choose for her. She's told you about Chris – well, after that she was frozen, afraid even to try and predict the outcome of her actions. She's with Simon for all the wrong reasons – and if that's not bad enough, now she's going to marry him.'

He steadies himself against the worktop. Out in the lobby the letter-flap snaps and his newspaper flumps on to the mat. 'That's that, then.' His voice is flat. 'I'm very pleased for her. Be sure and give them my congratulations.'

'Adam!'

'If that's what she wants, there's nothing I can do. She goes her own way. You know she does.'

'No, she doesn't. What exactly has she told you about Chris?'

He takes a moment to remember. He hears her voice in his head and echoes her words. 'The usual stuff. Her compromises weren't his. The relationship meant more to her than it did to him. In the end he went back to his wife.'

'No. She lied. It wasn't like that. Oh he went back to his wife for a while, but he couldn't hack it, any more than he could hack the idea of leaving his marriage. He went back to his wife, and then he went back to Ellie – only by then she'd stopped trusting him. How could she believe anything he said when he'd let her down so many times? I don't blame her. Chris was a selfish bastard. She had to protect herself.'

'What happened?'

'He turned up, banging on the door in the middle of the night, but she wouldn't let him in. She sent him away, so he left her house and went to the river. He couldn't make up his mind. He'd left it too long, and he'd lost her. No. He didn't lose her, he threw her away. And then he threw his life away.'

18

With a broad-bladed knife Adam slices the aubergine and courgettes and deseeds the peppers. He arranges them on a baking sheet, brushes them with oil and pops them in the oven to roast. He ties cutlets of lamb into neat noisettes, then peels and slices the celeriac and sets it to steam.

Today, Eleanor married Simon. Adam and Jessica had received a joint invitation. 'She knows we spent Christmas together,' Jessica explains. 'She's selling us to Simon as a couple; it's a way of bringing you into the circle. She wants you there, Adam.'

'I'm not going.'

'Well, you can always change your mind.'

'I have no intention of changing my mind. What the hell does she think I am?' He glares at Jessica. Why is she allowing herself to be a party to this? Her motives are so mixed these days, he's not sure even she understands them. He half suspects she's begging for a drama. She'd like to see him striding up the aisle in black cape and beard, ranting about just cause and impediment.

Except the ceremony will not take place in a church, and crimson-lined capes and Sir-Percy tactics don't sit well in a registry office.

He spends the day of the wedding checking over a restaurant he's thinking of buying. As soon as he heard it was coming on the market he got in touch with Rickie and invited him to lunch.

'I have to hand it to you, Adam, the way you've turned this place around, it's amazing. I never could have done it myself. And as for this,' he flicked a napkin at the murals. 'Hitching that artist to your wagon was a master stroke.'

'I'm glad you approve.'

'Certainly I approve.' He raised his wine glass and considered Adam over its rim. 'But you haven't brought me here to talk about the past, have you now?'

They took their time over lunch. Figures present, past and projected were bandied back and forth. Kay would have been in her element. Rickie scraped his spoon across a goblet of apricot sorbet. 'Well, it sounds very promising,' he said. Adam waited. Rickie liked to orchestrate his concessions for maximum effect. 'I have a suggestion,' he continued at last. 'How about you go ahead and do the legwork – look at their figures, check out the equipment, the clientele and the area. Let me know what you find and then, if the scheme's a runner, I'll reinvest.'

'I was hoping you'd say that.'

'You'll need a coherent theme, of course. Make a splash, stir up some publicity. Can you rope in the artist again?'

'It might be difficult. There's been a change of circumstances . . .'

'I have every faith in you. You'll sort it, I'm sure.'

Adam took his time viewing the new restaurant, checking out the premises and cross-questioning the staff. He lunched with the vendor and spent the afternoon going through the books.

And all the while, in a parallel realm, he watched Eleanor's wedding. Not the registry office wedding, but an alternative ceremony in her abandoned church with the grisly candles and Holy Ghost dropping birdlime on Simon's shoulder. He saw Eleanor and Simon side by side, and a profusion of flowers, and a gold ring slipped on to a long finger.

Back at Jangles he went over his plans with Tom. He intended to put Tom in charge of the new venture. 'Do some costings,' he said. 'Put together a specimen menu. You'll be running the show, so I want you to have some input.'

'This is great, Adam. You won't regret it.'

'I don't intend to. As for this evening, can you cope on your own? I've some business to attend to.'

He has no business to attend to, he simply wishes to be alone. He tests the celeriac with a skewer. It's ready. He pounds it with butter and lemon juice and black pepper. Why hadn't Eleanor confided in him about Chris? She hadn't exactly lied, but she'd told a selective version of the truth that invited him to make assumptions.

'I thought it was brave, ending it like that,' said Jess. 'She was really cut up about it. She loved him – God knows why – but she couldn't take any more of his shit. There's only so much prevarication and rejection a person can stomach. 'The funny thing is, it was Chris who couldn't cope. Six months after he'd gone back to his wife he turned up late one night, shouting, waking the whole street. Eleanor had worked too hard to go taking him back like that, with no guarantees and every chance that in a few weeks his guilt would kick in and he'd be off. So she told him to bugger off. "Go back to your wife," she said. "It's all you're fit for. You don't know how to live."'

'And he took her seriously?'

'I don't think so. There has to be more to it than that. I don't suppose we'll ever know the real reason. When they found him he'd been in the water for days. It must have been awful. I don't envy the wife – but it doesn't excuse what she did. Can you believe it? She turned up, blaming Ellie, and Ellie – well, she'd already started down that path, and she believed her. I think she still believes it.

Like I told you, it's one of the reasons she's marrying Simon. He's her penance. He's what she deserves.'

'Jessica, that is pure melodrama.'

'Melodramatic? Me? How dare you? Shall I tell you what she said when I asked her about you? "Oh no,"' she mimicked Eleanor's horror. '"I could never be with Adam. I'm jinxed, Jess, and anyway, he's far too good for me."'

He opens the oven to check on the peppers. They are ready. So is the lamb. He puts the meat in the warming oven and adds a dash of marsala to the juices in the pan. He opens a bottle of Fleurie.

At which point, Jessica arrives. He is not expecting her. She's still in her wedding gear, a grey suit and green tights. In the crook of her arm she cradles a bottle of wine. 'I thought you might appreciate some company,' she says. 'No strings, I promise.' She sniffs the air. 'My, that smells good. Any chance of a bite? I'm starving.'

It's easy to stretch the meal; when working at home he always cooks too much. Jessica wolfs her portion, then finishes his. He says, 'I take it the wedding buffet wasn't up to much.'

'Asparagus rolls and stuffed apricots at Farraday's – it's not what I call food.'

He opens another bottle of wine. 'So how did it go, the wedding of the year?'

'I kept hoping you'd turn up and put a stop to it.'

'I thought I'd leave the drama to an expert.'

'Me?' She laughs. 'And Ellie.'

'Meaning?'

'The bride wore black. Can you believe it? We went out a couple of weeks ago and bought this stunning little cerise number – and then she turns up looking like Lily Munster. But you should have seen Babs. Babs wore white. Eleanor's mother – you know? She had this wonderful white suit and a white hat and an overblown white rose in her lapel. Did you ever meet her? She's great. You'd love her.'

'Pity she couldn't talk Eleanor out of this.'

'She probably tried. But if Babs says don't marry Simon and don't wear black, Ellie'll go straight out and do just that. She can be a bit perverse where Babs is concerned; she says she's too bloody interesting.'

'What about Simon? How did he perform?'

'Nervy. Defensive. Wanted to know if you were coming. Probably hoping you'd pop up and stop the proceedings. I was tempted myself, but I don't think "Simon's a little shit" has any legal standing.'

There is no pudding, only fruit. Jessica nibbles on the grapes and Adam makes coffee. They go through to the living room and Jessica returns to the subject of the wedding. It disturbs her as much as it does him. 'I meant what I said, you know. It really was like Simon wanted someone to stop it, like he never really meant to marry her, as if the thing had run away with him. Weird, right?' She stops. He places the tray on the coffee table. 'I'm talking too much, aren't I? The thing is, you see, I think we'll both find ourselves out in the cold after this. I can't see Simon being all that chuffed at having us nosing around in his marriage.'

'I have no intention of "nosing around" in anyone's marriage.'

'Okay, but you know what I'm getting at. They're a couple now. You and me, Adam, we've got to get on with our lives.'

He lights up a cigarette. 'Jessica, d'you mind if we change the subject? I've had a bellyful of Simon Whitburn.'

'I know you have. Sorry.' She touches his shoulder as she crosses the room. 'How about some music? What have you got?' She shuffles through his CDs and laughs. 'There's a lot of Puccini here, Adam . . . and Donizetti. Let's have *Lucia*.' She snaps open the case and flips the disc into the machine. 'You really are a terrible romantic, aren't you?' She flops on to the sofa and hooks her arm in his. 'Not the wishy-washy sort who has an ideal of the world and ignores all discrepancies, but the thinking variety. The kind of man who measures the ideal against reality and sees all the gaps and broken bits, but still won't give up.' She squeezes his arm. 'Am I right?'

He looks down to where her hand rests on his arm. The skin is flaked and cracked. The upholstery twine has made red weals in the flesh. Suddenly he sees Eleanor puncturing her thumb with a broad-bladed needle – and is with her again in the old church, by the light of the candles, his face in her hair, the feel of her and smell of her. And Simon also.

What sort of a romantic is he – if at all?

He rests his head against the sofa and closes his eyes. Jessica has described him accurately. It's why he's in this mess. He lays his hand on hers. He feels its cuts and calluses. 'You're right,' he says. 'I am. It's why I had to let her go.'

19

Chris loved the view from Hungerford Bridge. Or so he said, though why believe this, when so much else was false?

But Hungerford Bridge is important to her and so this morning, the morning of her wedding, Eleanor goes there to say goodbye.

Every Friday Chris had a business meeting south of the river. She'd go with him as far as the middle of the bridge and they'd stand and exclaim over the view. Rain or shine, every time, they'd gaze along the river towards the city and St Paul's, and she would insist the light was such that, despite modern intrusions, she could still sense the spirit of Canaletto.

And Chris would laugh and nuzzle her hair, and she would feel the cool trace of his lips against her temple.

It is a long time since she's paused on this spot. She considers it a symbol of her new-found strength that she is able to come here.

The first year after his death had almost been easy. She had to cope, and so she did cope. But something happened with the passing of the first anniversary. Nothing obvious. An intangible something, a dropped stitch. Her life began to unravel. No. Not her life. Life is external. This was something inside, so deep she couldn't locate it. Couldn't catch the stitch.

A sense of dislocation was how it began. She would lose herself in the middle of a conversation, then return several sentences on. A day might move from wind and sun to sleet and gloom, and she not notice the transition.

Chris's wife said his death was her fault. Perhaps. Maybe if she'd let him in that night he wouldn't have gone to the bridge. But if not then, it probably would have happened some other time. Chris was selfish, he lacked courage.

It was not her fault. Had his marriage ended because of her, she would have stood by him. He would have come through. But he hadn't trusted her. Oh, he'd come back in the end, like a thief in the night, treating her as a last resort, but it was too late. She didn't want him by default.

At first anger and indignation carried her through, but then she woke one dead of night with her throat glut-full of panic. She scrabbled for matches to light a candle. With light came understanding. His wife had been right after all: it was her fault. She'd said she'd stand by him and he'd come to her, and she had turned her back. She was selfish, it was she who lacked courage.

I am to blame.

She remembers her terror, the way the scale of life changed. The world became a bigger place. Walls and ceilings flew outwards and upwards. People and buildings grew taller, her viewpoint lower, until all she could see were the undersides of chins, the bulge of a crotch and a damp gusset.

But the environment hadn't changed. It was her. She'd become smaller, less visible. Soon she'd be a speck of dust on a strange man's jacket, to be dismissed with the flick of a hand, sent soaring through the air and over the rail and into the black river.

How had she come to be there, on the bridge, at night?

The world turns. The scale adjusts. She's the right size again, but still nobody sees her.

She stands at the rail and thrills to the view and the night-time river running black as tar, to the bustle and noise and the fairy-city loops of light flooding from the banks.

It is November, bitterly cold and clear. The air is black glass, reflecting the light and sending the sounds – the hum and cough of traffic, the see-saw of voices up and down, loud and soft, shrill and deep – rebounding back and forth from bank to bank.

So many people. They go round her and over her and through her as if she doesn't exist. She wants to call them, tug at their sleeves, but she can't speak, can't move. She watches them. They are mostly couples – men and women, men and men, women and women – foreigners on a cheap winter break, provincials down for a mid-week visit.

And Eleanor, whose lover died because of her.

So many people heading across the bridge to spend the evening listening to music or watching actors play let's pretend. She lifts her head. She can move again, and so she joins with the flow, mingling unnoticed in their company.

She walks along the promenade. On her right is a glittering palace, and crammed behind the yellow glare of its windows, the people gather and raise their glasses and kiss the cheeks of new arrivals.

Despite the cold, some linger in the open. A man extinguishes a cigarette, clumping it against the paving with his heel. Closer to the river, a girl in a teddy-bear coloured coat over a yellow and red dress, switches on a portable cassette machine. The music moans. Indian or Turkish – a continuous wail, a needle stitching the fractured air – a long glittering needle of sound to mend her broken mind.

The girl starts to dance. Her hands explore exotic shapes in the air. Her hips take up the threnody and begin to swing and she starts to twirl and her skirt flies out and its uneven hem is studded with bells that chatter and match the tap of her heels until one or two, then three or four people stop to watch.

The people see her. They do not see Eleanor. She moves on.

Further along the promenade, still within reach of the strains of the music, Eleanor starts to dance. She's awkward at first. The music is unfamiliar and her shoes are uncomfortable, their heels too high. She kicks them off. They soar in an arc. One falls in a clatter on the pavement, the other goes into the river.

You see, Chris? Your wife threw flowers on your grave, but a shoe in the river is more true to us.

She hears the bark of her laughter and her toes curl against the paving, exploring the alien texture of the concrete. She moves, swaying just as the girl sways. She gathers the rhythm until it becomes a part of her. She flings away her hat, and then her crimson scarf. For an unreasonable moment it hangs like a banner, frozen above her head.

And now she's getting the feel of this. She no longer holds the rhythm, the rhythm holds her. It fills her up, artery and vein, tissue and bone. Her body moves of its own accord. She risks a twirl. It feels good. A man stops to watch. She bites her lip. She tastes blood. She continues to dance and as she does so she reaches behind to unfasten her plait. She throws herself into a violent spin that sends her black hair flying out to merge with the night.

More people have gathered. Faster she goes, and faster. She is aware of herself, of the structure of her body, muscle and bone, the tabasco sting of her blood, and the heat – she's so hot. She throws off her coat and the crowd grows, and she spins again till the faces blur and the eyes, blue brown and green, become a single speckled eye.

Oh the joy of it, and the pain – the physical pain in her head and her bleeding feet, and the cleansing pain as the centrifugal force sends all her misery and grief and her guilt flying away across the city. She's spinning so fast that she is no longer attached to the physical world. The needle of the music snags the thread, drawing her upwards, spinning like a bobbin high, high, high above the pavement and the faces of the people are turned to her and she reaches towards them, but cannot touch them.

And the music stops. The air is cold. The thread snaps and she drops to the ground and her knees buckle and her hair settles round her bare shoulders, clouding her breasts, and her skin prickles with the cold and the people advance towards her.

Try as she might, she can remember nothing after that.

Eighteen months on, she still cannot remember. On this spring day, her wedding day, she gazes down at the water glittering in the morning sunlight, and thinks of Chris and his weaknesses and her own failings. She tells him she's sorry. She tells Adam she's sorry.

And then she turns her back, and heads for home, and Simon.

Dark Tide Rising

It's high summer and Adam is clearing his garden. Birds chatter and insects buzz and the past is reduced to a faint shadow. His only thought is the task in hand. Polruan. Eden. This is where he belongs.

His land rises steeply from the road, but to the rear it drops gently to the boundary hedge. Nowhere is he able to work on level ground. He is amazed at the degree of physical contortion this requires, and at how readily his body adapts to these conditions. He is much fitter than when he arrived. It's not that he doesn't feel the strain, but he has learnt to accept it. Pain defines.

The sun is high and unbearably hot. He pulls off his tee-shirt. Over the past weeks his work-hardened body has moved from pallid to crimson to caramel. The sea breeze makes his skin smart.

The garden is a tangle of roses. There is an astonishing variety of bushes and trees; a rambler scrambles over and round a dilapidated trellis arch. It must have been spectacular in its prime.

When he told Pam he intended to clear the garden, she was horrified. 'You can't. We can salvage something, surely?' He let her take a batch of cuttings. 'Who knows? They might take.'

'I doubt it.'

'You're such a pessimist.'

'I'm a realist.' He hesitates. Jessica says he's a romantic, and she's right. A man with his feet planted in the real world would not have done a bunk to Cornwall. 'Anyway,' there's a blustering note to his voice as he tries to cover his confusion, 'aren't roses more complicated than that? Don't they have to be grafted, or something?' Pam doesn't know. She's no more a gardener than he is, she just hates the idea of outright destruction.

Since neither of them has the necessary skill, eradication is the only solution. The roses have gone untended for years and have degenerated to a tangle of deadwood and suckers. He will hack them down, dig out the roots and burn them.

He hefts his billhook and takes a vicious swing at a particularly stubborn tuber.

'Still hellbent on murder, I see.' Pam stands with hands on hips, all dressed up in a flowery dress and a straw hat. She doesn't look like Pam, she looks like Pam pretending to be someone else.

'I'm an unfeeling bastard, you know that.'

He lights a cigarette. Pam unlocks her car. The blast of heat makes her wince and step back. 'I thought as much the first day I saw you.'

'The eyes are such a giveaway.'

'And thin lips speak volumes.' She shades her eyes and peers up at the cottage. 'It's coming along nicely, your Eden. Almost habitable. Do I see curtains?'

'Curtains, towels, sheets on the bed . . .'

'Your wife should be arriving soon.' He looks away. 'You can't keep putting it off. Winter isn't a very nice time to move in.'

'I suppose not.'

'So, when's it to be?'

'I send regular progress reports. It's up to her.'

'I'm really looking forward to meeting her.' She waits. He has started to confide in Pam. Not in detail, but a snippet here, a fragment there. It's a game. Her aim is to find out as much as possible without asking direct questions. This is the only rule. They might strike up a round at any time, in any place. Over the months the urge to tell has grown steadily stronger.

Suddenly his past, which had begun to feel as though it belonged to someone else, is before him again. He says, 'I've been up since daybreak, I'm whacked. I made a fresh batch of lemonade last night. Good and strong, the way you like it.'

'That's nice.' Pam runs her hand over the bonnet of the car. The metal is hot. She examines her palm. 'But I have to play grown-ups today.' She lifts her skirt between thumb and forefinger and gives an exaggerated twirl. 'I'm driving to Oxford.'

'Why?' The car is cooler now and she tosses her hat on to the passenger seat. 'Who do you know in Oxford?'

Pam laughs and jangles her car keys. 'How come the "direct question" rule never applies to you?'

As soon as she's gone he goes indoors. He sluices his face and neck with cold water and pours a glass of lemonade. He's tempted to add a dash of gin.

So what's Pam up to, off to Oxford, dressed to the nines? Maybe she's got a man in tow. He's never asked. It isn't like her to be mysterious.

'One mystery at a time is all Polruan can handle,' she tells him. 'And just at the moment, that's you, Adam Mason, coming down here with your town ways . . .'

But Polruan does have another mystery. It lurks on the cliff-top, in the rocks and in the sky. It is a mystery even Pam doesn't suspect.

She should. She was here. She may have seen her, spoken to her. To both of them.

The idea takes hold – that they'd had a conversation of which he is ignorant. He cannot bear it. He must ask her. The moment she returns. He cannot believe that she has not mentioned such an important incident.

He drains his glass. The lemon is tart and satisfying.

She hasn't mentioned it because the conversation never happened.

Or it had, but she suspects. Yes. That's it. She knows who he is and why he's here – but she wants him to tell her himself.

He goes back to his roses. The idea that in healing Eden he might heal himself is turning out to be more effective than he'd ever imagined. Nor is it just his mental and emotional health that is improving. He has changed physically. Until a few months ago his most strenuous activities were chopping carrots and counting his takings. His first weeks in Polruan left his muscles flayed and torn, but they have mended in a stronger configuration. He is leaner now, fitter. Added to which, he is able to think of the past without flinching. Almost.

Some of the tangled roses have managed to bloom. Gasping through the deadwood and the weeds, the flowers seem disorganized, the petals randomly applied. They barely look like roses.

Babs had worn a white rose at Eleanor's wedding. Jessica had been wrong to think he might have influenced the outcome. Eleanor wasn't so easily swayed. Once set upon this path, nothing was likely to shift her. Okay, there were times when she seemed indecisive but, like so much else about her, it was an illusion, perhaps even a deliberate illusion. She liked to pretend that her actions arose organically from the situation. If she could establish that there was no deliberate intent on her part, then she wasn't to blame when the situation went out of control.

And things did spiral out of control with alarming regularity where Eleanor was concerned. Only now does he understand it had little to do with circumstance, and everything to do with Eleanor. Indecision pursued with such single-minded dedication is itself an exercise of will.

Pam returns late on Saturday afternoon. She parks her car in the lane and the doors open, and two noisy children tumble out and tear across to her cottage. The wooden gate crashes on its hinges. Pam shouts for them to take care.

The little girl is about seven, the boy a year or two younger. Pam waves to Adam. 'Come over,' she calls. 'Come and meet my grandchildren. I'll put the kettle on.'

He retrieves his tee-shirt from the brambles and follows her. The children run in at the front door, straight through the cottage, out the back door and into the garden. They race round and round the enclosed space, snuffling away like puppies exploring new territory.

'Alice and Peter.' Pam points first to the girl and then to the boy, as if Adam might have trouble telling them apart. She opens the fridge. 'I can make tea if you like, but personally I fancy something cold. I've beer in here, or you can pop back home for some of your lemonade.'

'Beer's fine.' She hands him a can and he snaps the ring-pull. 'I had no idea,' he says, gesturing to the children.

'That I'm a grandmother?'

'I didn't know you were a mother. I don't think you've ever mentioned your children.'

'Just the one, a son. Anyway, I'm more interested in your past than my own. And let's be honest, so are you.'

'You think I'm selfish?'

She pats his arm. 'Probably with good cause. Let's settle for preoccupied.' She reaches a couple of glasses from a cupboard. 'Here we go, we can't expect the great chef to drink from a can.'

'Pam, I'm sorry. I have been selfish.'

'Don't be silly. My past isn't that interesting. William has his own life. We were never close. He's married, he's got two kids, and he lives near Oxford. End of story.'

'You don't see much of him?' She shakes her head. 'Oxford's not a million miles away.'

'He doesn't like coming down here – wonders why I have to live in the back of beyond, and I confess I bridle at having to make all the running.'

'It still seems a shame.'

'You're getting all sentimental on me, aren't you? I can feel it coming. Mothers and sons. I'm sorry, Adam, you'll probably think this a terrible thing to say, but I don't much like William. He works in computers. We have nothing in common.'

'But surely . . .'

'He takes after his father, and his father was a dead duck years ago.'

'But the children?'

'Ah. Cantankerous and eccentric I may be, but I do have my uses. William and Anne like to take holidays in places that aren't terribly suitable for young children. It's Egypt this year. Tough on the kids, but I get to spend some time with them.'

In the garden, Alice is gathering stones and making a pattern on the grass. Every so often Peter jabs them with a stick and disrupts her design. She fends him off. They fight.

Adam glances at Pam. 'Shouldn't you intervene?'

'If I do, I'll be playing referee for the next fortnight. They must sort out their own battles. It's a hard world they're growing up in. Don't look so stern, Adam. I see you disapprove of my parenting techniques.'

'It's not that —'

'I daresay you have methods of your own.'

Indirect question. 'I don't have much experience,' he says. 'I was an only child.' He pauses. The statement is a lie. It is almost a lie. He feels her watching him. It's as if she knows.

You never get over a death. You think you do. You sift it down deep in the memory's subsoil and year upon year you build new structures on top of it. You get on with life. But the life you have grows out of your past and, like it or not, his own past includes his brother's death.

Right from the start his mother knew her baby would be a boy.

She was thin as a bean when she sat Adam on her lap and told him he was to have a brother. 'His name's Robert,' she said, as if he were just in the next room. 'Bobby.'

'Baby-Bobby, Bobby-Baby . . .' Adam chanted. It was a silly name. He didn't want a brother. He liked things as they were.

When Bobby died, he was glad.

It seems insane from this distance. What a callous little boy he must have been. He talked to Gran about it shortly before she died. 'You mustn't torture yourself,' she said, pouring the tea. 'It's perfectly natural.'

'I don't see what's natural about it. It's evil.'

'Now I'm sorry, Adam, but that's silly and self-indulgent. You really should know better, at your age.' She offered him a plate of chocolate digestives. It was intended to bring him back to earth, but it brought him up short in quite another way. The biscuits had come from a packet. Gran was getting old. Not for all the world would he allow her to read his thoughts. He smiled and thanked her, and took two biscuits.

'The thing is,' she returned him to the subject that had brought him here. 'It's not as if you knew Bobby and willed him to die. He barely existed for you. Everybody told you he was coming, then everybody said he was gone. That's all you knew.'

But he knew his mother's grief. And his father's. Although they never met, Bobby changed his life.

When the ambulance took his mother to the hospital, Gran came to look after Adam. That's when it took root, his love of food and cooking. Bobby's death, and his parents' trauma, fixed that time in his mind.

Life is a branch that might sprout from any point. Because of Bobby, it sprouted here, in his mother's kitchen, at Gran's side.

Everything he has done in his life, originates here.

Even Eleanor. If he'd had to tend his baby brother, maybe he'd have taken better care of her. There were times when she'd come to him, bleeding and broken in body and mind – a wounded animal he'd nourished and healed.

And then he lost it. Again and again he proved himself incapable of sustaining the effort.

Because Bobby died, Adam has never grown up. The process of

domestication limits a cat's development, locking it into permanent kittenhood. Just so has he remained a child. He is a man who has never learnt to nurture another being.

Until now. Eden. The white stucco glitters in the sun. The windows wink at him. He has healed this house, and he has healed himself. Soon he will turn these new skills to his marriage.

Dust to dust. The decayed remains of human life and animals and plants contribute to the fecundity of the earth. So too can the deaths of the past enrich the future.

If he believed in a God, he would go to St Saviour's and offer a prayer. Instead he goes to the headland. The sea is perfectly calm. A thin thread, like silver wire, marks its meeting with the sky. A ship stands at anchor. It is very still. Unreal.

He closes his eyes. Although close to the point where the cliff drops into the sea, he has no fear. He is not the man he was six months ago.

The peace is broken. The thread snaps. The screech of the gull is the cry of a child. He has a long way to go. His dead are not yet at peace.

1

'So what about it, Adam, will you take me to this private view, or not?' Jessica's voice shivers with enthusiasm. She has tracked him down at Jangles-Two and Tom has vacated his office so that Adam can take the call in private. He wedges the handset against his shoulder and leans back in the chair. It is a modern chair with a padded back. It swivels. Fixtures and fittings. He cannot quite get used to the new regime. When Rickie retired from Jangles, he'd quickly set about marking the territory as his own. At first he concentrated on the little things, rearranging the table layout and shunting the desk from one side of the office to the other. Not until Simon's mural was his identity established once and for all.

But Jangles-Two is different. It both is, and is not, his. Tom's desk is orderly, and whereas Adam's provisional menus are usually scribbled in his personal shorthand on whatever scraps of paper happen to be lying around, Tom's menu for the following day is displayed on the computer screen. Adam doodles as he reads. Tom is offering a set price meal of wild mushrooms with tarragon and cream, followed by sautéd calves' liver with red cabbage, and an autumn fruit salad with fromage frais and honey.

'Adam?' He has lost the thread of their conversation; his mind is a market stall jumble of red cabbage and raspberries. 'Are you listening?' A radio crackles in the background. Jessica must be ringing from her workshop. 'The exhibition . . .'

'Private views really aren't my sort of thing.'

'But you don't even know what the subject is. It's not paintings this time, it's sculpture. There's this woman called Andrea Harding – apparently she had a show at Farraday's the first time Ellie went there. She says she's fantastic.'

'And this is Eleanor's idea, is it?'

'No Adam, it's mine.'

'I know nothing about art.' He fixes his attention on the blue computer screen. The white cursor flickers impatiently. 'I'm a chef,' he says. Calves' liver and red cabbage. He must remind Tom to feature the fact that the cabbage is braised with wine vinegar and red peppercorns.

'Well I shall go, whatever you decide.'

'Fine.' Tom's menu taunts him. There's no need for consultation; he'll add the extra ingredients to the screen himself.

'What are you doing, what's that tapping?'

'Nothing. Sorry.' He pushes the keyboard away.

'Adam, how long are you going to keep this up? You can't go on avoiding her forever.'

'Why not?'

'Because it's childish. Is that really what you want – never to see her again?'

'Yes. No . . . I don't know.' He swivels his chair to turn his back to the screen. 'If I'd wanted to see her I could have used the Jangles-Two mural as an excuse, but I didn't.'

When the time came to commission the mural, he'd arranged to meet with Brian Farraday on Eleanor's afternoon off. Brian was sceptical at first. 'I'll do what I can, Adam, but I doubt even I can pull off the same stunt a second time. You know what Simon's like, he's still pretty ambivalent about his murals.'

'Will you at least talk to him?'

'Certainly I will, I'm simply warning you that I can't guarantee the outcome.'

'Well, make sure he knows I'm not expecting a freebie this time.'

'Ah, is that so.' Brian steepled his fingers and leant back in his chair. 'Now that puts a different complexion on it altogether. I had assumed we were talking the same terms as last time, but the prospect of a fee could well turn Simon's head. He's having a conversion job done on his flat – structural stuff, enlarged windows, roof lights, that sort of thing. He's even made part of it into a temporary exhibition space. Eleanor has sold him the idea of having open days. By Simon's standards it's a hell of an investment. He won't see a return for a while, and that's your bottom line, Adam – Simon needs the cash.'

Their approach worked. Simon was first tempted, then seduced by Adam's offer. The negotiations were completed through Brian. Eleanor was not present at his meetings with Simon, and he kept well away from the restaurant while the work was in progress.

He smiles and reassures himself. He doesn't need to keep avoiding her. He has passed the test; he has nothing left to prove.

But it isn't true, he admits to himself much later that night. He does have something to prove. He hasn't seen Eleanor in almost a year, not because he's good at avoiding her, but because they have not been fated to meet. The fact is, he has courted the possibility of a chance encounter.

No. Even that's a lie. Chance would mean finding her somewhere neither of them customarily go, whereas on several occasions – and more frequently with each passing month – he has made deliberate excursions into Eleanor's territory.

Eleanor's favourite places. Together they had fed the feral cats, so now he goes there alone. Tipping out a bag of kitchen scraps, he stands back to watch the scrawny, infested creatures feed. Eleanor said sometimes volunteers corral the cats and take them away to be neutered. A tabby with bulging eyes and jutting hindquarters glances over its shoulder. Reassured by Adam's stillness, it returns to its food, burying its runny nose in a mixture of lamb bones and chicken fricassee.

He also tried the church. He went there on different days, and at different times. The first occasion was back in the summer. He was self-conscious about breaking in. Eleanor had always taken responsibility for gaining entry. Like the stray tabby, he glanced over his shoulder to check for danger, then eased back the board and stepped inside.

The panel sprang into place behind him. Holy Ghost flapped up above, sending down a benediction of feathers and dried bird shit. Guttered stubs of burnt-out candles lined the altar rail. He's startled to find evidence of another intruder. Footprints in the dust. Footprints leading to and from the chancel. Although quite small, they are too large to be those of a child. A woman, then. Eleanor. And only the one set, so she hadn't brought Simon. Not recently, at least. Had she ever brought him?

This place is special to her. She had shared it with him and he has no reason to doubt that she would share it with her husband.

Husband. He hates the word. It doesn't fit.

No, if Simon had been here, he'd know it, he'd be able to smell him. He sniffs the air like a tracker dog. His hackles fail to rise.

So if Eleanor was here, it was for a reason. Favourite places – where you go when the world gets too much. Her marriage had driven her here.

How dare he presume so much. Life goes on. She eats and drinks, goes to work and comes home again. And sometimes she comes here. End of story. No big deal.

And anyway, who's to say the footprints are hers?

He went to the church again last Sunday. The air was heavy with newly extinguished candles. In the hollowed stubs on the altar rail, the wax was in the process of solidifying. It had a tantalizing, translucent quality. He had only just missed her. The air he breathed had circulated in her lungs only minutes before. If he left now, if he ran, he might catch her.

2

The gallery is packed when they arrive. Jessica clings to his arm and it occurs to him that, physically at least, they are as mismatched as Eleanor and Simon.

Brian spots them; he waves and heads in their direction. 'Great,' he says. 'Fantastic. Dragged you here kicking and screaming, did she, Adam? Good to see you. Now, let's see about getting you a drink.'

They follow him. Jessica is still holding his arm. He concentrates on Brian's broad back, looking neither to left nor right. He does not want Eleanor thinking his first instinct is to seek her out.

'I advise the red.' Brian hands them each a glass. 'I have to say, I'm a mite disappointed with the white. I must get Eleanor to speak to our suppliers. Perhaps you could recommend someone, Adam?'

'With pleasure.' His response is automatic. Brian, like Jessica, seems keen for him to re-establish a dialogue with Eleanor.

Jessica cranes around the room and says, 'You've pulled in a great crowd tonight.'

'That's Eleanor for you. One way or another, she knows how to whip up a storm. She's got a genuine instinct, has Eleanor. She's like me in that. It's a sort of sixth sense for judging works of art and the people that make them, the people that buy them. I knew she had the knack the moment I laid eyes on her.'

Adam swirls his wine in its glass. 'This is starting to sound like a sales pitch.'

'I think he sounds more like a lover.'

'Chance, Jess my sweet, would be a fine thing.' Brian pats her shoulder. 'Now see what you've done. Adam's looking all worried and green about the gills. Come on,' he takes them by the arm, 'let me introduce you to Andrea.'

Andrea Harding, who is small, round and sixty-ish, is deep in conversation with Eleanor. Eleanor is wearing a white dress with a scarf like a crimson slash across its shoulder.

When Eleanor glances up Adam sees at once that something is not as it should be.

Eleanor turns towards them. Her spine is stiff. The movement is jagged. She glances at Jessica, but doesn't smile. Jessica had predicted this coolness between them and he knows how much it must hurt. He gives her arm a little squeeze and feels the grateful nudge of her shoulder.

'Eleanor, would you look who's here,' Brian is as effusive as ever. 'And Andrea – this is Adam Mason. Eleanor's husband did the murals for his restaurants. You may have heard of them? Jangles-One and Jangles-Two? You've simply got to see them. In fact, I can't think why I haven't taken you there already. Now, where was I? Ah yes, this is Jessica Grant —'

'I revamped the chairs for Jangles,' she grins. 'Not quite in the same league as Simon's murals, of course. I must say, Andrea, I've been dying to see your work. Ellie's told me so much about it – and not a word of a lie, it's a fantastic show.'

'Thank you.' Andrea Harding stands with her hands folded tidily on her stomach. Her face is soft and friendly, but when she speaks her lips barely part.

'That one over there, for example.' Jessica points to a polished stone egg balanced on a brushed steel scoop. 'What a wonderful contrast, and the textures . . .'

'That's precisely what I love so much about them,' says Eleanor. 'I know touching them can be damaging, but surely their tactile nature is part of what they're about.'

'I think people should touch,' says Andrea. 'If the acids from our bodies corrode them, so much the better. To me, the sculptures are alive. If they are changed by your touch, then they live for you as well.' She stops. This is her longest speech so far. She is embarrassed.

'That's so refreshing. Galleries can be stuffy places sometimes, can't they? Not this one, of course.' Jessica laughs and squeezes Brian's arm. 'Andrea, I want to take a closer look. Will you come with me? I'd love you to talk me through it.'

Jessica's ploy is less than subtle. There is something going on here but although Adam senses the currents and tensions, he cannot identify their source.

The others drift away, but Eleanor remains. She is close enough to touch. He can think of nothing to say. If he waits long enough, one of the guests will doubtless claim her. Time passes, but nobody comes. Seconds become minutes, minutes expand into hours. His time is out of sync with that of the other guests. This is not credible, he must not give in. There is a scale to language; the space words occupy can be measured.

Turning towards her, he speaks mechanically. 'Eleanor. It's good to see you. How are you?'

Her face is utterly without expression, and as smooth as Andrea's sculpture. Except the sculpture has character, and Eleanor's face is bland, a pebble worn smooth by the relentless wash of the sea.

His flesh aches to the drag of the tide, to the undertow tug and rush of shingle.

'Fine,' she replies. 'I'm fine.'

'And Simon?'

'He's fine too.'

'He's not here tonight?'

'No. Other people's art . . .' She gives an awkward lift of her shoulders.

'I was sorry you couldn't come to the opening. The new restaurant.' His words snag. 'Both of you.'

'It didn't seem appropriate.'

'No.'

'And Simon, you know how touchy he is about the murals.'

'It's a shame. He's very good.'

'Yes.' She straightens her shoulders. It takes a visible effort. 'And what about you?' Her smile is a hard, straight line. 'Is the restaurant a success?'

'It seems to be going well. Tom's in charge of Two, and I've taken on a new manager for Jangles-One. She's very good. Her name's Yvonne. Yvonne Beck.'

Brian approaches with a client, a tall man with a bush of receding grey hair. Like the child on the pedalo lake whose time is up, Adam silently begs for one more go, a final circuit of the island . . .

'Lunch,' he speaks in a hurried whisper. He must persuade her before Brian arrives. 'Let's have lunch. Soon.' Although her face is still blank, something flickers behind her eyes. Whatever it is, it gives him hope. 'Let's make it very soon,' he says, touching her arm. 'I'll ring you.'

3

They take a picnic to Holland Park. It's October and rather cool, so they have the place to themselves. The day is sunny but cloudy. When the clouds pass over their patch of grass, Eleanor shivers. When the sun is restored, she laughs and stretches her neck to its warmth.

He has hollowed out a cob loaf and packed it with air dried ham and mozzarella, salad with herbs, olives and olive oil. He cuts her a wedge and wraps it in a white linen napkin. He'd been wary of suggesting the picnic – it seemed rather intimate – but to meet in a restaurant was too formal, too structured.

They eat slowly and sip their wine and discuss the restaurant, her job, Brian and Jessica. Not Simon. There is so much to say, but he's scared he'll frighten her away. He watches her greedily. He longs to touch her, but she holds herself aloof. This denial of their intimate past is unspeakably cruel.

He cannot bear it. His lips form words, but no sound comes. Forbidden words.

Eleanor wipes the last of the olive oil from her fingers and checks her watch. 'I should go,' she says.

A light breeze rustles the dying leaves on their branches. 'Not yet.'

'I have a meeting at two-thirty.'

'An artist?'

'Yes.'

'Will you tell Simon?'

'Tell him what?'

'That we met.'

She bites her lip. 'I don't think so, do you? That would be asking for trouble.'

'It would be truthful.'

She stands up and brushes the grass from her skirt. Looking around, taking in the trees and the grass, and the bisecting paths, she changes the subject. 'Do you remember the squirrels?' She smiles. 'Squiggles.'

'I remember.' He stands beside her. So close. There is a tightness round her eyes, and faint shadows that he suspects would be darker were it not for the efficient application of make-up. He tastes her breath. The rare intimacy of the moment paralyses him. It takes only the slightest inclination of her head for her to touch her lips to his.

It is the merest, most delicate contact – and as powerful as the sudden return of a forgotten perfume or flavour. Violets and lemon zest and olives. His fingers close round her wrist.

She stiffens.

'Eleanor?'

She shakes him off, and starts to walk away. He notes again a slight awkwardness, a difference in gait, a loss of fluidity. He calls her. She takes two more steps, then waits. 'Tell me . . .' He feels giddy. He stands on the brink. The cliff is sheer. 'Eleanor . . .'

'No,' she whispers. 'You tell me.'

'What?'

'About you and Jess.'

He stumbles back from the cliff-edge. 'There's nothing to tell. You know all there is. You tell each other everything.'

Women do that, they confide. His culinary skills and his dick. Isn't that what Jessica said?

'I don't see so much of her as I did, and anyway, she won't talk about you.'

'I see.' He is about to give up, but then it hits him that Eleanor is jealous. 'Jessica is a good friend,' he explains. 'I've certainly needed a friend these last months.'

'Is that all?'

'Yes.'

'Only you should know Jess can be a bit hit-and-run when it comes to men.'

'I'll consider myself warned.'

'Good, I'll stop worrying, then.' She forces a smile. 'And now I really must get back.'

'In a minute.' He catches her arm. She winces. 'You've had your question, now it's my turn. Why did you do it, Eleanor?'

'Do what? I didn't do anything. Let me go.'

'Simon.' Her head jerks and her plait skates across her back. 'Why did you marry him?'

'I came back from Cornwall . . . I had things to tell you, but you wouldn't listen to me. You jumped to conclusions . . .'

'Is it any wonder? You keep me at arm's-length, then let a complete stranger in. It hurt, Eleanor. It bloody hurt.'

'I know.'

'Then why?'

'It just happened.'

'You just happened to marry the man? This marriage didn't appear out of thin air. You willed it, you made a choice. I want to know why.'

'Why?' she repeats. Her face is white, the skin round her eyes and mouth is pleated and fragile. 'I'll tell you why. Because I recognized in him a part of myself. Because I needed him. Just as I needed you. It isn't a question of why I married him; it's the question of why you let me.'

She comes to the restaurant. He is in the kitchen with his chef and a supplier. Yvonne calls to him from the door. 'There's an Eleanor Bycroft to see you.'

He places the supplier's price list on the steel worktop and smooths it with the flat of his palm. 'Show her into my office, Yvonne. See if she wants coffee.'

He spends another five, deliberate minutes, debating the best varieties of potato for dauphinois and weighing up the benefits of flavour versus cost.

His office is a drab room. Yvonne would have turned on the lights, but Eleanor has switched them off. A grey light, the colour of old washing-up water, filters through the window overlooking the narrow side passage. Eleanor is a gawky stick-figure. She stands with her brow pressed against the pane.

He has not laid eyes on her in almost a year, and has now seen her three times in quick succession. This is not wise. There's no knowing where it might lead.

Although at a push, he might hazard a guess.

He places his back against the door. An instinct for self-preservation urges him to flee, but reason tells him to stay. He misses her. He pretends otherwise, has told himself over and over that she's wrong for him, can only do him harm. It's probably true, but he cannot make himself believe it.

She says, 'It feels odd, doesn't it, being here like this?' He can't speak. He nods. 'Strange that two people can be so close, so intimate, and then become strangers. How can such a thing happen?'

'You chose Simon.'

'Only because you didn't want me, and I couldn't bear to be alone. But it's not right, Adam. We shouldn't be strangers.'

She moves away from the window. He holds his breath as she crosses the room. They stand face to face. Their hands come together, blundering like moths. Her face is even paler than yesterday – and sharper, like folded paper. It is an origami face. Their hands cease fumbling. Their fingers lock.

Why did you do it?

Why did you let me?

The questions spin round his skull like the ball in a roulette wheel.

There are no answers. No choices. Like she said, it just happened, it's all chance.

You must take your chance, make your own choices. I am not your keeper, Eleanor Bycroft.

Jessica's rationale is that Eleanor finds it difficult to choose. She dare not advance one course of action over another because with Chris she had got it so terribly wrong.

No, that's just another cop-out. She's here now because she chooses to be – just as she chose to go to Venice with Simon, and then to marry him. And now, this very afternoon, it had been her decision to wait in his office, and then to cross the room and take his hand.

He presses himself against the door. The wood digs into his shoulder blades and spine. His self-control is slipping away – but who cares? This is what she's come for. He frames her face and slides his fingers down her cheek. She lifts her chin to expose her neck and he buries himself in her, the taste of her and the pulse of her in the soft hollows, all the fragile places where life heaves close to the surface, like a warm current in a cold sea.

Chris had drowned. He raises his head. Her eyes are closed but her face reveals a desire that matches his own.

No matter how many times he tells himself it's over, against the odds, hope lingers.

They shift position. They can no longer wait. They fumble and clutch and thrust against the wood. From beyond the fragile door comes the chatter of the restaurant, the crash of plates, the sucking pop of bottles being opened. Someone calls out, 'Where's the boss?' And Yvonne replies, 'In his office . . .'

He knows her so well, knows from the way she moves and the sound of her breathing the point at which she will cry out. He clamps his mouth on hers, silencing her with a clash of teeth and tongue, and they come with a gasp of stifled laughter. Her fingers bite into his shoulders. His hands clutch at her thighs. They cling to one another, burying their laughter in the folds of their clothes.

Relief floods him. He wallows in her, so familiar, her body, her voice, her movements, all her responses stored and treasured against this moment. How can he bear to let her go?

She moves, resisting him. Reluctantly, he loosens his grip and draws her neat underclothes over her moist skin and smooths down her skirt. Until the moment of her dressing the touch of flesh to flesh had been minimal. Hand to thigh, penis to vagina. A technical fuck. It is a tribute to the power of memory.

He strokes her cheek. She is shaking, a racking shudder that begins deep inside, rumbling to the surface until her whole body quakes.

What is this? His mind struggles to focus. She's like an accident victim in shock. He doesn't know what to do. He has no experience. He makes her sit down. 'Eleanor? What's wrong? Did I hurt you? I was a bit rough.' She gives a harsh bark of laughter. 'It's been a while, Eleanor . . .'

'No.' She touches his face and draws a finger through the tight curls of his beard. He feels the snag and rasp of her nail. 'Gentle Adam.' Her voice is a whisper. 'I'd forgotten.'

'You're pale.' He takes her hand. 'And cold. Should I get you something? Coffee . . .' She laughs. She's right. It's so banal. 'Brandy, then. Whisky? A Tequila Sunrise, anything – tell me.' She's still laughing. She shakes her head. 'Eleanor,' his voice is deep, grating in his throat. 'Something's wrong. You have to tell me.'

'No. It's shock. You should offer sweet tea. No,' her voice is unnaturally high, verging on the hysterical. 'It's all right. I'm going now. It's okay. Look at that,' she holds out her hand. Her fingers are splayed and rigid. 'I'm not shaking any more. I must go . . .'

'Wait, listen to me. When I saw you at Brian's – I knew. I knew something was wrong.'

'Nothing's wrong.' She struggles to her feet and pushes the strands of her hair back from her face. 'I've made a terrible mistake. I should never have come here.' She grabs her handbag and edges past him. She is a trapped animal frantic to escape – and yet she pauses for a moment when she reaches the door. 'It's always the same,' she says in a whisper. 'I never do the right thing, I never learn. I should have known. I've hurt you again, just when things were coming right for you, when you and Jess . . . I'm sorry, Adam, oh God, I'm so, so sorry.'

4

'How could she do such a thing?' Adam strides from one side of Jess's workshop to the other, scrubbing at his face with the palm of his hand, as if to erase the memory. 'How could she come to the restaurant, do what she did – and not explain, not say anything?'

'I don't suppose she could explain it, even to herself.'

'And that's it? That's supposed to shut me up, stop me asking any awkward questions? I don't know what to do, Jessica. Tell me what to do.'

'I'm not a soothsayer. I don't have the answers you're after and I'm all sold out of advice.' He stares at her. Her hostility bewilders him. It's not that she isn't sorry for him, but the man has the sensitivity of a brick. Imagine coming here and telling her all about Ellie – and in such graphic detail. 'It's your problem,' she spits. 'You started this.'

'The hell I did. It was you who dragged me to that private view, you threw us together. What in God's name did you expect to happen?'

'I didn't expect you to fuck her.' She turns her back and starts to roll up a length of webbing. She doesn't want him to see how much this is hurting. She's always had the upper hand when it comes to men, but with Adam it's different, and she doesn't like it – and what about Ellie? She's so scared for Ellie.

She glances over her shoulder. He looks so lost. She relents a little. She says, 'The thing to remember about Ellie is that she doesn't think ahead – she daren't. She went to you because she needed you. Then. At that precise moment. She can't see further than that.'

'So she's using me.'

'Not deliberately. Something's wrong, Adam. I don't know what, but something's not right in that marriage. She doesn't confide in me any more, but I thought she might talk to you. I made a mistake. I misjudged the weight of baggage you were carrying.'

'You're serious about this? You really do think she's in trouble?'

'You've seen her, what do you think?' He shakes his head and shrugs. Exasperated, she says, 'Well, would you describe her as the picture of health?'

'No.' He pulls up a stool. 'No, you're right, she's changed. She's thinner, unhealthy-looking, and very white. I thought her face looked empty, like a blank sheet of paper.' He leans forward. 'And the way she moves, it's like she doesn't know her body any more.' He stops. 'This is getting scary, Jessica.'

'I know.'

'We must do something.'

'Okay, but what? Discovering the problem has to be the first step.'

'Maybe I should go and see her again.'

'No,' she laughs unconvincingly. 'She'll just blind you with sex, like last time.'

'That's not how it was.'

'If you say so.' She wonders if he'll ever get Ellie out of his system. He's got to try. She doesn't belong there; she's an alien body, a virus in his bloodstream.

Too much remains unresolved between them. They ended their relationship too suddenly, before it had a chance to run its course. Such things should not be forced. There is no such thing as a clean break.

What is certain is that Adam will not abandon Ellie in her need, which means Jess must find a way to control the situation.

She says, 'I don't think you should see her again, not just yet.'

'I have to.'

'No. It's crazy, there's no point charging to the rescue when you can't see the hazard. It's asking for trouble. I know it's hard, but we need to tread more carefully, take it a step at a time. Ellie made the last move, perhaps if we hold fire for a bit, she'll make the next.'

The restaurant is closed for the night and Yvonne is cashing up. Adam pours himself a brandy. The glass clashes against the optic.

'Takings are up,' says Yvonne as she slams shut the till. He nods. She's pretty efficient, but he's less easy with her than with Tom.

She takes the money through to his office. Her cab arrives. Adam

228

locks the door behind her and stands for a moment peering into the darkness. There is someone loitering in the shadows across the street. He shrugs. If it's a mugging-in-waiting, well, the takings are in the safe and it's only three short steps to his car.

He returns to the bar, pours another brandy and goes through to his office. He always spends a little time alone at the end of the day. It is a time of contemplation, meditation, whatever.

What if he left London?

It is also a time when such foolish thoughts leap out of the ether.

Except it's not so foolish. He could go home to Northampton – not that he knows anyone there. His family have all died or moved on, and anyway, Northampton isn't terribly romantic. The fact is, he could go anywhere – Plymouth, Exeter, Norwich – sell the restaurants, start again. His goodwill together with Simon Whitburn's murals should turn a tidy profit. Or he might sell one restaurant and leave Tom running the other. It would provide an excuse to visit occasionally, drive down to London and look up old friends. Jessica Grant and Brian Farraday. And Eleanor.

Isn't that what Chris did? Come down, stay over, sleep with Eleanor, then back to his wife and children – did he have children? He knows almost nothing about Chris or his marriage or his relationship with Eleanor. What he does know comes mostly from Jessica. Eleanor doesn't trust him.

He has to put some distance between himself and Eleanor.

He finishes his brandy and buttons his overcoat. He will give serious consideration to the possibility of leaving London. But not right now. Now is not the time to be making important decisions.

He locks the restaurant and taking a couple of steps towards his car, aims the electronic key. The car bleeps, and the figure he'd seen earlier detaches itself from the shadows. He experiences a pleasurable frisson, a blend of fear and assembled readiness. The figure crosses the road and heads in his direction. Whoever it is, is tall, slender, and slightly stiff in their movements. He relaxes. He recognizes the outline and gait. Eleanor. Eleanor with her hands plunged deep in the pockets of her coat, and her hat pulled hard down to shadow her face.

'I thought you were a mugger,' he says. 'Were you waiting here earlier?' She nods. He wants to take hold of her, pull her close. 'You should have come into the warm. You don't want to be out here at this time of night. Come on, I'll take you home.'

She slides awkwardly into the car and buckles her seat belt. As he starts the engine, she speaks. 'Not home.' Her voice is muffled. 'I'm not going home.'

'To Jessica's, then?' She shakes her head. 'Okay.'

His flat is cold. He fiddles with the heating controls. Eleanor goes ahead of him into the living room and he follows and turns on the table lamps. One thing he does know about Eleanor is that she hates overhead lighting.

'Can I get you anything? A drink, or are you hungry . . .?' She laughs. It is a tight sound, like the squeak of a fat balloon. 'What's the joke?' he demands.

'Nothing. Just you.' Her voice is odd, muted. She keeps her back to him, face turned to the shadows. 'Food and drink are your answer to everything.' She takes off her coat and lays it across a chair. She moves like a doll, jointed only at the shoulder and hip. She pulls off her hat. Her hair is stringy and tired.

'It's a reflex,' he says. 'In times of crisis I get the urge to cook a three-course meal . . .' He stops. He feels foolish. If only she'd look at him. 'I just want to help,' he says softly.

'I know.'

'But it isn't easy, Eleanor. You turn up out of the blue, and I want to put you at ease, but I don't know how. I'm no good at this.'

'Neither am I. I'm such a fraud. I keep thinking, why should Adam help me, after what I did? I couldn't face Jess, and I've nowhere else to go.' Her hands clench at her side. He touches her shoulder and feels her start, feels the fragile slide of skin on bone.

'Look, Adam.' She returns. The lamplight is livid. Her eyes glitter, 'I want you to look at what he's done to me.'

5

He has never seen anyone sleep like this, so thoroughly, deeply and for so long. She is dressed in his pyjama jacket, and looks as vulnerable as a child.

Why has she come to him? It would have been easier and safer to go to Jessica – but then, nothing is ever safe or easy with Eleanor.

She sleeps with her face pressed into the duvet and her hair spread like weed across his pillows.

Tomorrow he'll ring Jessica. Jessica will know what to do.

No. If Eleanor wanted Jessica's help, she would have gone to her.

Last night she'd climbed his stairs and taken off her coat and exposed to him the inner Eleanor, the quaking child. 'Look, Adam,' she said. 'Look at what he's done to me.'

It takes a moment for his brain to register the image. He is distracted by the blue-jay flicker of her eyes, but then his focus tightens and he notes that her make-up is daubed and clumsy, and dark smudges like thumbprints mark the skin beneath. She seems proud of these tokens of courage. She tips her chin, and the shadows retreat like a dark tide.

She has a cut above her left eyebrow; the blood has dried and is almost black; a bruise like a stain seeps down her cheek and along her jawline; her lower lip is also cut and swollen.

'Did he do this?' he whispers. 'I knew things weren't right between you, but this . . . Eleanor, what happened, whatever possessed him?'

A half smile threatens to crack the wound on her lip. She presses her fingers to the split. 'Me. It's me, I possess him. We had a fight, you see, and Simon lost.' A kingfisher flash: Simon in a pool of blood, stabbed with the pointy-end of a paintbrush. The image is ludicrous, but powerful. A ratchet tightens in his chest. 'That's the thing about Simon,' she frowns. 'He always loses. Even when he wins.'

He cannot cope with her conundrums. It is his nature to be practical, and that's the only way to get through this. 'Put your coat on,' he says. 'I must get you to a doctor.'

'No.'

'You need to get these injuries recorded.' He hesitates. He has no experience of such situations, only hazy notions of procedure gleaned from the occasional police drama he's seen on television. He racks his memory for the appropriate course of action. 'After the doctor,' he says with a confidence he doesn't feel. 'After the doctor we'll go to the police. Get an injunction.' The artifice of it all makes him laugh. 'That's sounds okay, doesn't it? "Injunction" has the right sort of ring to it, wouldn't you say?'

'I don't want the police involved; they wouldn't understand. And I don't like doctors; they're intrusive and they make judgements.'

'Eleanor, we can't just let this ride. I'm at sea, I admit, I don't know how these things work, but we'll sort it, I promise. Tomorrow . . .' He stops. 'Eleanor, what are you doing?' She ducks her head and fumbles with the buttons of her shirt. 'Don't do that.' Her fingers are stiff. He should stop her. He should help her. The laughter returns, but he chokes it back. Caught between disgust and desire, he watches as the blue silk parts.

The bruising is a livid, fungal growth, creeping from ribs to abdomen. She parades her wounds, inviting his tentative exploration of the stain. Her flesh quivers at his touch. Goosebumps form. On her, as well as on him. He touches his lips to her tender skin. Her flesh tastes bitter. 'All right,' he says on a breath. He can feel her burning. 'All right. This obviously isn't going to fade overnight. Let's talk again in the morning.' He moves back and gently draws together the edges of her shirt. 'I think you should rest now. Come on.'

They do not talk the next morning. She sleeps deeply and he lies alongside her, chaste, protective. He wakes with a start when the alarm goes off, but Eleanor merely stretches and eases herself across the bed and into the warm patch he has vacated.

He eats breakfast in the kitchen, but takes his newspaper and second cup of coffee through to the bedroom. Reading the paper seems less intrusive than openly watching her, although it is still a pretence. He doesn't need to look to see.

She'd said the police wouldn't understand, but what is there to understand? Simon is violent. End of story. Except that if she will not act against him, Adam cannot force her.

He folds his paper and puts it aside. She is no longer sleeping peacefully. Now and again her face contracts and her breathing becomes shallow and she clutches the pillow. He wants to touch her. His instinct is to wake her, but sleep is supposed to heal. Perhaps she needs to dream this dream.

Food also heals. She'll make fun of him when she wakes, and he looks forward to it. In the meantime, he will cook for her. He boils stock, peels and chops vegetables, crushes herbs. It's a waste of time – ideally the soup will need two or three days to mature and by then she'll be long gone. He's not a fool; he's doing this for himself as much as for Eleanor.

It's time to leave. He sets a tray with a bowl, a spoon and a plate for the bread. And a note of explanation.

Between the lunchtime and evening shifts he dashes back to the flat to find that she has woken, eaten the soup, and returned to bed. He marvels at her capacity for sleep. This continues for three days, but the nights are very different.

There are no words. She comes to him in a tangle of sleep-heavy limbs. He is very gentle. Although sluggish and reluctant to speak, she's awake; he can tell from the way she breathes, from the little cry which, though distant, is the response of a waking mind.

He has a bad day at work. Because he is restless, he intervenes in the kitchen; because he is preoccupied, he curdles a sauce. During the lunchtime session he fails to placate a difficult customer, and just before the evening sitting he has a disturbing visit from Jessica. Finally, as he is preparing to go home, Yvonne waylays him. She's annoyed; she says she's been trying to talk to him for days. She wants to revamp the menu. What does he think? He doesn't say so, but he thinks she's trying to put her stamp on his restaurant.

He arrives home in a bad mood. He's resentful and distracted. Yvonne's suggestions do have merit. A less scrupulous employer would take the ideas and ditch Yvonne. He closes the door and draws the bolt. It goes without saying that he will do no such thing. He lets himself into the flat and reaches for the light switch.

He freezes. He hears voices. Eleanor has visitors.

6

Because it is easier to sleep than to talk, Eleanor fakes it when Adam is around. If once she begins to talk, she fears it may never end.

What's happening isn't really Simon's fault, it's the nature of their relationship. He just doesn't know when to stop.

No, that's not entirely true. There are two kinds of violence in their household. What had begun on the day she destroyed his painting, continued in Cornwall, and found its level in Venice.

They fight. It is what they do. They fight verbally and physically and the truth is, she finds it sexy.

In Simon her two selves merge, professional and personal – the dynamic is irresistible.

During their stay in Venice he bought her a mask, a black cat framed by a torrent of blue-black feathers. He presented it to her on Christmas morning. It looked quite sinister as she peeled back the wrapping; an exotic face with blank, staring eyes and funereal feathers.

Funereal or not, the feathers were gorgeous. She ran a finger from root to tip, then buried her hands in the shivering shower. She felt a tingling in her spine and with a fearful whoop, she stripped off her nightshirt and donned the mask.

'Magnificent,' laughed Simon.

'Do you think?' Balancing on the bed, she struck a pose in the mirror. She stretched her arms above her head and extended her fingers like claws.

'My turn.' He leapt to his feet and rummaging under the bed, produced another package. 'What d'you say to this, Nell?'

Simon's mask was a fine ginger moggy. He tied the silk ribbons at the back of his head, and flicked his mane and in a cod-Spanish accent said, 'My name is Pablo.'

They circled one another, spitting and yowling. Eleanor flexed her spine, poised to pounce. Simon leapt, preempting her. They engaged. Kicking and biting and squealing, they rolled back and forth across the floor, layering bruise upon bruise and scratch upon bite-mark.

And they laughed, oh how they laughed.

Afterwards, her skin glowed, rosy and warm. The marble floor was cool against her back. She rolled over. And over again, relishing the smoothness, the texture of the stone against her belly and breasts, examining the pattern, like marbled flesh when seen close to.

But this is only one side of their coin. There is another kind of violence. When Simon is thwarted, or thinks he's being slighted, something happens. He's like a dog she once knew, a bumbling cocker spaniel who could be as sweet as pie one moment, a semi-rabid lunatic the next. You needed to be aware of the look in his eye, of the sudden change – a darkening, a flattening of the pupil – that announced the onset of rage.

She has told Jess none of this, has avoided the kind of intimate encounters that might lead to a discussion of her marriage. But what about Adam, could she confide in him? Should she show him the mask – invite him to play?

No, it's out of the question. Such a confession would say as much about her as Simon.

If this is what I am, then why am I like this?

She huddles in the corner of Adam's sofa. I behave as I do with Simon because I need what he gives me – power and exhilaration – but I miss Adam, I miss his gentleness.

And yet she has not always been gentle with Adam. There have been times when he has looked askance and recoiled at her ferocity.

She must let him go.

She runs a hand lightly along her arm, echoing his touch. These last few nights have been precious. She will always savour the memory of their wordless lovemaking, the precious anonymity of it all. What an absurdity monogamy is. She needs Adam just as much as Simon.

'It's all a con,' Jess would say. 'When it comes to men, we've swallowed the myth, hook, line and sinker. A man should be like a nibble at a party – a canapé, a cheese straw or an olive to be snatched from the tray, relished and forgotten.'

Spit out the pips.

Tinker, tailor, rich man, poor man . . .

Thief.

Eleanor yawns and glances at the clock. It's time she faced up to Adam and told him the truth. She makes a pot of coffee and cuts a sandwich, and settles in front of the television to wait.

She is immersed in an American hospital drama – masses of blood and lots of shouting – when she hears Adam's key in the lock.

7

It doesn't take Adam long to realize the voices in his living room aren't real. He opens the door. The television flickers in the corner and Eleanor is coiled like a cobra on his sofa. Her hair is loose and she's wearing his dressing gown. There is a pot of coffee and a half-eaten sandwich on the floor beside her.

'Hello, Adam.' She lifts her head and manages a funny, lop-sided smile. He notes that the bruising to her jaw has begun to fade, and her lip is no longer quite so swollen. 'You look tired. Come and sit down.'

'I've had a bitch of a day.' He offers a glass of brandy which she declines, and pours one for himself. He joins her on the sofa. 'Never mind me. What about you, how are you feeling?'

'Much better.'

'You're looking better. I was starting to wonder if you'd ever wake up.'

She smiles and shrugs. There is a silence, a warm, stretchy silence, like honey. He cannot resist touching her. He strokes her long toes and they wriggle against the cushions. He encircles her ankle. She says, 'I've been a real nuisance, haven't I? Blundering in, taking over your flat like this . . .'

'Yes.' Her skin is cool, her bones fragile.

'Burdening you with all my problems. I don't deserve you, Adam. You've been a true friend.'

'No.' The fumes of the brandy make his sinuses tingle.

'No?' She frowns.

'I'm not your friend.' His fingers tighten round her ankle. 'It isn't possible for me to be your friend.'

'Of course it is. You know, it's better this way. It's something I've noticed, that friendships last much longer than all this other. Like me and Jess . . .'

'You're losing Jess.'

'We'll be okay, we always are.'

'And we were always more than friends. Don't demean what we had, Eleanor, don't try to make us less than we were.'

'I'm not. That isn't what I meant at all. You confuse me, you always do. Maybe that's why I married Simon.' She pulls her foot away. 'He's so much more straightforward. Everything's black and white for him – and that's good for me, I need his focus.'

'And the rest?'

'What rest?' She is defensive now, and angry.

'Pain sharpens the mind?'

'You don't understand.'

'No, I don't. I don't even know what you're doing here. Jessica came to see me today.'

'Did she really.' She feigns indifference.

'Apparently Simon's been trying to contact you. He couldn't get an answer from the house, so he tried the gallery and Brian said you were off sick and suggested you might be with Jessica.'

'I see.'

'And that's it, is it? Don't you have anything to say?'

'What did she tell him?'

'Nothing. She doesn't know anything.'

'Well, then . . .'

'So what about Simon?'

'What about him?'

'He told Jessica he's in Edinburgh – what the hell is he doing there?'

'He's got an exhibition coming up.'

'You haven't told him, have you?'

'Told him what?'

'That you've left him. Jesus Christ, the poor bastard's up there planning his exhibition, and he doesn't even know. I suppose he'll come home and find a note propped on the mantelpiece . . .'

'I never said I'd left him.'

'What?' He's gripping the brandy glass so tightly that surely it must break. 'You're beyond belief, Eleanor, you really are. You turn up on my doorstep in the middle of the night, looking like death warmed up, like some gothic ghoul . . . What was I supposed to think?'

'How should I know? I'm not inside your head. I never said anything about leaving him.'

'You used me.'

'I love you.'

'No. Words, Eleanor, that's all they are. You needed a change, a bit of sympathy – good old Adam, always a reliable touch for a cup of tea and fuck.'

'Don't.'

'Don't what? Don't speak the truth? What do you want from me? One minute we're just good friends, the next you love me. Today we're lovers, tomorrow – what?' He drains his brandy and crashes down the glass. 'You're going back to him, aren't you?'

'I've already told you,' she speaks slowly, with exaggerated calm. 'I haven't left him. We had a row, he went to Scotland and I needed to get out of the house for a bit.'

'My God.' Realization begins to dawn. 'This is what you do to him. You keep him in the dark, then spring some cruel surprise – it's why he flips . . .'

'You don't understand.'

'So you keep saying. What was the fight about anyway? You never said. Tell me, Eleanor, I need to know.'

'It's none of your business.' She tugs at the dressing gown, smoothing it over her knees.

'You came to me, I have a right to know.'

'No . . .'

'Why did you come here? Why not Jessica or your mother or Brian? I'll tell you what I thought, shall I? I thought he'd found out

238

about us, about you and me.' Her face is empty – as though she has forgotten everything to do with him and her. He wants to grab her and shake her and make her remember.

Is this the key? Is this how she provokes Simon?

'There isn't any "us".' Her voice cuts through him.

'Then why come here? You know I'm not interested in saving your marriage . . .'

'You could have stopped it, but you didn't. And now you want to break it.'

'Breaking marriages? No, that's your speciality.' She flinches, and her fingers brush the healing mark on her brow, trail the lingering trace of the bruise along her jawline. 'I'm sorry,' he mutters. 'I shouldn't have said that.'

'Simon and I,' she begins. 'It's like that with us, volatile. Sometimes it gets out of hand, like it did that night. He left the next morning before I was awake. I spent the whole day tying myself in knots. I kept thinking, why can't I be like Jess? She says we live in the modern world where a woman doesn't need a man, not full-time.'

'Jessica says that?'

'And she's right. Look at my mother – she brought me up on her own, I hardly saw Dad after he left. That's a hell of a role model. Why can't I follow it? I try. You see, that was what Chris was about. He was a canapé, a fat olive – something else Jess says – but Jess is wrong. That's not a complete diet, is it?' She yelps with laughter and plucks at the sleeve of the dressing gown. 'Everywhere I turn I see couples, people in relationships loving one another and hating one another – it almost doesn't matter which. At least they're not alone. But I wanted to be alone, or a part of me did. Then I met you and it would have been so easy to slip into being with you always. When I came back from Cornwall, I was going to tell you that, but you stopped me. So I chose Simon, and that's better really, more practical. Where are you going, Adam?'

Her words numb him. He cannot listen any more. He leaves the room and slams the kitchen door.

His lighter is in his jacket pocket, but he has no cigarettes. He must have left them at the restaurant.

He drapes his jacket on the back of a chair and goes over to the stove. The pan of soup is half full. He turns on the heat and gives it a stir and starts to cut some bread. His hands are shaking. That day in the church, his future had spun like a wheel, rolled like a dice – and he has ended up here, when he could so easily have been somewhere else.

He pushes the breadboard away. He isn't hungry, he's angry. Her arrogance takes his breath away. Nothing she has so far said gives any indication that she is concerned for his well-being. Her wants, her needs are paramount.

The door opens. He feels her presence behind him, the blunt nudge of her silence, like a fist in the small of his back.

She leans against him and her breath is warm on his neck. Her lips brush the lobe of his ear. Her hands slide along his flanks as she pushes him gently, irresistibly against the worktop. He presses his hands hard down on the stippled surface. His fingers are splayed. Hands, fingers, knuckles and nails. They look grotesque, out of proportion. He takes a breath. He says, 'I thought I meant something to you. Even after you went off with him, I thought . . .'

'I didn't mean to hurt you.'

'But you did, and I don't learn, I keep putting my hand back in the flame.'

'I know. That's why I want you to understand. What I did, I didn't just do it for me. It's better for you, this way. You don't know what I am.' She presses against him. His vision blurs and the crush of her breasts, the deft, caressing movements of her hands immobilize him. 'Adam,' she exhales his name, then tips her pelvis to gently trap his erection against the drawer front. He holds his breath. He half expects her to push again, but is unable to prevent her. 'I hurt people, Adam. I don't mean to, but I do. Chris died because of me.'

'No.'

'You mustn't believe Jessica. It was my fault. And you, you're such an innocent.' She slides her arms around him and presses her hands to his chest. His heart thumps against her palms. 'Not like Simon. Simon can look after himself.'

'Then leave him.'

'You don't really want me to, and anyway, I can't. You're not listening to me, Adam. I do love you. How can I make you see? If you could measure it, tip it in a jug, run a rule along it, even then you wouldn't believe how much. But I need him, I need Simon. God, this is so difficult. You still don't get it, do you? Okay, okay.' She

240

takes a breath; it's as if she's thinking out loud. 'I know what to do. I'll show you.'

He cannot move. He watches with cold dislocation as she reaches past him to grasp the bread knife.

'You see, this is what it's like with Simon. All the time. Sharp edges. Definition. Look, I'll show you.'

Her breath becomes jagged, it burns his cheek. His body shudders, his guts convulse.

Quick – like a fish in the shallows – the knife darts.

'Pain defines.' They lie curled in his big bed. He cannot remember how they got here, how they come to be in this chaste, this spurious embrace.

His body tingles with pain. His and hers. Has she cut him, or just herself? The flesh parts and the blood wells. He sees his disembodied hands, one grasping her wrist as the other twists the tap. The water is streaked with blood. Tabasco, cochineal, Cabernet Sauvignon. The chill stems the flow. Calm descends.

When the wound is clean, he is amazed at how slight it is. How innocent. Like a paper cut.

She's out of her mind, is his first coherent thought. *Pick up the phone – call the men in white coats.* But then he looks, really looks, and sees how composed she is. There is nothing manic here. He has always accused her of hiding, but not any more. In the simplest, most effective way she has shown him her true nature.

'Sometimes,' she explains, moving closer in the half-dark, 'I lose track of who and where I am. Nothing is real. The world goes . . .' she searches for a word and finds it with a laugh, 'spongy. And this,' she pinches his arm, 'brings me back.'

'You've told me this before.'

'But you didn't believe me. You didn't understand.'

No. He had not understood. She slides closer. Drawing her hand down his chest, she curls her thumb in a wide arc across his belly. He responds predictably. 'This too,' she says, as he rolls over and presses her against the bed. 'This also defines.'

8

Eleanor returns home. It is important she should be there when Simon gets back from Edinburgh. She will think up some excuse for her flight – she'll cite Fowey and Venice, and her many city walks. He will be angry and they'll fight, but it will be no worse and no better than usual.

She feels the first rush of adrenalin, a wash of anticipation. Fear and desire.

There is an uncanny hush to the house. Oscar does not run to greet her. He has become more wary of late, as if concerned that Simon's rage might be turned on him.

She moves from room to room, upstairs and down, touching objects, pleating curtain fabric, breathing in the familiar smells – coffee and cat-food, paint and polish. It is important for her to re-establish her presence.

When the ritual is complete, she rings Brian to say she'll be back at work tomorrow, then she takes a bath and washes her hair. She is in the process of drying it when Simon arrives.

She can tell his mood from the creak of his step on the stair, and from the harsh rasp of his breath.

Clenching her fists, she bunches the towel in her lap, and turns to face the door.

9

'You're still seeing her, aren't you?' Jessica's voice is thick with disapproval. She's re-covering a Victorian nursing chair. Burying a fabric-covered button deep in the padding of the back, she tugs and pleats the crimson velvet to create a diamond design that scuttles like a spider from button to button.

'You said we should find out what was going on. Well, now we know . . .'

'Okay.' She turns to face him, hands on hips. 'But this way you just make matters worse.'

'I only want to help.'

'And if Simon finds out how you're helping?'

'You should have thought of that before throwing us together.'

'I asked you to talk to her, not start it all up again. It'll backfire, Adam – I guarantee it – and don't come running to me when it does.'

'Not in a million years . . .' he says, and stops. Her face is sharp with rage. Or maybe it isn't rage. He says, 'Christ, just listen to us. We shouldn't be fighting. We're flying blind, we should be helping one another.' She fastens another button and snaps the twine. 'Jessica?'

She looks up. Her eyes are black with grief or fury. 'I've had enough of this.' She pushes a dusty hand through her hair and kicks the leg of the workbench. 'She's my friend, Adam, and she's supposed to care about you – but look at what she's done. We're trapped. We can't go forward and we can't go back. She's screwed us both. We should cut loose. You and me, off into the sunset. How about it? No,' she stamps her foot. 'You know as well as I do, we won't do any such thing. We're too bloody responsible.' He is amazed by the flood of anger, by the unexpected tears that she dashes away with the flat of her calloused palm. 'And you, look at

243

you, you're no better than me. She kicks you in the balls and you cry out and nurse it better, and then you turn around and let her do it to you all over again.' Her face is red and contorted. 'She's my mate, Adam, the best mate I ever had, but sometimes I bloody hate the woman.'

10

Eleanor has a key to Adam's flat. She waits for him on her afternoon off. When he arrives they make love almost at once. Afterwards, all he wants to do is lie quietly beside her and feel the slide and rasp of her skin. 'You taste of the sea,' he whispers. She also smells of Simon, but he does not tell her this. He pulls the duvet more closely round them, and tries not to see Simon's stamp on her body.

The afternoons are never long enough or idle enough. All too soon Eleanor becomes restless. She pulls away. His flesh aches at the separation. She says, 'Come on, we can't stay indoors like this. Look, the sun's shining. We should go out.'

Or, 'Listen to that, it's raining. I love to walk in the rain.'

It seems anything is preferable to the extended intimacy of an afternoon in his bed.

She loves to walk. She thrills to the slap of her heels on the pavements. She takes him to musty second hand bookshops with towering, crowded shelves, to grubby backstreet cafés where they drink weak tea from thick china cups. It is a form of torment. Jessica is right. He should cut loose.

Then early one morning they visit the market where he buys his vegetables. It's February, and crushingly cold. 'You look fantastic,' he greets her. It's true, but bizarre. She has pulled her hat hard down over the tips of her ears and is wearing her Cornish coat. A double-wrapped scarf forms a nest for her chin. His breath plumes from his mouth to hers as they kiss. He tweaks her scarf. 'Is this to keep you warm, or are you in disguise?'

'I doubt I'll meet anyone I know down here.'

'Wish I could say the same.' There are familiar faces all around, and here and there a flicker of curiosity. He says, 'What about Simon, what excuse did you give for coming out so early?'

'I didn't need to, he didn't wake up.'

'But when he does, and you're not there?'

'I'll say I went for a walk.'

'And he'll accept that?'

She shrugs and turns away. 'He knows me, I do that sort of thing. Now for heaven's sake, Adam, do you mind if we move about a bit, before I freeze to the pavement?'

The plastic covers to the stalls crackle with cold. A man in an army surplus parka and fingerless mittens rummages in a crate of sprouts. They rattle like bullets as he drops them into the scale pan. Eleanor flexes her frozen fingers and clings to Adam's arm.

Although he's not one of Adam's regular suppliers, the man seems familiar. Adam puzzles for a moment, and then it comes to him: he is an older version of Simon. He has grey hair and his unshaven skin glints with a second frost. His hands are rough and the nails ragged; the coarse skin is ingrained with soil rather than paint. The resemblance is distorted, but powerful.

Eleanor draws him further along the row of stalls. Her breath feathers the air. She laughs and with a little bounce, swivels to take in the spectacle. 'This is great, Adam. I must bring Simon here. Imagine what he'd make of it, the colours and textures, the shapes – can't you just see it?'

Anger. A sour taste in his mouth. The day is spoilt – first by his own thoughts, now by her. He remembers Jessica's words. *Sometimes I hate the bloody woman . . .*

'Yes,' he snarls. 'That's just the way you like it, isn't it?'

'I was only saying . . .'

He jerks her arm, pulling her closer. She teeters. His face is close to hers and it's hard to focus. 'You do this to me all the time, offer just a little something of yourself, then use Simon to smash it.'

'No.'

'It happens too often to be an accident. But that's okay. Bit by bit I'm getting the hang of you. You're just like him . . .'

'I told you, that's why I married him.'

'Not Simon. Chris. You're like Chris.' The shock silences her. The name hangs between them like a mist. 'You want it all. You want Simon and whatever your marriage provides, and you want a bit of me too – but not too much, because it frightens you. Isn't that ironic? Simon's the psychopath, but it's me who scares you.'

'He's not a psychopath.'

He continues as if she hasn't spoken. 'D'you know why I frighten you? Because I represent the real world, and you're not comfortable with that. You take everything Simon hurls at you, but reality scares the shit out of you. And we were real, you and me. Flesh and blood. You loved me. You said so. Say it again.' He gives her a little shake. 'Go on, Eleanor, say it.'

'I love you.' Barely a trace of vapour escapes her lips.

'If only it were true – but you don't have the guts to follow through.'

'It's not that simple.'

'We could make it that simple. No one forced you to marry Simon. You did it because he hurts you and you like that – but all those cuts and bruises, what are they for, Eleanor?'

'They're not for anything, and there's no need to concern yourself with my marriage. I can handle Simon.'

'Look in the mirror and say that.' He laughs. 'And as for the rest, you don't fool me. Pain is a barrier, a wall for you to hide behind . . .'

'No, don't say such things. You don't know, it's so complicated – now please, I want to go home. I'm cold and I'm tired.'

'Bullshit, you're no fainting violet, Eleanor. You're stronger than all the rest of us. But you pretend. It's time you stopped pretending.' He tightens his grip. 'I'll tell you what's real.' He wonders if she might cry. Her lips part, her whole face seems on the point of collapse. 'This is real.' His voice is hard, he must hold firm. She was born to manipulate and he must resist the tenderness that will suck him down. Her coat is puffy. His fingers dig in a long way before they bite her flesh. Her sharp intake of breath draws stares of curiosity. He is known here. He feels exposed. And yet, because he is known, no one intervenes.

'Adam . . .'

'Suddenly,' he says, and there is new wonder in his voice, 'I see it all. You keep saying you want me to understand, and I think at last

I'm getting there.' He experiences a kick of excitement and an inappropriate urge to turn and explain to the assembled company – but they've lost interest and have returned to their trading. He leans closer. 'All that stuff about not being part of the world, and pain and how it defines, it's rubbish, bullshit. This is what defines.' He snatches at her hat and drags her scarf from her face. She cries out. Her cry condenses on the air. 'Do you feel it?' he hisses. 'Feel the cold gnawing your flesh, scraping your throat – oh, that's real, Eleanor.' She twists her head away. He holds on to her arm. He imagines a hierarchy of bruises, his fingers obliterating Simon's marks. 'It's a bit too close to the real thing, isn't it? And that's not what you want, you want your seedy little artist to come along and make it safe. He'll paint it for you. Get the viewpoint right. The colours spot on. But he drains all the energy. He kills, Eleanor. Don't you know that? Why put up with the dirt and cold and noise – and all that messy emotion getting in the way? Love! Jessica's right, who needs it, eh Eleanor? Only the weak and the mentally impoverished. Hell, why settle for the genuine article when Simon can knock up a fake at a moment's notice?'

'You don't know Simon, what he is and what he does – and why.'

'You're a fake, Eleanor.' He is breathless. Pain replaces anger. 'Look at you, look what he's made of you. This,' he tugs off her mitten to display the white scar left by his kitchen knife. 'What he does to you, what he forces you to do to yourself . . .'

'He doesn't force me.'

'This isn't you, Eleanor. Where are you? I look and look, but I can't find you any more. Where is my Eleanor? The Eleanor I love. She's vanished, changed, hidden, and all I see in her place is canvas and varnish and paint, a stage set, a carnival mask – a pantomime horse.'

11

Big ginger Pablo confronts his black mate – Hell's Kitten, Simon calls her. Eleanor has augmented the mask with a black feather boa that swings and scours her bare breasts and her belly. 'We're two of a kind, you and me. Look at us.' He pulls her on to the bed and, nipping her shoulder, fans out the drawings he has made of them: a pair of surreal pussy cats with human bodies and tangled limbs. 'This is the best.' He proffers the largest drawing. 'I'll frame it, shall I?'

It hangs on the wall at the foot of their bed. It is a reminder and a prompt.

They fight often; it has become a way of life. Sometimes the battle is mutually joined, but sometimes he just hits out.

Returning from Edinburgh, he found her sitting on their bed with her hair wet from her bath, and the towel bunched in her lap. He braced himself in the doorway. She knew better than to speak. She waited. A pulse pattered in her throat. Life is so fragile.

Releasing the doorframe, he crossed the room. He collected the hairbrush from the dressing table as he passed. He sat beside her and took the towel from her hands, and set about brushing the long, damp strands of her hair. Between strokes, he touched his lips to her bare shoulder and his fingers skated a bruise.

Pain, more anticipatory than real, flickered like lightening. The pain gave her pleasure. He is right. They are two of a kind.

His anger can dissipate as swiftly and as inexplicably as it comes, and there are many kinds of violence in Simon's repertoire. Sometimes two well-matched bodies are aroused by a shared act, but when their battles get out of control, there is real malice in the conflict. It was like that in the run-up to the Edinburgh trip, and it was like that last night.

When she woke this morning, he had already left the house. He can rarely face her after such a brawl.

And after such a brawl, she is always glad to have her house to herself. Time alone is precious. She loves to indulge in a solitary bath, closing her eyes and tracing the outline of her body until every extremity tingles with life. Afterwards she dresses slowly and repairs her make-up, taking her time. Perfection is all.

But today her bath is less than relaxing. A bruise on her shoulder makes it difficult to lie comfortably. Her make-up barely conceals the signs of last night's violence. She can't remember how it began. The most casual remark can be enough to set it off. His face changes as the sea alters when a squall descends. Closing her eyes, she sees again his saliva-specked lips and the joyless smile splitting his face like a wound.

It's frightening, this capacity she has to provoke rage in those she loves. Adam and Simon and Jessica.

There is nothing she can do or say to deflect Simon's rage; it will either dissipate or explode. Either way, his fury is a barrier her reason cannot circumvent. And so she responds in kind.

Last night she hit him in the face with her hairbrush. She hears once more his yell as the nylon bristles dig into his cheek.

She tugs on her dress. A thread catches in the zip. She jerks the tab down, then up. She wants to rip the dress, scrub away her make-up, crawl back to bed.

She goes downstairs to feed Oscar and make a cup of coffee. She leans against the sink, waiting for the kettle to boil. Her body aches. Her mind is numb. Oscar moves away from his bowl. He has spilt some food and she clears it up. As she takes her coffee to the table, she collects the calendar from its hook by the phone.

Flipping through the pages, she checks off the dates. Her periods have a natural cycle averaging fifty-two days. If one month is twenty-four days, the next will be twenty-eight. She cannot recall a time when the rhythm has faltered. She keeps a record. It is important to her, this function of her body. Whatever she does, however far she drifts or uncertain she feels, this is something that can be relied upon to bring her back. Although oblivious to the different phases of ovulation, she is recalled to the cycle by the headache that marks the run-up to her bleeding. On the day itself there is a dragging ache in her belly and a rush of blood – a strawberry swirl in the pan, an unfertilized egg, a failed harvest.

Last month there had been no bleeding. She told herself she was off colour. Stress does strange things to a person. But stress has never affected her like this. Her cycle was twenty-five days the month Chris died.

If last month's bleeding had arrived on schedule, this month's should have arrived last week.

She counts the days. She is afraid to think. She goes to work.

The gallery is busy. She has phone calls to make and meetings to arrange. At the end of the morning she tries again. She opens her desk diary and laboriously adds one day to the next. Perhaps a different calendar will yield a different answer.

It yields the same answer.

She tosses the diary aside. Work. She must contact next month's exhibitor. He hasn't confirmed his carriage arrangements. Next she chases the printer for the catalogue. Through the plate-glass wall of her office, she sees a sprinkling of browsers. She should be out there, selling.

Brian arrives. He glances round the gallery, speaks to one or two of the clients, then strides into her office.

'What's going on, Eleanor? There are serious buyers out there.' She closes the file and places it in her basket, on top of the discredited diary. Brian extricates the diary. 'You'll be looking for that later.' He peers at her and frowns. 'What is it, Eleanor pet? You're looking decidedly peaky.'

'Yes.' Her skin is clammy and there is a burning sensation at the base of her neck. Brian lays a chubby hand on her shoulder and leans over her. He smells of tobacco and wine. He's a kind man, and his concern is genuine. What was it Simon had told her about Brian and Irene? Strange to think. Think what? Her brain flounders. The thread is gone. Her mind slows to a sluggish drift. A new thought pushes against the current. She doesn't know what to do. She needs to talk things through. But not with Brian. Or Adam.

The pub is almost empty. Eleanor rotates her drink on a stained beer mat. The table is varnished but a single, raking scratch reveals the raw wood beneath.

Eleanor was surprised Jess agreed to the meeting. She'd have been perfectly justified in telling her to get lost. But no, she'd never do that. Friendship matters to Jess.

Good for Jess – but why had she insisted on meeting here?

Neutral ground, that's why. Eleanor glances at her watch. They'd agreed two-thirty but now it's nearly three. Perhaps Jess isn't coming after all. She orders another drink. On the wall facing her, a blackboard declares the day's menu in a lurid pink and green scrawl. Jacket potatoes with chilli, coleslaw, tuna and corn. Underneath, a gaming machine flashing green and yellow and red, lures no one.

Gin and tonic. Adam says there are ways and ways of making a good gin and tonic. The ice is important. 'Surely ice is just ice?' Adam had laughed. Also, he said, lime is better than lemon. No chance of lime here; she'd had to fight to get the lemon.

Hurry up, Jess. What's taking you so long? Adam says she's losing Jess. Most likely she's already lost her. You can't go on treating a person like shit and expect them to keep bouncing back. No, sensible Jess has finally wised up to the fact that Eleanor is using her. She won't come. Who can blame her? You're a selfish bitch, Eleanor Bycroft.

Right. That's that, then. She'll finish this drink and go home. She hasn't lost anything – it's not as though Jess can change things. What's done is done, it's all a mess from first to last.

She drains her glass. She shouldn't be drinking at all. Too late now. As she reaches for her bag, Jess arrives.

'Hi. Sorry I'm late.' She dumps her bag on a stool and digs out her purse. 'I had a last-minute phone call. How are you?' She drops a cool kiss on Eleanor's cheek. She's doing her best to pretend nothing has changed. Eleanor admires her adaptability. 'Shall I get you another?' She gestures to Eleanor's glass.

Jess drinks beer. She bangs down a half-pint glass on the table and slides Eleanor's gin across to her. No lemon. Eleanor splashes in the tonic. Just a splash. No point drowning it.

Chris had had two children. Boys. Children do strange things to people. Change them. They become selfish and self-righteous. She has observed this, and not just in Chris.

She leans over and swirls her drink in its glass. The ice is cloudy and there is too much of it wedged too tight. Adam says the ice should be clear. How is that done? In some ways Adam and Simon are alike. For them the world has structure. Simon sees a landscape

251

or face in terms of light striking a plane, of colour thickly applied or smeared like margarine. Adam can tell a good ice-cube from a bad one, can look at a jumble of vegetables and spices and herbs, and before he's even raised a knife he knows which to put with which and how the dish will taste.

She is not like them. She knows nothing until she experiences it, has no anticipatory sense. She must try, taste, everything. She prods and jabs at life, like a child with a frog on the river bank. If its limbs convulse, then it is alive.

But life can be simulated. Stimulated. Pass an electric current through the frog and its legs will twitch. But it isn't alive.

'Ellie, you've not listened to a word I've said.'

She surfaces. Jess leans towards her, hissing urgently. 'I was saying, it's time I practised what I preach and got Adam out of my system. So, what about him at the bar – don't look now, Ellie. Glance across all casual like in a second. He's been watching. What d'you reckon? Shall I give it a go, ask him over?'

'Not now, Jess.'

'Well, it's either that or get out my knitting. You're lousy company at the moment.' Her ice-cube is melting and diluting the gin. She downs it in one. 'Another?' Eleanor shakes her head. 'What's this about, Ellie? Only I do have work to do.'

'I'm sorry. I'm taking liberties dragging you here . . .'

'Don't be silly.' Jess softens a little. 'If you need me, I'm here, you know that.'

'But get to the point, right?' Eleanor manages a smile, then looks away. 'I've something to tell you, Jess.' She grips her glass, concentrating on its coolness and smoothness. She knows the score, the dates speak, but she has yet to say it aloud. 'I'm pregnant,' she whispers.

'Jesus.' Jess's reactions flicker across her face like trophies on a gaming machine. Disbelief, amusement, alarm – three in a row, she hits the jackpot. 'Are you sure?' Eleanor nods. 'Wow.' Jess leans back and runs her hands through her hennaed hair. It stands on end. Eleanor wants to laugh, but fights it. 'Now there's a turn-up. So, is it Adam's?' Eleanor stares. 'No need to look like that. I know you've been seeing him.'

'Given you all the grisly details, has he?'

'Match highlights, action replay, the lot.' She stops. 'No,' she says with a shake of her head and a sigh. 'Of course he hasn't. Not a word.' She dabs some froth from her beer and sucks it from her finger. 'But in broad terms we're talking Wednesday afternoons, his flat, right?' Eleanor nods. 'So is it his?'

'It could be.'

'But it could just as easily be Simon's. Tricky, that. What will you do?'

She lines up her options like drinks on a bar. She could nominate one of them to be the father, and live with the myth. Or she could take some tests, or she could abort.

'Ellie?'

'I don't know.'

'If there's the slightest chance it's Adam's, you must find out. He has the right to know.'

'I don't suppose he'll care. He hardly has the lifestyle for fatherhood.'

'He hardly has the lifestyle for sex, but he seems to manage it.'

'Jess!'

'Well, you can be such a heartless bitch at times.'

'I'm just trying to be realistic.'

'It's not realistic to think Adam won't care. If you believe that, then you don't know him at all.'

'And you do?'

Colour flares across Jess's face. 'He'd make a great father. You should talk to him.'

'I can't.' She sees him again at the market, his rage and his misery. 'A pantomime horse,' she whispers.

He'd called her a fake, and he'd think her faking now, using her pregnancy to taunt him. But this is real. Too real. I don't want this, I want it out of me – this thing. This clash of cells, this lump of jelly.

With a gasp she grips the edge of the table and buckles forward, yielding to a sudden cramp and a wave of nausea.

'Ellie? What is it? Are you all right?'

'Stupid question.' She speaks through locked teeth, rocking back and forth, willing it to go away, the sickness and the pain – and the source of the sickness and pain. 'Stupid, stupid, stupid . . .' she shouts, and Jess is standing over her, supporting her, propelling her forward as she runs for the Ladies where she vomits into the sink.

12

Now she knows what she will do. She lies curled in her bed. A sickly grey light filters through the drawn curtains. There was a moment when she thought the foetus that refused to leave her body by the conventional route, might be expelled through her gullet. Her body racked and strained, voiding itself of everything but that of which she most longed to be rid.

Jess clung to her, stroking her hair. Friendship above all. How could she ever have doubted Jess?

The sickness passed, and with it the pain, but she was still shaking violently, cold on the outside, burning up within. Jess called a taxi and took her home and put her to bed. She wanted to get the doctor but Eleanor said, 'No doctors. I hate them.'

'Sooner or later you're going to have to see one.'

'But not now, not yet.'

'Well, let's see how you feel in an hour, shall we? I'll make some tea.'

She makes fennel tea. How does she manage that? She must keep emergency rations in her handbag. Eleanor smiles and takes a sip. She knew Jess would make it better. She can already feel the tension slipping away. The muscles in her stomach and shoulders begin to unclench. She inhales deeply. The air is fragrant with the fumes of the tea and she begins to doze.

A banging on the front door wakes her. Voices. First Jess's, then Adam's. Jess shouldn't have done that. Eleanor draws herself into a sitting position and adjusts her pillows. Oscar is curled at the bottom of the bed. He's a big cat getting bigger, and he weighs down the duvet. She gives it a tug. He opens one eye and scowls at her, then stretches a long forepaw, yawns, and marches up the bed to settle heavily in her lap. She traces the curve of his back, feels the delicate knobs of his spine pushing through the thick fur.

She knows what to do.

She slides her hand round Oscar's flank. He rolls over, exposing his tummy to the caress. Suddenly everything is sharp and clear. She no longer desires to be rid of the alien within. She'd experienced a moment of nausea-inspired panic at what lay ahead, but the panic had fled with the nausea, to be replaced by a remarkable certainty.

This event will change her. The rift in her menstrual cycle means an invisible, internal process, will now intrude upon the outside world. The blood in her veins is no longer the same; it is richer, thick with hormones like cream clotting milk. And to think it started weeks ago, without her knowledge. Her body, its life its own, has secreted another life. Cells divide. What stage has this child reached? Does it have limbs? A sex? Is there a new consciousness already flickering inside her?

Killing her baby is no longer an option. It is part of her. Not in the obvious sense that she is its host, but in a profound way she cannot yet grasp.

'Ellie?' She starts. Her hand jerks and Oscar glares reproachfully. Jess looks uncertain. Well she might. 'Adam's come to see you.'

She laughs. So strange that Jess should send for Adam and not Simon. Her laughter startles Jess. This certainty is exhilarating. She has never known anything like it. 'It's all right,' she says, sitting up and pushing back her plait. 'Don't look so worried. Let him come in.'

She cannot judge his mood. His face is closed, his eyes hooded. She gestures an invitation and he perches on the bed like a great black crow that might take flight at any moment. No. He's too fine, too glossy and well-hewn to be a crow. A raven, then. The ravens mustn't leave the Tower. She smiles at him. What she has to say will hurt him – in the short term at least – and she regrets that, but she has no choice.

Adam will bear it. He is her tower of strength. She touches his hand. His beautiful hand. Still he refuses to look at her. A muscular spasm flickers in his cheek, just above the line of his beard. He tightens his jaw, quelling it. He doesn't speak. That's good. She wants to prolong this moment.

She feels so strong.

He fusses Oscar, tickling the top of his head. Oscar acknowledges him with the twitch of an ear. Behind him is Simon's painting of human pussycats. When he turns to leave, he will see it, and it will confirm all the bad things he has ever thought of her.

He says, 'Jess rang me.'

'She shouldn't have done that. She should have let me do this in my own time.'

'She's worried. She says you're not well.' His attention remains fixed on Oscar. She studies the crown of his head and spots three grey hairs, more wiry than the rest. She wants to touch them. Because she hasn't responded, he looks up. The muscle in his cheek is on the move again. This time he ignores it. 'Are you better? You look . . .' His voice trails. He takes a breath and starts again. 'Jessica says you won't see a doctor.'

'I don't need to. She's told you, hasn't she? She's told you what's wrong with me.'

'Yes.'

'She didn't trust me to tell you myself.'

'Would you have done?'

It is her turn to study the finer points of Oscar's anatomy. 'I didn't want to believe it. I was going to tell you that morning at the market. But you called me a pantomime horse . . .'

'You knew then?'

'I suspected. I wanted to talk about it.' She is lying. Does it show? Is there a physical telltale of which she is unaware, an equivalent to the twitch in his cheek? She is doing this for his sake, so he'll feel better – but the lie carries blame on its back. He had stopped her 'confession' by calling her a pantomime horse. She can see in his face that he accepts the blame.

'You must tell me, Eleanor. Do you know, have you any idea . . .?' He pauses, frowns. He thinks the question self-explanatory and so it is, but her silence forces him to continue. 'Me or Simon? Can you tell from the dates? How does this work . . .' He falters. His ignorance and confusion delight her, but still she says nothing. He struggles to adjust, he tries to take charge. 'It'll be all right,' he says. 'You mustn't worry, we can sort this.'

'There's nothing to sort, and I'm not in the least bit worried.'

'But I need to know, Eleanor.'

'No.'

'I'm sure it's quite easy, these days. There are tests, aren't there? Blood tests, DNA . . .'

'Why?' She is becoming impatient. He must let go, can't he see that? 'Why is it important for you to know?'

'It just is. How can we decide what to do next if we don't have all the facts?'

'I've all the facts I need.'

'But you haven't . . .'

'I know what I'm doing and where I'm going. Establishing the paternity of this child won't help you. What do you want? To avoid responsibility, or claim it?' She laughs and it's an ugly sound, but she can't help herself. 'Either way,' she tugs at the duvet and Oscar jumps down, 'it doesn't matter. No tests. Not those kind of tests.' Her voice is tight. She cannot give him the tiniest scrap of hope because she knows, beyond doubt, that this baby will be her salvation. 'I don't need tests to know who this baby belongs to. She's mine. Not yours, not Simon's. At this very moment, look,' she raises her arm and, ignoring the cluster of fresh bruises, indicates the tangled blue rivers of unoxygenated blood. 'At this very moment it is my blood flowing in her veins. All her nourishment comes through my body – it's nothing to do with you or Simon. This baby is mine.'

13

Adam works. What else can he do? He dare not think of Eleanor, or the baby, or Simon. He has adopted Yvonne's suggestions regarding the running of the restaurant, and is revamping the menu for Jangles-One. He works till the early hours trying out new recipes. He makes notes, does pricings. Should he impose the new menu on Tom, or offer it for discussion? It's good for Tom to have some autonomy, but he must be careful; costs have a habit of spiralling.

It's too much. He's in too deep. He cannot split his mind so many ways. Two restaurants, Tom and Yvonne, Eleanor and Jessica, Simon and the baby.

He raids the bar. A double brandy. He goes back to the kitchen. The mess reproaches him. He gulps his drink and clears up and goes home.

He cannot sleep; he sees her everywhere. The echo of her. His office. His flat. The market. Even the darkness is full of her. And the light. He cannot understand this perversity that makes her cling to Simon. They are not suited. Even if he turns out to be this baby's father, what sort of parent will he make? If the baby gets in his way, if it cries at the wrong time, he will react on reflex. He will hurt the child. He might even kill it.

It makes no sense to dwell on such things. There is nothing he can do.

He must turn his mind to other things – though not the restaurant; that clearly doesn't work. Kay. He saw her last week, as she passed on the other side of the street. She waved, but didn't stop. Then he thinks of Jessica. It's over a month since he last saw her. He is very fond of Jessica.

And Jessica is more than fond of Adam. She's always telling Ellie to be more independent when it comes to men, but where Adam's concerned, she's just as bad. She thinks about him a lot, about how it might be between them if it weren't for his obsession with Ellie. Yes, obsession's the word, though not in any sinister sense. Ellie's like that, she gets under your skin. And now there's this business of the baby. What chance has Adam got?

He's avoiding her, she's convinced of it. He associates her with Ellie, so when things are troubled there, she gets shoved out of sight as well.

So what? I don't need him.

Her phone rings. As she crosses the workshop she catches her foot in a rogue ball of upholstery twine. 'Damn. Hello.'

'Jessica?'

It's Adam. 'Wait a minute, can you? I've got caught in a cat's cradle here.' She fumbles with the twine. 'Right, I'm back. What d'you want?'

'What is it? You sound hassled.'

'Do I?'

'Is something wrong?'

'No, Adam, everything's hunky-dory. Why shouldn't it be? I haven't seen you in ages.'

'I realize that, it's why I'm ringing. I thought maybe if you were free tomorrow evening . . .'

'Tomorrow?' she interrupts, pretends to consider. Play it cool, don't sound too keen. 'I don't know, Adam, I'm not sure . . .'

'How about supper? Here at the flat. I've been looking over the winter menu.'

'Winter?'

'The restaurant.'

'Well of course the restaurant, but it's June, Adam.'

'I have to think ahead in my business. I'm working on a wild boar and venison terrine. I'd like your reaction.'

She arrives at the flat a little after eight. Adam is nervous. He pecks her cheek and pours a gin and tonic. She pulls a face. Eleanor's drink. He apologises. Not a good start.

They eat in the kitchen. He's concerned she might get the wrong idea if he treats this as a dinner engagement, so he presents it as a professional encounter. He wants her opinion as a punter. Is the terrine good, or is it not?

Jessica sits facing him. She's wearing a white shirt and an emerald waistcoat. The top two buttons of her shirt are open and around her neck is a leather thong. An amber bead nestles in the hollow of her throat. 'The terrine was great,' she says with a wave of her fork. 'And so's the chicken.'

He's not interested in the chicken. It's an old recipe; he'd wanted the main course to be relatively bland so as not to detract from his cocktail of wild boar and venison, juniper and cranberries. 'What about the wine, do you think it goes well with the terrine?' What is he playing at? He doesn't care what Jessica thinks, she's no connoisseur.

She raises her glass. 'I do. This is nice, Adam. Supper, wine, chat – it's been a while.'

'I've been busy.'

'I can imagine. It's difficult, I suppose, things being the way they are . . .'

What can he say? She wants him to talk, and he'd like to talk, but he doesn't know where to begin. He tops up the wine. He has grown so isolated. He fingers the stem of his glass. He raises it to his lips, but he doesn't drink, he inhales.

Jessica says, 'Okay, let's stop playing games. Whatever's on your mind, let's get it into the open. I know I'm not here for my scintillating company – or for the terrine.'

'I enjoy your company, you know that.'

'I'm very glad to hear it, but that's hardly the point.'

'No.'

'Well, then?'

She is here because she's Eleanor's friend, and for no other reason. 'It's difficult,' he says.

'Ellie . . .' she prompts.

'Eleanor, yes. You're back in her good books, are you?'

'For the time being.'

'I don't know why you put up with her.'

'It's called love, Adam. I know I spit and cuss, but d'you know what scares me more than anything? Boredom. Now, how can I ever be bored with Ellie around?'

'True, but it's not easy, is it?'

'Now there's an understatement.'

'How is she?'

Jessica laughs and sketches a swell in the air. 'She's big.'

'I was hoping for a little more detail.'

'Whatever you say. She's looking good, fantastic, in fact. And she's still working. Makes you sick, doesn't it? But you know Ellie, she doesn't let her standards drop.'

'And Simon?'

'Simon's loving it, he's playing the expectant daddy for all it's worth.'

'Is he leaving her alone? Because if he isn't, if he so much as touches her . . .'

'What? Go on Adam, tell me, what will you do?'

He shrugs. 'I don't know. Probably nothing. I'm not handling this at all well, am I? I've never been in this position. You've got to help me. What can I do, what can I say to convince her? If only she'd take these tests . . .'

'She won't do that, Adam. If there's one thing I know about Ellie, it's that nothing'll make her shift on that score – and don't expect sympathy from me. For once I can see where she's coming from.'

260

'I'm damned if I can.' He stands up and pushes back his chair. He starts to clear the table, crashing the plates as he stacks them. 'What happens when this baby's born? What if it looks like me?'

'Well, it's not going to pop out with a beard, a hook nose and a recipe for wild boar terrine clutched in its mitt, is it now?'

'I suppose not.'

He loads the dishwasher. Jessica stands close, stroking his back. 'Come on, Adam, act like a grown-up. Smashing your dinnerware solves nothing.' He shrugs her off and slams the dishwasher door. 'We'll get through this. I'll help you – only don't shut me out, Adam.'

He goes through to the living room. She follows. 'Okay,' she tries again. 'Look at it another way. What if Ellie takes these tests you're so keen on,' – she can tell from the set of his shoulders that at last she has his attention – 'and it turns out the kid is Simon's after all?' He turns and stares at her. 'It could be.' His eyes are black with pain, his pupils gaping as if trying to swallow the enormity of her words. 'Would knowing that make you feel any better?'

'No.'

'So you're making all this fuss and pother on the assumption you'll get the answer you want.'

'There's a fifty-fifty chance.' He is stubborn.

'But if Simon gets the jackpot?'

'Then I'll leave.' His anguish makes her heart beat fast and the amber bead jumps in the hollow of her throat. 'I'll go away, sell up. I've been thinking about it on and off for ages, I've just never put it all together.'

'So what will you do?' she spits. 'Leave the country, leave London – move to a different street? Get real, Adam.'

'I can't see another way out. In fact, I'm starting to think I'll do it anyway, tests or no tests. I need to take control of my life, start living again.'

'Okay, agreed, but not like this.'

'Can you think of a better way? No, don't look like that.' He takes her by the shoulders. His face is close and his expression is tender. No, not tender. Kind. 'Don't be sad,' he says. 'We're friends, you and me, we won't lose touch, I promise. I'll write.' He laughs. 'I'll send you a postcard.'

14

It's ages since Ellie and Jess had a girls' night in. These days Jess hardly sees her without Simon in tow, so she issues the invitation in the form of a challenge, with the tacit accusation that Ellie is neglecting her friends.

Ellie understands the rebuke. She's contrite. 'Of course I'll come, only I can't drink. I mustn't take any risks with this baby, you do understand that?'

'Of course. It'll be strictly fruit juice, I promise. And a video.'

Jess knows this isn't going to be easy. She has a favour to ask, and she hates to be indebted to anyone. But in this instance, she has no choice. Only Ellie has the power to make Adam stay.

The video she selects is Francis Ford Coppola's *Dracula*. She slots the cassette into the machine and hits the play button. In the opening sequences Vlad the Impaler is busy impaling, the love of his life leaps from the battlements, and a broken Cross gushes blood. Jess and Ellie huddle on the sofa, sipping fresh orange juice and sharing a jumbo packet of cream cheese and chive flavoured crisps. At one point Ellie nudges her and whispers, 'Top hats and tinted specs do not a vampire make.'

'But so romantic.' Jess gives an exaggerated sigh. 'Did you hear what he said? "*I have crossed oceans of time to find you . . .*"' she speaks in a husky, hauntingly lascivious tone.

Eleanor gives her a sideways glance. 'Can you imagine the effect this is having on the baby? She's in a foul mood, kicking like hell. Give me your hand. Feel.'

'No.' Jess pulls away. 'That's disgusting, Ellie.'

Ellie laughs and, helping herself to another handful of crisps, settles back against the cushions.

The film ends with the grieving Vlad being decapitated by the woman he loves. Jess flicks off the set and rewinds the tape. Ellie has drifted into a trance. She's leaning back against the sofa with her eyes closed, stroking her bulge in the kind of self-satisfied way that makes Jess's gorge rise.

She fights her revulsion. 'I've really missed our evenings.'

Ellie smiles languidly. 'Me too.'

'We should make an effort, do it more often.'

'It isn't easy, what with Simon and the baby.'

'I suppose not.'

'And anyway, things have been a bit tense between us, haven't they? This business with you and Adam, I'm never sure where your loyalties lie.'

'Nor am I.' Jess considers for a moment. 'No, actually, that's not true. I've been turning myself inside out trying to be loyal to both of you. You know my views on friendship.'

'And men.'

'That's taken a bit of a battering too. The thing is,' Jess plunges on. 'I was rather hoping to talk to you about Adam.'

'I haven't seen him in ages. How is he?'

'He's going away.'

'Where?'

'I don't think he knows.'

'I doubt he means it.' Ellie fidgets in her seat, adjusting the cushion in the small of her back. 'He's got too much to lose. Look at how he's built up the restaurant, and Jangles-Two. He won't turn his back on that.'

'I'm not so sure. He'll make quite a profit on the restaurants, what with Simon's murals and the goodwill. He'll do it, I know he will. But you can stop him, Ellie; you're the reason he's leaving.'

'I can't.'

'I've never asked you for anything, have I?'

'No, but . . .'

'Well I'm asking this. You owe me, Ellie. He means to go and I know what'll happen – in cutting you out of his life, he'll cut me out too. He says not, but he won't be able to help himself. Talk to him.'

'The baby . . .'

'Let him be a part of that. It's all he wants.'

'It's too much . . .'

'You could do it.'

263

'You really want it that much?'

'Running away solves nothing, you know that. He'll listen to you.' Jess holds her breath and waits. She's going to refuse, the bloody woman's going to turn me down. 'If he stays,' she tries one last time. 'Who knows, he and I might finally get our act together . . . I know it's against my principles, but he matters to me. And even if we don't have a future, I still don't want him to leave. Do this for me. Talk to him, make him stay.'

15

Jess arranges for Adam to call at the workshop. 'He thinks he's meeting me,' she tells Eleanor. 'I told him three o'clock, so I'll get away well before. I don't want to bump into him.'

'Fine.' Eleanor is preoccupied. She's not convinced this is a good idea.

Jess says, 'I'll give you about an hour. Will that be long enough? Ellie? Are you listening?'

'Yes, of course. An hour will be more than enough.'

Jess leaves. Eleanor paces the workshop. She is moved by the strength of Jess's feelings. She'd no idea she'd become so completely entangled. The spider snared. She smiles. Jess is a good friend, and she must do whatever she can to help her.

But at what cost?

Who's counting? Don't be niggardly.

She leans against the workbench and fiddles with Jess's tools. She arranges the needles in a row, grading them by size. She gathers the tacks into a little pile, then scatters them again, forming the pattern first of a star, then a sailing boat.

Then all at once she glimpses the future, sees herself and Simon and Jess and Adam – four friends, two couples, dining at one another's houses, having days out and maybe even holidays together.

Maybe, maybe not.

She checks her watch. It is almost three. So strange, being here on her own. The hum of machinery drifts across the yard from the dry cleaner's. The roof of the workshop groans in the afternoon sun, and she remembers another occasion – a needle, a bubble of blood, a spike of misted steel.

Is Adam really planning to go away? It seems so extreme. She cannot imagine what it would be like, never to see him again.

The door creaks open. Adam. He sees her, and is taken aback. Perhaps he'll turn tail and leave? No. He leans against the door and digs his hands deep into his trouser pockets. She senses a difference. The Adam Jess knows is not her Adam.

How is he changed? He is more casual. His shirt is open at the neck, his tie hangs loose, his face is flushed with the afternoon heat, and his brow gleams.

She says his name. She would like to say more, but the heat, the dust from the hessian and horsehair and wadding, clog the air. Her throat is swollen and her lips dry.

At the sound of her voice he is transformed. He becomes her Adam again, stiffer, more wary. His tone is curt as he says, 'I was expecting Jessica.'

'We tricked you, I'm sorry. I need to talk to you.'

'What do you want? I don't have long.'

'Jess has told me . . .'

'What?' He is impatient, angry.

'That you're going away.' He says nothing. She moistens her lips. 'Is it true?'

'Surely you are not surprised?'

'It seems excessive.'

'When one is no longer wanted, one should make a dignified exit.' He is so formal. He is using language to put a distance between them.

'But it isn't true,' she says softly. 'You are wanted. You can't do this, Adam, you can't turn your back on us.'

'It is not a subject for discussion, Eleanor.'

'So it's all finalized, is it? The flat, the restaurants . . .'

'They have been valued.'

265

'But you haven't put them on the market?'

'I intend to do so tomorrow. The day after, at the latest.'

'Adam, no.'

'Give me one good reason why I should stay.'

'The baby —'

'—is nothing to do with me. You've made that perfectly clear.'

'You're too severe.'

'I'm only following your lead.' She wants to reach out, take his hand. Perhaps a flicker of movement gives her away, because he relents a little. 'All right,' he says. 'What about the baby?'

Now she comes to the difficult bit. She has something to give, but not as much as he would like. 'Well,' she begins tentatively. 'First of all, I have to tell you I meant what I said, about not having any tests . . .'

'Jesus.' He gives a harsh, gagging laugh and turns his head away, as if avoiding a bright light. Perspiration breaks out afresh, curling the hair on his brow. He says, 'Have you any idea how hard this is? I can't be this close . . .' The nerve throbs in his cheek. She wants to touch him, lick the salt from his skin. 'This close,' he continues, 'and be excluded. Try to understand what it's like, knowing and not knowing, being part of it and apart from it. If you cut me out, I have to go. Survival, Eleanor. That's all it is.' He laughs without amusement. 'It's nothing personal.'

'Listen to me. I care about you. I don't want to lose you. All week I've been going round and round in circles. Then suddenly it came to me. If this baby is mine alone – if it isn't Simon's . . .'

'Isn't it?'

'I said *if* it isn't his, and it isn't yours —'

'What?'

'Then it's as much yours as it is his.' Exasperated, he shakes his head and turns to leave. 'Adam, wait, please. I'm making a mess of this. What I'm trying to say is that in a funny way, you're equal, you and Simon.'

'Equal? Tell me, who will your child call father? Who'll be there to help it walk, tie its shoes, teach it to talk? Not me. Simon. Your husband. Now tell me we're equal. There's nothing for me here.'

'Simon thinks you and Jess are an item.' He stares; he thinks it's a digression. 'I've encouraged him to think that.'

'Why?'

266

'Because it's almost the truth, and because that way you're not a threat. Adam, if you stay, we can make it work, I promise. Please, you must stay. I couldn't bear it if you left.'

16

The summer is long and unbearably hot, and Eleanor cannot wait to be rid of her burden. She is impatient to meet her daughter.

Simon remains a cause for concern. In the long term, she's not sure what she'll do about him. The baby changes everything, but until she is born, Eleanor refuses to make any irreversible decisions.

Simon is obsessed by the birth, intrigued by the processes of her body. He insists she describe every sensation, the queasiness, the soreness, what it feels like from within. He wants to share her swollen breasts and taut flesh. At night he traces the lines and curves, exploring her body, crevice and crease, concavity and convexity. He says she is an art form, body-sculpture.

Lately he has taken to sitting on the edge of the bed with his hands clenched between his knees, talking and talking and talking about her and the baby and the future. His white-lipped intensity makes her stomach contract.

Eventually there comes a day when her stomach contracts more violently than ever.

Simon is a patch of darkness blocking and diffusing the glare of the hospital room – and she must find a way to tell them, tell the nurses how terrible it is, how she has always been afraid of the dark.

Because darkness is absence. Please, somebody, make him absent.

In a corner of her pain-locked mind, she is lucid enough to wonder what this means to him. Will the colour of her blood enrich his palette? Will the smudged head of her daughter pressing her passage into the world inspire a new sequence of paintings?

And then another crack of pain convulses her. Pain. A white light

– a light that brightens even Simon's corner so that now she understands how terrible this is for him.

She sees what he sees, as if through his eyes. He observes her agony, but is not a part of it; he witnesses the warm gush of her blood as it issues from a wound not of his making. Here in this hospital room, he is confronted with a new truth. Georgie's power to inflict pain exceeds his. Simon's blows rain from the outside. Georgie ruptures her from within.

How will he bear it? She clings to his hand. He clings to her hand. Her knuckles grind. The uneasy truce of the past months strains thin as a caul.

When she told him about the baby she had almost believed in his gentleness. 'This is great, Nell. It'll change everything. I know I go too far, but I can learn to control myself, I know I can. Christ, Nell, I love you so much. I'll make it okay between us. I'll never hurt you again, just you wait and see.'

Irene spoke of change as well, but she thought it would be for the worse. 'I suppose you know what you're doing,' she said. 'Frankly, Si, I'd have thought your career was at a critical point. Hardly the time to start a family.' She glared at Eleanor, as if it was her fault. She wanted to laugh. It was her fault. 'What does your mother make of it?'

They had given Babs the news in person. She poured thick tea into green and gold cups, then tucked the teapot back under its camel-shaped cosy. 'That's marvellous, dear,' she said, looking from one to the other. 'Your old cot's in the loft. All it needs is some oil and a lick of paint. No point spending money just for the sake of it. Then there's your christening gown . . .'

Eleanor glanced at her mother's tangerine and green kitchen and asked, 'What colour is it?'

'White of course, dear. I did rather want to make it myself. I saw some lovely gauzy material,' her fingers fluttered to convey the flutes and frills. 'Pink,' she said with relish. 'With little blue velvet dots, like beauty spots. Only your father interfered – he hadn't a scrap of originality, that man.'

Simon treated the slatted sides of the cot as a single picture plane. Sheep on a hillside. Eleanor thought the sunset rather bloody, but liked the way the gaps between the bars fragmented the image.

As for Simon's career, the Edinburgh show had been a huge

success and he is flush, he's being courted. There have been press write-ups and commissions and one or two enquiries about murals which he greets with his usual sneer.

With one exception. An American hotel chain has offered a bucket of money for an entire series. Simon is tempted. He lists the pros and cons. The arguments war across his face like two personalities battling for control. 'It could be good. What d'you think, Nell? Maybe we'll get an exhibition together – coast to coast, LA to New York. What d'you say? Reckon we could pull it off?'

She runs a self-conscious hand over her growing bump. Her sense of identity increases with her girth. The baby accentuates her physical presence. Her baby will save her.

Simon leans forward, prompting a response. 'Maybe,' she ventures. Her voice is distant. The woman who speaks neither knows nor cares. A flicker of movement. Simon's hand. A ripple of apprehension. The baby feels it. The movement is checked and transformed. Simon's roughened, paint-stained hand strokes her thigh, then slides down her calf. She recognizes the caress. He is learning her with his fingertips, as if by that trick he might transfer her to canvas. His touch is gentle, but cold. Shocking to think that, with rare exceptions, they can be intimate only in the way bickering children are intimate.

17

Adam decides not to leave London. Adam decides, Adam chooses – it's a delusion. His decision, such as it is, rests not on his relationship with Eleanor, which he accepts to be a thing of the past, but on her child. Just as his mother had known about Bobby, so Adam knows in his heart that Eleanor's child is his.

When the baby is born, he and Jessica visit Eleanor in hospital. Simon is with her and the three of them cluster round the bed.

Jessica arranges pink flowers in a yellow jug. Yesterday, Adam bought his daughter a teddy bear. He's rather taken with the little fellow, he's even named him, but Eleanor is scornful: 'Honestly, Adam, you haven't a clue – it's far too big. It'll suffocate her. And as for "Nigel", for heaven's sake, whoever heard of a bear called Nigel?'

Simon laughs, enjoying Adam's discomfort. He is holding the baby. Georgina, Georgie. Jessica edges closer. She's wary; she doesn't like babies, but she's curious about this one.

Adam is curious as well, and wary for a different reason. He remains at the foot of the bed, clutching Nigel to his chest. He can't take his eyes off Georgie. Is it his imagination, or does she look a little like him? No beard, of course, and no recipe for wild boar terrine – but even so.

He doesn't like the way Simon is holding her. He struggles against the sudden urge to snatch the baby from his arms. He doesn't trust the man. What if he's holding her too tight? His eyes blur, and he sees a dancing cluster of blackberry bruises on the tiny arms and legs. He cannot bear it.

Eleanor glances up and smiles at him. Her lip trembles. He is almost certain he no longer wants her for himself, and yet the loss of intimacy is a dragging ache in his belly. How have they come to be so far apart? He tries to reconstruct the route that brought them here, but like the wake of a ship, it dissolves into the sea.

There is a commotion as Simon's parents arrive. Adam relinquishes Nigel, placing him at the foot of the bed. Jessica makes a space for them at Eleanor's side and, joining Adam, takes his arm. The Whitburns' arrival is an excuse to leave, but Eleanor won't let them go. 'You must stay,' she says. 'Say hello, at least. Adam, you haven't met Simon's parents. This is Irene.' Irene Whitburn is small and has dyed blonde hair. Adam shakes her hand. Her skin is dry. Like her son, she has an aura of turpentine. 'And this is George.'

George Whitburn's grip is firm. His fingers are white and delicate. Adam is polite, but insistent. 'We must go. Isn't that right, Jessica?'

'We'll come again,' she promises.

'I'm going home tomorrow,' Eleanor says.

'We'll call at the house. I'll ring.' Jessica squeezes Adam's arm. He is straining to escape. 'Just to make sure you're up to it. Okay, Adam, I know, I know – you're in a hurry. Stop fidgeting.'

He leaves the hospital in a fury. There is only the one thought in his head. Eleanor has named their daughter after Simon's father. How could she do such a thing?

Jessica herds him across the road and into a coffee shop. 'Don't make such a fuss. It's not that bad.'

'Yes it is.' She pushes him into a cubicle and orders two strong cappuccinos. '"Don't go, Adam,"' he mimics. '"I don't want to lose you . . ."'

'What did you expect?'

'I didn't expect her to name our daughter after a Whitburn.'

'It's no big deal, Adam.'

'It is. For me it is. What the hell is she doing to me? Sometimes I think I'm no better than him. I want to shout at her, tell her what I feel, what she's doing to me – shout it to the street.'

'Like Chris.'

'Yes.' He punches the table top. 'Just like Chris.'

18

Georgie's christening is to be celebrated at George and Irene's house. It isn't really a christening because there's no church service; it's more of a welcoming party.

Adam collects Jessica from her flat. She's wearing a red seersucker dress with a seaweed tangle of necklaces and green Doc Martens. She laughs when she sees him. 'A suit?' She tugs his lapel. 'Isn't that a bit over the top?'

Eleanor accepts their presents – a silver necklace from Jessica, a vintage edition of *Larousse Gastronomique* from him – and greets them with a kiss on the cheek. She looks Adam up and down and, pinching his hand, says to Jess in an exaggerated undertone, 'What on earth have you done with him? Why has he come dressed like a waiter?'

In the living room, Irene hands them each a glass of wine and

Simon waves a greeting. He has a new, spiky haircut and an eau-de-nil jacket. His shirt is the colour and sheen of melted chocolate. As Irene moves on to the next set of arrivals, Jessica squeezes Adam's arm and says, 'I don't care what Ellie says, I'd rather look like a waiter than something left over from the dessert trolley.'

He laughs and feels better. He mingles with the other guests, and he and Jessica become separated. Like a medieval court, the party progresses to the garden. The garden is long and narrow and the far end is overshadowed by an ancient apple tree. 'Bramley,' George Whitburn confides. 'Past its prime, I'm afraid, like me.'

Adam lingers beneath the canopy of the tree. The branches are knobbly and arthritic, the leaves dried up and curled and brown at the edges. A table has been placed in the shadow of the tree. On the table is a Moses basket. In the basket is Georgie, with his teddy bear snuggled at her feet. Eleanor has re-christened the bear Big Nigel.

Adam towers over the basket and brushes the rim with the tips of his fingers. His hand is disproportionately huge. Can Georgie focus yet? If so, he must be an alarming sight.

A crumpled leaf has caught in the blanket. Moving slowly so as not to startle her, he removes it. Georgie blinks. Emboldened, he tweaks Big Nigel's ear, and feels a bizarre rapport with the bear. It is his ambassador.

His daughter lies on her back. Her body is swaddled and stubby, her arms bent above her head, her fists clenched. Her hair is dark and short and it clings to her scalp like fuzzy-felt. He takes in every detail. The texture of her skin, the blue veins skimming like swallows beneath the surface. There is a yellow encrustation in the corner of her eye. He wants to pick her up and take out his handkerchief, and clean it away.

He does no such thing. Eleanor might think he was staking a claim. Even standing beside the basket, he dominates her. He steps back. His shadow shifts across the blanket and Georgie stretches her fingers and tries to grasp the phantom shape. A voice behind him says, 'Look at that now, isn't she a sweetie? Just like my Ellie.' The woman brushes past him and hoists Georgie from the basket. She strokes her back with a deft, practised hand. 'Let me see now,' she turns and considers him with her head cocked on one side. 'You must be the chef, Adam, am I right?'

He has heard about Eleanor's mother, mostly from Jessica, and is partly prepared for the vision in yellow confronting him. In appearance she couldn't be less like her daughter. Above the voluminous dress her face is round, and her bobbed grey hair is held off her face by an orange headband. A russet chrysanthemum, identical to the cluster growing in Irene Whitburn's border, has been tucked behind her right ear. Georgie purses her lips and suckles one of the thin petals. He says, 'Should she be doing that?'

'No you shouldn't, should you, you naughty girl.' Babs adjusts her hold. 'You're going to be a right trouble to your mum, I can see that.' She rests her chin on Georgie's shoulder. Her gaze makes Adam uncomfortable. 'I never would have thought it, you know. Ellie's always been so independent, I never imagined she'd make me a grandmother.' Adam's smile is awkward and stiff. Babs says, 'So what about you, Adam?'

'Me?'

'Yes, dear. Would you like to hold my granddaughter?'

Babs doesn't wait for his answer. With a knowing smile, she places his maybe-daughter in his arms. He is shaking inside, but his hands are steady. She is so soft, somehow both fragile and substantial. His huge hand makes a nest for her head. She rests against his shoulder and nuzzles his beard. Her hair is dark and her eyes are blue.

'Eleanor's colouring,' says Babs. 'That's nice. I'm sure Simon is all very well, but I wouldn't really want my grandchild to look like him.' She laughs, and takes Georgie from him. His arms gape, empty and cold. 'Now don't you go telling Eleanor I said that, will you dear?' Babs scowls. 'She can be so touchy at times.'

'I won't breathe a word.'

'Of course you won't. I can see I can rely on you.' She peers at him. 'Now then,' she says. 'I want to ask you something. About Jess . . .'

'What about her?'

'Well, where is she, dear? I haven't spoken to her all afternoon.'

19

Eleanor is in a state of anticlimax. She has spent months engrossed in the functions of her body, she has monitored every change in shape and texture, the presence or absence of discomfort and pain. All these she knows. Her sense of self and purpose has grown steadily along with her baby.

And now Georgie is here. The pain had been glorious, but afterwards – nothing.

Her blood and Georgie's are no longer the same. Her daughter produces her own blood. Such a complicated process, red cells and white, platelets and corpuscles. Unaided, Georgie's digestive system processes Eleanor's milk, extracting nutrients, expelling toxins. The realm of the body, distinct from the mind. Georgie will grow, and will grow away from her, until the day her own reproductive cycle kicks in. Then Georgie's eggs will travel to Georgie's womb, to be fertilized or not, nurtured or vented.

There is so much in this little body, actual and potential. No wonder she cries at night, screaming beneath the press of her future.

Eleanor may have misgivings about the future, but she's happy in the here and now. Her truce with Simon continues, Jess and Adam seem to be getting along, and she has her daughter.

God, she loves this child. All she wants is to look and look, to memorize every wrinkle and pore; every movement, voluntary and involuntary. Georgie changes day by day, hour by hour, and Eleanor doesn't want to miss a moment. Babs always complained that Eleanor grew up too fast, but Eleanor had paid it no mind; it was just something mothers said, it had no meaning. Until now.

But now, oh now . . . she wants to stop all the clocks, swing from the hands of Big Ben and hold back time to keep Georgie like this, for herself alone, for always.

It cannot be, of course. She has her career to consider, work to do. She's not back at the gallery yet, but Brian brings work to the house and a fortnight after Georgie's party she is in the middle of checking the proofs for the gallery's latest brochure, when Adam calls.

She greets him with a cry of pleasure. She really is very fond of him. He's so tall and looks so awkward standing in her doorway. He says, 'Am I disturbing you?'

'No, I'm due for a break.'

'I don't want to interrupt . . .'

'It's okay, Adam. Come on in.' He follows her through to the sitting room where Georgie is asleep in her basket. His face changes when he sees her. All the angles and sharp planes melt, and Eleanor experiences a moment of weakness. Maybe she should look into which of these men is Georgie's father.

No. Any such knowledge would bring in its wake a demand for rights. It is better this way.

Adam goes over to Georgie's basket and, bobbing down, strokes Big Nigel's arm. 'You were so scathing about him at the hospital,' he says. 'You said he was life-threatening.'

'I wasn't sure how Simon would react. She's become unaccountably attached to him. Big Nigel, that is, not Simon.' Adam laughs and adjusts Big Nigel's position. He looks so right, leaning over Georgie. He looks as though he belongs. 'Come away from there,' she says. 'You'll wake her.' He glances up, startled. More gently, she says, 'Come to the kitchen, I'll make some coffee.'

Oscar is perched on the draining board. He glares at her; he's jealous of Georgie. She brushes him off and runs the tap, and spoons instant coffee into a mug. 'No Chagga, I'm afraid.'

'In that case, I'd prefer tea.'

'Fine.' She rinses the mug and starts again.

'That was quite a party you had. Simon's parents did you proud.'

'Yes. They're a strange pair. Irene can be a bit snappy, but she's okay really.'

'I liked his father very much.'

'Me too. George is a butcher.'

'So he said.'

'Whereas Irene is virtually vegetarian.'

'I thought I might put some business George's way.'

'He'd appreciate that.'

'Eleanor, why did you do it? Why did you name her after him?' She straightens her back and grips the edge of the sink. What a fool she'd been, to think he wouldn't notice. 'You gave her his father's name.'

She stares out at the little courtyard garden. The autumn weather has finally turned, and a light breeze spatters the rain against the window pane. She says, 'My mother really liked you.'

'Eleanor . . .'

'I'm sorry. Georgie is not a subject for discussion.' Her tone is curt.

'You said I could be a part of her life.'

'So you are.'

'If this is all there is, it's not enough.' The kettle boils and the automatic switch clicks off. The cat-flap bangs twice, once as Oscar goes out, again as he returns in disgust at the rain. 'Eleanor, how long can you cling to this charade? You only have to look at her . . .'

'To see what?' She turns. 'That she looks like you? No, Adam, she looks like me.'

20

October, November, December. It is a Tuesday afternoon and Adam is playing with Georgie. She's sprawled on a blanket in front of the fire watching him make a tinsel bow tie for Big Nigel. She chuckles and clutches at the glittering strand.

Simon rarely plays with Georgie. Simon never plays with Georgie. He draws her, sitting for hours while she sleeps, his sketch-pad propped on his knee, his charcoal working to and fro. Sometimes he tries to sketch her while she's awake. It makes no difference to Georgie. She plays alone in a room silent but for the swish of charcoal on paper.

Adam says, 'She's growing.'

'Yes.' It is a detail that seems to have slipped right by Simon. Elbows on knees, Eleanor pulls her plait over her shoulder and tugs at the tuft at the end. Adam calls round once a week. Simon does not know about this, although sooner or later he is bound to find out. He might return early and discover Adam and Georgie together, or perhaps a neighbour will comment on the regularity of Adam's lone visits. She treads a dangerous line. It cannot go on indefinitely.

But this had only ever been a temporary measure. She had hoped that his relationship with Jess would formalize itself so they could visit as a couple. They would be Auntie Jess and Uncle Adam. Perhaps one day they'd produce a cousin or two.

It might yet happen, but they're taking too long. She must act. Georgie is the focus of her life. Everything that has happened, all the pain and uncertainty, was worthwhile because it resulted in Georgie.

But how long before Simon's anger fixes on Georgie? His jealousy is already apparent. She must protect her daughter.

What are her choices? She could leave him. She married him for all the wrong reasons and though she understands his weaknesses and is fond of him – still, despite everything – they are a danger to one another.

What about Adam? Her feelings for him are confused and she doubts they can ever be untangled. But she is sure of one thing: they no longer have a future.

If she leaves Simon it will be down to her and Georgie.

Yes, she rather likes the idea, there is a rightness to it. And yet part of her is afraid. Every time she nears a decision, she remembers Chris. It's all too easy to make the wrong decision.

In the end, Simon provides the answer. They cannot stay together as things stand, but a major change in their lives would give a whole new framework to the relationship, allow them to start with a clean slate, a blank canvas.

It is decided. She will stay with him, but not here. Adam can keep London and his restaurants and his flat, it is she who will quit the country.

And so this afternoon she watches him play with his daughter and tells herself over and over that it is the right decision. He is getting too close to Georgie. Sooner or later someone is going to get hurt.

He perches Big Nigel on his knee and makes him wave at Georgie. Eleanor's eyes prickle and her throat aches with the knowledge that she is about to tip his world upon its head once more. This time he will learn to hate her, and that will make what she's about to do easier – for him, not her. She cannot bear to think of his hatred.

Georgie has reclaimed Big Nigel. She sucks at his ear. 'She's gumming him to death,' says Adam. He looks up, inviting her reaction. His laughter dies. 'You're very serious this afternoon. What is it?' His tone sharpens. 'It's not Simon, is it? Because if it is . . .'

'No, Simon's fine. He's being very sweet at the moment. He promised to change and who knows, he might just manage it.'

'I'm very glad to hear it.'

'You could sound a little more convincing.'

'I might, if I was convinced.'

'Actually,' she twists her thick plait until she feels her hair straining at the roots. 'I want to talk to you about Simon. He's been offered a job.'

'Lucky Simon. Doing what?'

'A series of murals.' He raises a doubtful eyebrow. 'I know, ironic, isn't it? It's for a hotel chain in the States. It could be the making of him. You know what Brian says: money enables.'

'Well, that's great news.'

'I'm glad you think so. It's sort of semi-permanent. The chain goes right across the country. It's a lot of work, and we'll be away for a long time. Years, probably.'

He has been slow on the uptake, but now it hits him. Even Georgie senses something. Her mouth gapes and Big Nigel tumbles from her grasp. 'You're going with him? You and Georgie?' She nods. 'No,' his voice grates like rough metal. 'You can't be serious.'

'He can't afford to turn it down.'

'But you don't have to go with him . . .'

'It's the answer to everything – you remember what you said about starting again? We can let this place, and Simon's studio . . .'

'Eleanor, no.' He's standing now, looming over her, over Georgie. 'You've done it again. You've let me into your life – her life – just a little, just enough to really hurt when you do this. How can you be so cruel?'

'You're putting Georgie and me in jeopardy – can't you see that? – and it's coming between you and Jess. Believe me, it's better this way.'

'Better for who? For you? You want to burrow into your marriage, pretend it never happened, pretend she's his – you can't, I won't let you. It's a lie. And what about Georgie, d'you think she won't know? Growing up in a household like yours, violence and lies – what sort of an upbringing is that? You can't do this.'

He's right. She cannot do this to either him or Georgie. There has to be another way. They are standing so close and she feels it again, the debilitating desire that got her into this mess.

The thread tightens, drawing them closer. His face fills her field of vision, his breath is on her lips, his eyes lock on to hers. It's as if there is nothing and no one else in the world worth seeing. And the heat of him, radiating from a body that scarcely touches her.

Then Georgie squeals and the thread snaps. She scoops her up and adjusts the blanket. Adam touches her. The back of her hand. Her cheek. Georgie's shoulder. She leans towards him. She will go with him, be with him. The three of them.

'What the fuck's going on?'

Simon. How long has he been there? Neither of them had heard the door or his tread – just suddenly his voice, and his face transformed into the angry hunted Simon of a year ago.

The adrenalin flickers like fire. Fear and anticipation, a muscular contraction that makes Georgie cry out.

Simon lunges. Adam snatches Georgie.

It has been so long. She is hungry for this, for the locking of limbs, the burn of his grip, the rush of energy making an animal of her.

They are two of a kind. She is dimly aware of Adam backing towards the door. Georgie's screams take on a sing-song quality. And then she forgets Georgie and Adam, knows only the battle in hand, the roar of her blood and the pain, the skitter of raked nerves and burning flesh – and because they'd abstained during pregnancy, in this also she and her daughter are separate. Georgie will never know the thrill of it, the rapture of flight, the roar of the victor.

'Get out, Simon. I want you out of my house. Now.'

They career down the hallway, cannoning off the walls. Their bodies fuse, but they strain to separate. She struggles with the door, grazing her knuckle on the bolt. He thrusts her into a corner and there is a sick thud as her head cracks against the doorjamb. She squirms away but he pins her arm behind her back and bites her shoulder and she twists and brings up her knee.

And now the door is open and she is thrusting his convulsing body out into the street. He reels and crashes against the gate. The violence of this breach is the greatest pain yet.

And so he wins. He has beaten Georgie.

She slams the door. He is gone. With fumbling fingers she slips the chain into its housing and leans against the wall. She closes her eyes. It is done. Tears force themselves between her lids.

Her skin glows. Her racked breath scours her throat. She is incapable of thought. The passing seconds are marked by the pump of her heart.

One, and two, and three, and four . . .

Thought returns in a crimson blur. Where is Adam? And Georgie? She throws back her head and struggles to concentrate.

She climbs the stairs slowly, clinging to the banister. She is distanced from her surroundings. The walls, the stairs, the door ahead lack substance; they have the flatness of projections on a cinema screen.

Adam is in her bedroom. He looks lost, like an actor who has forgotten his lines. Georgie is sprawled against his shoulder and his large hand strokes her back, soothing her. When he raises his eyes, Eleanor sees that they are black with rage.

At last he speaks. 'You like it.' His voice is low so as not to distress Georgie. She would prefer him to shout, for his anger to clash with hers and with Georgie's screams. Then she could hate him more easily.

Is this me, is this what I am?

No. It's what I've become. But I can fight back, reinvent myself. Why not? I've done it before. I have a new role. I am Georgie's mother.

'Jesus Christ, you really do enjoy it, don't you?' His voice is thick with emotion. 'It gives you a kick, a buzz . . . I should have realized. It was all there. That time in the church, the knife – I had all the clues right in front of me, but I couldn't see. I didn't want to see.'

Her dizziness returns, and with it the pain. She must go slowly. There is a ritual to this. Her mind explores her body, assessing the damage. Mostly bruising, by their standards, fairly minor. But she is also bleeding. She touches her fingers to the tickling trickle of blood at her temple. She is mildly indignant that Adam should show so little concern for her well-being.

She wipes her fingers and leaves a smear of blood on her skirt. She forces a smile and holds out her arms. 'Give her to me.' Adam takes a step back, but is blocked by the bed. 'It's all right, it's over, Adam.'

'If you think,' he takes a deep, shuddering breath. 'If you seriously think I'll let you take her out of the country after this – no way, Eleanor. I'll stop you, I'll do whatever it takes. She's my daughter . . .'

'I'm not going, not now. When I said it was over, I meant for all of us, you and me, me and Simon.'

'I don't believe you.'

'It's the truth. Now, give her to me.' She moves closer, close enough to see that his face is white, his cheeks wet. She wants to dry them, kiss them . . . no, she must be resolute. There is nothing he can do, he has no rights over her or her child. Very gently, she prises Georgie from his arms.

All the anger has gone out of him, and with it his strength. He relinquishes Georgie.

'She'll be all right, Adam. No harm will come to her. I promise.' She holds her baby close and tucks her head beneath her chin. 'This is how it should be, it's just me and Georgie now.' He has to believe her; she must make him understand. Georgie is the one good thing in her life, her only reality. 'I know what you think of me,' she says. 'I find it so hard to make the right choice – even the smallest decision has momentous consequences. But this is different. I know what I have to do. I should have done it from the start but I couldn't, not without Georgie. I can't choose for myself, but I can choose for her.'

'What about Simon?'

'He's not like you, he's not possessive about Georgie. In a week or two he'll be gone and he'll forget her. In the meantime, I'll change the locks, get a court order – buy a dog if necessary. He won't get near her, I promise.'

'And me? Us?'

'You don't want that. Look into your heart, Adam – you don't want to be a part of what I am.'

'Christ, I'm so confused, I don't know what to do.'

'But I know. I know everything now. What goes for Simon goes for you too. Remember what I told you at the start, that this baby is mine? I was so certain, but I didn't see the full picture and so I couldn't follow through. I was scared of being on my own and I compromised by staying with Simon. I was wrong. And now it's over. All of it.'

He understands. She can tell from the dead light in his eyes. For the last time she rests her hand against his cheek and draws her fingers through the tight curls of his beard. 'It's the right decision, for once I'm certain. And I can do it,' she touches his lips with the very tips of her fingers. She has to fight her desire for a last kiss, a final embrace. She steps back. 'With your help,' she whispers. 'If you and Simon let me be – I can heal myself.'

Last Rites

Adam cannot breathe, he gags on the stifling air. He cannot see. He stretches his eyes wide. Nothing. Like being tied in a sack. Not a glimmer.

No light, but sound. The distant whisper of malicious children. Snickering and snide, jeering at him.

And behind their cruelty, despair, such a terrible, grieving hoard – a raft of drowned children clustering the Cornish coastline like flies on a corpse. They clutch the black rocks, they reach for him and mock him.

When he wakes the malignant babble continues but the rest, the enveloping blackness and pitiless, grasping ghosts, are gone.

Sometimes it's hard to distinguish what is real from what isn't. Memories are real. So is this, a sudden cramp and spasm of nausea ejecting him from his bed. The sickness comes in waves, breakers mounting one upon the other, higher and higher, then crashing in an outrush of vomit.

Just in time. He pushes himself back from the toilet pan and struggles to his feet. He is shaking and dizzy. He leans on the sink and turns on the tap and swills out his mouth. The chill of the water and its sour taste sets his stomach heaving again. He has nothing left to void, yet still his muscles clench and knot and the bile stings his mouth and throat. His nose is running. And his eyes. He is crying. It is almost two years since she broke his world in two. Only now does he cry.

He is cold. Shaking violently, he edges along the landing. His fingers lodge in the cracks and crevices. He presses his cheek against the wall. The exposed stones are cold. Gritty. Real.

Three steps to the bed. He collapses. He is still crying but his mind races. A door has been breached. Light floods the archives. Dust stirs and paper crumbles. Order. Yes. He has a sense of cause and effect, of time passing and time stood still.

Don't lose this. This is important. He struggles against the fading light and the dust that chokes him. His chronology is hopeless. He must concentrate. Simon spent almost five years in the States and two years ago he returned to England. To Eleanor. And she destroyed them. All of them.

It isn't true. Time doesn't heal. The events and actions that caused pain in the past, cause pain in the present – even though the source of that pain, his love for Eleanor, is long dead. He has dragged himself from the battlefield, but his wounds are deep. His memories, like shrapnel, stay buried until a sudden movement works them free to pierce his gut and draw blood.

But something has changed; he recovers more swiftly. A thought that once would have felled him, provokes no more than a stagger now.

They had blundered back into his life, Eleanor and Georgie, and Simon – and broken his world not in two but into three, a dozen, a thousand fragments. A broken mirror, a smashed vase. A wanton act.

'What's past is past. Time to move on.' This is Pam's view, but Pam doesn't know.

There was a time when he had loved Eleanor. Then he'd stopped loving her. Finally, after years of separation, he had lost her. That's when he came here, to Polruan and Eden. Here his future is ready-made, he has a wife and a child. This is what Pam thinks. It is all she knows. Unless he tells her, how can she know what it was like for him to be lost so long in the bleak no-man's-land between past and future?

But the rift is mending. He is almost healed.

He pulls the covers up to his chin. Moonlight glimmers across the ceiling. He hears the sea. Here are no ghosts, just salt water governed by wind and tide, crashing against the rocks.

He must sleep. He'll feel better when he wakes. He tries to relax, but another spasm convulses him. Curled in a foetal ball, he occupies his mind with a list of everything he has eaten and drunk these past three days. Something must be causing this.

He buries his head in the pillow. He dozes – and dreams himself a strip of webbing that Jessica is stretching across a chair frame. Muscles strain, sinews stretch and snap.

He wakes next to a grey dawn. Rain swishing against the window is the sound of the wind in long grass.

Nothing is what it seems. Nothing is forever.

He no longer feels sick, but his twisted guts ache and his skin is clammy. He's dizzy. Daylight spreads across his ceiling.

It is a bad time to get ill. Eden is finished, inside and out. The bulk of his furniture will arrive from Suffolk tomorrow and his family is scheduled for the day after.

The house waits, everything in its place, immaculate. The sketch Pam made of him falling off the ladder has been worked up into a watercolour. Two days ago they held a little ceremony, hanging the painting above the fireplace and toasting it with an exceptional Australian Chardonnay.

Pam is impatient. She can't wait to meet his wife. 'You're too secretive, Adam. You make a mystery of everything.'

Beyond his window, simmering clouds heave themselves into unlikely shapes before disintegrating like scum on a stockpot.

To remember, and then forget.

This is what he came here for, and he has succeeded. He remembers it all – up to the very moment he stopped loving her.

Eleanor.

She sent him away. 'I can heal myself.' With those words, something shifted inside him – a physical sensation, a cracking twig. He would leave her. And Georgie. The identity of Georgie's biological father was no longer an issue. She belonged to Eleanor.

Simon left for the States, and Adam put his restaurants on the market. Simon's recent publicity, including a magazine feature on the Jangles murals, stirred up a lot of interest – far more than the agents had anticipated. They adjusted their expectations, and suggested an auction.

On the day of completion Adam was like a parrot in a cage. He blundered round the flat – kitchen to living room to bedroom, then back again. He made coffee, but couldn't drink it. He lit a cigarette, but managed only a single puff before stabbing it out.

He picked up the phone and started to punch in Jessica's number, then slammed the receiver back on its cradle.

Eleanor, Simon, Jessica. To hell with them all, he's out of his

287

depth – a Northamptonshire lad with a passion for cooking who'd come to London with the bull of ambition pawing at his stomach, who'd achieved his dream and made his fortune.

All over. Gone. There is no purpose to his life, no more ambition.

He snaps up the blind and, lighting another cigarette, leans against the worktop. On the other side of the street an old lady trundles a shopping trolley. The wheels bounce on the uneven ridges of the paving stones. Gran had a trolley. She would drag it behind her like a reluctant mongrel – and Adam too, clinging to her hand or the rim of the trolley. He remembers a particular day. They called at the corner shop where Gran bought him some sweets in a white paper bag, twisted at the corners. Rubbing his tongue against the roof of his mouth, he feels it again, the gritty sugar and acetone tang of the rose-coloured pear-drop.

And hears again the quiver in Gran's voice as she tells him the news, that his baby brother is dead.

You can't argue with death. Bobby had gone and nothing would bring him back. But he had argued with Eleanor – until he witnessed the fight with Simon. Once he'd seen that, come face to face with the pleasure she derived from their violence, he was done with her.

It's time to move on.

He heads north out of London. He will go back to his roots and start again. Northampton. It doesn't sound too enticing – Jessica's right, he's a romantic – but then it need not be Northampton. He has not committed himself to anyone or anything; he could go anywhere. For the first time in his life he has real freedom.

He reaches the M25, and turns east instead of west.

The A14 goes to within six miles of Newmarket. He bypasses the racing town and continues towards Bury St Edmunds.

At Georgie's christening he'd taken an immediate liking to Babs; she'd lodged herself in his memory and now she looms large, a benign presence, a yellow-swathed magnet dragging him eastward.

Arriving in Bury, he found a hotel and booked in, and then rang Babs.

'Adam, how lovely to hear from you. Where are you staying? Nonsense. You must pay your bill first thing in the morning and come here. I insist. I've got a lovely spare room. Ellie would have a go at me about the wallpaper, but then she and I have never seen eye to eye on that sort of thing, whereas you strike me as a very accommodating individual.'

Babs gave him shelter, cooked bizarre meals – pilchards and spaghetti – and took it upon herself to show him the town. 'I'm afraid that's not quite as exotic or erotic a prospect as it sounds,' she chuckled.

When he told her he was thinking of settling in Bury she said, 'Well, if you wanted to be sure of never bumping into Eleanor, you couldn't pick a better place – but what about Jess, dear? Where does this leave her?'

By mid-morning his vomiting is replaced by diarrhoea. His body rattles like an empty gourd. He should be taking fluids but the water from the tap tastes foul, and he can't face the effort of going downstairs.

He cannot even get back to the bedroom.

He sits at the top of the stairs, his head sunk on his knees, his hands gripping his ankles. His mind buzzes. Strange, this frenetic activity in his brain when his body is dying. How long has he been sitting here? He imagines days passing. His body will become a dehydrated husk with just a few strands of hair like dried grass clinging to his leathery scalp.

Banging.

Fists banging on the door.

Answer. He opens his mouth. His tongue cleaves to his palate. No sound comes. And who cares, anyway?

More banging and a voice shouting through the letter-flap. His name. Someone calling his name. He doesn't recognize the voice. Or the letter-flap. Or the stairs. His fingers clench. His nails dig in. Pain defines. Blood seeps from the scratch. Children kick and scratch. Bobby died.

'Adam?' Hands on him, forcing his head up, making him focus. Strange face, all lined around the mouth. Pudding-basin hair. Pam.

She helps him back to bed and calls the doctor. She feeds him soup from a can. Even in this state he knows. He wants to tell her, he wants to laugh. He sleeps. It's dark when he wakes. His mouth is dry and his eyes prickle. More soup. Watery, with machine-chopped vegetables. Dry bread. Tea.

He feels like an old man. There are ridges in his skin. His bones are all honeycombed; they have no substance. They will drift away. Float on the tide, winking like cockleshells.

Pam reads to him from a Daphne du Maurier novel. His mind meanders between the words, snakes up along the sentences, seeking gaps between phrases. Nothing makes sense, but now and again his mind anchors itself to a word or an idea that strikes up an echo somewhere deep inside. The words are like barnacles clinging to the shell of his brain. He wants to laugh. He imagines a cackle.

And then another idea, a very particular idea, fixes his attention. To the heroine, Janet, a son is born – a child calling to her before birth and beyond death. He shifts his position. Pam pauses and lays aside the book. She pours fresh water from the jug and hands him the glass. 'I think you should sleep, now.'

'Sentimental rubbish,' his voice cracks; it's the voice of a cantankerous old man. He takes a sip of water.

'If you'd wanted gritty realism, you should have said. I didn't think you were in any fit state.' His smile stretches his dry lips. His tortured body throbs. 'Adam, are you sure you don't want me to ring your wife?'

'No.'

'I know she'll be here at the weekend, but if she knows you're ill she'll probably come sooner . . .'

'Don't fuss, Pam. I'll be fine by tomorrow.'

'If you say so. But I'll fetch them, shall I, from the station?'

'They're driving down.'

'I see. Fine. I must say, I'm looking forward to meeting them – your wife and your little girl. You know,' she considers him. 'It's odd, but I don't think you've ever told me her name.' She drapes a napkin over the water jug. 'Your daughter . . .'

He closes his eyes. It's true, he has avoided names; it is a way of keeping the pain at bay. But there is no longer any escape. No more games. She'll know soon enough. He sees a pair of pale blue eyes and a haze of blonde hair. He feels the weight of her body against his shoulder, her tiny fingers lost in the palm of his outsized hand.

'Her name is Eve,' he says, opening his eyes.

'Eve . . .' Pam muses. 'That's nice. And what is she like, does she look like you?'

'Not in the slightest. There's no reason why she should. I'm sorry, but I lied to you, Pam. Eve isn't my daughter.'

290

1

The wicked witch lives in the walls of the house where Georgie lives. Georgie knows, she hears her cackling, hears her scrabbling in the night as she moves from room to room, thin as a broomstick, spying and casting spells, her crooked fingers and scratchy nails scoring the plaster, piercing the paper, reaching, groping . . .

She wants me, wants to take me with her, into the walls, into the dark, never come home, never see Mummy ever, ever again.

Scream. Georgie screams. Then she wakes. The screaming goes on; and the shouting too. Her mother's voice. And another.

Georgie snuggles her teddy bear close and tucks his head into the warm safe place beneath her chin. His name is Big Nigel and he smells of damp dog. Mummy keeps threatening to wash him but he doesn't like water, he says it makes him feel all heavy and sad. She and Big Nigel tell each other everything. Mummy doesn't understand. Sometimes Georgie thinks she's jealous. Georgie loves her mummy, but she loves Big Nigel too. He always knows what to do.

Big Nigel says, go see.

Georgie slithers out of bed. Her nightie rucks round her bottom and she tugs it down and clutches Big Nigel more tightly. She bites his ear. He doesn't mind, he understands that if she hurts him, it's only because she loves him. Owlie Night-Light watches and waits. Three steps to the door. No slippers. No time. She can still hear the voices. Angry voices – no screaming now. She reaches for the handle. It's cold. She creeps on to the landing. The light from the hall turns the banisters to cot bars.

Big Nigel says, go down.

One step, two step. Pause. Listen. The voices are quieter now. She can't hear what Mummy's saying, but understands her tone. When Georgie's been naughty and been told off and wants to be friends

again, but Mummy is still angry, she sounds like this, as if she can't
hear the Sorrys and the Please Mummys, can't feel the tug at her arm
and the nuzzling at her knee. That's how the man sounds, like he's
sorry for something and wants to make up.

Georgie tiptoes to the bottom of the stairs. There's a leather jacket
on the hallstand. Georgie hasn't seen it before. She wants to touch it,
scrunch the creaking sleeve in her hand, breathe in the dark smell
like wet earth and pepper that will catch in the back of her throat.
Mummy hasn't got a leather coat, but Georgie knows just how it will
feel and smell.

The voices from the front room are loud again. The man speaks
quickly, urgently. Mummy sounds like she's making fun of him. The
door is open just a crack and a needle of yellow light pierces the hall.
Georgie's afraid. She shouldn't be here. Mummy will be cross.

But it was Mummy who'd screamed. It had to be Mummy, it
couldn't be the man because men don't scream.   Go closer, says
Big Nigel.

The blue dress Mummy's wearing is Georgie's favourite. And
she's got her hair loose, too. That's nice, like a glossy black river.
Sometimes Georgie clambers into bed with her and snuggles up
close. It's one of her favourite things to do. She likes it because they
both smell nice, and because they're all soft from their bath. And
most of all she loves to go to sleep with her fingers tangled in the long
black strands of her mummy's hair.

Big Nigel wriggles. He's getting impatient, he wants to see.
Taking care not to make a noise, Georgie leans against the door. It
opens a crack wider, enough to see the man. He's standing very close
to Mummy. Mummy has her back to Georgie, but she can tell how
angry she is because her liquorice hair is snaking like a whip and
she's standing with her head back and her neck and shoulders all
stiff. Then Georgie sees the man has stopped wanting to be friends.
He's got yellow hair and he's shorter than her mummy. Georgie
wants to giggle. They look silly. She chews Big Nigel's ear, scared to
make a sound.

And then the room explodes. Her mummy says something in a
low, unkind voice, and the little man yells at her then pounces like
Oscar with a mouse. But her mummy's not a mouse and she fights
back and the man has hold of her arm and he swings her round and
hits her and shakes her and throws her to the floor.

Georgie screams and bangs back the door and flies to the rescue. She hurls herself at the man, clinging to his bucking back, biting and kicking and shouting, 'Stop it, don't do that, leave my mummy alone.'

Eleanor sits hunched on the floor. She's shaking inside, a high-intensity tremor. Her blood surges, whipped to a frenzy by the fight. It has been so long. Take it easy. Deep breaths. Don't let it show, don't let the fear come through.

Or the thrill.

The front door slams, followed by a car door. The car roars away. City silence. They are alone now, the two of them. Eleanor and Georgie. She must try to make light of it, mustn't let Georgie see how serious this is.

But Georgie knows, Georgie drew blood tonight.

Simon. She hadn't expected to see him again. Five years ago she'd kicked him out of her house, just like tonight. She'd changed the locks and when he came back, banging on the door and shouting for all the street to hear, she'd shouted back. She said if he didn't go, she'd call the police. 'I've bruises to show – and a witness. Don't think I won't . . .'

'Well fuck you, Nell.' He kicked the door. 'And fuck Mason too.'

What have I done? This is Chris all over again. Fists pounding on the door, a lover dismissed, a husband evicted. But Simon is not the suicidal type.

No, Simon is unlikely to go jumping off bridges, but what else might he do? What if he goes to the restaurant and makes a scene? Adam would hate that.

Later. Eleanor wakes in the night, scared as a child. Fumbling with the matches, she lights a stub of candle. The yellow glow spreads, warm and reassuring. She stares at the ceiling, striving to divine answers in the wavering shadows.

There must be something very wrong with her, perhaps the same loose connection that confounds her love for Babs. What sort of woman is loved by two men, and drives both of them away?

By the time Adam left, he no longer loved her, Eleanor is certain of that. What had happened between him and Jess? They could have made a go of it, if only she'd not blundered into their path. Adam is the one man Jess doesn't despise, but these days Jess never mentions him.

Eleanor doesn't mention him either, nor does she think about him much. She pretends he's dead, and Simon too. Like Chris. This little delusion has worked quite well until now, but now she finds that her dead are not buried.

This evening she'd opened the door expecting Jess or a hawker, and found Simon on her doorstep clutching a bottle of wine. Simon comes a-courting as though nothing has happened, no time passed. He hasn't changed. He's as scruffy and shifty as a child who's done wrong and thinks he can bluff and endear his way into the right. And like a fool, she lets him in.

She should have known better. He'd not been in the house five minutes before her precariously sustained self-assurance began to unravel and she had to defend herself in the only way she knew. By mocking him – his way of life, his principles, his art.

Never sneer at a man's car, his art or his penis.

There had been a moment, a fraction of a second lasting an hour, when they'd squirmed together on the bare boards, a jumble of limbs clashing and bruising. Her dress caught on a splinter and she felt the tug of fabric and cool wood against her thighs – and Simon above her, heavy and hard. His breath rasped, a thread of saliva joined upper lip to lower; rough stubble scraped her cheek as he thrust downwards, spread-eagling her, pinning her wrists to the floor. She heard noises, sounds from the street, youngsters heading for the pub and laughing as they passed. So close. She wanted to call out, but couldn't. She was losing this battle. She was out of practice, not as strong as she thought – and more than that, her body's responses betrayed her. Bad blood. A deadly cocktail of rage and desire.

And then Georgie – her mother's daughter with her shrill war-cry and the hard impact of her determined little body. Georgie to the rescue, catching him off guard, sending him flying. What a blow to his ego. She laughs and lifts her head and rakes her fingers through her hair.

Georgie is still in the room, huddled cross-legged on the floor, watching her mother through a muddle of curls. She has brought Big Nigel with her. For protection. They are inseparable.

Georgie returns her smile, but there's a tremor to her chin.

Eleanor wants to tell her it's all right, that Mummy's in control, but it would be a lie.

She takes a breath and bunches her hair back off her face. She is distracted by a bruise on her upper arm. She examines the growing cluster of smudged finger-marks.

The jack-in-the-box jumps out of his box.

Where there was numbness, now there is pain. She fingers the spreading blackberry stain. Long ago, with Simon's help, she discovered the value of pain – its power to define, to peg the boundaries, mark out the territory of the body.

Who am I? This is who I am. Simon paints a line on flesh, blue-black and mustard.

But now there is Georgie and Georgie is Eleanor – a reflection, a shadow. No. Georgie's not a ghost, she's my other self.

Georgie shuffles forward and strokes Eleanor's fingers where they lace the bruise. Eleanor examines her face, eager to detect a resemblance beyond colouring. 'Your hair,' everyone said when baby Georgie's hair was a dark fuzz, before it began to spring into defiant curls. 'Your eyes.'

'Does it hurt, Mummy?' Georgie leans closer and squints into Eleanor's face. Eleanor nods and shrugs. 'Will he come back?' She proffers Big Nigel, as if he's the one asking the question. 'Don't let him, Mummy. Me and Big Nigel don't want him to.'

Anger also defines. How dare he. She should have known he couldn't stay away forever. Once again she has to make a choice. Not for herself, but for Georgie. If Simon inveigles his way back into her life, it will be disastrous for both of them. She has seen Georgie respond to him in kind. Her paternity is not in doubt. His genes and hers jangle a discord in Georgie's blood. Adam's daughter would not have joined the fight.

She cannot allow it to start again. She must stop it before it begins, this game as predictable as Russian roulette, in which sooner or later one of the chambers – his or hers – must fire.

2

'Evil little bitch.' Nursing his sore hand, Simon raids the bathroom cabinet. Empty. Shit. Bloody tenants, they haven't left so much as a bar of soap, let alone a packet of plasters.

He tries the kitchen. No joy there, either. Just a ragged green scouring pad, a few knives and forks, a bottle opener and a broken garlic press.

It shook him up, being attacked like that. Not that he didn't deserve it. He's only been back five minutes and already he's gone and lost his cool with Nell. It's like he's never been away. He just can't help it, all his good intentions go for nothing when she comes over all cold and superior.

And then the kid bursting in on them, grabbing hold of him and hanging on, fierce as hell. He'd shaken her off like she was one of those ratty little dogs. He'd thought she was a dog at first, coming out of nowhere.

He rubs his hand. She's broken the skin. Trust Nell to go and breed a little vampire. There always was something a bit gothic about Nell. He'd tried to paint it once, while he was in the States. He'd been drinking. Leaving Nell and the kid had been hard, but she was right, they were a danger to one another. He'd always meant to go back, try and patch things up, but his programme of work was relentless. Nell didn't answer his letters. He let it slide.

I missed you, Nell. Both of you. Just because I let it go, doesn't mean I didn't care. There was so much going on, you've no idea.

He'd never worked so hard. When he wasn't up on the scaffolding physically applying paint, he was working on the scheme, composition and palette for the next job. Weeks passed. Months. The new country was both familiar and unfamiliar. At first he clung to the things he understood. Anything remotely corresponding to his old life – aspects of language, dress, the layout of a supermarket – was seized upon. Then gradually it dawned on him that he was no longer trying to match the images of the new world with those of the old. He had begun to court the unfamiliar.

Like the pattern on a fabric stretched too long in the sun, his memories became blanched and indistinct. Eleanor and Georgie appeared translucent, faded. Soon they would disappear altogether.

Scary. Shit, I need a drink.

But he had the power to reverse the process; he could give them back their substance. He would paint them. Baby Georgie tugging at her mother's breast, making the nipple all swollen and red, suffused with blood, raw. The kid had got a taste for the stuff, ingesting it with her mother's milk. Raspberry ripple ice cream. One of these days he'll take her to McDonald's.

He laughs out loud. What a kid. He re-examines his injury, this time with admiration. It has become a trophy. Spunky. Bet no one fucks with my Georgie.

He takes the bottle and corkscrew through to the studio. He flicks on the light. It glares – no shade. No matter. He's worked hard and made a packet. He'll buy a new flat in a better part of town, see if he can't impress a few people.

That's why he'd called on Nell, to impress her.

No, who does he think he's kidding? He'd called to talk. He thought they might put an exhibition together, get the old partnership back on the road. Him and Nell and Brian Farraday.

She wasn't interested. He tried reminding her of the other team – the two of them and Georgie. She flew into a rage. 'We're not a team. We never were. I'm warning you, Simon, if you come anywhere near us, if you even try and approach Georgie . . .'

'Approach? She's my daughter, Nell, I haven't seen her in five years.' He stops. He knows this route, straight down to hell. 'All I'm saying—'

'Five years – and not a word from you, nothing. Oh, payments in the bank, fine, thanks a bunch, Simon. It's no substitute.'

'We were supposed to go to the States together, make a new start, remember? But then you and Mason – you kicked me out, changed the locks . . .'

'You know, it escapes me – why did I do that, I wonder?'

'Okay, I was a bastard, I admit it, but that's all in the past. I'm different now. I promise. You've got to trust me, Nell.'

'I don't trust you. I can't imagine why I ever did. You think you're special because you've been out of the country earning Mickey Mouse money – but doing what? Blood will out, Simon. You don't fool me; you're nothing but a third-rate decorator and I don't want anything to do with you . . .'

With a vicious tug he opens the wine and hurls the cork at the window. It rebounds into a pile of crumpled newspaper. The flat's a mess. Yesterday he'd gone round to Irene's to pick up the stuff she'd stored during his absence, and now the room is a mêlée of half-unpacked boxes and dismantled stereo equipment and canvases and folders stacked unevenly against the walls.

He drinks the wine straight from the bottle. His anger and defiance ebb a little. He's lost. Displaced. He's been away too long. I'm a changed man, Nell. Honest.

'No, you're just the same. I know you, Simon. This is what you always were, a spiteful little boy.'

He sees himself in the night-darkened window, the prisoner in the mirror.

Fantastic view in the daytime, though. He takes another mouthful of wine. Roofscapes. Real source of inspiration. There's a hotel restaurant – where? Connecticut? Maybe. All the towns and states merge after a while; only his images remain distinct. No matter. This restaurant out in the country has a wall covered with roofs. It gives him a buzz, does that. A little bit of London transported. Not the obvious bits, oh no. Not Tower Bridge or red telephone boxes, but everyday grey slate. He painted it seeping moss, fractured, streaked with birdlime. And chimney stacks, a whole forest of them. He'd worked hard to get the exact shade of brick, a subtle transition from ochre to cream. Important to get it right, this counterfeit reality. He'd silhouetted the roofs against a dawn sky with just the suggestion, the merest ghost of an aeroplane. Or an interesting cloud formation. You pays your money and takes your choice. Oh and yes, the shoe. Mustn't forget the shoe. A white trainer with a panting tongue, lodged in the gutter. Now that was real. He'd seen it from this very window. How the hell had it got there? Who cares. It's great stuff, grist to the mill and all that. Mind you, the Mary Poppins angle sold the idea.

And now he's back, and he's not sure quite where he goes from here. Still, no rush. He'll take it slowly, consider his options, put out some feelers. Maybe work up a few old sketches and get Farraday to hang them. Nursing the wine bottle, he plucks a folder from the stack against the wall and drops cross-legged to the floor. He clears a space with a swipe of his arm, opens a folder and fans the crisp sheets in an arc.

Eerie. Hands. Sheet after sheet covered with the things. One or two have been done in washes, but most are charcoal, sweeping strokes, beautiful hands – but ugly, too. Long and slim, the little finger extending almost as far as the others. Creepy, that. Deformed, almost. No, they're neither beautiful nor ugly, just amazing. Fingers extended, fingers crooked, beckoning, fending him off, tracing shapes in the air. He's never been able to get it right. The hours he's spent – and it never stops, not even after all these years.

He has never captured her convincingly. Only her hands. Yet from the moment they met everything he has painted – colours, textures, shapes, figurative or abstract, even a bloody bowl of fruit for God's sake – has been his way of trying to get hold of her, pin her down, define her.

The only time he ever got close was with the Cornish seascape.

He shuffles the papers back into the folder. There's no future in this. He takes another swig of wine. When he told Irene he was going to call on Eleanor, she'd shaken her head and said, 'What for? What is it with you? Have you never heard of sleeping dogs, Si?'

'She's my wife. Why shouldn't I see her?'

'Water under the bridge.'

'And Georgie?'

'In all these years, how much thought have you given to your daughter?'

'It hasn't been easy.'

'It hasn't been impossible either. Forget Georgie.'

'I didn't abandon them. She was supposed to come with me, but she changed her mind. I tried writing, I sent them money. What else could I do? Okay, so it's a mess and it's my fault and I'm sorry, but I'll make it up to them. She's my kid, Mum, and Nell's my wife. I have rights.'

'You're an absentee father and an absconder. You're my son, Si, and God knows I love you, but you always were a fool.'

3

Eleanor takes Georgie to the nursery. So far as Georgie is concerned, today is like any other day. She skips ahead, a little Medusa with her baby-snake curls of black hair writhing. She's singing. Eleanor doesn't recognize the song; she probably learnt it off Jess's radio. She spends most afternoons at the workshop. Eleanor worries about sharp implements.

The song becomes shrill. Georgie waves her arms in time to her music. It's as if she has no memory of Simon's visit.

Georgie is the only person Eleanor has ever really loved. Adam and Simon were just a means to this end – sad, but true. Georgie. Blood of my blood. Eleanor smiles, and tears start to her eyes. Her daughter's vulnerability terrifies her. She wants to tie her down, shut her away in a safe place. She frets about needles and knives, cars and scalding water. She tries telling herself these are not threats, but lessons waiting to be learnt, and that children are marvellously resilient. Chris had refused to see this; he could measure his own worth only according to his children's needs.

She has not thought of Chris in a long time. He is still a part of her life, but only in the form of a dull ache that will never quite disappear.

Which means it may not be true what she tells herself – perhaps once she did love somebody other than Georgie.

It doesn't bear thinking about.

What about this business with Simon? She really should have seen it coming. Life progresses in a series of cycles. She has observed this.

Things she knows for certain: the earth orbits the sun, the moon orbits the earth and the earth spins on its axis. Sooner or later everyone turns up somewhere they've already been. When the planets form a line, there is an eclipse.

Events are lining up now. Simon is back and Jess is pregnant.

When they come within sight of the main road, Georgie stops skipping and loiters by a lamppost. She always waits here, in front of her favourite house. It has a flamenco doll in the window. The dancer has black hair and red lips and a cascade of crimson flounces. Georgie says it's the most beautiful thing in the whole wide world. Babs would be proud.

Babs thinks Eleanor has mishandled the whole business of Simon and Adam and Jess.

As they approach the main road, Eleanor catches hold of Georgie's hand. Ever since they left home this morning she has half expected Simon to leap out of a doorway and spirit Georgie away – which is strange, because if he wasn't interested in her as a baby, why should he want her now?

Who knows how Simon's mind works? She cannot take the risk.

The traffic roars. Babs says London is a terrible place to bring up a child and she's right. Dog-dirt and traffic, drugs and alcohol.

I should move away. She imagines somewhere rural, a long dirt track stretching between tall, dark hedges, and at the end a five-bar gate, and behind the gate a house. A house made of stone. Solid. Impenetrable.

Georgie tugs at her hand. Eleanor quickens her pace. Georgie giggles and pulls her along even faster. Eleanor laughs and tries to hug her, but Georgie pushes her away. 'You mustn't do that, Mummy. Stop it.' She's indignant. Embarrassed. She's growing up too fast.

They reach the nursery gates. Next door is the big school. Children play, squabbling and screeching like tomcats. A ball is kicked against the fence. The chain-link yields, then resists. The ball drops back and a boy skids across the asphalt to retrieve it. Eleanor herds Georgie into the relative safety of her own playground.

Once again, she is visited by certainty. She knows what to do. The idea of starting again is terrifying, but she will make the choice, not for herself, but for her daughter.

4

When Adam moved out of London, he almost left without saying goodbye to Jess. It was Ellie who told her he'd put his restaurants on the market, and she read in the local paper that they were to be auctioned.

She had been close to Adam – okay, not as close as she would have liked, but even at the level of friendship you don't just bugger off without a word of goodbye.

Men are such cowards. She scrunched up the newspaper and stuffed it in the bin. A complete waste of space – insemination is all they're good for. The sooner we replace them with machines, the better.

That's what her head tells her – pity her body won't listen.

She drove round to his flat. The removal van was parked outside. Inside, two lads were manhandling a sofa down the stairs and she had to press herself against the wall to let them pass.

Apart from a couple of crates stacked in the hall, the flat was empty. She wandered through the living room to the kitchen, then back again. She found Adam in the bedroom, sitting on the floor with his back to the wall. His eyes were dull and flat, and he was smoking a cigarette.

He acknowledged her with a glance and she hunkered down beside him. The room was hazy with smoke and the ashtray had a sad little mound of dog ends. He looked haggard and tired. Damn the man.

The lads returned for the crates and there was a great deal of heaving and scraping and cussing. When the front door finally slammed behind them, Adam rested his head against the wall and closed his eyes. 'That's that, then,' he said with a sigh. 'I suppose it's time I was on my way as well.' He roused himself and stabbed out his cigarette. 'I'm very glad you came, Jessica.'

'Then why on earth didn't you ring me, or call round? You were going to just up and leave, weren't you?' He shrugged. 'We're supposed to be mates, Adam.' He turned to look at her. She felt herself redden.

He said, 'It's complicated.'

'Isn't everything?'

'Don't let's fight. Please. Not today.'

'Okay, not today.' She took a breath. 'So. Where are you going? Where will you start this new life of yours?'

'I don't know. I've put the furniture into store.'

'You're serious, aren't you? You're just going to drift off into the wide blue yonder. This is Eleanor's fault . . .'

'She can't help it, Jessica, it's the way she is. I'm sorry.' He takes her hand. She stares down at their twined fingers, his long and shapely, hers stubby and calloused. 'I really am very sorry.'

They go downstairs. They linger on the doorstep, their hands still linked. He kisses her at the corner of her lips. She wants to clutch at him, demand more, but she doesn't, she lets him go.

She hasn't seen him since. She knows where he is. Every so often a postcard arrives from Bury, but she doesn't reply. She has no address. She could find him if she wanted, but if he needs her, he has only to pick up the phone.

5

Hardly a day passes when Eleanor doesn't quake at the thought of how close she'd come to losing Jess completely. She had abused their friendship terribly and yet as soon as Simon and Adam were out of the way, they set about recapturing the magic of it.

'I don't deserve you,' she tells Jess often.

'We none of us get what we deserve,' Jess replies.

These days the only real discord concerns Georgie. Jess insists she doesn't like babies and, up to a point, Eleanor believes her. She remembers how it was when Georgie was born, how Jess had made a visible effort to be pleasant. 'She's quite sweet, I suppose,' she conceded. 'In a squidgy, dribbly sort of way.'

It amused Eleanor to watch her circling Georgie like a cat stalking a bee, reaching out to pat or stroke, then withdrawing quickly, as if afraid of being stung.

But there is a difference between babies and children. Last summer they went to Richmond Park and Eleanor has a photograph of Jess in orange shorts and a baseball cap, playing ball with Georgie. In another photo Georgie is hysterical with laughter as Jess rolls her in the grass and tickles her. When she grew tired of being tickled, she snatched Jess's cap and ran off to chase butterflies. Eleanor and Jess sank back in the grass. All around them rose the shouts and laughter and occasional screams of children at play. Fronds of pale grass bordered their contracted horizons and prickled their ears. There was a constant, close-range humming and buzzing. Ants skittered up the stems of the bobble-topped plantain. Immobile clouds in shades of white, silver and grey hung above them, weightless sculptures in a Magritte sky. A bird darted across their line of sight.

'Imagine you're a spaceman,' mused Jess. Eleanor rolled her head sideways. Jess sucked at a stem of grass. 'You come from Neptune or wherever, and your next-door neighbour tells you Planet Earth is *the* place for your hols . . .'

'Man-from-Mars?'

'Exactly. So you hop off the Neptune charabanc, and here you are and it's great and it's sunny – only you've never seen a bird before. What would you make of them?' Eleanor shrugged. 'Are they missiles? Robotic satellites? I think they'd be terrified. Look at them, blundering through the air, screeching and shitting like there's no tomorrow.'

'Hammer horror, the sparrow from hell. Jess, this is why Georgie loves you. It's like you never grew up. You really should have kids of your own. The pooping stage doesn't go on all that long . . .'

'Thanks but no thanks. Don't get me wrong, Georgie's great, but I wouldn't want to spoil the fun. If I had a kid of my own, quite apart from the dribbling and the nappies and the sleepless nights, I'd have to give sensible answers to its questions.'

'I doubt it.'

'You're right, I wouldn't – and imagine what a screwed-up little tadpole it'd be. No, I can't be bothered, Ellie. Not full time.'

'Georgie adores you.'

'Sure she does, and I think she's scrumptious, but I've known her since she was born, and I know her father – whoever he is. She's yours, Ellie. We're virtually bringing her up together. And that's the point – other people's children are great, but who needs it twenty-four hours a day? Listen, I didn't ever tell you about this guy I lived with back in the mists? Steve his name was. Well I told him, Ellie. I said, if I start getting broody, it'll only be hormones, it won't be real. Be buggered if I'll let my body dictate my life.'

The picnic at Richmond was at the tag end of last summer. The following February Jess broke the news she was pregnant.

They had put Georgie to bed and eaten their supper, and were curled on the sofa, sharing a bottle of Rioja and watching the late film.

Eleanor was enjoying the film and she protested when Jess aimed the remote and killed the sound. Jess punched another button and the video recorder kicked in. 'I was watching that.'

'You can see it later. I want to talk to you.'

'Okay . . .'

'I've been trying all evening, but I can't seem to hit the right moment. This isn't the sort of thing that crops up casually.'

Eleanor draws her knees up under her chin. 'If it's a man, that's great. You're too choosy these days, Jess. I know you think no one measures up to Adam, but he wasn't so special, you know . . .'

'It's not that. Not directly, anyway.'

'Then what?'

'I've been thinking about some of the things you say about Georgie. The two of you have really got something there and you know what, I'm just a bit jealous.'

'There's no need. Georgie tells the other kids at school that she's got two mummies. She knows how close we are. I think it's great.'

'It's not the same, though.'

'So?'

'So maybe I should give my own hormones a whirl.'

305

'What the hell does that mean?'

'It means I'm pregnant, Ellie.' Eleanor's first thought is to wonder what Adam would say but Jess interrupts. 'Now,' she says, 'if I've got this right, you're supposed to congratulate me, shower me with advice, bootees and educational toys.'

'I didn't know you were seeing anyone.'

'Come on, Ellie, that's got nothing to do with anything. It's just a question of genes.'

'I don't understand. There must be a father . . .'

'There certainly is. His name's Rob – he's gorgeous, Ellie. There'd be no point, otherwise. Remember Dirk Bogarde in *The Spanish Gardener*? It was on TV a while back. You must remember.'

'Vaguely.'

'That's Rob. Lean. Dark – feral.' She gives an exaggerated shudder. 'The ultimate canapé —'

'—for someone who's been on a starvation diet. You're crazy, Jess.'

'If I am, then so are you. Pots and black kettles, Ellie. Look, these last few years I've watched you and Georgie, I've seen what you get from her – and when I think of my own life, it's going nowhere, and as far as my body-clock's concerned, we're talking Big Ben here. Don't you see? This fits with everything I've ever believed. You, me, the kids – what more do we need? Rob doesn't matter. He's just a bag of chromosomes, Ellie – hand-picked.' Her laughter is a fraction too high. 'I promise you, Baby Dirk is guaranteed to be beautiful.'

'Don't do this, Jess, don't do as I did.'

'That way madness lies, huh?'

'I'm serious. I screwed up, big time. I married Simon because I was scared of him and scared of my feelings for Adam and what I might do to him – and I was ratty with him for not chasing me to Cornwall, and then, when he accused me of having been with Simon I thought, okay, why not? Go for it. I'm a failure, Jess.'

'Okay, maybe you began with failure, but you pulled a success out of it. Georgie's a great kid.'

'Why didn't you go to Adam?' Jess stares at her, finally rendered speechless. 'I know how you feel. When he left, you should have gone with him.'

'He didn't want me.'

'Not then, but later – if you went to him now—'

'Ellie . . .'

'You know where he is, Jess, don't pretend. You could have gone to him, had his baby – he'd have loved it. There was no need to get tangled up in some half-baked substitute.'

'He's not. I didn't. Anyway, Adam and Simon, they turn everything inside out. We don't need them, Ellie. You and me, look at us, we help each other, care for one another . . .'

'Jesus Christ, and I thought Adam was the romantic.' They glare at one another. Every taboo of the past five years has been breached in this conversation. Eleanor says, 'Okay, I'm sorry. Look, I know it must seem like a solution.' She pauses. Jess's face has an angular, stubborn look. 'But think about it. It's not so easy, detaching yourself from the father, bringing the kid up alone . . .' She reaches for Jess's hand. Somehow she must make her see what a tomfool thing she's done – that silver linings tend to have a dark under-cloud, and Spanish gardeners are best confined to Spanish gardens.

'Well, it can't be undone,' says Jess. 'Or rather it can, but that's not me, I won't go down that road. As for Adam, if he'd given me a chance we might have made a go of it – but that's not what he wanted, and when push comes to shove, I don't want a man hanging round full time.'

'They have their uses.'

'Hark who's talking. No, they're like dogs and kids, too much of a tie and a face-aching bore. Tell me this, did you ever know a man with a scrap of imagination? I don't mean Simon and his paintings, I mean the real thing, full-blooded and alive. Men are cripples, Ellie, narrow-minded and petty and emotionally immature – and yes, okay,' she punches the arm of the sofa. 'I'm exaggerating. It's an excuse, I know that. But I can't do it. I'm no good at relationships. The nearest I got was with Adam, and I'm so grateful I can blame the fact that I fucked up on you. So. This is the best solution. It's what you did, and you made it work. Come on, Ellie, don't pull such a face. You had two men hanging on your tail and you sent them both packing. That's power, Ellie.'

In the corner of the room the television flickers soundlessly. Oscar tracks a spider round the skirting board. At last Eleanor says, 'It's not power, it's incompetence.'

'No. Listen to me, everything I ever said about friendship, I meant it. The way we've stood by one another these past few years . . .'

'It's been touch and go, at times.'

'Show me a relationship that doesn't hit the rocks now and then. No, like I said, we stick by one another. I needed you when Adam left, just as much as you needed me, and I need you now. I want Baby Dirk so much but every time I think of what's in store, it scares the shit out of me. Never mind looking after the kid when it comes – what about the run-up? I'm going to get big and blubbery, I won't recognize myself. When I was nine, maybe ten years old, I'd see pregnant women in the street and wonder how they could bear to go out looking so gross.

'And that's not all. It's going to hurt, isn't it? I'm a coward, you know that. I don't even like going to the hairdresser.' She laughs. It is a shrill sound, like scraping metal. 'Ellie, don't abandon me, not now. I really need you.'

6

It is not a good idea for Georgie to remain in London, not now Simon is back. She must do something, she must act – but what can she do, what sort of action will convince him that he has no place in their lives?

She spins first this way, then that. Her mind is not on her work. She fails to return an important telephone call, and spends an hour hunting for a set of exhibition photographs. Brian joins her for coffee. Pulling up a chair, he tops up her steaming mug from an engraved silver hip flask.

She confides in him. Brian is a sympathetic listener; he is also a compulsive fixer. She can see his mind buzzing away behind those puppy-dog eyes. He grins and says, 'Eleanor, my pet, I think I have an idea.'

That evening Jess comes to supper. She arrives as Eleanor is getting Georgie ready for her bath and they spend half an hour splashing her and fighting to wash between her toes. Georgie loves it. She wriggles her toes – long toes, like her mother's – and squeals and slaps her palms on the water when Jess dabs bubble bath on her nose and threatens to dunk Big Nigel.

Eleanor prepares supper and Jess reads Georgie a bedtime story. The house rings to a symphony of stifled laughter and shrieks. Jess hasn't quite grasped that these stories are supposed to induce sleep.

Eleanor smiles and mixes the salad dressing. Adam taught her how to make it, which herbs to use, the proportion of oil to lemon juice. She tosses the lettuce and takes it to the table. She tests the pasta; it's almost ready.

She is calm now, she feels in control. Brian's plan is not ideal, but if Jess plays along, it could be fun.

Over supper, she tells her about Simon's visit. Jess gives a low whistle. 'What a nerve – what does he want?' Eleanor pushes her blouse aside to reveal her bruised shoulder. 'Jesus, Ellie.' She reaches to touch the bruise. Her fingers are light, reverent. 'The bastard hasn't changed, has he? D'you think he'll come back?'

'I don't know. Probably.'

'Men are like that; always out to claim their rights. Take Rob,' Jess leans back and slides a hand over the dome of her belly. 'Did I tell you I'm having trouble with Rob?' Eleanor stares. 'My prototype Dirk, remember? The bloody man wants to play Daddy – but I told him. Screw that, I said.'

Eleanor mops up the last of her pasta. 'So,' she pushes her plate away. 'We've got much the same problem. We should do something, Jess. Make a stand, fight back.'

'I'm all for fighting back, you know me.'

'Good, because I've been talking to Brian, and you know what a fixer he is.' She crosses to the sideboard. 'Brian's got a plan. I could do it alone.' She returns to the table with biscuits and cheese and a bowl of grapes. 'But it wouldn't be the same without you.'

'How very mysterious, do tell.'

'How would you react if I suggested a change of air? The four of us – you and me, Georgie and Baby Dirk.'

'Move away?' She prises some grapes from the bunch. 'It worked for Adam, I suppose. We could try south of the river. I've a client who could give us some pointers . . .'

'I thought somewhere further afield. Like I said, I've been talking to Brian. I admit I had doubts at first, but we needn't commit ourselves outright. I can let this place, then there's the money Simon sent from the States – I haven't touched it, it's my rainy day money. I rather like the idea of using Simon's money to escape Simon . . .'

Jess cuts a lump of brie and eats it straight from the knife. 'So we move away – where to? Where will we live? Rainy day money's all very well, but we'll need an income.'

'Brian's got a friend who owns a gallery in Bury.'

Jess jabs the brie with the cheese knife. 'Bury? Would this be Bury as in St Edmunds, as in Suffolk?'

'Okay, it's not perfect, and I know I'm always moaning about the place, and it's sod's law this guy is based there – but it's a start, Jess, and we don't have to live in the town. In fact I'd rather not be too close to Babs.' She stops. Jess isn't listening. She's studying the tablecloth and her face has gone all pinched and pointy. 'What is it, Jess, what's wrong?'

'Nothing.' She looks up and forces a smile. 'I'm just thinking it all through. This friend of Brian's, he's definitely got a job for you, has he?'

'Part-time to begin with, but Brian knows somewhere we can live rent-free. You'd be amazed at the connections he's got. It's an arty area, I suppose – Gainsborough, Constable . . .'

'Ellie . . .'

'What?'

'I'm not sure. It sounds too good to be true, and far too convenient. Why would you want to go back to Bury?'

'I don't, it's just how it's panning out – and you must admit, knowing the way I feel about Bury, it's the last place Simon is likely to come looking for me, and even if he does, the house Brian's found is pretty remote.'

'I'm a city bod, Ellie, I'm not sure how I feel about remote . . .'

'When I say remote, we're not talking Russian steppes, here. It's between Bury and Newmarket, within easy striking distance of both. I know the village.'

'Do you know the house?'

'No, does that matter? According to Brian the owner's working abroad to make enough money to do it up. He doesn't like it standing empty, so we'll be sort of house-sitting.'

'Squatting in some dank dump in the middle of nowhere, more

like . . .'

'It'll give us time to decide whether we've done the right thing before committing ourselves, and Babs is always going on about never seeing Georgie, and you want to get away from Rob – come on, what about it, Jess? We won't burn our boats here. We can come back if it doesn't work out.'

'Like I said, it's all a bit too convenient.'

'But that's the whole point, everything's just falling into place. I love it when that happens. Like it's all meant.'

'I've a business to run. I can't just up sticks and go.'

'I remember when we first met you told me you could do your job anywhere. Be your own boss, you said. All you need is a bag of tools and you can set up in any town, anywhere in the country. Think about it.'

'It's crazy.'

'Of course it is. Totally. But what's to lose? You're the one with all the fancy romantic notions about friendship – and what have we got here that's so great? Think of Georgie and Baby Dirk – it'll put you out of reach of Dirk senior and get Simon out of my hair . . .'

'But Suffolk, Ellie – I hate the country. You know that. Grass and bugs and birds – pheasants, great lumbering things, flapping and screeching and blundering into cars. I've been to the country, I've seen it, I know what it's about.' She starts to laugh. 'God, Ellie, you break me up, you know that?' She retrieves the knife and cuts another hunk of brie. 'Okay. I give in. Change one thing, change it all. You, me and the kids. What the hell, let's go to Suffolk. Fuck the pheasants.'

7

'Adam dear – how are you?' Babs's voice lacks its usual elasticity and her question ends on a downbeat. The lunchtime sitting at

Jangles-Three has ended and he leaves Janice clearing the tables while he takes the call in his office.

'I'm fine,' he says. 'Very busy, but fine. How's the decorating coming along?'

'It's all finished. You haven't been over in weeks, or you'd know.'

'Are you ticking me off?'

'Yes, dear, I rather think I am. So, how about this afternoon?' He hesitates, sensing this is not a straightforward invitation. 'I'll be honest with you, Adam, it isn't only that I want you to admire my new curtains. I have some news for you.'

'What sort of news?'

'I thought you'd want to know straight away. It's Eleanor, dear, she's back.' He shifts his position and his chair creaks. From beyond the closed door comes the clatter of pans and the crash of crockery. 'Adam, are you there?'

He shuffles through a pile of bank statements and locates a crumpled packet of cigarettes. His lighter flares on the third attempt. 'Is she with you, at the house?'

'Dear me, no. Cats in a sack, that'd be.'

'Well, then . . .'

'I thought you'd want to know.' She's a little defensive. 'I did wonder whether Jess might have told you.'

'I'm not in touch with Jessica, you know that, and Eleanor's comings and goings are nothing to do with me.'

'Adam . . .'

'I'm sorry, Babs.' Despite his denials, the old wound starts to throb. 'But it's the truth.' Eleanor and Jessica are no longer a part of his life. He has all he needs – money in the bank, a successful restaurant and a string of failed relationships. What more could he ask?

'Adam?' Babs is insistent. 'I know how hard this is. You think I should mind my own business – but she's back and that's bound to affect you. Come and talk to me, Adam, please.'

A clipped privet shields Babs's garden from the road. The lawn has a border of roses and the crazy-paved path is edged with measured loops of green wire.

He parks the car. Adjusting the rear-view mirror, he straightens his tie and runs his hand over the stubble of his hair. These days he keeps it cropped close to his scalp; it's cooler that way, more easily managed.

'Why is he dressed like a waiter?' The voice from the past is sharp, resonant.

Babs's gate stands open. A green and yellow gnome peers at him from beneath a frowzy pink rosebush. Freddie is the shape of things to come. He is heavily whiskered and although he carries a fishing rod, there is no pond.

Eleanor's mother has strong views when it comes to good and bad taste. 'What you must ask yourself,' she explained one afternoon over tea and a gaudy slice of Battenburg, 'is what you mean by "bad". The Parthenon is supposed to be an icon of good taste, but I was reading the other day that it used to be a riot of red and blue and gold. Such wonderful vulgarity, it makes the heart sing. And then I thought, if the Greek government restored it to its original splendour, they'd lose their tourist trade overnight.'

'Or double it. Think of Disney.'

'Well yes, maybe. But the principle's the same. Our entire concept of taste is based on a fallacy. Norman churches, for example . . .' She'd taken him to Ely once, to show him the vestiges of crimson paint clinging to the cathedral vaults.

He smiles at the memory. He's still smiling as Babs opens the door. She's wearing jeans and an orange shirt and a green plastic apron with a pattern of cherries.

'Adam, good, you're here. I wasn't expecting you quite yet . . .' She flutters her hands, fending him off as he tries to embrace her. 'No you don't, mind my hands, I'll make you all messy. I've been oiling my sheep. You go on in, make yourself at home.'

The sheep stands in the middle of the kitchen, marooned on a raft of newspapers. It is the size of a half-grown labrador and made of wood. The shop had told Babs to oil it regularly, otherwise it was likely to crack.

Babs returns minus the apron. Her hands are clean, but still stained. 'Sit yourself down.' She edges round the sheep to the sink. 'So how are you?' She fills the kettle. 'Everything going well?'

'Yes.'

'And how's that nice girl you're seeing – Julie, isn't it? Very Botticelli, very *Birth of Venus*, though I've not seen her without her clothes, of course. The real thing this time, is it?'

'No.'

'Well, keep an open mind, do. I worry about you, Adam. I'm not sure you'd recognize the real thing if it popped up in your toaster one bright morning.'

'Babs —'

'Cover it with butter and honey, you would . . .'

'Julie and I are finished – all over bar the shouting. And Julie isn't why I'm here.'

'Of course not. You know me, never go straight to the point if I can take a nice trip round the houses.' She turns her back and, opening the cupboard, produces a cream-coloured teapot with orange poppies painted on the side. The lid is green and it doesn't fit. She has to hold it on to pour.

On the windowsill behind her is a photograph. Adam leans to one side to get a better view, but Babs gets in the way as she fetches the milk. Slopping some into a jug, she dumps both jug and carton on to the table. She tops up the pot and covers it with a tea-stained, camel-shaped cosy. Only now does she sit down.

He tries to imagine an adolescent Eleanor sharing this house with her mother. Babs treats life as a colouring book and delights in scribbling her baroque presence all over it. But if Babs is baroque, Eleanor is gothic. He remembers St Mark's. A building can be a metaphor for a person – that's what Eleanor said. The notion had struck him as self-indulgent at the time, but now it occurs to him that her precious church had itself been a metaphor for another age. It was a neo-gothic, Victorian pastiche – a fake.

Eleanor and Babs have more in common than either is prepared to admit. If Babs has a sense of drama, so does Eleanor. The difference is that Eleanor's natural flamboyance is countered by a more urgent need for control.

And that, he acknowledges with a kick of distaste, is Simon's particular magic. He'd freed her, enabled her to lose control and indulge her wilder side. When Adam called her a pantomime horse, he'd not been far from the mark. Simon is her *fasnacht*, her *carnevale*, her lord of misrule.

It is not in Adam's nature to take on such a role.

He silently damns her but it does no good, the memories cascade – his London flat, his kitchen, the flash of the knife and her wound, the way she'd held out her hand, presenting the prize, her blood a crimson rosette . . .

Her every action had begged him to displace Simon. She'd wanted him to follow her to Cornwall; she'd tried to share her dark side, but it repelled him. He cannot take pleasure in pain. Now, as then, she frightens him. He cannot give her what she needs.

'Is your tea all right?'

He snaps to attention. Digging around in his pocket, he produces a packet of cigarettes. 'Babs,' he forces a smile. 'I know you've given up, but I really need this. I'll go outside if you like.'

'Of course not, in fact I'll join you. One won't hurt. Times of crisis and all that . . .' She gives a nervous shrug and a laugh.

He flicks his lighter and holds it out to her. 'So that's what this is, is it? A time of crisis?'

'Not really.'

'Come on, best get it over with. Tell me about Eleanor.'

'Well,' she inhales her cigarette with exaggerated satisfaction. 'It's much as I said on the phone. She got back last week. They're living in some dreadful wreck in the middle of nowhere. Her and Jess.'

'Jessica is with her?'

'Very much so, although things have changed there, as well. Jess is expecting a baby. I believe it's due some time in autumn.'

'I see.' He has barely absorbed the news about Eleanor, and now Babs hits him with this. Eleanor once told him that Jessica was a bit hit-and-run when it came to men. He wonders what sort of man has finally snared her. He says, 'About Eleanor . . .'

'Yes of course, where was I? Oh that's right – the house. It belongs to some crony of Brian Farraday's.'

'And Georgie?'

'It's not ideal for young children – it's a bit dilapidated, the staircase needs looking at – but it's better than where they were. I was never happy with her being brought up in London.'

He cradles his cup like a bowl. 'As I said on the phone, this has nothing to do with me.'

'So I shouldn't have mentioned it?' He tightens his grip on the cup. 'And if one day she comes to Bury to do her shopping or whatever, and you happen across her?' The cup is fragile. Any minute it will collapse in on itself, crumbling like eggshell.

Babs is right. He's played the game often, seen himself walking along Buttermarket, and Eleanor coming out of a shop, tall and fierce, intent on some errand and seeing no one. Or sitting on a bench in the Abbey gardens, her head bent over a book, her long, perfect fingers rustling the paper as she turns the pages. He would watch for a moment. And then he'd go up to her.

No, he wouldn't. He would walk on past, pretend he hadn't seen her.

Babs says, 'I suppose we should have been prepared for this.'

'You said she never came here.'

'And she hasn't, has she? Not in all these years.'

'Then why now?'

'She has her reasons.' She hesitates. 'No, I'm sorry, dear, I've gone as far as I can. You must ask her yourself.' She becomes brusque. 'Now then, are you ready for another cup of tea?'

He watches her pour. The liquid trickles in a tawny stream. He remembers Jessica's tea, aromatic fennel, pale as air.

Once again the photo on the windowsill catches his eye. It is propped against a bowl of china fruit. Tomato-coloured apples, egg-yellow bananas, an iodine orange.

Babs fetches it. Handing it over, she says, 'I took it last time I was down there, a month or two back. What d'you think?'

Georgie. He holds the photograph by the edges. The little girl's head and shoulders fill the glossy rectangle, but he can't look at her directly. He flirts warily at the edges, taking in the wispy ends of her black curls, then working his way via Eleanor's wide mouth, the soft baby chin and cheeks pushed up and rounded by her grin, to wide, laughing, cocktail-blue eyes.

'Well?' says Babs on a breath. 'Say something, dear.'

'She's just like her mother.' With emphatic care, he props the photograph against the sugar jar.

'She's growing up fast.'

'It doesn't seem possible.'

'Five next month.' Babs retrieves the photograph. Leaning her elbows on the table, she examines it closely. 'Children are like that,' she says. 'Blink and you miss something vital.'

'Babs . . .'

'She's pretty, don't you think?' She touches the photographed cheeks with the tip of a chipped fingernail. The whorls of her fingerpads are stained with the oil from her sheep. 'I never would have called Eleanor a pretty baby. But Georgie . . . that hair, those curls.'

He puts down his cup. He says, 'I have to go, Babs. Thank you for the tea. And the warning. I'll be in touch.'

'Adam, wait.' She places the photograph face down on the tablecloth. 'You'll think I'm interfering, but please, sit down for a minute. You must go and see her. Don't look at me like that. I'm serious. For your sake as much as hers, you must talk to her, Adam.'

8

Irene is right, Simon decides. He should let them go, Nell and her vampire child. Let sleeping dogs lie. What's done is done. Let bygones be bygones.

The clichés cluster. They do not help.

He doesn't need Eleanor. These past few years have proved his independence. Both personally and professionally, she is superfluous.

He examines his hand. Georgie's wound has more or less healed. His self-disgust is glazed with regret.

Let's bury the hatchet, look to the future. Just the three of us – what about it, Nell?

It won't be easy, getting back together. He feels it again, the total humiliation of his last visit as he stumbled out of her house, defeated by a feisty four-year-old.

He must be crazy even to think about trying again. He's just setting himself up to be rejected again. It's not worth it. She's not worth it.

Yes she is. Nell in that dress the colour of her eyes, her hair, her hands – God, it's so fresh, the thrill of it, and the dread.

He takes a cab. He gets a buzz from that. He never took taxis in the old days; Irene's lessons in thrift had rooted well. But everything's different now. He wants Nell to see that. And Georgie. We'll go out for the day, a picnic, a boat to Kew. Come for a ride, Georgie Girl.

Eleanor's street is lined with cars. Trees are planted at intervals along the edge of the pavement and at their bases pockets of earth, grey as charnel ash, are piled with votive mounds of dog dirt. Shards of broken glass litter the gutter. This is no place to bring up a sensitive kid like Georgie.

But the house is okay, Nell keeps it nice. The polished windows reflect the sunlight back at him. He pulls his sunglasses from the pocket of his shirt. The privet is in flower, covered with little greenish-white, sickly smelling cones. The wrought-iron gate squeaks. The front door has dimpled glass panels that rattle as he pounds on the wood, harder, then harder still when she fails to respond.

He squints through the letter-flap. He calls to her. Nothing. Nell all over, this is. It's what he loves about her, and what he hates. She's always a little out of focus. She's probably hiding behind the living-room door, willing him to go, daring him to leave. That's my girl . . .

Jesus, Nell, can't we get past this? Okay, I know, I know. Don't get paranoid. I can hear you. You're not hiding, you're just out. No car, so you're at the gallery, of course you are. What a moron. I know.

'You selling something or what?' He spins round. The woman wields a pushchair. Strapped in the pushchair is a toddler clutching a dirty pink and blue bunny. 'Whatever it is, I don't want none.' The bunny's mutilated ear has been fastened to the side of his head with a nappy pin. 'You're in my way.'

'Are you coming in here?' He gestures weakly at Nell's front door.

'What of it?'

'She's out . . .'

'Who's out? I bloody live here, don't I?'

'Since when?' There is a tingling sensation behind the bridge of his nose, a tightening in his chest as a succession of images assemble in his mind. He sees a series of giant safety pins – ear to bunny, bunny to child, child to mother . . .

'Don't see it's no bloody business of yours,' snarls the woman.

She has frizzy hair, a swarm of silver earcuffs and a mouth like a wound. Her lipstick is the colour of dried blood.

It's typical of Nell, wrong-footing him like this. He's swallowed his pride and come looking for her to say he's sorry – kiss and make up, this time it'll be different – but she's upped and gone, and now what's he supposed to do?

And what about Georgie? The kid must think he's a nutter. He's got a lot of making up to do there. Years ago, before he left for the States, she was nothing. Not a person, not a somebody. Screaming and puking everywhere. You'd think a kid of Nell's would know better. That's what he'd expected, that she'd lie in her cot, straight and tidy with the cover tight under her chin, feeding when she was supposed to, sleeping the night through. Turned out she didn't do any of those things and instead of freaking out, Nell had gone along with it. She'd cleared up the sick and got up in the night when the baby cried. The kid only had to blink and she was there – but what about him? He could jump up and down with a knife at his throat and she wouldn't notice.

It'll be different now. I've grown up, travelled, seen a thing or two. I can hold my own with anyone, even you, Nell.

He smiles at Blood-Lips. 'Listen to me,' he says, and his voice has a new authority. 'I know a woman who lived here. Tall, skinny type, long black hair – know who I mean?'

'Rent the place from her, don't I?'

'Well, she owes me money.' He slides his hand into his back pocket and eases out his wallet. 'And I need to get in touch a bit sharpish.' He smiles, and flicks open the wallet. 'So do you have a forwarding address?'

9

Babs draws Adam a map. She folds it in half, then folds it again. He holds out his hand. Still she hesitates. 'This was your idea,' he reminds her. 'I thought you wanted me to go and see her.'

'I do. But I'm a little worried. She doesn't know you're here, or about the restaurant, or anything. Don't look so amazed. You know what she's like. Nervy. I never know which way she'll jump. Just tread carefully, Adam. It'll be a shock, you turning up out of the blue.'

'You could ring and warn her.'

'I could, but she can be such an ostrich. If she knows you're coming, she'll go into hiding. Best get it over with, catch her unawares.'

'If you say so.'

'I do. Now, take the map and off you go – and don't put it off, because the longer you do, the harder it'll be.'

She's right, of course. Best to get it over with, before he has the chance to think too much and too deeply about the possible consequences.

Pulling out on to the dual carriageway, he accelerates past an animal transport lorry. The lorry grunts. Its slatted sides display a rash of glistening pink snouts. He tries to concentrate on the road, but the memories edge in. The grand opening of Jangles-One, Eleanor in her electric blue dress with the plunging back. She'd looked stunning, but even then he could see through her. The carapace was almost perfect; it dazzled and deceived the eye, drew attention from the weak spots, the seams and the apertures.

Oh yes, he'd seen through her all right; he just hadn't understood what it was he was seeing.

Not until that final day, the fight with Simon, and her eyes bright with the thrill of it.

Strange to think she knows nothing of his life now, is ignorant of everything that has happened to him since their parting.

A sudden thrill, his hands clench the steering wheel. She is utterly unprepared. He'll stand on her doorstep and ring her bell – and watch for her first, unguarded reaction.

Unless, of course, she knows. Two or three times a year he sends Jessica a postcard, usually of somewhere in East Anglia, always with a Bury postmark. He's never been quite sure why he does this. She doesn't respond, and he doesn't want her to – but at least she knows where he is; she could find him if necessary. The question now is whether she has ever spoken of this to Eleanor.

He'll know soon enough.

He leaves the main road and drives through a succession of

straggling villages. He passes a sign, black on orange, 'Don't Kill Our Children – Watch Your Speed'.

Whose child had died? And how, and where?

He turns left at a whitewashed pub. The stone porch is smashed, as if someone has driven into it at high speed. The road narrows. The tall hedgerows give glimpses of stud paddocks bordered by threadbare belts of trees. Beyond the trees is what passes in this region for a hill – in fact no more than a faint, yeast-dough swell of the land. A little further on the hedges thin and the sun melts the hill back into the paddocks.

He rounds a corner. Eleanor's village. A modern, single-storey school is surprisingly located in the Y of a road junction. He sees himself with Georgie, hand in hand, swinging along the road.

At the centre of the village is a trickle of a stream and a ford. Alongside the ford a flint packhorse bridge leaps the near-dry river bed. He pulls into the side of the road and examines Babs's map. Eleanor lives in Laburnham Lodge. To reach it he must cross the ford, turn right, then go up the little road running alongside the church. He can see the church from here, squat and Saxon with a knobbly flint tower.

He edges along the lane. It's very narrow. The banks are high and crowded with trees that meet overhead. The sun blazes through the leaves and the road is a luminous lime-green cavern. The leaves shimmer and the light flickers, and the asphalt ripples like water.

He almost misses the house. The trees obscure the entrance and he has to reverse back along the tight funnel of the lane. There is a gatepost, but no gate. The green paint is peeling. At the base of the post are two empty milk bottles. One has a note fastened to its neck with a wooden clothes peg.

Driving through the overhung gateway he parks alongside a silver Renault. The house is in a bad way. It probably started life as a rectory and in its prime would have been tended by a little band of servants polishing the floors and laying the fires and keeping the grounds in order. Now the guttering hangs away at one corner, the chimneys need repointing and there is a cracked pane in the lunette above the door.

He gets out of the car. Stunted weeds push between dusty gold chips of gravel. There is an iron boot-scraper with a leaping dolphin frozen above a scalloped tray. Curtainless windows range on either side. The Georgian frames are original, but the paint is flaking and the putty has come away in great chunks, leaving the glass sitting precariously in gap-toothed gums.

Over to his right, a range of frost-flaked redbrick outbuildings shamble away into the trees. The house is surrounded by trees. They wash against it in a fierce green torrent. Over the years the flow has eroded the fabric. Soon there will be an almighty crack and the rock will split and the house will crumble.

He has a tendency to be fanciful. It is a ruse, a ploy, and today its purpose is to delay the moment of confrontation.

In all the scenarios he has concocted, the little playlets in which he comes across her unawares, he has never envisaged actively seeking her out.

The house waits. If she sees him from a window, he will lose the initiative.

There is no doorbell, only a blockish iron knocker, a hand grasping a ring. It is a rather brutish hand, and he is reluctant to touch it. Fool. He takes a breath and lifts the knocker with the minimum contact. He allows its weight to drop against the door. The wood absorbs the thud. He doubts it can be heard from inside. He tries again. This time he is less fastidious. He grasps the iron hand that grasps the ring and bangs the knocker hard down on its plate. The door opens almost at once.

She's so tall. He'd forgotten. Her startling, blue-jay eyes are almost on a level with his. She's wearing a white shirt over jeans and a plum-coloured waistcoat woven with gold thread. It seems too much for such a hot day, but even as the thought forms he feels the cold air and just a taint of damp emanating from the house.

He is taken aback at how immediately upon his second knock the door opens. He feels cheated, robbed of that unique moment, the flare of first recognition. He can scarcely think; the heat has liquefied his brain. He clings to the image of her, is stunned by how little she has changed. Her hair is pulled tightly back from her face. The style is so severe he can feel its tug at the butterfly-veined skin of her temples. She's smiling, but it is a tight smile, a mask to hide her alarm. He says her name. She draws the door towards her, narrowing the gap. He tries to reckon up the years and months since they were last together. There was a time when he knew it to the minute.

He rubs a hand along his jaw and is comforted by the rasp and scratch of his beard.

She watches. She waits for him to speak, but he cannot think of anything to say. His mouth is dry. What if she grows tired of waiting? 'How are you?' he blurts, a verbal foot in the door.

'I thought you were Jess.' He frowns. 'She's out,' she explains, 'touting for business. I thought maybe she'd forgotten her key.'

'No.'

'No,' she agrees. She looks him up and down, puzzled to see him here, which must mean Jessica has not told her about his cards.

He says, 'I heard you were back.'

'You heard,' she repeats. 'Who told you? Did Jess tell you? Or Babs?' She speaks like an automaton, a brass cage and a bright, mechanical bird that jerks and chirps and fails to simulate reality.

'Yes,' he says gently. 'Babs.'

'I didn't know . . .'

'I live here now, in Bury. I moved there after . . .' He stops, takes a breath. 'I've a restaurant. Jangles-Three.'

'She should have said. Babs should have told me. And Jess,' she stops. 'Jess knew, didn't she?'

'Your mother wasn't sure how you'd take it. You can be a bit . . .' he hesitates, '. . . volatile.'

'Volatile as custard, that's me. Jess . . .?'

He shakes his head and smiles and thinks of burnt custard and custard spiked with Kirsch, and hopes he doesn't look as though he's lying.

She says, 'I suppose I should ask you in.'

'That would be nice. Babs generally offers me a cup of tea and a biscuit. On a good day I get a slice of Battenburg.' As he speaks, he sees how the delicate skin round her eyes is fragile and tight. Her lips are white and her hooded eyes look past him. The sighing trees wash against the house. The leaves paddle sunlight across her cheeks. He remembers the feel of her skin, how fine it is, and how easily bruised.

'Eleanor?'

She rouses herself, and blinks. 'Don't you think it's lovely here?' she says, and there's a feathery, uncertain quality to her voice. 'Jess says it's creepy, but you know Jess, she's a bit weird when it comes to the country. It gets lonely sometimes, but it's better than London. For the children especially. Jess is having a baby, did Babs tell you?'

'Yes.'

'What else has she told you?'

'Nothing.'

'Nothing at all? Really?' She is distracted, looking anywhere but at him.

There is a movement in the shadows behind her. Georgie. No, not Georgie. A huge black cat emerges. 'Oscar,' he murmurs. Oscar head-butts Eleanor's shins before stepping over the threshold to roll on the gravel. 'He must like it here, he's put on weight.'

'He hunts.'

'Back to nature . . .'

'I thought I'd cracked it, Adam.' The non-sequitur makes him frown. 'Do you understand?' He shakes his head. 'I thought I'd broken the circle but all I did was buckle it a little. Paint it another colour, hitch it to a different wagon.' She narrows her eyes, peers at him. 'I'm sorry. I'm not making much sense.'

'No.'

'That's how life is, these days. Disjointed. Nothing makes sense. You know how baby turtles hatch and scuttle down to the sea? Well, it's like I've hatched and I'm scuttling for all I'm worth – but away from the sea, in the wrong direction. No, don't look so worried. It's okay. I'm talking nonsense. You'd better come in, and I'll make that tea.'

The cool air drops round him like a net. The smell rising from the flags is of rain on hot stones. The lower steps of the staircase flare into the hall like the train of a wedding gown. As his eyes adjust to the gloom, he sees how dilapidated it is. The uncarpeted treads are dipped and worn. Some of the banister spindles are missing, some broken. Their splintered remains tilt and jut.

Eleanor closes the heavy door. They stand side by side, not touching, not speaking.

And still no one mentions Georgie.

Her closeness unsettles him. Their past is a mirage but when he touches her arm it stabilizes in the present. He no longer loves her, yet in a way, nothing has changed. This treacherous sense of belonging baffles him. It is the same for her, he's sure. The past has imprinted itself indelibly on their cells and they slip too easily into their old ways.

With an irritated wiggle of her shoulders, she breaks the mood.

She crosses the hall. He follows. The hall is large, and unfurnished apart from a massive bog oak chest pushed against one wall. He trails his fingers along its edge. The gleaming wood is almost black, and deeply furrowed. There is a telephone and a blue and red Chinese bowl filled with petals – faded pink, yellow and cream, their edges rimmed with brown. He dips his hand among them. They rustle, frail as dry skin. The edge of the bowl is chipped. It is an old chip, grey, ingrained with time. Hanging above the bowl is Simon's Cornish seascape. Eleanor calls it her portrait. He has never understood.

She calls to him, 'Are you coming, or not?'

She waits. The faceted garnet doorknob gleams and her long fingers press against the matching glass finger-plate. He stands behind her. The wingspan of a moth separates them. She glances at him and a dusty fluttering deep inside responds to the thrill of a shared breath.

She turns back to the door. Her plait swings. The tip reaches almost to her waist. He has a schoolboy urge to tweak it. He resists. She turns the handle.

He knows what's on the other side of this door, and Eleanor knows why he's here. He has not come for her, he has come for Georgie.

She pushes the door and stands back. The room beyond is large. French windows open on to the garden. There is a patch of brown lawn and a watery wash of trees patterning the dried grass. She moves past him. The walls are inappropriately covered in red flock. The furry surface is an exotic mould and in places the paper has peeled away to hang in tatters. There are wall lights without shades, sad candle bulbs screwed into cheap brass. There is very little furniture. An armchair stripped to its wooden carcass, a scattering of hardback chairs and a music stool. The floor is bare boards, dusty and splintered.

Eleanor leads the way. Her canvas shoes scuff the wood. At the far end of the room, in front of an austere marble fireplace, is a square of ruby-coloured Turkey carpet. Here, surrounded by dolls and clutching a teddy bear with a well-chewed ear, is Georgie.

He would have known her anywhere. He towers over her. The shiny black curls crowd her face. She regards him with suspicion, hostility, even. What has he done to make her feel this way? He hasn't spoken since entering the room. Maybe that's the problem. Or perhaps she's shy and doesn't like strangers. He promises not to be a stranger for long.

Eleanor chivvies her, 'Georgie, this is Adam. Come along, come and say hello.'

Georgie's eyes flicker from him to her mother, then back again. Blue eyes, black lashes. She is still hostile, but also calculating. He swallows a desire to laugh. None of Babs's stories have prepared him for this. With her stern gaze this knowing child sweeps away his delusions of innocence. Behind those eyes, a mind is working full pelt.

Georgie bites her lip. It is her mother's habit and it rips the breath right out of him and brings it crashing back, a moss-green, foam-flecked floodtide of memory. Georgie newly born. Georgie's christening. The feel of her body, the smell of her, milk and soap and urine. And Eleanor, and Simon.

He bobs on to his heels and strokes Big Nigel's paw. He levels with the suspicious blue gaze. He smiles and says, 'Hello Georgie. How are you? My name's Adam. I bet you don't remember me.'

10

Red-Lips scribbles Eleanor's address on a crumpled scrap of paper. Back at his flat, Simon spreads the paper on his knee. Suffolk. He fetches a map and looks up the village.

How about that – she's near as dammit scuttled home to Mum.

What next? He could hop in the car and go to her now, or he could hold fire for a bit. It's probably best to wait. She's done a bunk, gone into hiding. He's angry enough now, but if he sees her, he's bound to lose his temper.

When in doubt, delay.

He fetches a sketch-pad. He thinks of Red-Lips and her brat and the poor bloody bunny. When he was a kid Irene painted a devil-bunny on his bedroom door. The rabbit had black fur, glowing garnet eyes and floppy ears matched to a pair of crimson horns. Beelzebunny.

You're sick, Irene. No wonder I'm so screwed up.

He incorporates Beelzebunny into his drawing. Irene steals from him, so what the hell, she's right – there's no such thing as an original idea.

He will go to Suffolk. Not tomorrow because he's meeting Brian, and the following day it's lunch with Irene and George, but if he can get away by mid-afternoon he can be with Nell by teatime.

But lunch drags on. Red bean lasagne and tofu salad. His parents want to hear all about his time in the States. 'Come on, lad,' says George, 'don't be coy. Bet you've got a tale or two to tell . . .'

Irene can't be bothered with travellers' tales; she wants a catalogue description of every mural, every exhibition. 'I hope you've kept cuttings. Did you take photographs? Really, Simon, you are the limit, why on earth didn't you bring them?'

It's dark by the time he gets to Suffolk. He finds the village easily, but the house is harder to locate. He stops at a pub and orders a whisky, and asks the way to Laburnham Lodge.

He edges the car through the narrow gateway. The gravel churns beneath his wheels. It is the sound of the sea. A car and a van are parked under the trees. No lights show at the front of the house.

He gets out of the car. The air is cool, and heavy with night-time scents. Moist earth and damp grass. The trees whisper. He's nervous. A thread of alcohol spirals in his bloodstream.

He'll get it right this time. She won't provoke him. There will be no more violence and no more blood.

Shit, but it's creepy. Trust Nell. Bloody dark, as well. The night is intense. The village lights do not stretch this far. Darkness is not a force, but an absence. Absence of light. Stepping away from the car, he steps into a void.

What should he do? Knock on the door, ring the bell, throw stones at her window? Which is her window?

He will do none of these. He will explore.

He moves slowly, as if afraid. Of what? The darkness – he is afraid of dislodging the darkness, of sending it tumbling off the edge of the world.

327

He approaches the house. The door is shut fast. He peers through the letter-box. A glimmer of light shines beneath a door on the far side of the hall.

Gingerly, he allows the letter-flap to close. He is perspiring. His breath racks in time to the sigh of the trees. He creeps down the side of the house and pauses at the corner. One more step. Light. A pale, wavering glow spilling over broken flags. He edges along the terrace, keeping close to the wall until he reaches the window. There are no curtains and he can see straight into the room.

There is a fireplace, but no fire, a rug and a pile of cushions enclosed by a ring of candles – fat and cream-coloured, like church candles. In the centre of the circle, Eleanor lounges on the cushions. Jess is there too. She is pregnant and sits awkwardly on her cushion. In front of her a bowl is suspended above a candle. The bowl contains water. As he watches, she unscrews a tiny brown jar and adds a few drops of its contents to the water.

Eleanor laughs and reaches for a bottle of wine. She tops up their glasses. They are drinking from huge baroque goblets with green and red stems and honey-coloured bowls. The wine is red. Simon's mouth puckers with anticipation. Eleanor is magnificent, lying propped on her elbows with her hair loose and her eyes glittering in the candlelight.

I belong here. The knowledge roars through him. He's been spinning like a dervish, careering through life, looking neither to right nor left, fixed only on the quest for success and experience – and all the while, everything he's ever hungered for is here. He is a gaudy spinning top, and she the pin at his centre.

Now, suddenly, he is still.

He leans closer to the window. Jess says something and Eleanor frowns and looks up. He presses his fingers against the glass. The wood creaks. The women start and turn. He ducks out of sight.

He's shaking and sweating. Playing the role of intruder, he feels an intruder's panic at the threat of discovery. He presses his palms against the grainy brickwork. There is a chattering in the trees and movement in the undergrowth. He hates the country.

A door opens. Light splashes across the terrace like water tipped from a bucket. It's Jess. He holds his breath and presses himself harder against the wall. Jess calls to Oscar. He wants to laugh, but manages not to. She calls again, then steps off the terrace and into the garden.

Slipping behind her, he enters the house.

The door to the drawing room is open. Eleanor is lying back against the cushions. Her eyes are closed. He creeps closer, pausing when he reaches the perimeter of the candle ring. The shadows make a living sculpture of her body. Why must he see everything through the prism of his art? He is a long-term drunk who has forgotten how the world looks through sober eyes. He would love, just once, to see her as she really is.

He gazes down at her and wonders, is she really asleep? Only moments ago she was awake and laughing. There has been a shift in time; it loops back on itself, a tangled cat's-cradle of mismatched memories.

He gazes down at her, and the sea is in her hair. It cascades across the cushions, rippling in time to the roar of the waves in the trees surrounding her house. He sees again the angles of the cliffs in the planes of her cheeks. The flickering candle-shine is the play of the sun as it dodges in and out, playing tag with the clouds.

And then the sun goes in. The waves crash down. They smash the rocks. Darkness descends.

Darkness is absence.

11

It is almost a week since Adam called on Eleanor. He had thought the visit a success; certainly Georgie had taken to him. Eleanor made tea, not one of Jessica's specials, but a Typhoo teabag in a mug, and they sat round the kitchen table and Georgie clambered on to her mother's knee and nibbled a chocolate digestive. Her face was very serious. She fidgeted, wriggling her bottom and looking from one to the other as he explained how he came to be living in Bury.

'Have you been to Grandma's house?' She reached for another biscuit and Eleanor reprimanded her with a tap on the wrist.

'Certainly I have.'

'Grandma's going to get me a Freddie-brother.'

'Freddie is a garden gnome,' Eleanor explained.

'I know.' He grinned at Georgie. 'Freddie and I are great friends.'

Eleanor did not offer more tea, and he had to ask for a second cup – not because he wanted it, but because he was enjoying being with Georgie, and he half hoped that if he hung around long enough, Jessica might appear.

Jessica did not appear and he was in danger of outstaying his welcome. He finished his second mug of tea and made his excuses. As he buckled his seat belt, he glanced back at the house. Eleanor and Georgie stood in the doorway. He caught Georgie's eye and she laughed and, breaking free of her mother's embrace, she ran to him and offered Big Nigel for a kiss.

He is glad Georgie likes him, but it makes him uneasy, partly because it may alienate Eleanor, but also because during these last few years his life has settled into a routine. He is successful. He has no attachments. This state of affairs suits him well. But he knows full well that patterns recur. Julie. Julie has gone the way of all his relationships, and that's okay, that's fine. It is better to be alone than to be with the wrong person.

Julie was definitely the wrong person, as was Kay. And Eleanor.

Life inches forward. He makes little ground, but he survives and he succeeds. Five years ago he locked his memories and his feelings for Georgie in a deep vault. He is a practical man and there is no point grieving for something that cannot be altered.

But now it seems it can be altered.

It is Wednesday afternoon and the restaurant is closed and Janice is clearing up. Adam is at the bar checking the evening bookings when someone knocks on the door. He glances up. A familiar face bobs under the 'closed' sign to peer inside. Much lower, a tiny palm presses against the glass.

His hand is unsteady as he unfastens the door. 'Hey, Adam, how are you? Is now a bad time? If it is, we can come back later.'

'Jessica.' She's wearing yellow dungarees and she looks like a pregnant daffodil. 'No, now is perfect. Come in.' He closes the door and turns to look at her. Her smile is a little too bright. It has taken as much courage for her to come here as it had taken for him to call on Eleanor. He says, 'It's been a long time.' She nods. 'Did you get my postcards?'

'Every one.'

'I should have written.' He glances down at the swell of her child. Her hand flickers self-consciously over her belly. So many questions clamour in his head, and the first amongst them concerns this baby's father.

'Hello.' Georgie's voice, sharp and demanding, fills the void. She is swinging on Jessica's hand. She's being ignored and she doesn't like it.

Adam laughs, and his relief is reflected in Jessica's face. 'Well hello, Georgie,' he says, swinging her above his head and kissing her. 'And how are you today?'

'I'm hot. I want an ice-cream.'

'Do you, now? Okay, well I'm nearly finished here; why don't we go to the park? Would you like that?' He looks at Jessica and she nods and smiles. He fills a bag with stale bread and they set off. 'We're going to the Abbey Gardens,' he explains as Georgie swings down the hill between them. 'Where there's a river with ducks and, if you're lucky, swans and maybe geese as well.'

'And ice-cream?'

'Georgie,' Jessica chides her.

'It's okay,' he says. 'Yes, Georgie, ice-cream too.'

They pass under the crenellated gatehouse and he points out the arrow-slits and the portcullis, and Georgie screams with delight and terror. Once inside, she forgets all about the ice-cream and scampers ahead.

Jessica slips her arm in his. It feels good and he gives it a little squeeze. 'I have to say, Adam Mason, it's surprisingly nice to see you again.' He glances sideways and she laughs. 'Don't look so sceptical.'

'It's been a long time.' As soon as he speaks, the questions start up in his head again. Who is her baby's father, where is he? He says, 'So much has changed.'

'That's for sure.'

There is a squeal and Georgie runs at them and skids to a halt. 'Where are the ducks?' she shouts. 'I want to see the ducks.' She grabs Adam's hand and swings on it and pulls at him. 'Show me, show me.'

'Okay, okay. They're over that way, look.' He points towards the river and she gallops off. 'And don't fall in,' he calls after her. 'Your mother will kill me.' To Jessica he says, 'A fine baby-sitter you are. Come to think of it, why are you Georgie-sitting? Where's Eleanor?'

'Out and about, you know Ellie.' She releases his arm. 'Come on Adam, look lively, where are these ducks?'

They cut across the lawn. 'See that,' he points to a roofless hexagonal building, like a miniature house with flint walls and stone windows. 'It's part of the old abbey, it's a dovecote.' He speaks in a rush; he has a sense that he is teetering on the edge of something, and that his vertigo is in danger of returning. 'And this,' he points ahead, 'is the River Lark. There's also a River Linnet. Isn't that beautiful? Lark's tongue pie, four-and-twenty blackbirds . . .'

'Adam, that's disgusting.'

Georgie has reached the river. She crouches down and dibbles a stick in the water. On the far bank, the ducks gather in a suspicious cluster. 'Try not to frighten them,' he says. 'Give them this.' At the sight of the bag, the ducks miraculously shed their fear. They skid flat-footedly through the mud and set off across the river in a little phalanx. Georgie squeals and breaks off bits of bread and tosses them into the water. The ducks squabble and dive and splash. They are joined by two swans who send their sinewy, muscular necks snaking down among the rippling green weed to retrieve the bread the ducks can't reach.

'All gone,' says Georgie, shaking the empty carrier bag. The last crumbs drift down like spring petals. Georgie flops on to the grass and scrunches up the carrier bag and thrusts it at him. He sits next to her. Her brilliant blue eyes study him. She stretches a hand to his face.

'Georgie!' Jessica is strict, he suspects more for his sake than for Georgie's.

'It's okay.'

'I want to touch.' Georgie scowls. He nods. Her fingers tug and stroke the tight curls of his beard. The sensation goes straight to the pit of his stomach. It is a pleasure and a pain so acute that his throat constricts and the nerve in his cheek starts to throb. Georgie brings up her other hand and presses her fingers to still the flickering. He sits, locked into wonder, his face framed by his daughter's tiny hands.

And then she laughs and jumps up, and runs off. 'Don't go far,' Jessica calls. 'Stay in sight.'

The ratchet in his chest loosens and he stretches out on the grass and closes his eyes. The sun turns his lids to crimson. The sounds of the garden, the rustle of the trees and the water and the distant voices of the children, make him sleepy.

He is roused by a rustling and a little splash close at hand. He opens his eyes and shields them against the sun. Jessica is beside him, digging stones out of the grass with her bare fingers. She tosses them into the river. She bows her head, concentrating on a particularly stubborn flint. Her hennaed hair gleams like polished wood. The bone at her nape is as delicate and pale as a shell bleached by the sun. He wants to touch it. He looks away. Her hands are small and strong, the fingers stubby, the nails short.

Suddenly aware of him, she looks round. 'What is it?' she demands.

'I was thinking about Georgie,' he lies. Georgie is several feet away, busy with her stick, excavating the mud at the edge of the bank. 'She's amazing.'

'She's just a kid. Don't be sentimental.'

'It's not sentimental, it's an observation. What do you suppose she'll be when she grows up?'

'An archaeologist . . .'

'If she's making mud-pies, she might turn out to be a cook.'

'Or a painter.'

'Jessica . . .'

'You're making assumptions again. You haven't changed.'

'No.'

'And neither has Ellie.'

'About Eleanor – why is she here, Jessica?'

'She hasn't told you?' He shakes his head. 'She's running away again, just like Cornwall. Simon's back. He went to see her and they had this fight, and she's scared he might get difficult over Georgie. She's so possessive about Georgie.'

'Christ.'

'So Brian found her a house and a job and she thought she had it made, but it turns out she can't get away from it, from any of you. You're here . . .'

'You knew that, you could have warned her. So could Babs.'

'She didn't consult Babs. Anyway. It's not just you, it's Simon. He's followed her here, that's where she is today – out with Simon, doing the rounds of the galleries.'

All at once, his rage erupts. For years it has been locked in the vault with Georgie and Eleanor, but now they're back and Jessica's pregnant, and his anger is on the loose and he doesn't know what to do with it. It buzzes round his head like a rabid mosquito – and there's Jessica, just look at her, all smug and yellow, stroking her bump like it's a sleeping pussycat.

Oblivious to his mood, she smiles and says, 'Baby Dirk's on the move. Would you like to touch?' She takes his hand and tries to place it on her belly. He pulls away. She laughs, 'I used to be like that, when Ellie wanted me to feel Georgie. I thought it was disgusting . . .'

'It isn't that.'

'Then what?'

He doesn't want to feel her child because it is a stranger. He says, 'Are you going to tell me what's going on? Is Dirk Senior around?' She stares at him. 'Only I wondered. No one's mentioned him, so I suppose it's safe to assume you've abandoned the poor bastard.'

'That's none of your business, Adam.'

'Of course not, how could I ever have imagined it was? Put it down to fellow feeling. Another poor sod shoved out in the cold because we all know women have the prerogative when it comes to parental devotion – Jesus Christ, you've really got it taped, haven't you?'

'So that's what this is about. Georgie.'

'No. It's about us.'

'What's this "us"? Some mythical beast, a unicorn . . . Okay.' She stops. 'Okay, let's stop playing games. You're right, I left him. I had to. Ellie wanted to come here, she needed me and I couldn't bear to think of her and Georgie being so far away – and yes, I knew you were here. If I was a true friend I suppose I'd have told her and we'd have gone somewhere else. But I've missed you, Adam, I wanted to see you. As for Rob, he'd started getting these strange ideas . . .'

'About the baby?'

334

'It was never a relationship. This was all I wanted, he knew that.'

'You're doing to him what she did to me.'

'It's not the same.'

'It is. You can dress it how you like, but it's exactly the same.'

'Ellie made a mistake and did what she had to to get out of it – and it worked. Georgie is the most important thing in her life, you've only to see them together. You don't understand, I can see you don't. How can you – you're just a man. I wish I could make you see. Look at this,' she massages her pod, 'it's so intimate. You can't share it and I can't describe it, so you'll never understand . . .'

'I can't understand because I'm only a man! Isn't that convenient? Me and your kid's father, and Simon. God, I'm sick of this shit, of the sheer bloody arrogance of you women. You think because you carry the thing in your body you've an absolute right to determine its future.'

'Up to a point.'

'No. You don't. Look at us, Jessica – you and me, we're the same species, male and female, interdependent, but you're so bloody self-righteous, you think it's a holy vocation carrying a child.'

'Not holy, but special.'

'You're a host, nothing more. Like a cat with tapeworm. A seedpod. A baby has to grow somewhere and by a biological fluke it grows in women. But that doesn't entail special rights, not so far as I can see, and it doesn't make you a better parent. It's a question of expediency, nothing more – nothing less.'

'Okay, maybe it begins that way – I'll go along that far – but honestly, Adam, carrying a child all those months, the moment of birth . . .'

'Bullshit.'

'Don't shout.' She glances at Georgie. 'And don't swear.' Georgie continues to play.

He lowers his voice. 'If carrying the child inside you creates a special relationship, can't you see that exclusion produces its own bond? Do you really think I've nothing to offer Georgie? She's my daughter.'

'You don't know that.'

'Whether she is or not, I still don't have any rights. Women like you and Eleanor use a freak of nature to deny men a meaningful role in their children's lives. It's immoral, it's wrong, can't you see that?'

'I had no idea you were so bitter.'

'No, neither had I.' As suddenly as it had come, his rage is gone. Jessica's eyes are bright and her face is close to his. 'I'm sorry,' he mumbles as she slides a comforting hand down his back. 'I shouldn't have said those things. Not all of them, at any rate.'

'I'm glad you did. It's strange, I've never thought of it that way. We tend to take it for granted. This whole process – we live with it all our lives, from the age of eleven or twelve onwards. A perpetual cycle, month after month. It does make a difference, Adam.'

His throat is tight, he can't answer. Georgie concentrates on her excavations. A little boy has joined her. She tosses her stick into the water and a naïve but hopeful duck swims across to investigate.

He is acutely aware of the bulk of Jessica's presence. Her skin is pale, like milk, her lashes short and dark. Her hand is warm on his back. He says, 'It shouldn't be like this, so much division.'

'No.' She leans closer and kisses him. 'It shouldn't, it doesn't have to be.'

12

'This is my wife, Eleanor.' Eleanor and Simon have spent the day exploring local art galleries. They find them tucked down backstreets, located in private houses and in barns. They have coffee in Clare, lunch in Long Melford, tea in Lavenham. 'We've just moved to the area,' says Simon. The proprietor of the gallery shakes Eleanor's hand, but his attention remains focused on Simon.

Wife. She smiles politely, and wanders off to look at the paintings. There is a part of her that wants to shout and protest that she is no longer Simon's wife, but she doesn't have the energy. Something strange is happening to her; she is a butterfly in regression, returning to its chrysalis stage.

It began with Adam. Jess, Babs and Adam – there's no doubt

about it, they're in cahoots, all three of them. Why do they take his side against her? It isn't fair.

Like a creeping tide, her lethargy thwarts her anger. She does not pick a fight with Jess, which is just as well, because hard on Adam's heels, comes Simon.

She had not expected him. There'd been no premonition, not so much as a glimmer of forewarning.

Nothing new in that, she has never been able to think ahead.

She remembers that night. It had been Jess's turn to put Georgie to bed and read to her. *The Little Mermaid* is Georgie's favourite story. Eleanor hates it. The Little Mermaid relinquishes everything for love of her prince. She loses her voice, and though the Witch of the Sea gives her legs in place of a tail, every step is agony. Even so, she suffers it gladly for the sake of her prince. But the prince marries another and the Little Mermaid dies.

Georgie relishes the tragedy, wants to hear it again and again. Eleanor protests, 'Can't you find something a bit more gentle to read to her?'

'Certainly not.' Jess is indignant. 'It's a wonderful moral tale and I hope she takes the lessons to heart. Lesson one: you can't make bargains with life. Lesson two: all men are bastards and are not to be relied upon.'

They eat supper in the kitchen and afterwards take their wine through to the drawing room where Eleanor arranges candles in a ring. She moves round the circle setting taper to wick and the candles take up the light until the glow surrounds them like a burning fuse.

She misses her dusty old church, Holy Ghost, the smell of incense and the candles.

Jess places a bowl of water above a night light and scatters the surface with bergamot oil. They toast one another. 'To a new life,' says Jess. They lean over the bowl and inhale the fumes.

Later. Later she sinks back against the cushions and closes her eyes. Jess has gone to look for Oscar – a city cat more used to hunting half-eaten bags of chips, he is overwhelmed by the abundance of country life. She smiles; she is content. Adam is no⁺ a problem. He is a good man and he would never do anything to hurt either her or Georgie.

337

Jess. She can hear Jess calling to Oscar, her voice becoming more distant as she descends into the garden.

Then all at once, another sound. Closer. A movement. Her eyes snap open. Simon. Standing over her. A thrill of fear. His smile. She mistrusts his smile.

He doesn't speak. He steps inside the candle ring. She has no strength, her bones are water, her flesh flows like melted wax.

He kneels beside her. He touches her. So gently.

And today he calls her his wife.

The owner of the gallery is thrilled to meet Simon. 'I've heard of you, of course. You've been in the States, right? I read an article . . .' He is hesitant, but eager. He has a proposition. 'I wouldn't want you to think me too forward, but I've got this mixed exhibition coming up at the end of the year and it'd really make a difference – it would be wonderful if we could hang a canvas or two.' Simon is doubtful. 'I'm sure we could come to some arrangement, make it worth your while?'

On the way home, Simon asks her what she thinks. 'Is it a good idea, or not, Nell? It can't do any harm to set up a base round here, establish a presence, can it? I'll ring Brian, shall I? See what he says. What d'you reckon?'

'It sounds a very good idea. Yes, you should do it.'

'Isn't this great? Hey, Nell, you're really something. Look at me, I'm a success.' He snatches her hand from the steering wheel and kisses her wrist. 'And it's all down to you, you and those bloody murals. I kicked and spat, but hell, you were spot on – and guess what, I even enjoy doing them these days.'

'Good. I'm glad.' Her lips make the shapes and the words pop out, but her brain barely intervenes.

'D'you suppose they're still there?'

'What?'

'The murals. I mean, that's the problem, isn't it? If you turn against a painting, or it becomes unfashionable, you can give it away, or sell it, stick it in the attic. But you can't stick a wall in the attic, can you? If Mason wants a change of image, all he has to do is buy a can of emulsion.'

'He didn't do that. He sold up. He left London not long after you.'

'Is that right? So what about the new owner? You see, my theory still holds. The buyer is bound to want a change of scene, and there

goes all my hard work, flushed away – just like that.' He snaps his
fingers.

'No,' she says.

'No?'

'Adam auctioned the restaurants and they sold for well above their
market price – because of your murals.'

'Shit.'

She grips the wheel. Simon hasn't changed. It's still there, the
seductive energy, the lurking anger. Contradictory feelings war
across his face. He is thrilled to discover his murals commanded a
premium, furious to think of Adam reaping the benefit.

They arrive home and she goes ahead of him into the house. As
she opens the door, a smell of cooking fills the hall. Bacon and garlic.
The sound of laughter comes from the kitchen. She hears Georgie's
voice, and Jess's. And another.

She crosses the hall and pushes open the door. Lights glare, pans
bubble on the stove. Jess and Adam sit at the table sharing a bottle of
wine. Georgie is perched on Adam's knee. He has his arm round her
waist. She dips a finger in his wine and, like a puppy at the teat,
noisily sucks it dry.

13

Jessica wanted Adam to come back and cook supper and when he
resisted, she enlisted Georgie's help. 'Adam's a chef,' she explained
to Georgie. 'Do you know what a chef is?' Georgie shakes her head.
'It's a kind of cook.'

'Like Mummy?'

'Not quite,' says Adam with a glance at Jessica. 'This is not a good
idea,' he says. 'Eleanor won't like it, especially not with Simon
around.'

'Don't be feeble. Look at him,' she grins at Georgie. 'He's frightened of your mum. Come on, Adam, Ellie won't bite.'

'She might.'

'If Mummy bites you, I'll bite her back.' Georgie pulls at his hand. 'Come with us. I want you to. Make him, Auntie Jess.'

'I can't, he's scared.'

'Scaredy-cat, scaredy-cat.'

Eleanor's kitchen is magnificent; a huge room with a deal table at its centre and a massive solid-fuel range with an old-fashioned electric stove moored alongside like a battered dingy. There is a butler's sink with a wooden draining board, and a walk-in pantry with a mesh-fronted meat safe. He goes from feature to feature and Jessica laughs and says, 'You're loving this, aren't you? Like a kid let loose in Lapland.'

'It's amazing.' He swivels on his heel. 'You know what the restaurants are like. Surgical. I work with stainless steel, everything pristine. This is a holiday camp for bacteria, and inefficient as hell. Look how far you have to walk from sink to stove.' He paces the distance. 'But I love it, Jessica.' He catches her hand and swings her round. 'I love it to bits. The art of cooking began in places like this.'

'I want to eat, I'm hungry.' Georgie bangs on the table.

Jessica squeezes his hand and he feels the soft nudge of her belly. 'You'd better tell us what we're having,' she says. 'Or you're liable to have a riot on your hands.'

'In a kitchen like this it should be roast goose stuffed with apples and prunes . . .'

'Prunes!' shouts Georgie. 'Yuck.' Adam swings her up and perches her on a cupboard. 'I hate prunes.'

'Everybody hates prunes,' shudders Jessica.

'Even the goose' giggled Georgie.

'Prunes,' Adam insists. 'Followed by syllabub. D'you know what that is, Georgie? It's cream curdled with brandy and wine.'

'I think you eat horrible things,' says Georgie. 'I hate curdled. I don't want you to make it.'

'Okay, let's see what we've got instead.' He examines an array of tired vegetables. 'There's not a lot of choice here.'

'Cooking's hardly Ellie's strong point.'

'My mummy cooks lots of things. She does custard and fried egg and crumpets and hot chocolate and sausages.'

340

'Pasta.' Jessica rummages in a cupboard.

'And bacon,' Adam contributes from the fridge. 'And mushrooms. I think we're in business.'

'Big Nigel wants to help.' Georgie kicks her heels against the cupboard. 'And I want to help too.'

'Okay, but be careful with the knife.' Under his direction, she places a mushroom precisely at the centre of the chopping board. The knife is too large and he exchanges it for a smaller, paring knife. He shows her what to do. She looks up at him, her blue eyes filtered by dark lashes. 'Are you ready, Georgie?' She nods. She is very earnest. 'Good. Now pay attention. I'm going to teach you how to cook.'

14

Eleanor fills the house with light. Electric light. Candlelight. Lamplight. The candle-ring, lit for fun only days before, has become a serious effort to keep the darkness at bay.

Jess says, 'Don't burn the house down. I don't want Baby Dirk born homeless.' It is only partly a joke. She drags her furniture carcasses to the far end of the drawing room.

Jess had no business bringing Adam here. All that shit about friendship, it was just her way of biding time till she could get Adam back. The betrayal sickens her.

That evening she'd gone into the kitchen and found them there, Jess and Adam and Georgie. Like a family. Laughing. Surrounded by sharp edges. Knives of all different sizes scattered across the table. Georgie on Adam's lap. She had been wrong to think that Adam wouldn't hurt them. Look at his face. So happy. Proud. He thinks she belongs to him. She doesn't. Georgie belongs to me.

Words. These are only words, they are not accompanied by feeling. She is numb. Cold. Dying from the feet upwards.

Why are they staring at her? Why does nobody understand?

The people who fill her house – her one-time lover, her one-time husband, her friend and her child – they are detached from her. Indifferent.

Jess had come here because Adam was here. She'd known all along, Eleanor is certain of it. She had put her own want before Eleanor's fear. Friends before lovers, she used to say. Whatever happened to that?

She should have known. Nothing is forever. She has succumbed to her biological destiny. Jess wants Adam. Adam wants Georgie.

But Georgie is mine.

Simon, what about Simon? He says he's here for me, it's me he wants. I don't know whether to believe him. Not that it matters, because I don't want him, do I? It's been good, these past few years, just me and Georgie and Jess.

Such stillness. Yes, that's what I love. Tranquillity – a pond in winter, a summer sky. Over and over again, stillness follows pain, and there has been so much pain in my life.

But nothing lasts.

What should I do about Simon? Wait and watch? Yes, see which way he'll jump, and then react. It is important to initiate nothing. Hold on to the silence, cherish the calm.

Simon says he'll paint her bedroom, would she like that? She thinks maybe she would. It is a large room, but then all the rooms in this house are big; they have high ceilings and broken plaster cornices and spider-garlands woven into the shadows in the corners. Her bed is a mattress on the floor, a sad island on a sea of oak. There is a chair, a wardrobe and her candle-pricket, and nothing else. Just space.

'It's a bit grim, don't you think?' Simon wriggles down the bed till his head disappears under the covers. 'We should brighten it up.' He nuzzles her breast and nips her nipple. 'I'll paint it for you, a mural, a sort of thank you for all you've done for me. What d'you say, Nell?' He plunges his hand between her legs. 'You'll like that, won't you? Christ Nell, you still do it to me, you know that?'

He spends the following morning ransacking the outbuildings and she arrives home from work to find his treasures scattered across the drive. There are two wooden stepladders, a plywood table with a drawer and an undertier, and a pile of floorboards from which he says he'll make a working platform. The centrepiece of his collection, squatting like a heap of mouldy meringue, is a quantity of faded green canvas. 'Thought I'd cover the floor with this, it's cheaper than polythene.' He gives the mound a hearty kick. It's stiff and resists the blow. Dead leaves cling to cobwebs spanning the creases and a crumpled spider, translucent in death, produces an irrational convulsion. 'Hey, Nell, you scared of spiders, then? I never knew that.'

Jess thinks she's crazy. 'Why are you letting him do this? The man's history, Ellie, you can't let it start all over again.'

She has no intention of letting it start again; she's not a fool. But she'll let him do the mural, why not? Where's the harm in getting her bedroom jollied up?

Simon goes on a buying spree and when he gets home he stacks his purchases in the hall and calls her to come and take a look. There are brushes everywhere, some as broad as his hand, others as fine as a pencil; there are cans of primer and a flat-bladed scraping tool, a plasterer's float and a tub of ready-mixed plaster.

He starts work. 'Can you believe it?' he complains. 'I've stripped off five layers of wallpaper this afternoon.'

He stuffs the paper in black plastic bin bags which he lines up along the landing. Fragments poke out of the tops – some are damp; some are dry and stiff and leave a chalky deposit on Eleanor's fingers. There is a piece from the nineteen-fifties – a grey ground patched with closed and open squares and rectangles, blocked in red and black. Another has a pattern of purple pansies. She delves deeper. A design of green and yellow stripes divided by a thin strip of embossed gold reminds her of Babs. She folds it in two and tucks it in her pocket.

Simon has put a lock on the bedroom door. He still won't allow her to see work in progress. She hates this sense of displacement and migrates from room to room, pacing the empty spaces, measuring her territory step by step. She leans against the banister. It creaks and sags a little. She runs her hand along the worn rail and worries at a splinter. She goes outside. The garden is overgrown. The grass is tall, but dying. Brown fronds wave in the breeze. The trees wash against the house. She goes among them. The bark of one is deeply grooved, another is smooth and silvery. Her feet snag in their roots. She thinks of Daphne who became a laurel to escape Apollo's clutches.

343

Somehow, she must escape. She has had five years of peace, and now this. Simon. Adam. It must not happen.

The breeze becomes a wind. The tops of the trees whip and whistle. Like the sea. Like the gulls. She goes back inside. Simon's seascape hangs in the hall, above the bog oak chest. She touches it, tracing the line of the cliffs, the curl of the white-topped breakers and the tangled weed.

She loves the play of light on the sea, the changing colours and textures. Blue and silver and green.

A catwalk array.

And grey. Suddenly the sky is so grey. The wind whips the clouds, piling them up like dirty washing.

But this wind is good. It shapes her. Sharp edges, lines of definition. I will break free.

15

Adam is working on a new pudding. His previous chef had been a tad territorial and preferred him not to get too involved in the kitchen. His new chef, Neil, is more flexible and today's joint effort arose over a late-night glass of Amaretto. It is a variation on a theme, a classic creation incorporating coffee and almonds and liqueur. Neil whips the eggs. The dribbling addition of hot milk is at a crucial stage when Adam is called to the phone. 'I can't talk now,' he snaps at Janice. 'Get the number, I'll ring back.'

'She says it's personal, it sounds urgent.'

Jessica. He has a flickering vision of water and blood and pain. Pain defines. Bobby.

Christ.

'Okay. I'll be right there.'

He hasn't heard from either Eleanor or Jessica since his impromptu supper two weeks ago. At Jessica's suggestion they had eaten in the garden, sitting on the dead lawn, balancing plates on their laps. Eleanor barely spoke but Simon prattled endlessly about some exhibition he'd been offered. Georgie leant against Adam's arm and, spiking a mushroom on her fork, sucked it like a lollipop until it was mangled beyond recognition, then waved it at Eleanor and said with pride, 'I cooked this.'

As soon as they'd eaten Adam made his excuses and prepared to leave. He towered over them as he brushed the scraps of grass from his trousers. Georgie wanted to wave him off, but Eleanor caught her round the waist and held her tight. 'No,' she said, nuzzling her cheek. 'It's time you were in bed, Georgie-pud.'

'I'm not a pud!' Georgie shouted and wriggled and her screams followed Adam and Jessica across the garden.

At the corner of the house he paused and glanced back. 'Will she be all right?'

'She'll be fine,' said Jessica. 'She's disappointed, that's all. She gets her own way far too much.'

'Next time you bring her to the restaurant I'll show her a real kitchen in action . . .'

'Don't go making too many plans, Adam. Ellie can be stubborn. I think she might dig her heels in after this.'

'She can't do that. Jessica, if she shuts me out again . . .'

'Maybe she won't, I'm just being cautious.'

It seems she was right to be wary. He hasn't seen them since, and now Jessica is ringing him at work. He takes the call in his office. His hands are sticky. He wedges the handset against his shoulder.

'Adam?'

'Jessica? Are you all right? What is it? Baby Dirk . . .'

'No,' she laughs. 'Not yet.'

'They said it was urgent. Is it Georgie, then?'

'That was me, I said it was urgent, I'm sorry. It's just that when people say, "Mr Mason's busy" in that sniffy way, it gets my goat.'

'I was in the middle of something. I was making a bavarois.'

'A what?'

'Never mind.'

'Adam, listen, I need to see you. It's not Baby Dirk or Georgie or anything sinister, I just have a favour to ask. Can I come over?'

He is taking a reservation when she arrives. She leans on the bar and waits for him. He ushers her towards a table, aware that glances are being exchanged behind his back. His employees gossip about him – he has given them cause. Julie had worked here, as had others before her.

He holds Jessica's chair for her and she glances up at him and pulls a face. He grins. She's right – this is play-acting. He sits facing her. She leans forward. 'Your staff,' she says softly, 'are trying terribly hard not to stare. Perhaps we should have gone somewhere else.'

'I'm sorry if you're uncomfortable.'

'I was thinking of you.'

He decides to clear this up straight away. He says, 'Do you remember what Eleanor always said about you, that you were rather hit-and-run when it came to men?'

'I still am,' she laughs. 'Ask Rob.'

'I'll take your word for it, but you see, round here they say the same about me.'

'Adam Mason!' She pretends to be shocked. 'Is that so?'

'What I'm trying to say . . .' he hesitates, searching for the right words. They are on the brink of something and he doesn't want any misunderstandings. 'I want you to know how things are with me.' He speaks in a rush. 'There's been nothing long-term or serious, not since Eleanor.'

'Right.'

'I thought you should know.'

'I see.' She smiles, and it goes through him like a hot brand.

He changes the subject. 'When you rang, I assumed Baby Dirk must be on the way.'

'Not yet.'

'I'm looking forward to meeting him.'

'I'm glad, but be warned, there's no guarantee he'll be a Dirk.'

'I thought you knew.'

'No.'

'My mother knew.'

'Well I wanted a surprise, like Christmas.'

'I mean, she knew without being told. About Bobby.'

Their first course arrives: baked goat's cheese on a raspberry coulis. He offers to replenish her wine but she shakes her head and shields her glass. She cuts into the cheese, but doesn't taste it. She pushes a pale fragment back and forth in its carmine sea. 'Would you prefer to have something different?'

'No, this looks lovely.'

'Then try it.'

'In a minute. Adam, I need to ask you a favour, but all this talk about me being hit-and-run and the rest, I'm not sure how to take it.'

'We're not likely to fall out, are we? I know we argue, but . . .'

'We disagree. It's not the same.'

'Then come on, if you've a favour to ask, spit it out.'

'Okay. It's like this. I've another couple of weeks before the pod pops, right?' She spikes a piece of cheese and nibbles one edge. The coulis stains her lips. 'Top marks, by the way.' She brandishes her fork. 'This is delicious.'

'My own recipe. Jessica . . .'

'I know, I know. Get on with it. Well, the way things are at the moment – you know, with Ellie and Simon – it's all a bit odd. No, it's okay, not like that. They're getting along fine. They seem to be working something out and I want to help, but all I seem to do is get in their way – and Ellie's angry with me, though I don't know why. She won't talk about it.'

'Still, I'm sure they appreciate a referee.'

'They don't need one. Simon's different. I almost like him. He's doing this mural and he won't let her see it, and she hates that, but they don't fight. Eleanor's different, too. Quiet. I've never seen her like this. I don't know where any of this is going, but they need some space to work it out and I think the best thing I can do is get out of their hair for a bit. Which is where you come in.' She takes another bite of cheese and speaks as she chews. 'So what about it, Adam, do you have a spare room in your cottage?'

He sips his wine, playing for time. He both does, and does not want Jessica in his house. 'I have a room, yes, but Jessica, are you sure this is a good idea?'

'I promise not to be a nuisance. I'll clean the bath and make my own bed – yours too, if you like. And I'll leave as soon as the baby arrives. It'll only be for a week or two.'

'What about Georgie? Are you happy to leave her with them?'

'That's part of the plan. Simon won't harm them, but I don't think he can keep up this good-guy act indefinitely. Georgie's a sweetie, but she's demanding. Like her mother. I reckon if we leave them to it, he'll be off to London or back to the States in a couple of months.'

347

16

Eleanor is in the garden with Georgie. The lawn is dry and hard and brown. If she bangs it with the heel of her palm, it makes a dull thudding sound. She thinks of underground caverns. Sealed and dry.

She has borrowed the family biscuit tin album from Babs, and scattered all around her are photographs of herself as a child. Eleanor at six months, naked on the sofa, kicking her feet; Eleanor swooping down a slide, falling off her little three-wheeler bike – and Eleanor at eight, on the quay in Fowey, feeding the gulls, Babs's camera case on the harbour wall beside her.

Georgie chatters away, telling herself a story as she plays. In the middle of the lawn is a stone bird-bath. Its rim is encrusted with green and brown lichen, but the bowl is empty. Georgie feels sorry for the birds and she fills a galvanized watering can from the standpipe by the back door and staggers across the lawn. The can is too heavy and she splashes water everywhere. Droplets glitter like opal, like broken glass.

Eleanor looks from the photograph to Georgie, and back again. She overlays the images, attempting to fuse the child in the photos with the child in the garden. They are the same; she can match them to one another, feature by feature, gesture by gesture. What Georgie is doing at this moment is exactly the sort of thing the young Eleanor might have done. She is trying to impose order on her world.

Eleanor picks up a photograph and traces the glossy line of her childish cheek. Up until this moment, everything she has done regarding Georgie has been the right thing. Having her in the first place, refusing to identify her father, bringing her up alone . . .

She lifts her head and laughs out loud. Georgie turns and waves.

She pushes some loose strands of hair up off her brow. She hates this cloying heat; it would be cooler inside. She had a shower only an hour ago but already her nape is sticky and she can detect the salty tang of her sweat. But she will not go in. She cannot. For one thing, she has come to hate the smell of paint. For another, Simon's secrecy taunts her. He is obsessed. He spends his days locked in her bedroom, reappearing every evening like an overworked goblin released only at sundown. He looks ill. He's pale, saggy-eyed and exhausted, and spattered with a stomach-churning mix of green and brown and yellow paint.

If Jess were here they would make up silly stories as to what he gets up to all day, but Jess has moved in with Adam.

A good thing too. I don't want her here.

Jess had said, 'He's putting me up for a few days, a week or two at most.'

'Putting you up?'

'In his spare room.'

'And when the baby comes?'

'I'll come back here . . .'

'If that's what you want.'

'That was the whole point of the move, wasn't it? You and me and the kids. I just need a bit of a break, Ellie.'

'So do I. What about Adam?'

Jess shrugs and misunderstands. 'What about Simon?' she says.

Georgie doesn't like Simon. She barely speaks to him, and she wolfs her meals so she doesn't have to stay too long in the same room.

'Come on, Georgie, tell me what it is you don't like about him.'

'I don't like anything. I like Adam. Why doesn't Adam come any more?'

Eleanor bundles her photographs back into the biscuit tin. Georgie has grown bored with splashing water and is digging around in the overgrown borders, looking for flints. Flints are her latest discovery. The colours excite her; pale gold like sand on a beach, dark amber like wet sand. And blue and black. Like bruises. They are gritty on the outside, but where they have split the inner surface is hard and shiny. Eleanor explains that in the days before there was bronze or iron for tools, they were chipped into axe-heads and arrow-tips and skinning knives. Eleanor gets a book from the library and Georgie draws pictures of cave women killing and gutting animals. The women are surrounded by a tangle of scribbled blue entrails.

Georgie has a whole collection of flints which Eleanor helps her to arrange along the windowsills like exhibits in a gallery. She shouts that she's found another and presents it to Eleanor like Oscar offering a mouse. Eleanor weighs it in her hand. 'This is a beauty,' she says. 'Best yet.'

'There's more.' Georgie rises to the challenge. 'I can find lots more.'

She disappears into the shrubbery. Simon is thrilled with Georgie's drawings; he has pinned them to the kitchen walls. Simon's presence oppresses her. He is changed, so passive. She has nothing to push against.

But she too has changed, and at a fundamental, cellular level. Her bones are no longer porous and light, but solid metal. A femur sliced through would show a hard, shiny cross-section.

Or flint. Her bones are not steel, but flint. This is another, more alarming form of regression – and these are dangerous, destabilizing thoughts.

It is not safe to stay here – who knows where such a metamorphosis might lead? She should go away. Why not? She's done it before. Nobody needs her, only Georgie, and Georgie belongs to her. Georgie is Eleanor.

But where could they go?

London. Venice. Edinburgh. Fowey. Any of these, or none of them.

17

Adam wakes in the middle of the night, aware of someone in the room with him. There is the scuffle of a body, the sound of breathing, erratic, almost gasping. 'Adam? Wake up, Adam.' It's

Jessica. 'I'm sorry, but I think I'm going to need your help.'

She sits on the bed and waits while he pulls on a pair of jeans and a sweatshirt. It is all terribly calm. She winces and smiles up at him as he helps her to her feet and eases her down the stairs. There is no need for frantic phone calls or screaming sirens; he simply helps her into the car and drives very carefully to the hospital, and there the staff take over.

He rings Eleanor from a phone booth and she promises to visit Jessica in the morning. He's edgy; it's almost as if this child is his own. He feels helpless. He paces to and fro exactly as expectant fathers are supposed to do.

A vending machine dispenses watery tea into a plastic cup that burns his fingers. He pulls out a packet of cigarettes. The No Smoking sign reproaches him. Above the sign is a clock. The face is white with big, institutional numbers. The chairs are moulded grey plastic with metal legs. Stackable.

He tries not to think too much about what Jessica is going through. She's suffering, yes, but his argument stands. One or the other, male or female, is required to play host. The fact that Jessica is in the delivery room instead of Rob, is a biological fluke. With sea-horses, it is the male who gives birth. Another fluke.

If motherhood is a freak of nature, what about fatherhood? Does it matter whether Georgie is his daughter or Simon's? And Baby Dirk. Rob is no longer part of Jessica's life. Adam is. He is here now, and his presence is a significant factor in Baby Dirk's life. As significant as Rob's absence.

A nurse stands in the doorway smiling. 'Mr Grant?' He doesn't correct her. 'You've a little girl. Would you like to see her?'

Jessica's narrow face is bleached white and her hennaed hair is like a shock of dried blood. She doesn't look at him; she's looking at the bundle in her arms. He perches on the edge of the bed. Jessica adjusts her hold on the baby. 'I'm going to call her Eve,' she says, smiling. 'Do you mind?'

Of course he doesn't mind, he's thrilled. This is what counts. Being with them, like this, gives him a stake in Eve's life. An emotional stake. What does blood matter? It is commitment and love that counts.

'You can hold her, if you like.' He wants to, but he's afraid. Afraid he might hurt her, and afraid because he cannot bear to think of

351

losing her as he has lost Georgie. Jessica says, 'It's okay, Adam.' She knows what he's thinking and wants him to be reassured. 'Really it is. Come on, take her.'

She places Eve in his arms. He moves instinctively to protect her head. His hand is so huge, her skull so tiny. He revisits the sensation experienced when he held Georgie for the first time, a curious combination of substance and fragility. A sudden tenderness and a sense of his own vulnerability spiral through him and nudge aside the little part of him that had once belonged to Georgie.

And Jessica, what about Jessica? He looks at her, and knows what he wants. His mouth is dry with the fear of commitment – because commitment is what she'll require of him. Jessica doesn't allow people to get too close, not men at any rate, and he must not let her down.

She is watching him, and it is as though she is following his thought processes, waiting for him to say the words they both know are at this moment forming in his brain. He takes a breath. 'Look at us,' he whispers. 'The two of us . . .'

'I'm looking.'

'We've wasted so much time.'

'You,' she gives a little shake of her head. 'You're the time waster, Adam Mason, moping around after my best mate all these years.'

He nods and smiles. 'I've been a fool, right?'

'Right. You see? I told you – we don't fight, we are beginning to agree on everything.' There is more to say, he feels it welling inside him, but Jessica is wise. 'Give her here,' she says, beckoning for the return of her daughter. She is right; they have all the time in the world.

He places Eve in her arms and for a moment their faces are close, and they breathe the same air. Jessica laughs softly and nuzzles her baby's head. She presses a finger to Eve's palm and raises the tiny hand to her lips. 'Well now,' she says, speaking low so as not to disturb her. 'Tell me what you think, Mr Mason. Are these the fingers of a first-class cook, or a grade-one upholsterer?'

18

Simon's mural is finished and Eleanor wants to see. 'Soon,' he says. He is reluctant. She sulks. She goes into the garden.

Georgie has built a tent. She has raided the house for towels and strung them between the bushes. She has also found a little red and black Persian-style rug and she sits cross-legged in her glowing pavilion, like a princess from *A Thousand And One Nights*.

Eleanor ducks under the canopy. The air is musty, a combination of crushed grass and orange juice and the sickly sweet scent of little girls. She has to hunch up small. Georgie laughs. The sunlight filtering through the towels is orange and red and green. A thistle prickles Eleanor's thigh and she wriggles and squirms to get comfortable. A butterfly has followed her into the tent. It flutters and blunders against the towels and Georgie cups it gently in her hands, and releases it back into the garden.

A door bangs. Simon is unlocking one of the outbuildings. He disappears inside.

Georgie shuffles back into the tent. 'I hate him,' she says. 'I wish he'd go away.'

'So do I.' Eleanor strokes her daughter's dark hair. Burrs have become caught in the curls and, like a monkey grooming its mate, she sets about removing them. 'Maybe we should go away instead,' she says. 'For a holiday.' She pauses in her grooming and rests her chin on Georgie's shoulder. 'What do you say to that? Would you like that, Georgie?'

Georgie considers. 'With Auntie Jess?'

'Of course.'

'And Adam, can Adam come?'

'I don't know. We'll see.'

Simon goes back into the house. Georgie is once again absorbed in play, assembling a meal for Big Nigel. Using a flat-faced flint as a plate, she makes an arrangement of plantain and grass and clover. She sprinkles dry earth for pepper.

Simon is clearing the bedroom. He reappears, kicking and shuffling the canvas floor-covering across the terrace. He heads for the outbuilding. As soon as he is out of sight, Eleanor gives Georgie a quick kiss and says, 'You stay here, Pud.' Georgie draws breath to protest, but Eleanor places a finger against her lips. 'Be good,' she whispers. 'I'm going inside.'

The hall is cool as a pool and the stone flags chill her bare feet. Shallow water, a beach ribbed by the tide. The tide turns.

Looking up, she sees the bedroom door is ajar. Simon has grown careless. Step by step, her shoulder pressed to the wall, she climbs the creaking stairs. On the landing she pauses. The house is silent but down in the garden Georgie is singing. Her voice is shrill. It cracks as she strains for the high notes.

She pushes the bedroom door wider, and steps inside.

Green. Shades of green. Earth green, verdigris, lime and sage. Sunlight screened through trees makes the room flicker and glow; the air sparkles – he has painted water, he has climbed inside her head and painted her fear. Although bright on the surface, glittering like sequins in the sun, this sea is dangerous and dark beneath.

And he knows – none better – that she has always been afraid of the dark.

The ceiling is the surface of the sea, the plaster cornice the bright foam. The sun strikes like a knife. Bright silver and hammered pewter and polished bronze. She is surrounded by water. Four walls to her prison. High up, the water is pale. Lower down it becomes darker and darker still, sucking her in, sucking deep, deep, deep . . .

Coral and weed and angelfish weave sinister patterns. They seem benign, but she knows, oh yes, she knows better. Come, they say, be a part of us, be one with us. But humans cannot live beneath the sea. The Little Mermaid knows.

She turns. The corners of the room dissolve into shadow. Rocks loom. Tentacles wave. Hot waters. Tropical waters. Her shirt is soaked all down the back and between her shoulder blades. The weight of the water is crushing, intolerable. She moves sluggishly against the stubborn thrust of the tide.

Her brain protests. Illusion. Touch. Feel. She drifts towards the wall. She presses her hands against cool plaster. The wall resists. It pushes back. Boundaries.

But the light deceives; it dapples and shifts and there is a sound like the rush of the tide, and beneath her feet the rug-pulling suck of the current's undertow.

She turns slowly, oh so slowly, rolling against the wall. It is solid. Or it is not. Perhaps the wall and its substance is also an illusion.

Then she sees her face. Her own face, so clear, like looking in a mirror.

But not a mirror. He has captured me.

Ever since they met he has been trying for this. At last he has succeeded.

She sees her own eyes. Blue. Cocktail-blue, blue-jay. Tawdry. Hair like weed drifting in the current. Long neck, white neck shading to black.

Her face, but not her body. He has imprisoned her, immobilized her, bound her in black skin, a strait-jacket snake. She recognizes her face framed by drifting hair, but her pale neck is transformed, transmuted, moulded to the form of a serpent. It has a rib along its back and a cruel, whipping, tapering tail.

'Conger-eel.' He laughs from the doorway. 'Hey, Nell, what d'you think?'

She pivots like a floating ballerina. He is holding out his arms. To embrace her. He wants her and he wants Georgie. This cannot be. Why did he have to come back? They were doing so well, the two of them.

'I understand it all now, Nell.' His manic face grimaces. 'I worked it out, you see. All this time I've been trying to paint you, and that was wrong – because you can be anything you want to be, Nell, that's the magic of it. It's what you are – a blank canvas . . .'

'No.'

'We've got it made, you and me. You and me and Georgie, what a team, eh Nell?'

The water numbs her. Its weight, its tropical chill. She moves towards him. His lips part. He is still speaking, but she can't hear him now, she doesn't want to hear him. His words lay claim to her and Georgie – but no, her life is her own; she knows who she is and what she wants.

His words dissolve in a rush of bubbles. She laughs. He frowns; he doesn't understand. She shakes her head and her hair floats out like weed on the surface of the sea. He takes a step towards her – this must not be. She launches herself; they collide. Eleanor and Simon in a sluggish embrace, still hindered by the crush of illusory water, they stumble backwards and she thinks nothing, hears nothing. Until his scream. 'Jesus, Nell – stop!'

They hover, hanging over space. Air above, below and all around. Stillness. Such glorious stillness in this moment of stasis.

Their aching bodies press against the banister rail, heaving it, breaking it as water bursts a dam. There is the sound of splintering wood and a rush of air. Their arms lock. He screams, she is silent. He breaks her fall. She hears the sickening crack of bone on stone.

Pain defines. She lies still, cushioned by his body. She is damaged. She is familiar with the slow spread of pain. She waits. Pain suffuses her, but it is a gradual ache. There is no immediate point of impact; there are no broken bones or ruptured organs.

She moves. She will live. What about Simon?

She lifts her head. Georgie stands in the kitchen doorway. She clutches Big Nigel to her chest, peering at Eleanor between his well-chewed ears.

She scrambles to her feet. The pain pulsates. Dull. The hammer thud of molten metal in her veins.

Simon's face is very white. There is blood on his head. One leg is bent at a silly angle. He is unconscious, maybe he is dead. Yes. Clearly, Simon is dead.

Next move? Choose.

No need, Simon chooses for her.

Georgie stands over him, waving Big Nigel in his face. 'Georgie, don't do that.' Her voice sounds strange. It vibrates deep inside her. Her vocal cords twang like guitar strings.

Georgie bends over the body of her maybe-father. 'Look,' she points to the wound on his head. She bobs down and her skirt rides up and her bottom skims the flags. She probes the gash with the tip of her finger. She laughs and, looking up at her mother, touches his blood to her lips.

19

Jess sits on her hospital bed waiting for Adam to take her home. Not back to Laburnham Lodge, but back to his cottage. 'What d'you think of that, little tadpole?' She traces the line of Eve's ear. 'He says we can stay with him. Should we go the whole hog, d'you suppose? Maybe I'll marry him, what d'you say to that?' Eve blows a bubble that becomes a dribble. Jess laughs. 'I'll take that as a yes, shall I?'

She cannot believe this, that she has this child that pukes and shits like any other child, and yet is not disgusted by it. In fact, it's rather touching to watch this new body struggling to come to terms with the complicated functions life requires of it. 'I think I'll buy you a Running In sign,' she whispers, shifting her attention from Eve's ears to her hairline. 'You know, little tadpole, your Aunt Ellie is going to make my life hell after all the things I've said about babies . . .'

There is a movement at the foot of the bed. She looks up. The nurse seems very young and Jess feels rather foolish. She grins and says, 'I suppose all new mums go a bit barmy, don't they?'

The nurse smiles. 'Do you need anything?'

'No, I'm fine – except, have there been any phone calls?' The little nurse shakes her head. 'You will tell me straight away if there are, won't you?'

It's probably nothing, but it's strange that Ellie hasn't been in touch.

It's possible she's sulking. They'd come to Suffolk together, Ellie and Jess and their children, but then Jess had gone and moved in with Adam. Maybe Ellie sees that as a betrayal. It's the sort of twisted conclusion she's likely to draw – with never a thought to how she's allowed Simon to intrude on their idyll.

Damn you, Ellie. Get a grip, can't you?

Adam arrives. She's unreasonably glad to see him. He kisses her and strokes her cheek, then Eve's. She clings to his arm. 'I bet you're dying to get out of this place,' he says. 'Come on, where's your bag?'

'Wait a minute. Adam, about Ellie, you did ring her, didn't you?'

'I told you, she said she'd be in to see you.'

'But she hasn't and I haven't heard a word, not even a card. I'm worried.'

'What are you worried about? You said he'd changed, isn't that right? You said you didn't think he'd harm her . . .'

'I'm sure he won't. I don't know what it is, I just don't like it.'

'They've probably gone off on a jaunt to set up an exhibition or commission a mural or something. Once she gets the wind behind her the rest of us always get shoved to the back, you know that.'

Simon's car is parked in the drive. There is no sign of Eleanor's Renault. Adam glances at Jessica. 'I told you she'd be out. We should have rung.'

'I want to make sure.' She adjusts her hold on Eve and digs her keys from her bag. 'Here, take these.'

The gravel grinds beneath his shoes. He remembers the first time he came here, his excitement, his reluctance to touch the door knocker. No need to knock this time. He inserts the key and pushes the door.

Coolness descends. It takes a moment for his eyes to adjust to the gloom. He blinks, and takes a step closer.

A crumpled heap – a shop-window dummy dumped in a skip. Simon. 'Jesus . . .' He looks up slowly and sees where the banister rail has broken. It is not so high, yet Simon has fallen heavily.

'What is it?' Jessica is behind him. In the deadly silence he hears her sharp intake of breath. He would hear her heartbeat as well, were it not for the pounding of his own blood.

Simon. This is Eleanor's doing. It is too much of a coincidence that she is absent and Simon is here, broken and bleeding. He crouches beside him. He has never seen a dead body, let alone a ~~d one. He expects it to be cold, imagines flesh the texture of ~stry.

~ is warm. The fingers curl at his touch.

with him. I'll fetch a blanket.'

stands on the bog oak chest, next to the bowl of

rose petals. In this house and in this situation it should be a clunking great bakelite phone. It is not. It has buttons and a display panel. He punches in 999. He holds out his hand and splays his fingers. He is shaking. He asks for an ambulance and gives the address. He hangs up. He dips his fingers among the rose petals. They rustle, frail as dry skin. The wall above the chest is blank. He tries to remember what had hung there.

Jessica tucks a blanket round Simon. She looks up, 'Will they be long?'

'I don't know. As soon as possible, they said.'

'Adam,' her voice is unsteady. Eve begins to whimper. 'Where's Ellie?' He takes a breath. 'I knew it – you see? I told you something was wrong. What's happened here? And Georgie. Adam, where the hell is Georgie?'

20

The motorway ends at Exeter. From here on, the journey into Cornwall will be slower. Eleanor restricts her thoughts to practical matters, allowing her mind to dwell only on those things she absolutely has to do. She must buy petrol. Feed Georgie. Watch the traffic.

But there are some matters she cannot avoid. 'You mustn't tell anyone,' she tells Georgie. Georgie is very white. It's probably shock. She must keep her warm. She turns up the car heater and switches on the fan.

'Mummy, I'm too hot.'

'You mustn't get cold. You don't look well. Did you hear what I said, about not telling anyone?'

'I heard.' She's sulking, staring out of the window, tugging at Big Nigel's foot.

'What mustn't you tell?' she insists. They've got to get this right, synchronize their stories.

'About Simon falling downstairs.'

'And what else?'

'I'm not called Georgie any more. I think Lizzie's a horrible name.'

'It's just for a while. Until I get things sorted. It'll be all right, Georgie, just you and me. I'll look after you.'

But Simon is dead. That can't be sorted, and if they're found out, how will she be able to look after Georgie then?

They reach Liskeard. Liskeard, Lizard, Lostwithiel, Golant. The names down here are from another world. She needs this, a new world and a new identity. She clenches the steering wheel. Her knuckles and knees were grazed raw by the fall. At first they hardly hurt at all, but now they sting terribly. And she has a headache. She has been taking paracetamol at regular intervals to lessen the pain. They are almost at their destination. She will take no more pills; she will let the pain wash over her, allow the bruises to form. Rub lemon juice in her cuts.

But for now she must drive. Concentrate. No distractions.

Simon is dead, and it's her fault. She should have told someone. Rung for an ambulance. Anonymously. Phoned Babs or the police. But she hadn't. She'd crammed a muddle of clothes into a holdall and grabbed Georgie, unhooked Simon's seascape and run.

She had only two choices, stay or run. Instinct had prompted her to flight. Had she stayed, they would have taken Georgie from her.

She stops at a garage. 'Wait here,' she tells Georgie. 'I won't be a minute. Don't get out of the car and don't open the windows. You must stay warm, do you hear me?'

She pays for the petrol and buys a phonecard and a tube of Smarties for Georgie. She'll ring the house first, just in case Simon's up and about – a miracle cure, just a bit of a headache. Like her.

The phone rings three times before being picked up. Jess says, 'Hello?' Eleanor can't answer. There are voices in the background. Men's voices. And a crackling sound, like a radio. Police. 'Ellie, is that you? Are you okay? Ellie?' There is a scuffle. Then a new voice. Adam. 'Eleanor? Where are you? Speak to me.' She hasn't said a word. How come they're so certain it's her? 'Is Georgie with you? Is she all right?'

She can see Georgie from here. She's scowling, pressing her face against the windscreen, mouthing for her to hurry up. Georgie is mine, no one else's. My blood in her veins, my genes and DNA . . .

I can be whoever I want to be.

Adam is still speaking. He wants her to come home. What he really wants is Georgie. She slams the phone back on its cradle.

She takes a room in a hotel on Fowey Esplanade. They have a view across the river to Polruan. Georgie is thrilled by the boats and the gulls, by the huge tanker being guided out to sea by the little black and orange pilot boat clinging like a barnacle to its hull. But there is an edge to Georgie's excitement. These things are new to her. She's using them as building blocks to make a wall, to form a barrier to block out the picture of Simon bleeding on the flagstones. Eleanor knows this. She has used the technique herself. As a child, when her father left; as an adult, when Chris died. And today, gathering sights and sounds along the motorway.

But it's not enough. Nothing is big enough, dense enough to hide the scene. She has grown too tall. She sees over every wall.

Adam is coming.

Georgie is asleep. Her hands grip Big Nigel's paw. Her knuckles are white.

What have I done?

They are registered at the hotel as Miranda Grant and her daughter Lizzie. No one has questioned this or asked for identification, but when she pays her bill she will write a cheque or flash a credit card, and the name on both is Eleanor Bycroft.

Simon introduces her as his wife, but she never changed her name to Whitburn, so if the papers report his death, no one here will make the connection. Not that the papers will be interested. People die or are killed all the time. There is nothing distinctive about Simon's death.

Not so. It is news when a man is killed by his wife – and in the presence of his daughter. In her mind's eye she sees the headlines. What would Georgie's life be after that? She imagines her grown up, a wife herself, and a mother, desperate to hide her past and her genetic legacy from her husband and children.

No. She cannot think about it, it is too far in the future. What about now? She must decide what to do in the here and now.

They are Miranda and Lizzie Grant. Using Jess's name was probably a mistake but it had popped to the tip of her tongue without warning.

How can she hide? She is shackled to her past. She is responsible for Georgie. She needs money. Using her own accounts will alert the authorities.

She needs a job. Anything but casual work will involve forms, P45s and National Insurance numbers. And what about a doctor if Georgie gets ill? She doesn't know how to do this. How does a person hide? People manage it, but they are more resourceful than her. Her mind reels. She has taken only the first step, and already she has stumbled. They have assumed new names, but these will not hide them.

Every time she runs away, Simon follows. He found her in Suffolk just as he had found her here, in Cornwall. Adam and the police are unlikely to be less successful. However hard she tries, she cannot help but leave a trail. This evening at dinner the adjacent table was occupied by a middle-aged couple. The man stared at her through-out the meal. People do that, they notice her.

Why did she take Simon's painting? It's almost as if she wants to be found.

No.

Regardless of her intention, either Adam or Jess are bound to notice that the painting is missing. When they do, they'll tell the police and they will come here with their photographs and their questions, and sooner or later someone will say, 'Yes, I do believe I may have seen them . . .'

And then there's her car. If all else fails, they will trace her through the car.

They are trapped. She has sprung the mechanism herself by fleeing to the obvious place and making only the most superficial efforts to hide their identity. She estimates they have twenty-four hours, forty-eight at the most, before they are found.

Then what? They will take her away. Lock her up. Georgie. She will never see Georgie again. Georgie will not want to see her again.

It must not happen. Georgie scowls in her sleep. I won't let it happen. She touches her brow and pushes back the tangle of curls. Her skin is moist and hot. 'It'll be all right, Georgie Pud. You're mine, you know that, don't you? We'll always be together. You

362

mustn't be afraid, I'll stay with you, I'll never let you go. I'll sort it all out, I promise. I'll never leave you, Georgie.'

21

Georgie doesn't want to go for a picnic, she thinks it's a silly idea. 'My head hurts,' she whines. 'I'm cold. I want to go home. I want Auntie Jess, I want Adam. I hate it here.'

'You'll like it soon. Come on. It's a lovely day.'

Adam was always very fond of picnics. They went to Holland Park once; on another occasion they went to her church and sat on the pews and ate game pie and salad and drank rich red wine, thick as blood.

She buys crab sandwiches and a bottle of cherryade and a bag of apples.

They catch the ferry to Polruan. The little boat bobs and rocks and Georgie clings to her arm. It is September and the wind is strong and the water is dipped and textured like beaten metal. The tower of the blockhouse stands in sharp silhouette against the sky. Eleanor explains how a chain was once stretched from one side of the estuary to the other. 'So when the enemy boats came in, it snapped their masts in two.'

Beside the blockhouse is a tree. Its dark branches rise in layered shelves, like the design on an antique plate. Further out, beyond the promontory, is a boat, rusty and businesslike, a dredger perhaps.

When the ferry docks, Eleanor hurries Georgie away from the harbour and up the hill. Georgie drags her feet. She's not well; she should be in bed.

They reach the headland. Georgie grizzles. Eleanor's headache is worse. It probably means her period is on its way. She takes a couple of paracetamol and washes them down with a swig of cherryade.

It is a grim picnic. What on earth possessed her to come here?

Who knows? It is the need to be alone, to be away from the curious stares of strangers, to avoid polite exchanges laced with danger.

The wind has grown stronger. The sky is low, a gun-metal grey. The horizon glares. 'What d'you think, Georgie?' she says. 'Will there be a storm?' Georgie is sulking. She won't eat. She turns her back on the cherryade. Eleanor says, 'What would you like to do now? Shall we go for a walk? Just a little walk.'

The weather continues to deteriorate. Last time she came here, Simon followed her. Maybe if it had been Adam, everything would have turned out otherwise. Adam would like Fowey and Polruan. He could open a restaurant. A fish restaurant. Not that he'd like it up here. Adam is afraid of heights just as she is scared of the dark.

She slips her bag across her shoulder like a satchel and, taking Georgie's hand, pulls her to her feet and starts to walk.

'No. I want to go home,' Georgie protests. Eleanor doesn't answer. 'Not this way,' she insists, leaning back, resisting the tug of her mother's hand. 'I want to go back.'

But Eleanor is stronger than Georgie. They reach the edge. It is not really much of a cliff, not sheer. It is just the place where the land ends by breaking away into the sea.

'I don't like it here, Mummy. I'm scared. I'm dizzy. I want to go home.'

The wind buffets in from the sea. Like a heavy curtain it parts to allow them through. Her body's outline is shaped by the drag of the wind.

Beneath her feet, the headland vibrates with the song of the sea.

There is a path. Well, not really a path. A slope of scrubby grass leading to a rock shelf. Then a steeper, shorter slope. And more rocks.

'Let's go down, Georgie. What d'you say? We'll have an adventure. Look at the sea, isn't it beautiful?' She begins the descent. Georgie squeals. 'Don't be scared. It's okay. I'm here. I'll always be here.'

She kicks off her shoes. She tells Georgie to do the same, but she won't. 'It'll be easier, you'll be able to hold on. Look.' Her long toes grip the flaking boulders. Georgie shakes her head. 'Okay. Well, hold on tight then.'

They scramble lower. The shale lacerates Eleanor's soles. But that's all right. Pain defines. She lifts her head. For the first time in weeks she sees the world face to face.

She cannot go forward and she cannot go back. She is trapped. Not here on this rock, but in life. They will take Georgie from her. They will take her out of the world. She will stop being herself, become somebody else, and that will never do . . .

They slither down the next stage. Georgie is silent now, all her efforts concentrated on finding a foothold.

'It'll be okay,' Eleanor reassures her. 'Look. We're nearly there. All we have to do is reach the sea.'

Then what? screeches the wind.

She laughs and shouts, 'Who knows? Who cares? It doesn't matter . . .'

As the wind snatches and mangles her words, there is a tug on her hand. Her shoulder jerks in its socket. She turns. Georgie is gone. The stones and scrubby grass are scuffed and ripped where she kicked her heels. Eleanor stares at the empty space, and at her empty hand. How can this be? So suddenly.

Where is she?

Noise. Waves on rocks. Gulls on the wing. A slither of stones. But no scream. No cry of any kind, and no sign of her. It is as if she'd never been here. The indifferent sea scours the rocks. Eleanor cranes to see. There should be something – a body floating out to sea. Out, then back again to crash upon the rocks with every wave.

Nothing.

The Little Mermaid hurls herself from the bridal ship and becomes a spirit of the air.

Even as a child, Eleanor thought that a nonsensical, a contrived ending.

But if Georgie is neither the foam on the sea nor a spirit of the air, where has she gone? And how can Eleanor follow?

She feels no grief. Stillness follows pain. How strange. She feels nothing, only a sense of rightness and cohesion. Patterns recur. She has observed this. The earth spins on its axis, the moon orbits the earth, the earth orbits the sun. Sooner or later the planets align. Then the darkness comes.

Sooner or later, Georgie will be washed ashore. The body of a child shattered on the rocks. Bones eroded by salt, bleached by the

365

sun. Georgie's knuckles and toes and vertebrae winking like cockle-shells against the black boulders. And hair, strands like weed clinging to the cracks and crevices, rising and sinking with the tide.

She leans against the rock. She has come here for a reason – though even now she does not fully understand, except that her journey to Fowey and Polruan was no accident.

Any more than it was an act of will.

She eases down the last steep slope. At the bottom is an area of rock and shale that the tide has not yet reached. She finds a boulder and sits down.

She aches all over. Her shoulders and arms, her back. Her head. She opens her bag. She spills the remainder of her pills across the boulder. There are lots of them. She lines them up.

'I like the red ones best . . .'

'No, the blue, the blue!'

At the bottom of her bag is a packet of dental gum. She chews on a piece until the saliva runs. Then she starts to swallow the sweeties, one by one, orange and brown and green. She keeps the red till last.

The tide rises. She shuffles back on her rock, then slithers down behind. It's nice here. Out of the wind. Quieter. She curls against the rock. Like curling against Adam at night. Not Simon. Simon would crush her like the rock.

She never knew before that rocks had a smell. Like wet metal. She presses against the rock. *Redemption*. Andrea Harding and her foetal stone. She must tell Andrea about this. About the feel of it, and the smell, and the taste. She explores it with her fingers and her tongue as once she'd explored Adam's face. The sculpture lives.

But she is tired now. And that's okay. Her rock will guard her. Like a dog. A great black salivating hound.

The rising tide tickles her feet – splashing up, then sucking back. She wriggles her toes. It's good here. Georgie would like it very much. Here is where it's best to be.

You see, Georgie – didn't I tell you, didn't I promise never to leave you?

Are you listening out there, Georgie?

Can you hear me?

Georgie.

Blood Ties

It's two in the morning. It's eerie up on the headland. Dark and light, silent, yet also saturated with sound. The endless waters gather their radiance from the glimmer of the moon – which in turn borrows its light from the sun – and from ships and towns and villages. The greedy sea seizes its harvest from the Cornish coast and the French coast, sucking it from the air and distilling it on to a surface as sheer and brilliant as taut silk.

Torn silk. Ripped and shredded. Rocks like razors. A body rent.

He closes his eyes. The light goes out, but he can still hear the sea, a soft rustle and a heavy murmur, like a giant shifting in his sleep.

He'd needed to come here. Fresh air, a new perspective.

Stretched alone in his bed, the night had seemed endless. He misses Jessica so much, her laughter, her brisk no-nonsense approach to life. Her body, the smell of her and the taste of her. But he is also afraid. They spoke on the phone last night and the long silences ached between their words, and her laughter scraped like a spoon in a tin saucepan.

Or maybe it was just the straining of the telephone lines.

They will arrive today, Jessica and Eve. What will it be like to see them again? Eve will be shy, that's only to be expected. But Jessica? They will circle one another, afraid to touch, to embrace. He sees a little scene, Eve burying her face in Jessica's shoulder, Jessica using Eve as a shield.

These images dance in and out and round and round his sleepless mind.

He sits up. Alien shadows surround him. Huddled figures lurk in the corners of the room. This morning his furniture arrived from Suffolk. Jessica and Eve are due in just a few hours. They will start their new life together. If they can. Of course they can. It was her choice to join him, no one is forcing her. No one could ever force Jessica to anything. At least he can be certain that if she stays, it will be because she wants to, not because she feels she should. Her stubbornness has rankled at times, but now he sees it as a particularly incandescent form of honesty.

If she stays.

Will she?

A life together. They have tried it once already. After the funerals he had bought her a silver ring in the form of a snake. A new beginning. Slipping the ring on to the tip of his little finger, he said, 'I did think about a solitaire, but diamonds go with white dresses and churches and cars with ribbons, and that's not your style.' He wiggled his finger to make the ring catch the light. 'So I thought, how about a silver snake and a week in Vienna in December?'

'I'm not sure about the snake,' she said. 'Garden of Eden and all that. It's not a very propitious start, and we need all the help we can get.'

'I know, but if you're looking for omens, snakes also signify fertility, wisdom and the power to heal. I checked.'

Their snake wedding lasted a year and came to grief because he couldn't accept the truth of what had happened to Eleanor.

He has accepted it now. Eden has cured him.

He blinks. Lights dot the skyline. He can just make out the dark, cutout shape of a ship resting on the horizon.

The sea draws him, a living creature, hypnotic and luminous, bright as silver and sluggish as mercury. Day or night, it has a quality of light all its own. And Eleanor is a part of it now. Which is appropriate, given her fear of the dark.

He stands close to the edge and feels the hum of the sea in the rocks beneath his feet. The landmass shifts, its form changes. Nothing is forever.

He sits on a tussock of grass and grips his shins and rests his chin on his knee. His mind buzzes. The past. Eleanor and Georgie. The future. Jessica and Eve.

He almost lost them when Eleanor died. Not straight away. At first her death brought them closer. They clung to one another like children adrift in an open boat. And there were distractions, so much to be done. He is a practical man. He coped superbly and he fooled them all. He fooled himself. He spoke with the police, liaised with friends and relatives. Babs, Irene and George, Brian Farraday.

Simon. He felt responsible for Simon. So did Jessica. If they'd been more vigilant, less involved with one another, they would have seen how her mind was unravelling, and would not have left the two of them alone.

They had thought that any danger lay with Simon. But Simon had returned from the States a different man. Slightly different. Different enough.

Irene and George, Adam and Jessica gather round Simon's hospital bed. None of them knows what to say. The banalities catch in their throats. There are no reassurances. Nothing will ever be the same again.

'I kept telling her to get that staircase looked at,' he says. 'I told her so the first time I saw it.' His words crack the silence. Like splintered wood. 'What else can I say?' he defends himself. 'Everything is taboo . . .'

Only Jessica hears the note of hysteria. She lays a hand on his arm. 'It's okay,' she says, 'me too. I keep thinking about that. But you know Ellie, she wouldn't listen . . .'

Irene Whitburn is venomous. 'She was trouble right from the start, that woman. I knew she'd only bring grief.'

'Then it's a pity you didn't say something,' Jessica spits. 'I don't think hindsight's very helpful at this stage, do you?'

Simon's eyes are puffy. He can barely open them. The globe of his eyeball rolls beneath the swollen lid. There is a glint of blue as he manipulates his narrow gaze from one to the other. His skin is blotched, red and yellow-cream in colour, like mutton marbled with old fat. His voice is hoarse. 'Give it a rest,' he rasps. 'It's like a fucking cockfight in here.'

They laugh. He pricks their embarrassment, their bubble of rage.

He has a cracked skull and some broken ribs and his leg is broken in two places. He'll hobble for a while, but he'll be okay. People like Simon always bounce back.

He rolls his head painfully towards Adam. 'Has anyone heard?' he croaks. In the dead silence that follows they hear him swallow. 'Nell?'

'No,' Irene barks. Adam and Jessica exchange glances. Simon knows only that Eleanor and Georgie are missing.

'Try Cornwall,' he says, fumbling at Adam's arm. 'Fowey. She went there last time. I followed. Remember? It should have been you.'

'I remember.'

In the end, it is Adam who tells him. 'I spoke to the police,' he lies. 'About what you said, about Cornwall.'

'Did they find them?' Simon is excited. Eager. And then he sees the hard set of Adam's face. His own face freezes.

Adam says, 'Yes, they've found them. They were washed ashore. I'm sorry.'

'You're sorry?' Adam is silent. Simon gathers himself. 'Both of them? Georgie as well? Shit, Adam, not Georgie too . . .'

The police have questions for Simon. Just routine, they say, they want to get the picture straight. Simon insists on Adam being present.

Adam admires the change in him. The old, jittery Simon has vanished and he answers their questions, no matter how bizarre and apparently irrelevant, with clarity and dignity. He tells how he found her in the bedroom examining his mural. He describes her face. He tries to describe it. In the end he sketches it on the back of a get-well card. 'Look,' he says later, thrusting it at Adam. 'I never could get her right.'

He gives the details of her attack, but words cannot convey the terror of it. Her expression. The fear and the hatred as she propelled herself at him. The police want facts, not sensation. They are not interested in how it felt to fall against the handrail, to know with his mind that it cannot sustain their combined weight. To sense with his body its structural fragility, to hear and feel the creak and sag of rotten wood, and then the keeling ceiling and Eleanor's face and snarling lips, and a rush of air, and darkness.

'What do they expect?' he says after they've gone. 'You know, don't you, Adam? It's not about what happened then, it's about what happened the day before, the week, the month, the year. What the fuck do they expect?'

Something has happened between Adam and Simon. In a way he is closer to him than to Jessica. Their grief has more in common. At the funeral Adam sits at the end of the row, Jessica on one side, Simon's wheelchair on the other. He looks down. Simon's hands are shaking. His cheeks are wet. He is a wax candle, melting in the heat of his grief.

Adam cannot cry. When it's time for the hymn he stands very upright, his arm round Jessica, a hand on Simon's shoulder. His voice grates. The coffins slide through the hatchway to the fire. He feels a dull glow of remembered rage.

After the service they are ushered into the courtyard where the flowers have been arranged in a semicircle. Babs bends over to read the labels. She looks small and very grey today.

Adam and Jessica, Irene and George, stand in a huddle round Simon.

'I don't understand.' Simon cranes up at Adam. 'I keep going over it, but I don't see how she could have done such a thing.'

'She didn't. It was an accident.' They stare at him. This is the point at which he realizes he is the only one who believes this. He continues to believe it. For months.

But now he knows the truth. Sitting here on the headland he understands how he'd buried the truth because he could not admit that what she'd done had been a deliberate act of will.

'She's not capable of such a thing,' he'd shouted at Jessica. 'You know that. Any decision is potentially the wrong decision, that's what she thought, that's what paralysed her. After Chris, after he died – you said it yourself – she was frozen, so how could she ever have done this thing?'

'Something must have changed, something we missed. Face it, Adam, there's no way it was an accident.'

Their relationship foundered on this rock. He adored Jessica and he loved Eve, but Eleanor stood between them and he began to think she always would.

'Listen to me,' says Jessica. 'It happened. It was nobody's fault, but it certainly was no accident.'

'Yes, it was. Georgie fell, she lost her footing, that's all . . .'

'Okay, but what were they doing there in the first place? There was a gale blowing that day – and they went for a picnic for Christ's sake!'

Everyone condemns her. Surely they cannot all be wrong.

To find a person, one must go to the places that matter to them, that's what Eleanor would have said. So Adam went to Fowey and fell in love with the river and the estuary and the sea. He took the little ferryboat across to Polruan, and discovered Eden. And Eden

373

has healed him so that now, after all this time, he can say her name aloud.

His lips are dry as he whispers it to the sea. He moistens them. Again. Louder, this time. And louder still, till it becomes a shout.

Eleanor.

Jessica arrives a little after six. Adam has been watching for her, standing at an upstairs window, craning for a glimpse of the road and his first sighting.

The little van strains up the hill. He hurries out to meet her. Reaching the gate, he stops and waits. He mustn't rush this; he will take his cue from her.

Jessica stands on the verge, one hand resting on Eve's shoulder, the other pushing her hair back off her brow. She's wearing a loose green top over jeans, and a dangling tangle of beads. This is Jessica as she was when he first met her, way back, before he'd ever heard of Eleanor Bycroft.

Eve is grizzly. Jessica picks her up. 'She's dead tired,' she says over Eve's shoulder. 'It's been a hell of a journey. We had to start so early and your directions were crap. I took a wrong turning at Liskeard . . .'

'And ended up on the road to Bodmin?'

'Easy mistake, huh? You might have warned me.' They stand close. Just as he'd expected, Eve is shy; she buries her face in her mother's neck. Jessica strokes her hair, and studies Adam's face. 'My goodness, look at you,' she says. 'You certainly have changed, Adam Mason. And this,' she turns slowly and looks up at the cottage. 'It's not at all how I imagined it.'

He leads the way inside and gives them the grand tour. Eve wakes up enough to be excited by her bedroom, by the yellow walls and the golden sunrise Pam has painted on the ceiling. 'Pam's first mural,' he explains. 'She swears she'll never do another.'

Eve is at the window. She grips the ledge and stands on tiptoe to see the view. Adam stands beside her. He says, 'Can you see the river?' She looks up at him, oh so seriously, and shakes her head. He holds out his arms and she comes to him, and allows him to lift her up. He points out Polruan's harbour and across the river to Fowey Town Quay.

Jessica strokes Eve's hair and says, 'I think that's enough for one day.' She gives her ear a gentle tweak. 'It's time little tadpoles were asleep in their beds.'

Adam waits outside. He has placed a wooden bench along the side of the house and sitting here he sips a glass of Chardonnay and watches the sun go down along the line of the river.

Last night he told Pam about Eleanor and Georgie. 'You should have said.' She is amazed. 'Why didn't you tell me?'

'I could hardly tell myself. Sometimes I can't even say her name.'

'But I remember it happening,' says Pam. 'I was away at the time, but everyone was talking about it when I got back. Why didn't I make the connection?'

'There's no reason why you should.'

No reason why anyone should. They were not a couple. In the end they were neither lovers nor friends. Their only link was Georgie. Georgina May Whitburn, who may or may not have been his daughter. He will never know. He suspects that she was not, that she was Simon's. Or perhaps this is something else he needs to believe. A necessary delusion, and one he can live with because now he understands that the ties of blood are ties of convenience, nothing more.

The people who matter to him, those he loves the most – Jessica and Eve, Babs and Simon – are not related by blood. Their closeness arises from shared experience and deep understanding.

Jessica comes out of the house and dumps herself on the bench beside him. He says, 'Is she asleep?'

'Out like a light, the poor mite. She was whacked.'

'Will she like it here, d'you think?'

'She already does.'

'And you?' She turns her head to look at him. He loves her foxy face, her sharp brown eyes. 'Jessica?'

'The house is great, but then it was bound to be; you're such a perfectionist.'

'But?'

'But this place, the reason you came here . . .'

'I don't think about that any more.'

'Okay, but even without Ellie, you know what Babs says – she's always complaining that Cornwall is too far from everywhere. Do you really want to stay here?'

'I love the house, I've made friends, and there's a restaurant in

Fowey. It's been empty ever since I came here but they're putting it on the market at the end of the month—'

'Adam . . .'

'And Pam's heard of somewhere you could rent for a workshop – she's dying to meet you, by the way – and there are masses of antiques shops round and about, so I'm sure you'll drum up enough work.'

'Ah yes, Pam,' she changes the subject and gives his arm a reproving tap. 'All those postcards you sent, there wasn't room to say much and most of what you did say was about Pam. Pam this and Pam that. I'm telling you, I was on the verge of being jealous.'

'She's got grandchildren.'

'Has she? Well, you never mentioned those. I think you wanted me to be jealous . . .'

'No.' The word falls with a dull thud. He doesn't know what else to say. This is small talk. Jessica isn't remotely bothered about Pam, she's just using her as a smoke screen – but now the smoke has cleared and he can see clearly and his hearing is so attuned he can detect the lap of every wave, the rustle of the clouds. Jessica's hair has grown longer and the breeze blows a strand against his cheek. He says, 'Jessica, we really do need to talk. We haven't discussed this properly.'

'What's that? Discussed what?' She is brusque; she knows what.

'We agreed that when the house was finished you'd come down, and we'd talk things through, take it from there.'

'Yes, we did.'

'Well, now the house is done . . .'

'To perfection.'

'And you like it, and Eve likes it – you will stay, won't you?'

'I don't know.'

His belly turns to water. He has tried not to think that in coming here she is making a commitment to their future. He knows better than that. It is enough that she is beside him now; one day at a time is all he can hope for.

'I wish . . .' he begins, then stops.

Tentative as a child, she touches his cheek. 'I wish you'd grow back the beard,' she says, then laughs and shrugs and turns away again. 'And I wish I could tell you where we go from here, but the truth is, I don't know. Maybe we need to be together for a bit, get used to one another again.'

'It's a start.' He smiles. 'One day at a time?'

'On the way down here I was thinking about what you said in the Abbey Gardens that time, about Ellie and how she tried to buck the system and keep Georgie all to herself. Perhaps I can learn from her mistakes.' She nudges his arm and gives him a mischievous pinch. 'Men and women – a single organism, isn't that what you said?'

'Something like that.'

'Biologically speaking?'

'And in other ways.'

'But in other ways, singular. We mustn't lose sight of that.'

'Never.' As he speaks, there is a blood-curdling screech and a gull lands on the wall. It is an evil-looking bird with beady eyes and a long yellow beak, hooked at the end for killing and gutting. There is a flurry, and three more arrive. Their wings whip the air.

He looks down to where her hand has alighted on his arm. Her fingers curl, he feels the dig of her nails, and the snake ring catches the gleam of the dying sun.

Like Jessica, he knows that to survive, he must change.

That was where Eleanor had failed. She couldn't change. Her relationships with others – with Adam and Jessica and Simon – were constantly mutating. Alliances shifted, loyalties were called into question. She couldn't keep up. She had hoped that somehow Georgie would save her, set her free, but motherhood only bound her more firmly.

So Jessica must learn from Eleanor; she must bend a little to her genetic destiny, to pairing and to motherhood.

Yet do so without losing her essential self.

It is as if she hears his thoughts. Locking her fingers with his, she leans against him. Laughing, she says, 'Hey now, that's a tall order, Adam Mason.'